*T*wo women. One too many brides.
Only one knows it...

Powerful forces are about to hit. Irresistibly drawn to each other, fortune-cookie maker Blossom Sun and silver-fortune heir Brock St. Clair find love at first sight. They also find that every secret has a price. The problem: He's about to be married and she's engaged. The bigger problem: It's April 18, 1906, and a catastrophic earthquake and inferno are about to bring San Francisco to its knees. A Cinderella story like no other, *Blossom* will leave you breathless.

"A compelling story of the power of love in the face of an unprecedented disaster; of a man who has to choose between his duty and a love that transcends two cultures. Lentz writes an amazing story that brings the San Francisco earthquake to life—first rate!"

—ANNE CLEELAND, acclaimed author of historical fiction and contemporary mysteries such as *Daughter of the God-King*

Blossom

Book One of the Blossom Trilogy

Christopher Lentz

Blossom

ISBN 978-0-9962936-0-0

Copyright, © 2015 by Christopher Lentz
Cover and internal design by Bambi Crowell

This book contains an excerpt from the forthcoming book *Blaze* by Christopher Lentz. This excerpt has been set for this edition only and may not reflect the final content of the forthcoming edition.

Dedication

To my wife, Cheryl, for teaching me the meaning of love—and for kidnapping me to San Francisco for my 40th birthday—I dedicate this novel. It was that long weekend of exploration and romance in the City by the Bay that sparked this story. While the women of Chinatown who we saw hand-making fortune cookies did not resemble the young woman named Blossom in my imagination, their demure posture and rhythmic motions made an everlasting impression.

I thank Cheryl for supporting my dream of writing a novel, including what might have appeared to be endless procrastinating and incubating, as well as red-hot writing spurts that inevitably turned into slow productive simmers.

This novel is also dedicated to love. Though it took many seasons of crafting, *Blossom* is a love story written from the heart to the heart. For those who love and those who are fortunate to be loved in return, I sincerely hope that *Blossom* helps you bring back warm memories and look forward to the love that lies ahead.

> "'Tis a fragrant retrospection—
>   for the loving thoughts that start
> Into being are like perfume
>   from the blossom of the heart."

From *An Old Sweetheart of Mine* by James Whitcomb Riley, 1888

Chapter 1

$\mathcal{F}$ortune Favors The Heart

Saturday, April 14, 1906, 11:05 a.m.
Four days before the earthquake and firestorm

Brock St. Clair was only planning to get a bag of the newest craze from the Orient: fortune cookies. The request for the prophetic desserts sounded harmless enough to Brock when his fiancée made it.

Following an uneventful walk from Nob Hill, Brock was surrounded by red paper lanterns swaying in the San Francisco Bay breeze. The grey skies split apart and unleashed an explosion of warm sunshine. In an instant, everything gleamed. He squinted at the glistening parallel rails in the street, watching how an open-air cable car traveled along the defined track that had no visible deviations.

Brock thought about how his life was like a cable car. He continued to look at the tracks with an open hand raised near his eyes to cut the glare. *That's me. Always on track.* His thoughts were interrupted by the winds of change, literally. A gust stole his straw boater hat and playfully begged him to chase after it. The hat skipped and rolled away from him down a street he wasn't intending to take. "Hey, I jumped my tracks," he whispered to himself.

As he captured his wayward hat, Brock found himself on the fringe of

Chinatown. He slowed to study the cobra-like plumes of burning incense that wafted out of the open storefronts. Ginger and ginseng perfumed the air and grew more pungent the deeper he ventured into Chinatown.

"Looks pretty much like the rest of San Francisco," Brock said quietly as he noticed how rust wept out of anything metal. Chinatown's weathered fancy wood and brick Italianate buildings stood shoulder to shoulder unlike those in the images he'd seen of China. There were no pagoda towers, no dragon sculptures and no intricate tile roofs. Brock remembered learning in school that Chinatown was merely a downtown district that businesses had left behind in a migration to other areas thought to hold more potential.

"Looks better from up above," he added.

"What you say?" asked an elderly Chinese man who was passing by.

"Nothing...nothing at all. Pardon me."

Geographically, Chinatown was not far from Brock's world of wealth and comfort on Nob Hill, but he was aware that—in ways not measured by distance—Chinatown might as well have been located in China itself. Its few city blocks were a fortress for its people. It was self-contained and self-sufficient. And while Chinatown welcomed visitors and their money, its inhabitants were rumored to rarely stray beyond its borders.

Brock grew up knowing that Chinatown had a reputation as well-defined as Nob Hill's. However, Chinatown's opium dens, brothels and warring gangs were the topics of most conversations, rather than its respectable shops, restaurants and theaters.

This wasn't the first time he'd been here, but Brock was more aware of his surroundings. As he studied the streets and alleys, Brock saw how Chinatown was a ghost town reborn. While to some it was a hellhole, to many more it not only looked like home...it was home.

Though he didn't think the area looked foreign, the sounds—like the clickety-clack of a nearby shopkeeper registering his sales on the beads of an abacus—and, more specifically, the voices were worlds apart. Men barked orders at each other in abrupt-sounding words that were nothing like English.

However, finding someone to help him who spoke a little English didn't take as long as Brock figured. In fact, the first man he asked about fortune cookies gave him clear directions. "Go to Golden Palace. It small, but very popular. Look for yellow flag. It mean restaurant. Golden Palace run by Chang Sun and his mother. She called Grand Ma Maw."

After navigating the crowded streets and taking in their unusual smells, Brock reached the intersection of Clay and Dupont streets. *What died and how long ago did it die?* He kept his thoughts to himself this time.

People called out from open windows on the second and third floors to men down below. He noticed that the latest news must have just been posted on the exterior wall of the building because a group gathered to read, point at and discuss what appeared on colorful papers that hung vertically like unrolled scrolls.

Within the commotion, Brock saw one man turn his head quickly and his precisely braided *queue* pigtail lashed the man next to him, triggering a more heated exchange of comments. Each voice was heaping on the other to be heard, with undecipherable shouts fighting for attention.

Brock made his way down the street and found the three-cornered yellow silk pennant next to The Golden Palace's sign. He stumbled through the doorway when his boot heel caught on the raised threshold. The bell hanging above the shop's door helped announce his graceless arrival. An enticing sweet aroma rode on the backs of several warm breezes as they escaped the open door a few feet from him. A tall, thin man with striking ebony-colored hair—without a *queue*—approached him while humming a tune that sounded strangely similar to a song Brock heard in a saloon recently about "Irish eyes a-smiling."

The shopkeeper bowed and said in a choppy way, "*Ni hao*. How I help?"

Brock bowed in return. "Knee how," he replied to the best of his ability, assuming that the phrase was a pleasant greeting. "Hello to you. My fiancée sent me to get a special dessert. She thought it was called a moon cake. But then she said it might be called a fortune cookie. She wasn't sure. I was told you had fortune cookies here."

"How she know of moon cake? Wrong time of year for moon cake. Need yokes of duck eggs. Make shape of full moon—"

The shopkeeper violently slipped. His arms swung out in flailing and erratic ways as he reached for something to help break his fall. Brock was surprised not just by the fall, but the array of colorful glass marbles that ricocheted around the floor. *Marbles in a bakery?*

Brock lunged forward, but his effort was not quick enough as the man who was just humming yelled out, "Damn. Damn. DAMN!" He knocked several metal trays off of the counter, making for a dramatic fall. Brock's eyes darted to follow glimpses of baked goods as they took flight and sailed across the room in a chaotic airborne ballet.

Brock lowered himself to his knees just behind the shopkeeper's shoulders to be in a sturdy position to lift him. He reassured the shopkeeper. "Please, let me help you. That was a nasty fall. Is there someone—"

Brock's words stopped midstream as his eyes met those of a girl who emerged from the next room where the sweet-smelling breezes came from moments ago. She froze. She looked first at the man on the floor, and then at the one who was cradling him from behind.

His eyes locked with hers.

She allowed Brock's eyes to pierce hers, peering much more deeply than was customary.

In spite of the shopkeeper's growling and damning the marbles on the floor, Brock's eyes remained locked on hers. His heart pounded. *Breathe, make yourself breathe,* Brock shouted in his head.

She extended her hands to the shopkeeper without breaking eye contact with Brock. Together, they helped the shopkeeper to his feet.

"*Shay shay*—I mean, thank you," the shopkeeper said to Brock. He brushed off his clothes and kept his eyes lowered. The shopkeeper sent the girl to the workroom with a gentle nudge. She looked back at Brock as she passed through the doorway.

Brock's gaze followed her like a shadow. He moved closer to the doorway to see where she went. He noticed how she appeared startled and hesitated before looking down at her work. He wasn't in the habit of staring at strangers. He was raised with better manners. But this girl entranced him like no other. Brock saw that she needed to return her full attention to the task at hand because she'd suddenly burned a fingertip on the hot iron she was working with. She barely winced, however.

"Young man! Young man! Young man!" said the shopkeeper in what Brock noticed was a triple-repeat pattern. The shopkeeper picked up the metal trays and slammed them on the counter with a loud bang.

"If I might ask, what's she making?" asked Brock, never looking back at the man and continuing to watch the girl.

"Fortune cookies, of course!"

"Then I'll take one dozen, please. They will—"

"I give you happy price. Good value. Fifteen cent," interrupted the shopkeeper. "Some say Japanese make first. I no agree. Fortune cookie as Chinese as…as…me!"

Brock dug into his pocket and retrieved a dime and a nickel. He now looked at the man to deliver the coins without dropping them.

The shopkeeper placed a bag on the counter.

Brock's eyes darted back to the girl in the other room. She was looking at him even though her hands continued their work with graceful rhythm and movement.

"May I see how the cookies are made?" Brock asked. *I really want to see the girl who's making the cookies.*

"Fine. Come, come, come. Follow me," muttered the shopkeeper as he made a waving motion with his hand.

"This my daughter, Mei-Hua," he said standing tall, his shoulders back and a grin on his face. Brock thought how in a sea of people with brown eyes and black hair, the girl's deep brown hair and lavender eyes must make her stand out whether she wanted to or not.

"Her name mean beautiful flower. People call her Blossom. She beautiful, no?" He didn't give Brock a chance to answer. "My name Sun Chang. You call me Chang. In old times, family name come first to honor ancestors. Given name next. Now many Chinatown people put given name first."

Brock sensed someone else in the room. His feeling was confirmed as he spied two beguiling dark eyes peering around the corner of the wall behind Blossom.

"Well, hello to you," Brock directed to the corner of the room.

"Ting Ting. Come out, Ting Ting," ordered Chang.

The child, who Brock estimated was about six or seven years old, obeyed. She bowed and smoothed out her bright canary yellow shirt.

"This See Ting Ting. Her family live next door. Fireworks and tea, that their business. She spend time with us in afternoons, with orphaned... adopted...sister named Little Sunflower. She not here now. They sometime leave toy on floor, like marbles behind counter." Chang gave Ting Ting a stern look.

"Blossom like sister to them. When Ting Ting good girl, we call her Rose Bud. Not so often, though. Her little lips red like rose, no?"

"No, I mean yes," replied Brock.

Ting Ting scooted out and stood close to Blossom. The chubby girl's eyes twinkled above cheeks that appeared to have a dumpling stashed in each one. She whispered in what sounded like Chinese to Brock. Blossom smiled at the girl and patted her on the shoulder, drawing her in even closer. Ting Ting bounced back a bit when the hand that held her music box collided with Blossom's body.

Ting Ting slipped her feet into Blossom's unoccupied shoes. Chang looked down and noticed. Blossom was working wearing her socks. The music-making "hurdy-gurdy" had a hand-held metal cylinder with a tiny crank that had a shiny red bead on the end. Ting Ting examined the bright-colored paper that was glued around the cylinder. Brock could see that it featured circus acts.

Ting Ting turned the crank to play the signature circus tune, *Entrance of the Gladiators*, as Blossom got back to work.

With great precision, Blossom took the thin circles of dough and laid them on the hot metal pedestal. Using two sticks—not with her fingers, as she did before—she inserted a strip of paper and folded the dough into a three-dimensional crescent shape. She didn't look up once as Brock observed her work. He asked about the messages on the pieces of paper.

"Mostly happy messages put inside cookies. Some fortunes not so happy," pointed out Chang. *Was that just a warning?* Brock thought.

Blossom took the risk of speaking freely to the stranger in the presence of her father. "Sometimes fortune favors the strong. Other times, fortune favors the delicate. But always, fortune favors the heart."

Chang commanded Brock's attention by instructing, "Only eat cookies you break open. Must be offered to you. You pick cookie. You pick your destiny. Must be whole when in your hand. A cracked one bring very bad, bad, bad luck. No take."

Blossom smiled as she broke a cookie in two and looked up at Brock.

"Would you like a taste?" she asked. Her voice had a playful sing-song quality to it. She offered Brock the cookie as she slowly closed her eyes and opened them to again pierce his.

"If that broken one you're offering me will bring bad luck, then no thank you. But I would like to try one of those next to you," replied Brock, pointing to the pile of unbroken cookies to Blossom's right.

She grinned.

Brock couldn't stop looking at Blossom. As politely as he could, he studied the loose-fitting, jade-green silk blouse she was wearing. It had a high collar fastened together with gold-colored braiding shaped like a butterfly. *Seems like too nice a shirt to be working in.*

She had billowy pants, the color of purple iris. As he gazed further down, her white socks popped out not only because they were so starkly white, but because she had no shoes on.

She scanned the pile and selected three cookies. Blossom then offered them to Brock to choose from. He pointed to the one in the middle and she placed it onto Brock's extended palm.

He noticed how she looked at his rough hand against his elegant clothes with a questioning expression. *Not the first time someone's given me that look.*

Her studying gaze rose with the slowness of the bay breezes outside, from his hands to his necktie to his mouth and then to his eyes again.

"Well, go ahead. Break open!" insisted Chang. "Fate wait for no man!"

Brock blinked and shuddered. He clenched his fist and cracked the cookie.

"Open! Read paper aloud before you eat!"

Brock separated the halves of the cookie and pulled out the slip of paper. He sighed. He looked at Blossom and then at Chang.

"I guess this is my lucky day," he said and smiled at Blossom. His eyes returned to the paper, and he read, "Confucius say, 'Wherever you go, go with all of your heart.'"

He put half of the cookie in his mouth and bit down. "Hmm, it's sweet, crisp... more like crunchy." The crunching sounds echoed in his head.

"Can you hear that? Or is it just me?" *They must think my head's hollow!*

"Yes, we hear. Anything else you need today *before* you go?" asked Chang. Ting Ting observed the entire exchange, not cranking her hurdy-gurdy at that moment.

"No, I don't think there is—" Brock said in a voice that trailed off, though his mind raced. He couldn't stop staring at Blossom. He tried, but couldn't. He didn't care. He liked the way it felt, except how his face was hot and probably as red as the paper lanterns outside. Brock's hand clutched the paper bag that contained the cookies, and the crackling sound brought his mind back into focus.

"Thank you for the cookies, Blossom. I mean, *shay shay*. And Chang, *shay shay* for showing me how they're made."

Blossom lowered her head in what Brock figured was a gesture of thanks, while maintaining eye contact. Her lavender eyes were thieves, stealing his breath and holding it captive.

Get a hold of yourself, man! You're engaged. This is wrong. This…is… wrong. He knelt down so that he was face to face with the little girl. "It was very nice to meet you, Ting Ting. Even though you say a lot with your eyes, perhaps sometime you'll let me hear your voice in English."

Ting Ting smiled and bowed. Then she waved. As Brock began to leave the room, she cranked her music box's handle.

He put the fortune-telling slip of paper into his wallet and handed Chang a white rectangular card.

"Come again, come again, come again." Chang bowed and then walked toward the front door in what Brock took as a not-so-subtle way of ending their conversation. "Good day, Meester Brock St. Clair," he said, reading Brock's last name from the card in his hand.

Brock responded to the signal and soon found himself back out on the congested street.

"Blossom, Blossom, Blossom," he uttered in Chang's triple-repeat pattern of speech. He looked back over his shoulder at the front of The Golden Palace as he headed back to Nob Hill with a bag of fortune-telling cookies in his grasp.

Brock retraced his path through Chinatown. He noticed two different sights this time: a shoemaker and children playing. The shoemaker sat along the street and called out to potential customers. *Shoes made to order right here in the street*, Brock thought. The children were spinning tops on the ground and flinging yoyos in the air. As he walked by, laughter and chattering lingered in the air.

As Brock turned the corner and began to climb the steep slope, a cable car appeared. It was close enough for Brock to study its stained wood and high-gloss varnish. He noted how the sun reflected on the polished brass handrails. His eyes followed the car with its maroon, white and light blue painted accents. The cable car's grip man rang the bell for all to hear and heed.

Within a heartbeat, there was a metal-on-metal, shoulder-raising screech. Through squinting eyes, Brock saw passengers flopping around like fish just hauled in from the sea. An out-of-tune symphony of grunts, high-pitched squeals and "Good Lord" comments filled the air around the cable car that jumped its tracks.

Passengers instantly began to rearrange themselves and their packages. "Is everyone accounted for?" he heard the conductor ask. "Please step away. I don't want anyone to get hurt."

"Help us. Please help us!" Brock followed the voice around to the other side of the cable car. A young woman sat with her arms tightly wrapped around a toddler-age boy. They were seated on an outer-facing bench and their groceries were thrown onto the street.

Brock put his bag of fortune cookies on the ground. "Is there anything I can do?" he asked the woman as he'd already begun to reach down to collect the cans of fruit and butcher-paper wrapped packages that escaped the handled net bags that once held them prisoner.

"My son and I are fine, but I can't say the same for our dinner tonight," replied the woman.

"You'll have a lifetime of dinners ahead of you…but only one child like this one to keep a hold of," Brock said as he stood up and put his hand on the boy's shoulder. "You made the right choice. Now you two better get down onto the street!"

A crowd surrounded the action and several people helped collect the runaway food.

"Everyone, please stand back," announced the conductor as he flipped several coins in his hand that he likely collected as fares. He looked down at the groceries. "Saints preserve us! No one fell off. I've never been on one of these contraptions when it derailed."

"Thank you, sir. Your kindness is very much appreciated," the woman said to Brock. "Son, thank the nice man."

"Thank you, sir," he said and scooted closer to his mother.

Brock tipped his hat. "Glad to be of service."

When it was clear he was no longer needed, Brock brushed his hands on his pants and instantly realized he'd lost his prized possession. The bag of fortune cookies was nowhere in sight. He looked around the feet of the crowd and spotted a bag. He picked it up and looked inside.

A bag of fortune cookie crumbs. That won't do. Not for Clarissa.

Brock went back to The Golden Palace with visions of Blossom in his head.

He opened the door, lifted his feet higher than usual and did not trip on his way in. The bells announced his return.

"You back so soon!" said Chang.

"It's a long story."

"Long story?"

"I won't bother you with the details, but the bag of cookies I bought got smashed while I was helping a lady whose groceries fell off of a cable car. There was an accident down the street. Now I need another."

"Another accident?"

"No, I need another bag of cookies, please," replied Brock.

"Yes, yes, yes. More cookies for hero!"

"I wouldn't go that far, but I was happy to—"

The words that described Brock's recollection vanished as he looked into Blossom's eyes. She was peering around the corner of the doorway.

Chang looked at him and leaned forward as if to coax more words out. "You happy to do what? Be hero?"

"Oh, I was happy to help," concluded Brock. "Yes, I was happy to help."

"Fine then, here another bag. Fifteen cent, my hero." Brock offered Chang coins from his pocket and got a bag in return.

"Be safe. Stay away from cable car!" Chang said as he walked over to the doorway and opened the door. "Ten thousand thanks. Bye bye."

Brock's attention was solely on Blossom. *There's a hammer pounding on my heart and I can hear it in my head!*

"Back to work, my daughter. This instant!" She vanished.

Brock turned to face the doorway and discovered that Chang was there already with the door open.

"*Shay shay.*"

"*Shay shay* to you," added Brock as he left the bakery.

With the second bag of fortune-telling cookies firmly in his grasp, Brock got himself back on track to his fiancée's house. Unlike the grip on the bag, his mind did not hold such a firm grasp on Clarissa.

Chapter 2
Wisdom Comes With Age

Saturday, April 14, 1906, 11:47 a.m.
Four days before the earthquake and firestorm

"What you thinking, my daughter?" Chang asked in broken English. "Have you no sense? Have we not raised you to keep to yourself? To your work? To your *own* people? That white man…what you think he see when he look at you?"

Back at her workstation, Blossom readied herself to answer with a deep cleansing breath and weaving her fingers together. "Ba Ba, it's 1906, not 1806. People can talk freely now. That includes me and you." She did her best to be firm, yet respectful, though Blossom recognized that it ended up sounding preachy.

"Make cookies. Speak no more," said Chang now in Cantonese.

From down the hall came a clump-clump sound and another voice. "Climb off your high horse, my son," said Grand Ma Maw. "And you, Blossom, you make anger in your Ba Ba."

Blossom looked down at the worktable.

"She just full of fire, like always," said Chang.

"Yes, perhaps too much and too often," added the old woman. "Until I draw my last breath, it my duty to run this business and this family…

duty and burden at times like this. Chang, how many times I must tell you to speak in the English? The more Blossom hear and speak the English, the better her life be."

Blossom wondered what her father did to deserve a lifelong stream of sideways looks, heavy sighs and sharp criticism from Grand Ma Maw. Though she was a smart and shrewd woman whose wit could sharpen pencils, when it came to speaking with her son, she always seemed to have a harsh edge.

The loud thumping of her cane hitting the floor boards continued, prompting the old woman to point out, "President Roosevelt say: 'Speak softly, carry big stick.' I no speak so soft, but I carry big stick!" *Did she really just say that like she'd never said it before?* Blossom thought.

Blossom put down the uncooked dough in her hands and pushed back from her worktable. She knew she was in for a lecture of epic proportions, one she clearly had brought on herself.

"Ting Ting, you probably should go home now. Or go find Little Sunflower and play a game. You know how she looks up to you," said Blossom with the kind tone of a loving sister. "This may not be a conversation for you to hear."

"But—" Ting Ting replied.

"But nothing," interjected Chang in English. "Please leave now, my Rose Bud." He smiled, placed the flat of his hand on her back and gently pushed her out the door to the alley. Rather than going home, Ting Ting stood outside next to the door to listen to what came next. She knew English well because she went to the same English-speaking school Blossom attended as a child.

"Do you both expect me to do nothing for hours on end but make cookies and sell cookies, thinking about what I'm missing out there?" asked Blossom, pointing out the nearby window. "Is that the life you want for me? Is that why you came to America, to raise a mindless cookie-making, cookie-selling spinster by day and a restaurant waitress by night? Why did you send me to school every day? For this?"

It was not the first time they'd had this discussion. But the previous discussions never concluded to Blossom's satisfaction.

Grand Ma Maw crossed the room at a measured pace. Blossom watched her and could feel the rust in Grand Ma Maw's back and knees. She was old and did nothing to disguise it. She responded, "My precious one, you know your father and me only want best for you."

Her training showed as Blossom bowed in her grandmother's direction.

"But how do you know what's best for me?"

"Because we know you. We know the ways of our people, of ancestors who came before us," answered Chang.

"I honor your wisdom and your knowledge of our ways, but I don't want to be limited by our ways. There has to be more out there for me. I don't want to be a prisoner in this building and just watch life pass by without me," said Blossom with a sweeping arm gesture. "I feel like a lamppost bolted to the pavement and everyone else is going somewhere." She let the sentence die its own death. The air in the room was like quicksand.

Grand Ma Maw looked into Blossom's eyes, then into Chang's. "A *prisoner* you say? A *lamppost*? This what living in America come to? Never satisfied? Always want to see beyond your home? Challenging those with wisdom, who wish you not repeat past mistakes?"

Not repeat past mistakes echoed in Blossom's mind. *What mistakes? Whose past mistakes?*

Before Blossom could respond, Grand Ma Maw added, "Put shoes on! Always shoes on!"

"I apologize most humbly if my open mind and open mouth have offended you…and my shoeless feet too," said Blossom as she slipped her shoes back on. "But if I want to look at a white man and speak to a white man, I don't see why that's such a problem."

"You not act so familiar with someone we not familiar with. He here only to buy something mysterious to him: fortune cookies. He found more than he set out to find, but he not find it here again." Grand Ma Maw placed her hand on Blossom's hair and stroked it. "Why you act that way with him? That not like you at all."

"Oh, I have my reasons," replied Blossom. *It wasn't like me, was it? It was that stupid dare I took and the childish pinky swear I made yesterday at lunch. But then I couldn't help myself. Something changed. Something—*

"Wisdom come with age, but sometimes age come alone. Lucky for you, I have both," Grand Ma Maw said. "Many things end bad that began with innocent glance or kind word. Blossom, you hear but not listen too much. Now is time to listen. Listen to my words and know they come from this old woman's heart."

Chang joined the conversation. "These my thinks about this matter."

"You mean *thoughts*?" asked Blossom.

"My thinks, my thoughts…ugh, the English make me crazy. You be no reckless. You have man. He your future husband. What he think if he know how you act today?"

"Ba Ba, I don't have a future husband. I'm not engaged. You and Butch have an understanding and that's all," said Blossom.

Grand Ma Maw spoke up. "You like last kernel of corn in chicken coop. Too many men in Chinatown. Families still in China…especially women. You, my dear one, are a treasure."

"You be wife of Ming Yang soon," said Chang. "He excellent match for you."

Blossom looked at Grand Ma Maw. "Butch, I mean Ming Yang, he's the butcher who's the man of *your* dreams. Not mine. A butcher for a son-in-law who can supply fresh meat to you! And I become a baby-making factory. That way there can be more butchering and cookie making and table waiting for years to come. I don't know, maybe I don't even want a man. Maybe I'm meant to be alone. That's it! I'm supposed to be a spinster with calloused fingertips and an arched back that looks like...ah ...like the rolling hills across the bay."

"You too picky. Ming Yang be your husband soon," added Chang.

"But I want more than '*a husband.*'"

"You want what?" asked Grand Ma Maw.

"I...want...more."

"I hear enough. Now you work! Cookies not make themselves," said Chang. Blossom noticed how he scanned the card in his hand. "I expect we not see Meester Brock St. Clair in here again."

Then, with a flip of his wrist, he threw the card into the wastebasket and left the room. Grand Ma Maw followed.

Blossom placed some dough on the iron, but eyed the card on the top of the trash pile. She looked around the room for any witnesses who might see what she was about to do. All was clear. Without making a sound, she made her way to the wastebasket, picked up the card, slipped it in her shoe and returned to her stool. She looked around the area again, seeing no witnesses. *I don't see her, but Grand Ma Maw is watching. I just know it.*

As she had thousands of times before, Blossom reached for a fortune-telling slip of paper to put inside the warm dough. She paused to read this particular message, though, and its sentiment could not have been more appropriate and coincidental: "Confucius say, 'Wherever you go, go with all of your heart.'"

She looked out the window above her work surface and whispered, "I wonder if Mr. Brock St. Clair is going somewhere right now...with the cookies and *all* of his heart?"

Chapter 3
$\mathcal{T}$ime For A Pinky Swear

Saturday, April 14, 1906, 1:18 p.m.
Four days before the earthquake and firestorm

Blossom mindlessly selected yet another slip of paper for the soon-to-be-folded circle of dough. The slip—like all of its brothers and sisters in the pile—offered a prediction of a future overflowing with good fortune, dreams coming true or discoveries waiting to be made. Blossom felt like the unrelenting repetition of her life made her existence flow like a run-on sentence, devoid of punctuation…especially exclamation points.

As she completed another tray of cookies, she asked herself, "How many does that make? *Too* many, that's how many." She inhaled deeply to make a strong puff of air that she sent toward her left eye to dislodge an irritating strand of hair.

Blossom rested her chin on her elevated right hand, with her palm cupping her cheek. She peered through one of the shop's hazy window panes and let herself drift away on the forceful currents of her imagination, as she too often did, to someplace else…anyplace but here at The Golden Palace.

She thought back to the conversation she had with Monique and Anna Mae, her two best girlfriends, yesterday on a bench in the alley—the conversation that led her to be so flirty and coy with Brock today.

It started with a firm knuckle rapping on the window and a cheery, "Hey, chick-a-dee! It's lunchtime. See you out in the alley." The voice's body had already passed the confines of the window frame before Blossom was able to look.

Blossom made her way through the bakery to the kitchen. She scooped up a bowl of rice and steamed vegetables, and opened the door to the alley. Her foot almost didn't clear the raised threshold of the doorway. She jerked and almost dropped her chopsticks. Her friends were already on the bench, ready to share another meal. Leaning against a red-brick wall, the cracked-wood bench was the trio's island. Not like Alcatraz. It was an oasis, a refuge.

Blossom took her usual place in the middle. With a wavering voice, she said to Monique on her right, "I wish you wouldn't pound on the window and scare me. It's bad enough that I have to sit there for hours and daydream to stop from losing my mind, but then you come along and bang on the window and rattle me back to work!"

Monique jutted out her chin at Blossom. "You're most welcome."

Blossom leaned in. "So what's new with you?"

"Oh, it's been just another day in paradise." Monique rolled her eyes, stared straight up to the sky and continued. "My knight in shining armor swept me off my feet. Well, I wish he had." She stopped speaking, sat up and then relaxed into a slouch. She smoothed her charcoal black hair to ensure that all of the prisoners were still captive in a bun so tight that it further narrowed her already almond-shaped eyes.

"Instead, I had an early-morning encounter with a banker from Chicago, who spoke mostly German. He was polite enough, but there was a cloud around him of week-old sweat, wet wool socks and sauerkraut!"

"German sauerkraut? Monique, what do you know about that?" Anna Mae leaned forward.

"More than I wish to know."

Blossom was well aware that Monique's gentleman caller was one in a long parade of penises in her line of work. She was one of Chinatown's most sought after prostitutes. For as long as Blossom could remember, it was a profession for which Monique had made no apologies. "Someday, a man is going to want me for more than a few stolen moments. He'll want me for a lifetime. I have to admit, though, I've got a regular who lights a fire in my furnace, if you know what I mean. Maybe one day you'll be calling me Mrs. St.—"

She dammed her flow of words. "Oh, I'll just keep that to myself for now."

"Say, aren't you going to ask about my day?" asked Anna Mae.

"If you're the ultimate entertainer in town, Monique, that makes me the ultimate matchmaker. I've connected so many people already today that my fingertips and ears are numb." Blossom heard Anna Mae say this before, but she knew that being a telephone operator was a skilled and exhausting job that provided her incomparable intelligence about the residents of Chinatown.

"Numb fingers and ears…those you have," said Monique. "But you still don't have a man for yourself either!"

Blossom chimed in to lighten the conversation. "I guess that makes me the ultimate fortuneteller. Even if there are only a dozen or so different messages, those prophecies that I put in each cookie could change the course of humanity," she stated with a grand wave of her hand. "At least they might make some people change their plans for the day…or not." She shrugged her shoulders.

A Chinese woman walked by clutching the hand of a little boy, pulling him along at too fast a pace. But his smile beamed upward to his mother with a loving bond.

"You know, as a child, I was sure I was mailed to the wrong address," Blossom admitted in a flat, monotone voice. She poked at the vegetables in her bowl with her chopsticks and slowly stirred them. "I've always felt like a misfit, even in this misfit neighborhood."

Blossom pressed her lips together and paused. "I've been thinking a lot lately. I know that's a dangerous pastime around here. I've decided to go out and get my own future, one that I choose. Surely you've both felt that way?"

"Nope, I've *never* felt that way," replied Anna Mae with her head held high in an exaggerated way. She delicately patted her upturned nose, winked at Blossom and grinned.

"Me neither," added Monique. She chewed a mouthful of white rice, but couldn't hold back a cough that escaped her mouth before she could cover it. It snowed rice bits.

"Classy, real classy," said Anna Mae with a smirk. Monique laughed and took a quick drink of tea to clear her throat.

The conversation dried up. Blossom waited for the right words to reveal themselves to get the conversation going again, like panning for gold in her mind and coming up empty handed.

"It reminds me of the Yeh-Shen story," announced Blossom.

"The Chinese Cinderella?" Monique took another quick drink. "What reminds you of her...now?"

"Us. Our situations. We may not have her talking fish, sea-green silk gown, golden slippers or a king to whisk us away to a palace, but we're ready for some changes, true?"

"True," responded Anna Mae.

"True," added Monique with a single nod.

"Yeah, but now look at our reality. Smell our reality," added Blossom as she lowered her bowl and chopsticks to her lap.

"Oh Blossom, you're not going to start whining again about your unfulfilled life and how you're *craving* for something more out there... or over there," said Monique with exaggerated flair, pointing up in the direction to the hills and then down to the bay.

Blossom didn't need to look, because she knew the view from the alley was completely obscured by buildings, making it impossible to see up to the mansions of Nob Hill and down to the congested wharves. However, for the sake of the conversation, she and the girls looked in unison one way and then the other.

They saw three young women coming toward them who must have been on an adventure. Blossom could tell because they weren't from Chinatown and they definitely were not Chinese. Each had on an attention-grabbing outfit, hair styled to perfection and an immense hat crowned with ostrich plumes. Blossom studied how the feathers danced with each step they took.

They looked back at the Chinese girls on the bench and giggled. They huddled close and whispered something as they got a few steps away.

Again, the walking girls giggled.

The sitting girls did not.

"I wonder what their lives are like." Blossom asked, "Think they'd switch places with us for a day, an hour, a few minutes?"

A quick reply came from Monique. "Yeah, that's about as likely as me shitting a strand of pearls!"

The trio on the bench burst with laughter, prompting the walking trio to look back from a distance and chit-chat among themselves. Just down the alley, several crates crashed to the ground.

"Who's there?" Blossom yelled. "I thought I felt someone watching us."

"There's always someone watching…everything, everyone, all the time," said Monique.

"This time it felt different, in a creepy way."

Two cats ran out into the alley. "See, just some cats!" Monique pointed out.

Blossom noticed a group of men coming their way. "Say, those are Butch's friends. But I don't see Butch in the gang," said Anna Mae. "I wonder what he's up to…or chopping up!"

They kicked the crates out of their way.

"You can always count on the men of Chinatown to keep the streets in order," said Anna Mae.

As they got closer, Butch somehow appeared to be part of the group. Blossom couldn't miss the angry look on his face as they came near.

"Hello, ladies," they said almost like an all-male chorus.

"Blossom," Butch said as he passed.

"Hello, Butch," Blossom replied. *Where did he come from? He wasn't there a second ago.*

The girls watched the men turn the corner and disappear.

"Just look at us. We're twenty years old and still meeting on this same bench…in an alley no less! We've really got to make some changes."

"I have to admit that I'm tired of being patient and waiting for Mr. Wonderful to come along," Monique added. "Actually, I'm just tired." She looked down at the ground. "One of us is going to do something about it…today."

Her eyes zeroed in on Blossom.

"Honey, I dare you to…um…okay, I've got it. You must flirt with the next man who comes through the bakery door. Flirt like you've never flirted before. Use your eyes. Use your hands. Use your body. Use your voice. Make it impossible for him not to want to get to know you."

Blossom had a stunned, blank-page face at first, but summoned a comeback. "That's amusing. Anyone who walks through *your* doorway can have whatever and whoever he wants, not to mention however he wants it."

"You're right, but that's work. It's a fantasy for the men, but it's work for me. It's about paying for what he wants and moving on. I'm challenging you to taunt this man in your bakery with what he can't have, but letting him think he can."

"You have a platoon of men at your door. This is a bakery. How many men shop in a bakery?"

"So that's your challenge," announced Monique.

"I'll take the dare. But you two have to seal your lips. Don't tell a soul or I'll—we'll—be the talk of the town, and not in a good way."

"Deal," replied Anna Mae.

"Deal," added Monique.

"Then it's time for a pinky swear," said Blossom.

The three got up off of the bench and faced each other. Each girl crossed her arms and locked pinky fingers with the other girls, making an interlocked circle. It was a school-girl ritual they devised and continued to practice despite its childish appearance. No verbal instructions were needed to complete the *gou xiaozhi* promise. Together they chanted, "Cross my heart, hope to die, one thousand chopsticks in my eye." They broke their pinky chain, in unison kissed the top of each of their own hands and with their right hands knocked three times on the wooden bench.

Anna Mae looked at Blossom. "So how are we going to know if you followed through? And if Butch comes in, he doesn't count."

"You'll know. Trust me. I'll tell you about it right here on this bench if not sooner."

Monique took hold of Blossom's shoulders. "You're always saying that you're waiting for your life to begin. Now, it begins!"

Chapter 4

*E*verything In Its Proper Place

Saturday, April 14, 1906, 2:04 p.m.
Four days before the earthquake and firestorm

Brock found Clarissa Donohue, his fiancée, in the dining room of her parent's house, ever so carefully positioning place cards at each setting on the expansive table. He lingered just outside the doorway and didn't disturb her. She was beautiful, and the toast of the Paris of the Pacific's society.

At twenty-two years of age, Clarissa had completed her education, expertly played the harp and was well-read. She'd mastered the nuances of being mistress of the mansion and a perfect hostess. Everything appeared to be falling into place for Clarissa and her self-centered girlfriends who inhabited the city's thin layer of social veneer. Like a well-cultivated hothouse orchid, Clarissa was in full bloom.

Someone was singing a tune that was an unrecognizable blend of jumbled lyrics and sour notes. Brock leaned in and discovered Clarissa's mother. She was accomplished in many ways. *Singing was not one of them,* thought Brock. *She can carry a tune, but not very far!* He recalled stories of how Clarissa's father teased her mother by saying she had a singing voice best suited for selling fish in a street market. However, he always followed that criticism with a wink and a kiss blown in her direction.

Brock's movement in the hallway caught her eye and Mrs. Donohue stopped singing. "I didn't hear a thing," he said. "Not…a…thing!"

"You did too." Clarissa's mother, one of the leaders of the gilt-edged aristocracy of San Francisco, gracefully rose from her chair. As she exited the room, intentionally leaving the two without a chaperon, she said, "You two lovebirds are on your own now. I trust that you'll be on your best behavior."

"Yes, Mother."

Brock came through the dining room's entryway that was hung and swagged with burgundy silk cords and tassels that formed open-air portieres. "Here they are. I got a dozen. I hope that'll be enough. The table looks too perfect to eat at," he said and then kissed Clarissa on the cheek. "Here, these are for you!"

"Eleven red roses and one white. They're simply exquisite." Clarissa's face was incandescent.

"Yes, you're like the white one. You stand out even among a bouquet of roses," Brock replied.

Clarissa turned her head a bit, but kept her stare squarely on Brock.

"Zelda, please come here," Clarissa called out to one of the household's maids. "I know you're there in the hallway eavesdropping. Send someone to the flower market this very minute to get three dozen red roses."

"Yes, I'll do just that," could be heard from down the hall.

"If one dozen is good, then a total of *four* dozen will be better. I'll arrange them perfectly. You'll see," Clarissa said.

She turned and ran her fingers across the side of the ornately intertwined wires of the suspended birdcage that housed her pair of rosy-cheeked lovebirds, Romeo and Juliet.

"Hello, my tender hearts."

"Why are your birds in the dining room?"

"Oh, I just wanted them to keep me company while I prepared for the best party ever held…the best party held *before* our wedding, that is."

"I love how you see the world now," said Brock.

"Whatever do you mean?"

"For you, time is no longer measured by a.m. or p.m., or even BC or AD. Instead, everything is 'before our wedding' or 'after our wedding.'"

Clarissa's smile beamed at Brock. He grinned back at her and walked over to the birdcage.

"Don't you agree that animals deserve to be outdoors, even ones named Romeo and Juliet? Birds in a cage…one day you'll set them free, won't you?"

Clarissa wound her index finger around the gold necklace that draped from her neck. A silver and gold heart-shaped locket, a most cherished gift from Brock, hung from the chain. Actually, it was Brock's mother's idea for him to give the locket to Clarissa. In fact, she had it designed, engraved and gift wrapped.

"Your horses and cows are fenced in. How's that any different?"

"It's very different. They're outside and can move around in some open space. And the horses get to go to town with the wagons." Brock stopped there, realizing that it was not a discussion worth having.

"Anyway, don't you think the fortune cookies will make my party one that the girls will never forget, just like our entire wedding? I want it to be so *wonderful*, so *spectacular* that every girl in town dreams of having a wedding as *magnificent* as ours. Oh my goodness, the date April 21 will *forever* be known as our day!"

Brock was now certain that Clarissa could talk faster than he could listen. He mulled over his options for navigating this conversation, but it didn't take long to find his path. "Let's not get too full of ourselves," said Brock. "I want *our* day to be memorable, but not so grand that we may regret it later."

Clarissa's mouth began to fall open. She composed herself and smiled. Brock studied how her tortoise-shell brown hair was smoothed and swirled atop her head like meringue on a lemon pie. Her ivory-colored lace dress, tight at the waist and again at her ankles, provided clear hints about the curves of her body. She lowered her head and opened her deep bluish-green eyes widely and gazed into his eyes.

"My dear Brock, I want only the best for you. I want our wedding to be the *best* in the *worst* way," she whimpered and made a droopy shape with her lips. "But if you would prefer to scamper away and elope, that would be fine with me," Clarissa said, her voice trailing off. "As for our honeymoon this summer to Europe, well I'm sure we can scratch that off our list of things to do as well."

"Eloping doesn't sound half bad." Brock flashed a quick grin. "Seriously, I know you and your family want a big wedding to make up for the modest one your parents had, so I'm happy to do whatever's needed."

"Thank you. So how was your visit to Chinatown?"

All at once, Brock's cheeks flamed. "Oh, it was fine…just fine. It didn't take long to find someone who made fortune cookies and moon cakes. He was surprised that I knew about moon cakes because they're only made in the fall as part of some festival of theirs. They even put whole duck egg yokes in the center to represent the moon!"

"How perfectly awful! Can you imagine me serving my guests cakes with egg yokes plopped in the centers?" She made the face of a repulsed child who had taken a mouthful of castor oil.

"But how wonderful that you found the fortune cookies!" said Clarissa, anticipating a supreme social success. "What was the shop like… where you bought them? Was it clean? Please tell me it was clean."

"Yes, it was clean." He paused. "But there definitely was something different about that place. I can't believe we haven't spent time in Chinatown before. No need to, I guess. We just skirt around its fringes on the cable car or in a carriage."

Brock continued to share details about his afternoon's adventure. "It had all kinds of smells. Some were nice, I guess. The people were friendly enough, and there were lots of them on the streets, in the shops and looking out the upper-floor windows. They bow to each other, mostly when someone enters or leaves a room. I didn't feel uncomfortable, but it didn't necessarily feel comfortable either. And they don't speak English unless they're speaking to someone who's not Chinese. At least that's what I noticed."

He added, "I met a sweet little girl named Ting Ting. Her eyes twinkled, almost like sparks. The funny thing is her family sold fireworks. It was right next to The Golden Palace."

His thoughts flashed to Blossom and how his time with her was strange and thrilling. Even the thought of her now made him inhale deeper than usual and release the pent-up air in a sudden burst.

"Are you alright?" Clarissa rested her hand on the fireplace mantel and then ran her fingers through the row of hanging tassels of the lambrequin that dressed up the hearth.

"Not to worry. Now tell me about your plans for this evening." Brock knew that if he changed the subject to anything related to their wedding, Clarissa would refocus. And he did have an interest in what was planned.

Clarissa explained how the party was going to be a girls-only affair for her bridesmaids and a few special guests. Unfortunately for Brock, Clarissa went on in great detail about the setting of a proper table. He did his best to appear to listen attentively. He also did his best to stop his mind from wandering and keep anything from escaping his lips that should remain unsaid.

"First, the servants spread a felt silencing cloth on the table and then top it with a freshly ironed damask tablecloth. Snowy white is always best. The table's seating arrangements should be roomy. People don't wish to sit with their elbows pressed against their sides like trussed fowl." *She sounds like an etiquette book being read out loud*, thought Brock.

"The flowers come next," she said with confidence. He nodded in agreement.

"Then dishes of nuts and bonbons are added. These candles will provide just the right light for a festive table. The covers are then placed at each place setting."

"A cover?" asked Brock. *Asking a question always makes her think I'm interested.*

"Yes, when the servants use the sturdier versions at their table, they call them 'placemats.' Honey, I know you've spent time in the kitchen."

"Yes, I know what a placemat is."

Clarissa jumped right back in to impress Brock with her knowledge as the soon-to-be mistress of their household.

"Then come the dinner plates, with tri-folded napkins centered on them. Now Brock, you should know that napkin rings are rarely if ever used at a formal table. Do you know why?"

"Uh, no, I don't."

"In homes of families that are less fortunate than ours, *mismatched* napkin rings are used to identify each family member's personal napkin so it can be used more than once."

Mismatched. He looked at his fiancée with narrowed eyes, as if to sharpen his vision. *Are we mismatched like the napkin rings?*

His thoughts were interrupted as he again heard Clarissa sharing her knowledge. "That reduces the need to launder them. Isn't that sensible for those who don't have the means to enjoy linens as they were intended... used for just one meal and then swept away for someone else to deal with?"

"Oh yes, that's sensible." *Is she ever going to stop?*

"To each plate's right, with edges inward, is the knife for the meat, then a knife for fish, a tablespoon for soup and an oyster fork." *Apparently not.*

"Should I tell you more about the forks?"

Brock's response to this yawn-inducing question was to clear his throat and shake his head. "Do I have any duties tonight?"

"No, though you'll be the topic of discussion. I'm sure of it!" said Clarissa, knowing that she'd have plenty of opportunities to brag about her beau and their future together.

"Then I'll leave you to your preparations and party. Maybe I'll see what Austin is up to tonight. But I promise not to have too much fun without you," he said as he hugged her, kissed her on the forehead and walked toward the door.

"But I haven't explained the placement of glassware, tallest to shortest glass to the right of the dinner plate. What about the correct times to serve from the sideboard 'a la Russe' or 'en buffet'?" Clarissa's voice became softer as Brock escaped the dining-room lecture.

Clarissa returned to her work and muttered, "Just as Mother says, 'The work of a home is love made visible.'" Katie, one of Zelda's co-workers, entered the room. "Don't you agree, Katie?"

"Yes, Miss Clarissa. I do indeed agree."

"The things we do for our men!"

"Yes, Miss. If I had a man, I'd treat him right nice. I'd—"

"Katie, I know that I shouldn't talk to you about such things, but I'll bust if I don't."

Clarissa went on about Brock's rough-edged good looks and the rancher-type clothes he wears. She said how it frustrated her when people underestimated his social standing because of his appearance. Clarissa was well aware that unlike many of the nouveau riche who inhabited The Hill of Golden Promise above the city, he wasn't the kind of man who flaunted his family's good fortune or expected extraordinary treatment because of it. At twenty-five years of age, he was running his own business on the outskirts of town.

Clarissa gloated in detail about the couple's time together last Saturday. She described how they spent the entire day together, just the two of them, walking and talking and dining like a married couple. At least that's what she thought married couples did.

Clarissa took a moment to sit down at the dining-room table. She closed her eyes and inhaled deeply. Katie stood nearby, not leaning or sitting. Clarissa looked like a woman who was going into a trance at a séance, bringing back the ghosts from the past.

"The colors in the Conservatory of Flowers in Golden Gate Park were absolutely spellbinding. It transported us to faraway places. There were plants from the Amazon that had leaves the size of elephants' ears."

Clarissa waved her hands in front of her with exaggerated grace. "The air was heavy and moist, like it was pampering everything that was delicate and green and growing."

She pondered for a moment. "Katie, the clothes were as spectacular as the plants! Women were showing off their most elegant dresses and parasols as they strolled. I was wearing an ivory lace dress with a bright yellow ribbon around my waist. And my hat, oh my hat had pure-white ostrich feathers and yellow-ribbon streamers. If I do say, I looked like springtime itself," she confessed as she kept her eyes closed. Her hands swirled above her head.

Katie remained standing and listening. It was her job.

"Then we had a fashionably late luncheon at the Palm Garden of the Palace Hotel. The orchestra played on and on. Katie, anyone who wants to mingle with royalty, writers and heroes either stays or dines there. It's as close to being at a palace as we can get here in San Francisco…but my honeymoon with Brock will be filled with castles and cathedrals. You'll see!"

Clarissa rested her elbow on the table as she relaxed and then removed it. "No elbows on the table" rang out in her head. It was a phrase she didn't have to be told too many times as a child, though her mother reprimanded her father with it often.

She took Katie back in time to the Palace. "Picture this." Clarissa began to clearly recall the conversation she and Brock had during the meal to the point that she could hear it word for word in her head.

"Can you believe we're getting married in fourteen days?" asked Clarissa, hoping that Brock would reply with something romantic that would affirm his limitless love for her.

"I better believe it if you want me to show up!"

Clarissa did not disguise her lack of enthusiasm for his response. Brock noticed and added, "Who would have thought we'd be getting married if they'd been there when we first met…well, the first time we met and truly noticed each other?"

Clarissa smiled and threw her head back. "Yes, we didn't exactly get off on the right foot, did we?"

"Actually, I believe I stepped on your right foot!" replied Brock.

"You did. If Faye hadn't introduced us at that party, we wouldn't be here today."

Never one to like dancing, Brock was proficient as a result of lessons that his mother required be taken and completed.

Brock recalled, "You'd been travelling out of town a lot with your parents, and I was never one to go to many parties, except the ones that my mother made me and my brother attend. So when Lloyd Shelton introduced you and Faye Huntington to me, I almost didn't recognize you. You'd changed. You'd become a woman."

Clarissa grinned.

"Lloyd was hoping that I'd take a shine to Faye so that he could monopolize you that evening."

Clarissa laughed in a restrained manner. "You know, I've never told you this before, but Faye confided in me later that she wanted to be paired with you that night. Let me see if I can remember how she told me. I believe she said that her smiling lips were for Lloyd, but the smile *beneath* her smile was for you. Oh well!"

Clarissa noticed how Brock looked embarrassed, then uncomfortable.

"I guess both of their plans didn't work out. But you didn't exactly like me at first, did you?"

"You were a diamond in the rough. And I'm a girl who likes diamonds, rough or not! But, I have to admit that it wasn't love at first sight. You grew on me."

"It wasn't easy, with Lloyd interrupting our time together. Did you know he was trying to pay boys for their slots on your dance card?"

"Yes, Faye pointed that out a number of times during the night. I wasn't sure why she kept talking about it, as if I should be flattered."

Brock and Clarissa enjoyed the two dances that he was able to get on her dance card. The second dance ended when Brock stepped on Clarissa's foot. They spent the rest of the party talking at a table while others danced. She turned away her would-be dance partners.

Clarissa remembered how it was several weeks before the two met again, and their relationship developed slowly and properly. Their families knew of each other on Nob Hill and grew closer as the pair's engagement was announced and the wedding date was selected. While it wasn't a whirlwind of passion, the engaged couple came to accept that their match was supported by two overriding factors: their fortunes and their families.

The mansion's doorbell rang and Clarissa's insides jumped a bit. "Katie, you may go and see who it is."

She soon returned to the dining room. "Miss, it's another wedding-gift delivery. I'll put it with the others."

"Yes, thank you."

Clarissa focused again on her table setting. As she fussed with the placement and symmetry of the silverware, her mind soon wandered back again to last Saturday's time with Brock.

She smiled as she recalled how she acquiesced to Brock's need to be by the sea late that afternoon. They headed toward the ocean and strolled along the beach near the Cliff House Restaurant, an aptly named establishment that loomed above the shore at the very edge of a continent. She watched how Brock was fascinated by the seagulls as they wheeled about the rocks. Their raucous screeches intermingled with the thunderous percussions of the crashing waves. Clarissa had to admit that the air was fresh, though a tad too chilly considering the outfit she'd selected for the Conservatory and the Palace Hotel.

Before long, they decided the fresh air and walking had worked up their appetites, so they watched the sunset as they dined behind the protection of panoramic panes of glass that lined the Cliff House's main dining room.

Back in the present in her own dining room, Clarissa tucked her memories away for safe keeping. She rose gracefully from her chair and adjusted the position of the fork in the place setting next to her. She smiled at her thoughts of their day together around San Francisco, and she looked forward to her party that evening with her best girlfriends.

Just one more week and we'll be making new memories as Mr. and Mrs. Brock St. Clair, thought Clarissa with great satisfaction. She held the bag of cookies and grinned at the excitement their prophecies would bring to her guests.

Fortune cookies. What an amazing way to finish a celebration. This is going to be a night that no one forgets!

Chapter 5

Favor From A Little Brother

Saturday, April 14, 1906, 3:16 p.m.
Four days before the earthquake and firestorm

The St. Clair name was just a breath away from being included among the elite "Bonanza Kings" of the Comstock Lode, alongside James Flood and James Fair. Brock's father's silver-mining interests were the family's ticket to high society.

Nob Hill not only offered an escape from the rawness and rowdiness of the boomtown below, it allowed the newly rich San Franciscans to have homes on a pedestal. The "Big Four" railroad barons staked their claims and built their mansions, setting the pace for all who followed. Charles Crocker, Mark Hopkins, Collis Huntington and Leland Stanford constructed estates of architectural excess that lowlanders ventured up the steep hill to stare at slack-jawed and awestruck.

Brock was well accustomed to the St. Clair estate, dubbed "Silverado" by his father. For as long as he could remember, this house glistened with silver accents in just about any form that silver could be applied. From the front door knob to the light fixtures, even the toilet handles, if it could be solid silver or plated with silver, it was part of the grandeur of Silverado.

Constructed with the finest woods, wrapped in radiant stone and crowned with a tiara of towers, steeples and turrets, Nob Hill's magnificent homes and manicured grounds lacked comparison west of the Mississippi River.

Brock raced up the grand staircase, putting his hand around the waist of the silver goddess statue on the newel post—a superstitious act he and his brother had done since childhood. At the top of the mahogany staircase, Brock turned to the left and walked quickly to the second door on the right.

"Hey, Austin. Spent much time in Chinatown lately?" Brock knocked on his brother's bedroom door. There was no answer. He opened it, but Austin wasn't there.

Brock searched for his brother, who was younger by three years. The mission ended in the billiard room. No surprise to Brock. Austin lived life like a gambler, taking risks both calculated and on a hunch. So far, his luck held out. Brock was perpetually annoyed at Austin's talent for getting himself out of any situation just by flashing his pearly smile and doing some fast talking.

Brock, as well as his widowed mother, worried about Austin's prospects. Not that money or comfort would ever be an issue. They were concerned more about a direction and purpose for his life.

The billiard room offered every luxury a hard-earned—or even ill-gotten—dollar could buy. Brock observed his brother. Matching his jade-green eyes, Austin leaned on the green felt-lined game table over which hung a Tiffany lamp shipped from the East Coast, like so many of the home's furnishings. A lit cigar in his mouth completed the picture of a pompous playboy enjoying masculine pursuits.

"Spent much time in Chinatown lately?" Brock asked, breaking the room's silence. "Want to go today?"

"Why do you ask?"

"I was there this afternoon, running an errand for Clarissa. I met someone—"

"You did what? Were you whoring around? No, that wouldn't be something you'd do. That's what I do down there! Were you looking for a good game of poker?"

"I said I met *someone*," corrected Brock.

The room fell silent as Austin digested what Brock just said. He turned and looked into the massive mirror on the wall. He checked his teeth, and then up his nose to be sure nothing was there that shouldn't be. Brock noticed that even when Austin puffed up his chest like a rooster in the mirror, it did nothing to harden his slight build and delicate facial features he inherited from his mother.

"You mean to tell me that while you were running an errand for the woman you're about to marry you met another girl—a Chinese girl—who made your blood rush down to your—"

"Don't be crude. Someone might hear you, not that they'd be surprised by what falls out of your mouth. Besides, I'm still your older brother. I'm still bigger than you, and I can pound the life out of you just as easily today as I could when you were six years old." Austin backed off, recalling previous painful times that Brock had inflicted his sibling authority.

"Finally, my *real* brother surfaces," Austin announced. "What a relief. I didn't think it would ever happen. You're finally being impulsive. You actually want to do the opposite of what your intuition is telling you. You bad boy, you bad—"

Brock took control of the conversation. "Calm down. Her name is Blossom. She works in a bakery that's part of a small restaurant. Maybe you've been there. It's called The Golden Palace."

"Can't say that I have." Austin folded his arms and cocked one leg at a new angle. "But what if I had?"

"I just figured that you spend a lot of time down there and you might know."

"You figured wrong. When I'm in Chinatown, that really means that I'm at one whorehouse and one whorehouse only…with a whore."

"Could you possibly say whore one more time?"

"Whore! Whore! Whore! Whore! WHORE!" Austin grinned.

"Anyway, back to why I came to talk to you," Brock said. He stared beyond Austin at the wall and then gazed up at the ceiling. "I can't say exactly what it was, or if it was just one thing. But I can't get her face—her eyes—out of my mind. She isn't like anyone else I've ever met. I didn't set out for this to happen. But we connected." Brock did his best to describe the heady rush of early infatuation, a sensation he knew that he hadn't felt before.

"I know I'm taking a big risk telling you this. Keeping secrets is not something you're known for. But as my one and only brother, I want to trust you this time. Will you go with me?"

Austin rubbed his chin, caressing the well-manicured reddish-blond goatee that provided some much-needed masculinity to his face. "Are you sure you know what you're doing?"

"No, I don't. But I do know that I have to see her again. It could be a huge mistake…or not."

"You connected?" Austin asked. "Yes, you connected." He answered his own question with his lips dancing on the edge of a smirk. "Buddy, if you want to pluck an exotic Chinese flower, I know of a place and a *stupendous strumpet* who would be happy to take you…um—"

"God, you're an ass!"

"Brock, when I'm cold and rotting, then you can call me an ass, but not until then," Austin said as he waved a pointed finger. "Assuming Clarissa is a virgin and considering that you're a *sex-lifeless* corpse, helping you find some satisfaction may not be such a bad thing. Isn't that what a best man is for?"

The younger brother clammed up and returned his attention to the billiard table. Brock began to regret disclosing his newfound interest in Chinatown. Austin moved the pool cue with his right arm, causing a crisp clacking of colliding balls on the table with the red ball dropping into a corner pocket.

"Say big brother, how much cash do you have on you?"

"Why do you care? Did you burn through all of your money doing whatever you were doing last night?"

Brock knew how costly Austin's tomcat ways were, but the younger Mr. St. Clair prided himself by never being cash-poor.

"My pocket has plenty of money in it, like always. But if I go with you, you're going to owe me something and maybe—" He stopped talking to think a moment. "Yeah, it's *not* going to be cash, though. I'll call in that debt another time, I think."

Brock looked at his brother and wondered how the two of them could be so different.

"Hey, it's your life. And if you want to make a pile of horse shit out of it, I won't be the one to get in your way," said Austin. "I'm all too happy to oblige. Then, maybe I won't look like such a lost cause in Mother's eyes after all. So, when do we leave?"

Chapter 6
Back For More

Saturday, April 14, 1906, 3:52 p.m.
Four days before the earthquake and firestorm

"The girls may be having their 'hen party' tonight, but we're going to have our fun too, and then some," said Austin as he swaggered just ahead of his brother down the front steps of their house.

"Whoa, little brother," grunted Brock. "We're not going on that kind of hunt. Besides, it's hardly four o'clock in the afternoon. And her father works at the front counter. I doubt that we'll be making an evening out of it."

Brock and Austin took the cable car down to the intersection of Clay and Dupont streets, where the Tie Yick General Store displayed preserved meats in the open air for all to see. Brock enjoyed watching how Austin was disturbed by the sight of dried duck, pig livers and frogs. They ventured down a narrow alley.

"Where are you taking me? God Almighty, it smells like Hell's outhouse around here!" blurted Austin. "I've been in some alleys here before, but not this one."

Brock glared at his brother. "I was here a few hours ago. I'm sure this is the way. Remember, it's called The Golden Palace. Look for a sign."

"Just what are you going to say when we get there? Hello, the moon biscuits—or whatever you call them—were great and I'm back for the girl now. What's your plan? You have a plan, right?"

"Well…I don't…have a plan." Brock felt his stomach slosh. "I just know I need to see her again. You've always been the manipulator, the schemer, the—"

"Stop already," interrupted Austin. "Give me a second to think. Here's what we're going to do. Didn't you say there's a bakery *and* a restaurant?"

Brock nodded.

"Then we'll go in the bakery to get more of those cookies. We'll tell them we just *had* to have more. I'll ask as many questions I can think of to distract whoever's working the front counter so you can make time with the girl. If that doesn't work, we'll have dinner at their restaurant and hope your girl works double-duty in both the bakery and the restaurant today."

"Sounds good!"

When they arrived at The Golden Palace, Brock took a deep breath, only to have it knocked out as Austin slapped him on the back. "Relax! Come on. Let's get this over with."

The bell hanging on the top of the doorway announced their arrival.

Brock remembered to step up and over the raised threshold. He neglected to warn Austin, who tripped over it. "I did it too, earlier today," Brock admitted in a whisper.

Chang looked shocked when he recognized Brock.

He bowed twice, once for each of the shop's visitors. The brothers bowed in response. "My new friend, you back. Sorry about trip. Evil spirits travel flat ground. We raise doorway. Keep them out, yes?"

"Yes, no evil spirits here," replied Brock.

"You no like cookies?"

"No, I mean yes, we liked them so much that we need more."

"Wonderful, wonderful, wonderful. They full of delight." The pair turned to look at each other. "So sorry. I mean to say delightful." He went on, "You bring friend?"

"He's not my friend," Brock responded. "Well, yes, he's my friend, but he's my brother, too. He was so fascinated…yes…fascinated by what I told him about your bakery that he had to come see it for himself."

Brock elbowed Austin. "Uh, yeah, absolutely. I had to see The Golden Palace for myself," he said as he strained his neck to scan the next room for the mystery girl.

A rhythmic clump-clump sound preceded the arrival of Grand Ma Maw. She heard Brock's and Austin's clearly spoken English from a nearby room.

"Greetings. I am Grand Ma Maw…first Ma higher, second Maw soft if you please. How we help you two jen-teal-men?" she inquired with a slow downward nod.

"Fortune cookies, ma'am. I mean Grand Ma Maw. We'd like another dozen," said Brock with yet another bow.

"Ah, you discovered the goodness of our cookies, have you? Chang, please see to their needs." Grand Ma Maw leaned back to see if Blossom was at her worktable. The old woman sighed.

"Fifteen cent," said Chang as he handed Brock the bag of cookies.

Austin not-so-gently nudged Brock out of the way so that he could pay for the cookies. He pulled a large wad of paper money from his pocket. Despite his mother's repeated warnings, Austin always carried too much cash, a trait he picked up from a favorite and flamboyant uncle. Austin did it partly to feel secure that he could buy whatever he wanted whenever he wanted it, but mainly to impress people. It usually worked. It did with Chang, who stood motionless and stared with his mouth agape.

"Hey! Move! You like over-cooked fish, my son," commanded Grand Ma Maw.

Chang closed his mouth and passed a bag over the counter. After paying for the cookies, Austin blurted out, "My brother was telling me about how the cookies are made. Can I see too?"

"So sorry. Girl gone to prepare for work tonight in our humble restaurant," said Grand Ma Maw. She held out her hand. Three fortune cookies were offered to Austin. "Pick one," she instructed. Austin did as he was told.

"Please enjoy. Eat. Eat. Eat," ordered Chang. Austin obeyed, shoving the entire cookie into his mouth. He began to chew. Brock watched as Austin pulled a wet paper slip out of his mouth like a ticker-tape machine producing a message. He turned to face Brock. "Why would anyone want cookies with a chewy paper center?"

"That your fortune, my sir. Read it," instructed Chang.

Austin cleared his throat. "A surprise treat awaits you."

Brock smiled.

"Sounds like this message was meant for you, Brock. Say, are you hungry?"

"Starved, just starved."

"Let's stay and have dinner." Austin turned to Chang and Grand Ma Maw. "We've never had a meal in Chinatown. What time does your restaurant open? Will there be someone to help us order?"

"We open five o'clock sharp. Yes, we help pick from our most delicious dishes. The Golden Palace not grand like Hang Far Low Restaurant around corner. But our regular customers never complain," Grand Ma Maw admitted with pride.

"Then I guess this is goodbye for now. We'll be back after five," said Austin as he pushed his brother toward the shop door. They both paused to step up and over the threshold.

"You owe me for this. And you can bet I'm going to collect on this favor when it matters most," said Austin in a hushed tone.

"Actually, I'm going to start collecting right now," added the younger brother, pointing to a saloon a few doors away.

"Damn, it smells like *rotten* eggs," he remarked now in an insensitive loud voice. Brock pointed out that next to The Golden Palace was a fireworks store, out of which wafted a most potent scent of sulfur. He mentioned how the lighting of firecrackers was believed to drive away evil spirits.

"Just the same, I bet they serve rotten eggs in your new girl's restaurant! I guess I'm an evil spirit, because—lighted or not—the smell of those firecrackers could drive me away. But it's not going to today."

Chang made his way upstairs to tell Blossom about a change in the evening's plans. "You have night off," commanded Chang.

Blossom studied him. She couldn't remember the last time she got a night off unless she was vomiting, which was rare. Grand Ma Maw was not far behind and entered the room. The addition of her presence made Blossom even more uneasy.

"You work too hard. You rest now," said Grand Ma Maw. "Spend night in room. Relax."

Blossom now knew something was happening and they were attempting to shield her from it.

"What's wrong with the two of you? Maybe you should sit down and relax. Really, I'm fine," replied Blossom.

"No more talk. You…stay…here," concluded Grand Ma Maw with authority. Chang and Grand Ma Maw began to leave the room.

In a hushed voice, Blossom mumbled, "I'm *not* staying here!"

The old woman turned and clarified, "My hearing not so bad. You stay here, my dear one." She nodded to once again end the conversation, turned and moved on. She closed the door behind her.

Blossom did her best to let Grand Ma Maw have the last word. But she couldn't overcome the urge to say, "You forgot to lock the door on my prison cell. I can still escape! You know I can still escape."

Outside the door, Grand Ma Maw grinned.

"What's going on tonight that they don't want me to be part of?" Blossom continued in a whisper, "I can't stay here. I *won't* stay here."

Chapter 7
$\mathcal{D}$ining At The Golden Palace

Saturday, April 14, 1906, 5:09 p.m.
Four days before the earthquake and firestorm

Time passed quickly for Brock and Austin as wince-inducing shot glasses of whiskey were hoisted back in the saloon near The Golden Palace.

"Don't be such a little girl. Drink your fire water like a man," instructed Austin. "Come on, raise up that shot glass again. You'll be all loosened up for the next time you meet this mystery girl of yours. It'll take the edge off!"

Brock obliged, sending the liquid fire down to his belly.

"That's how it's done!" Austin praised.

They left the saloon once it was five o'clock, having heard the faint chiming of nearby church bells over the early evening conversations in the barroom. Austin took in the full sight of the alley and how cramped everything was. "This place is so stacked and packed it makes canned sardines look comfortable," Austin observed.

Upon their return, the pair discovered a line of customers forming outside The Golden Palace's door. Brock noticed the pair of large ceramic statues that were standing like sentinels at the doorway. Local diners all rubbed the ball in the mouth of one of the statues. A man turned to Austin and said, "Rub foo lion-dog. Good fortune yours."

Austin turned to Brock. "I bet none of them trip over the doorstep." He rubbed the ball and pet the statue on the head as he passed it, muttering softly with a bit of a slur, "Good dog. Stay!"

Chang greeted and seated customers while Grand Ma Maw perched herself on a stool nearby to keep a watchful eye on her business. He bowed slightly to each customer, saying, "You honor our humble restaurant with your presence, my venerable guest."

Austin and Brock waited to be seated. The sweet smell of vanilla had given way to the aroma of chicken broth and hot vegetables. They did their best not to stare or study their new surroundings too obviously, but Brock was fascinated by the watercolor paintings on the walls. With a few strategic strokes of paint and a few details added with ink, the artist captured ordinary objects and dreamy exotic scenes. There was even a stylized portrait of a girl who looked to be Ting Ting.

Grand Ma Maw walked toward the brothers and carefully placed a brimming bowl of uncooked rice on the shelf in the restaurant's waiting area. The white porcelain bowl was decorated with a cobalt-blue dragon.

The pair bowed to her, though Austin kept his eyes on the rice bowl.

"You see, jen-teal-men, in China, we have Mount Penglai…the land of the Eight Immortals. No pain and no winter there. Jewels grow on trees. And rice bowls never empty…no matter how much people eat from them. Our good luck saying here at The Golden Palace is 'May your rice bowl never be empty.' This our way to wish customers good fortune as they come in and go out. This bowl of rice remind us to be grateful."

Brock cleared his throat. "Thank you—uh, *shay shay*—for explaining. May your rice bowl never be empty."

"Yes, thank you, Grand Maaaa Maw," added Austin. Ting Ting giggled from her seat in the corner. She pointed to Brock and repeatedly curled her index finger to draw him in. Brock leaned over and she whispered, "Your brother just said her name wrong. It came out like he was scolding a horse!" She giggled again. Brock smiled at her.

"Brother, we better stick to English. I'll tell you later what you just said in Chinese."

"Fine idea," said Grand Ma Maw with a slight smile. "I humbly ask you to remember my name Grand Ma Maw...first Ma higher, second Ma soft."

Austin nodded to acknowledge the old woman's request.

"You like paintings?" she asked Brock. "My granddaughter make them. She put in only enough to let us see what she paint. Then let rest vanish, except for one or two detail. She talented, yes?"

"Yes, she is talented. She certainly sees the world differently than the rest of us. And I like it, especially this one of Ting Ting," he said, pointing to the little girl's likeness. *She's being really friendly. Maybe too friendly?* Brock asked himself.

Brock's eyes then gravitated to the unusual flower arrangement on the counter. It had one enormous white chrysanthemum, a few shoots of tall green grass, several sandy-brown twigs and some speckled-grey stones in a brilliant orange ceramic bowl. "I've never seen anything like it before," Brock pointed out. *It's certainly not like the arrangements Clarissa puts together.*

"Granddaughter make that too," replied Grand Ma Maw. "One flower each day. She get from old lady who sell flowers down street next to fortuneteller. For our humble restaurant, she make beauty with just one blossom every day since she was little girl."

Grand Ma Maw announced, "Chang, seat these jen-teal-men! It time now."

Chang scurried over to do as he was told.

Grand Ma Maw added, "Have long noodles for long life. In respect, oldest person at table eat first."

She paused. "End with orange slice. Mean you have sweet life up on your hill."

Brock noted how it was Grand Ma Maw's role to ensure her patrons were well taken care of from the moment they entered the door.

The telephone in the small reception area rang loudly, demanding attention and action. "Pardon me," she said as she turned to answer the phone. "Yes Anna Mae, I will take the call," she said into the phone's receiver. In a flourish, the old woman rattled off an endless stream of words in Chinese with energy and passion.

Chang approached and seated the brothers at a small table. It had no recognizable utensils other than porcelain ladles that they would soon discover were soup spoons and pairs of decorated bamboo sticks like the ones Blossom used to make cookies.

"So we got this far. Now where's the girl?"

Brock scanned the room for Blossom. She wasn't there.

"Compliment of Grand Ma Maw," said the waiter. "She order you whole meal. You no worry. You eat."

Brock attempted to make adult conversation to distract Austin from saying or doing something embarrassing. "I read in the *Chronicle* this morning that the life expectancy today for men is forty-seven years and fifty for women."

Austin replied with a clear sense of frustration about the current misuse of his evening. "Yeah, right…as if I'm really going to need that useless piece of information!"

Brock continued, "And President Roosevelt is in—" His flow of words came to an abrupt end.

There she was.

As Blossom entered the dining room, Brock's voice remained frozen. She carried two bowls and gracefully maneuvered through a maze of tables. All eyes were on her now, as if she was an optometrist's letter chart. However, her gaze was locked on Brock just as intently as Grand Ma Maw's focus became locked on Blossom. *I know I'm staring…and I can't help it*, thought Brock. *My face is on fire. Oh God, even my ears are hot and they're ringing!*

Austin followed Brock's eyes and discovered Blossom for himself.

Uncharacteristically, he drank in the sight and held his words. Blossom's flaming crimson silk dress shimmered as she moved. The color made her an unavoidable visual target in the room.

Blossom brushed right by Butch at his regular table. She didn't even see him, much less show any interest. "You're mine," he said quietly but with force.

"Did you hear that?" Austin looked around. "Someone said 'you're mine.'"

"Wasn't me," whispered Brock as he watched Blossom come near.

"Wasn't me either, but a deep voice in this room is staking a claim on someone."

"Shut up and get ready to claim whatever's in the bowl that Blossom puts in front of you. Don't you embarrass me. Promise?"

"Promise," replied Austin. "But you already know I'm not the best at keeping promises…or secrets!"

Chapter 8
Fortune-Telling Cookies

Saturday, April 14, 1906, 5:31 p.m.
Four days before the earthquake and firestorm

Clarissa knew to be on guard at all times tonight. The well-tended young women who sat around her exquisite, well-appointed dining-room table were all icebergs. Below the surface, there was so much more to be aware of—and that's how they wanted it.

The polite and controlled table conversation was melting into a mixture of laughter and gossip. Not all at one time. To these emerging society women, while the energy level may elevate and the topic of discussion may become more scandalous, deeply ingrained manners and the rule about one person speaking at a time reigned supreme. The one-upmanship competition to be the speaker at the table was fierce after they finished their early supper.

"Ladies! Ladies! May I please have your attention," announced Clarissa from the head of the table where her father usually presided. "I'd like to take this opportunity to thank each of you for attending our gathering tonight. I'm certain this will be an evening that we'll never forget."

The woman to Clarissa's right skillfully took full control of the conversation. "Girls, as you know, Clarissa is my sister by choice—not blood. Since she and I are closer than any of you, I want you to know the joy we're feeling right now."

Here she goes, Clarissa thought.

Faye Huntington, Clarissa's maid of honor, was by far the most demanding and outspoken of all at the table. Clarissa would agree with anyone who concluded that Faye was the undisputed champion in the sport of vying for attention. Once she had grabbed everyone's attention, she never voluntarily loosened her grip.

Dressed in her freshly starched evening serving outfit, Katie turned to Zelda in the hallway outside the dining room. "By the saints above, I swear that Miss Faye makes me crazy. She's over-privileged. She's self-obsessed. She's got too much time on her hands. And she uses words like *adore* and *delicious* far too much if you ask me."

"Well, I didn't ask you, but those are some highfalutin words you just used. Showing off your schooling, like always!" Zelda straightened her back, held her head a little higher and nodded vigorously. "And if I hear her tell the story about her rich relations, I'll wring her boney neck myself."

"You better get your hands ready. You know it's coming, don't you?" replied Katie. "She always brings it out to play like an elephant at the circus…in the center ring, of course."

Faye stood up, drawing even more attention her way. "Though Clarissa isn't from a family of fame, like me and my railroad empire-building relatives led by THE Collis P. Huntington, I'm certain that her wedding will be the absolute talk of the town."

Clarissa took a long look at Faye as she spoke. She was tall, slender, even statuesque. She had porcelain skin lightly powdered to perfection. Not one hair out of place, Faye was inescapably the object of appropriate glances and inappropriate stares. She wore green, and only green, nearly every day to set off her emerald-hued eyes, much to the envy of the more plain young ladies in her circle, Clarissa included. She continued to study her friend. Add her flaming red hair to the mix and Faye had a powerful, attention-getting brew at her disposal to intoxicate onlookers.

Faye took her seat and whispered to Clarissa behind her open palm, "Ho hum, what a gathering of lost causes surround us. These girls couldn't attract flies!"

"What a wicked thing to say, Faye!"

Katie turned her attention back to Zelda. "You know, she's the bitchiest bitch I've ever come across." Zelda's eyes opened wide and she dropped her arms in mock surprise. "We should thank our lucky stars that it's no secret or there would be more casualties on this battlefield!"

"I know," added Zelda. "I've seen her throw her words at people like stones if it suited her. And when she's polite, folks don't even know that she's showering them with insults like parade confetti."

Fawning over Clarissa in yet another attempt to redirect the table's conversation to herself, Faye gushed, "Oh, Clarissa, I've got my maid putting together the most adorably quaint thing for me to give you! I'd have kept it a delicious surprise, but I simply can't!"

She continued, "Once you have your wedding dress, I'll have her sew a pouch to the petticoat. Inside you'll find a small piece of cloth, the tiniest nibble of bread, a sliver of wood, and a single dollar coin. Each item will help ensure that you and Brock will always have clothes to wear, food to eat, a roof over your heads and money for the future. I guess it's something that poor people do, but isn't that the sweetest thing I could do for you?"

"Yes, Faye, it's the absolute sweetest thing I could hope for."

Faye raised her glass. "Girls!" she announced with crisp elocution as she stood up. After making a shushing sound and flapping her hands, she unfolded a sheet of paper.

"I've written a poem—a toast, if you will—to express our wishes to the bride." She cleared her throat daintily behind an open hand that covered her mouth.

"A toast to the bride-to-be,

Because she is about to wed, you see,

She will help us understand,

What it's like to find the perfect man."

A synchronized "Awwww" flowed from every girl's mouth as if it had been carefully choreographed. Faye went on.

"Tonight, even if one tempts her fate,

She knows her destiny awaits,

To meet her beautiful beau,

Because in the end, she will say, 'I do.'

Best wishes and regards, Clarissa,

We love you!"

Applause filled the room. "Faye, that was wonderful. Thank you all so much," said Clarissa. Faye basked in the moment. "And I'd like to add a thought to that poem. It's something I read recently," Clarissa continued.

"Happiness is not having what you want, but wanting what you have. With Brock, I know that I'll want for nothing because I'll have him. I can only hope that each of you will know this kind of contentment and happiness."

Again, a synchronized "Awwww" poured out with overlapping voices that sounded like a tuning orchestra.

Clarissa noticed that Katie and Zelda continued to stand near the dining room doorway, listening to the conversation. She caught Zelda making a dismaying face.

"My dear, being around you and Brock is like witnessing a happily-ever-after love story that's come to life," Faye said. She snapped her fingers at Katie. Faye pointed to her nearly empty water glass. "More. Now!"

"Don't be so bossy," said Emmaline, throwing caution to the wind in defense of Katie.

Faye turned to look at Emmaline, but it was more than a look that she gave. Clarissa recognized the intense and prolonged stare that Faye always had the ability to summon at moments of frustration like this one. She'd seen it used before with great impact, even during their childhood.

It looked like Faye was trying to make Emmaline burst into flames with her mind. *Poor Emmaline, with Faye's perfect memory, this is something she'll never outrun,* Clarissa thought.

Faye eventually broke her stare and addressed Emmaline. "I'm not bossy. I just know what other people should be doing, particularly for me."

Clarissa was keenly aware of Faye's questionable social games and evil tactics, but she tolerated them because of their long-standing friendship. Clarissa wasn't sure what Faye was up to this time, but she made a mental note to remember what just happened for future reference. She knew Faye would.

However, tonight was Clarissa's night, and she had a surprise to spring on everyone.

"My dear friends, I have a special gift for each of you," announced Clarissa.

The word "gift" brought all eyes in one direction. She waved to Katie who was now hovering in the butler's pantry.

"Katie will come to each of you with a platter of cookies, more precisely, *Chinese fortune cookies.* My dear Brock personally went down to Chinatown just hours ago to get them for us."

Faye looked at Clarissa with a tilted head and squinted eyes.

"As Katie passes, take one cookie. But choose wisely."

Everyone followed Clarissa's directions and waited in a curious sort of anticipation for what would happen next. They inspected the cookies, commenting about their odd shape and texture.

"My cookie has some paper stuck in it. May I choose another?"

Leave it to Faye to speak out before I'm ready to finish the instructions. "No," Clarissa replied before Faye could utter anything else. "That cookie and that paper hold your destiny." She emphasized the word "destiny" for added drama and mystery.

Faye set her cookie down on the table, pushed it away and then gave it an extra push.

"Go ahead and break your cookie in half and read the prediction that appears on the paper. Tradition says that you must read the message before you eat the cookie."

One by one, each girl squealed as she read her fortune aloud.

Amanda was delighted to learn that happiness was just around the corner. Crystal giggled when it was revealed to her that marriage was not far off. Maribelle already believed that wealth would be hers, especially since she stood to inherit one of the city's largest fortunes. But her cookie's message confirmed it. And Emmaline pretended to be stunned when it was revealed that she would discover a hidden treasure.

It was Faye's turn. "I don't want to crack it open or read it aloud. I've never liked fortune-telling. No message in a cookie is going to guide my life," she added, wincing slightly, as if the words were sharp in her throat. "Anyway, I get everything I want."

Maribelle asked, "Well, what do you want?"

"Everything," Faye purred.

As hostess, it was Clarissa's job to jump in. "Faye, don't take this so seriously. You don't have to open your cookie now." She scooped it up. "I'll set it aside for another time when you're ready to see what's inside. Is that a good plan?"

Faye fired back, "I don't know. Why don't you ask one of the cookies!"

Amanda came to Clarissa's aid. "Clarissa, open your cookie. Let's hear about what the future holds for you."

Clarissa cracked the cookie open and pulled out the slip of paper. "I'm truly fortunate to receive this one! Confucius say, 'Wherever you go, go with all of your heart.'"

The group applauded. For all to see, Clarissa folded up the slip of paper and placed it inside the silver and gold locket that hung from her neck. The letters "B" and "C" were engraved on the face of the heart. She handled it with great care.

The girls told their hostess it was the best possible message to get before a wedding. They pondered aloud about the possibilities of the message's words coming true for Clarissa and Brock.

Uncharacteristically, Faye remained silent as she witnessed Clarissa's shining moment.

Clarissa noticed how Faye's eyes wandered over to the sideboard, where her cookie rested on a plate with the slip of paper slightly sticking out as if to taunt her.

Faye sat back in her chair, a smirk overtaking her face. Clarissa had seen that smirk before and considered how this was a particularly bad time to see it on Faye's face.

Chapter 9
Confessing To A China 5 Phone Operator

Saturday, April 14, 1906, 5:37 p.m.
Four days before the earthquake and firestorm

Blossom arrived at the table and gently, from the knees, lowered her entire body as she placed the bowls on the table. Blossom and Brock never broke eye contact, except for a brief moment when she felt Brock's soup bowl begin to slide on her serving tray. She looked down in the submissive manner. She placed a bowl of soup in front of each brother. She turned to walk away as Brock said, "Hello, I'm back." *Now that was a brilliant thing to say. Brock, you're an idiot!*

"Yes, I can see that," Blossom said over her shoulder. She continued to move toward the kitchen door, not stopping to speak to anyone else.

"Brother, she's the one you 'connected' with? Hmmm. Pretty loose connection."

Brock stared at the kitchen door. "It's like a bee sting."

"You mean it hurts?"

"No, once you get stung, you can't get un-stung. There's nothing you can do about it."

Austin added, "I understand. I really do."

"You do?"

"Yeah."

Since when does he feel anything other than instant gratification and pain when he doesn't get it?

"Well, she's not much for conversation," said Austin.

"It's like she talks to me with her eyes. Maybe it's their custom, their way."

"I don't know if it's her custom or not, but she didn't seem to show much interest other than staring at you. Or did I miss something?" asked Austin.

Clearly, you did.

Aware of every move and conversation in the dining room, Grand Ma Maw slid off of her stool and shadowed Blossom as she walked through the kitchen. "Did we not tell you to stay upstairs?" asked the elderly women of the girl who had yet to stop moving.

"Yes, you did," replied Blossom. "But I could hear from my room that things were getting backed up here, and I assumed that orders were not going out. I came to help, as you have taught me. It was my duty."

"You find time to change outfit in such a crisis?" asked Grand Ma Maw as her eyes scanned the kitchen, which was not at all busy or backed up at this early dinner hour.

"Your Mr. St. Clair dining with us tonight, as you now know. And he bring his brother. It seem we make quite big impression on him today."

"Yes, it would seem so," said Blossom. Blood rushed to her face like flames in a growing fire. *Can she see me blushing? Of course she can.*

"I not like what is happening. You done now. Back to your room. Shoo!"

Blossom could hold her words only so long. "I ask this respectfully, but why?"

"It your place to be obedient," said Grand Ma Maw curtly, with a clear air of authority.

Blossom closed her eyes and composed herself before saying matter-of-factly, "If I cannot serve Mr. St. Clair and his brother their dinners tonight, then I will serve no one again in this dining room, including Butch."

With that, Blossom turned and headed upstairs to her room, leaving Grand Ma Maw standing with her mouth wide open with words needing to be spoken to a girl who had left the room.

Blossom changed her clothes yet again and slipped out the back of the building to the alley. She made her way through the crowded streets to a black door with a poorly printed sign: China 5 Phone Operators Only. She pushed the door open.

Her friend Anna Mae was fast at work at one of the telephone company's switchboards, shifting from English to Chinese and back to English with ease.

Seeing the look on Blossom's face, Anna Mae nonverbally signaled to the operator next to her that she needed a break. The girl waved her hand and pushed a cord into a socket—one of hundreds of sockets in front of her. Anna Mae was quickly on her way out the door to be with Blossom.

"Oh, that Kitty is such a tattle-teller and gossip. If I'm not back on time, everyone will know. What do you need?" asked Anna Mae as she zeroed her attention on her friend.

"I've really done it this time. I've done what's forbidden, and to top it off, I disrespected Grand Ma Maw. But she gave me no choice because—"

"Please hold the line, ma'am!" interrupted Anna Mae as if she was speaking to an incoming phone caller. She looked at Blossom. "What on earth did you do that made her so upset?"

"Well, I haven't done it yet. But I've threatened to do it just the same.

That's what Grand Ma Maw is probably fuming about right now."

"But you've always spoken your mind with her. And Grand Ma Maw always talks about honor and dishonor—and ancestors—and on and on. What's so different this time?"

Blossom looked around as she searched for the right words.

"Just say it. I talk and I listen for a living. It's not that hard," said Anna Mae, encouraging Blossom.

"This time it is. He came into the bakery—and then the restaurant— and looked at me the way every girl wants to be looked at by a man. It's like he peels away everything and really sees me, not just my hair and eyes… because they're a different color than all of the other girls. I tried to act as if he didn't get to me, but my acting isn't so good."

"Who is the 'he' that you keep talking about, Ming Yang…I mean Butch? He's just a dumb ox from Fish Alley. He breathes through his mouth and drools—literally— every time he sees you."

Blossom rolled her eyes. "No, no. It's not Butch." Blossom stopped talking while she thought for a moment.

"Come on! Tell me more. I'm only on a break."

"Alright, alright, alright. It's the dare. I followed through. I'm sorry that I didn't tell you and Monique yet!"

"Oh my gosh. I'm so proud of you. Now you have to tell me everything…at least the short version!"

"His name is Brock St. Clair. He's from Nob Hill."

Blossom reached into her handbag. "Here's his card. He gave it to my father. He'd just helped him off the floor after he'd fallen down."

"Wait," interrupted Anna Mae. "Who did the falling and who did the picking up?"

"My father tripped on Ting Ting's marbles…again."

Anna Mae smiled. "Got it."

"Anyway, I had to secretly fish it out of the wastebasket where Ba Ba threw it. That's all I know about him. He's sitting in our restaurant right now with his brother having what I would guess is his first Chinese meal."

"Well then what are we doing here? Let's go! Wait a minute," Anna Mae paused. "Is there anything else that could make this worse?" *Of course there is*, thought Blossom.

"He's about to get married. Does that make it worse? And he's not Chinese."

"I figured he wasn't Chinese when you said he was from Nob Hill! Could you have made this any more impossible?" asked Anna Mae with a face-filling smile. "Love is *wonderful!*"

"Love. Who said anything about love?"

"You didn't have to," she said like an aged matchmaker. "I can see it in your face. I can hear it in your voice."

Blossom was stunned by Anna Mae's words. They burst into laughter and hugged each other.

Blossom kept the conversation going. "I don't want to wake up years from now and wonder, 'what if?' I've already got my share of unanswered what-ifs, and he's not going to be added to that list. I'm going to find out where this could go, whether I like where it goes or not. Do you think I'm crazy?"

"No, just a headstrong girl who's learning to follow her heart."

"You make it sound so poetic."

"No, it sounds *insane.*"

"I can stay out for a few more minutes. Let's go to your restaurant and you can show him to me."

"Okay, but we can only peek in the window. I don't dare go inside. Grand Ma Maw will put me under lock and key for sure!"

"Fine."

The two hurried, dodging people in their way. Luckily, it wasn't dark yet. The last thing they needed, to top off the list of rules that were already broken, was to be out after dark without a family member or a proper escort.

"Hey, isn't that Monique?" asked Anna Mae as she pointed across the crowded street.

"Yeah, it is. Who's she talking to? She must be low on gentleman callers."

"That's putting it politely."

Blossom made a mental note to visit Monique to tell her about the dare and to get her take on men.

"Come on. Let's get moving. Remember, Kitty is covering for me. I don't want to be in debt to her or have her gossiping about my comings and goings."

When the girls arrived at the restaurant, they peered into the front window as discreetly as they could. Ting Ting scampered over from next door with her two upturned pigtails bouncing around. Their sprays of loose ends of hair looked like exploding fireworks tied at the base with red ribbon bows. Blossom always told her that it was an appropriate hair style for the daughter of a fireworks-shop proprietor.

"Who are we looking for? Blossom's sweetheart?" the little girl asked in a silly sing-song way.

Blossom shushed Ting Ting and looked back into the restaurant window.

"So where is he? The room is filled with the regular crowd. No one here looks like they're from Nob Hill," said Anna Mae loudly enough for a man passing by to hear.

"I'm from Nob Hill. Is there anything I can do to help you?"

Blossom turned around and was face to face with Brock. It was the closest they'd been. She felt his warm breath on her face. He was about a foot taller than she.

Anna Mae figured it out fast and smiled widely. "Well, h—e—l—l—o Mr. Nob Hill. I'm Anna Mae. This is Ting Ting. This is my best friend,

Blossom. But I see that you've already met."

Brock was still looking at Blossom and didn't blink.

Austin stepped up to advance the conversation. "Very nice to meet you. I'm Austin St. Clair. This is my brother, Brock. He met Blossom in the bakery earlier today and then we had a *fascinating* discussion with her at the beginning of our dinner. But she never came back from the kitchen to bring the rest of our meal." He elbowed Brock in the ribs. The pain forced Brock to break eye contact with Blossom and take in a deep breath.

For the first time in her life, Blossom was speechless. She could not find any words worth speaking. The tingly feeling she had all over her body kept her mind from working.

"We just ended our first Chinese dinner before it was supposed to be over, I think," said Austin to Anna Mae. "No orange slices. No fortune cookies. No slips of paper with *cryptic* messages," he said with a creepy tinge to it.

"What did you think of the meal?" asked Blossom.

Brock answered, "The soup was incredible. After that, I don't remember much."

Blossom smiled.

"So just what are you two fine ladies doing outside the restaurant where one of you works?" Austin asked. "And why are you looking in the window?"

"Oh…well…um…Anna Mae is planning a party and I was, yes, I was just showing her my family's restaurant as a possible location for her party." Blossom was back to being herself again and thinking quickly on her feet, even if the delivery of her words was uneven.

Anna Mae jumped in and addressed Blossom with a serious, businesslike tone. "Now how many people did you say the place could seat? I need room for at least 50 guests."

Ting Ting just stood there looking up, pivoting her head and grinning at whoever was speaking.

"Perhaps my brother and I should leave you to your business," said Brock, taking a step away.

"You don't have to leave. We were just finishing our conversation and I was about to walk Anna Mae back to work. It's not a particularly scenic walk, but would you like to join us?" asked Blossom. *I can't believe I just asked to walk with us!*

"We don't have any plans," said Austin. "Sure, we'll walk with you. Anna Mae, can you tell us again what line of work you're in?"

"I don't believe I mentioned it earlier, but I'm a telephone operator."

Brock and Blossom paired off, as Austin walked next to Anna Mae.

There are no secrets in Chinatown. I bet Grand Ma Maw already knows what I'm up to right now, and her temper must be boiling over.

They talked about the damp evening air and the items in the shop windows that were unfamiliar to the men.

"So what happened to the men telephone operators?" asked Austin.

"It's interesting that you should ask that. Almost all of the operators were men not too long ago, but they were not polite enough," explained Anna Mae. "So, they were replaced by young women called 'Hello Girls.' If men had been more polite, I wouldn't have my job I guess!"

"That's quite a lesson for us men, now isn't it?"

"Yes. You better mind your manners or a woman might just take your job."

Austin replied with a snicker, "I don't have a job, so there's nothing to lose or take!"

Once the group delivered Anna Mae back to her workplace, the brothers offered to walk Blossom home. She accepted, knowing that the decision was questionable. It was even more scandalous that a respectable and prized Chinese girl would walk openly with two white men than to walk alone. As a result, Blossom picked up the pace.

They said their good nights at Blossom's restaurant door.

"When may I see you again, Blossom?"

"Will your fiancée need any more cookies?" asked Austin of Brock as he pet one of the foo dog statues.

Brock looked at him with an uplifted eyebrow and a cocked head.

"I cannot say when we'll meet again, but I hope it will be soon," Blossom gently said.

"I *can* say when. We can steal some time to be together. We'll meet tomorrow at noon at the Tie Yick General Store at Dupont and Clay streets. The cable car goes by there. That's how we got here this afternoon. I want to show you my favorite place. Please be there at noon!"

Blossom hesitated, then nodded.

"Now go, before my Grand Ma Maw chases you away with a broom or her walking stick!"

Once the two brothers left, she ran around to the alley and rushed into the back door and upstairs to her room.

What have I started?

The clump-clump of Grand Ma Maw's approaching walking stick dynamited Blossom's dreamy recollections of the evening. She braced herself for what was sure to be a verbal lashing, if not something worse.

Though she didn't need to and Blossom's misbehavior certainly didn't make it necessary, Grand Ma Maw knocked on the door leading into the tiny room the two shared. She entered as quickly as she knocked, not waiting for a response.

"You foolish girl! What you did tonight cannot be repaired. Entire town talking about your little show. You know this, yes? Somebody's eyes always watching. No secrets in Chinatown, only hidden answers to questions yet to be asked. Can I ever play mahjong with my friends again without being asked about you and him?" Grand Ma Maw paused. "In one night, you undo everything we work on these many years. Your reputation—our family's reputation—now spoiled like chicken meat left out in hot sun."

"Grand Ma Maw, let me—"

"You…listen to…me! I not done. I only begun," said the woman, who for the first time looked truly old and vulnerable to Blossom. "I fear what you have done cannot be undone."

Chapter 10
All About Men

Sunday, April 15, 1906, 10:14 a.m.
Three days before the earthquake and firestorm

Under the guise of needing to pay Anna Mae a morning visit, Blossom made the risky choice to go see Monique to learn about men. Grand Ma Maw put up a strong defense, but cautiously agreed to give Blossom the freedom to go out alone.

Blossom was hyper-aware of her surroundings the entire time she traveled the streets and alleys of Chinatown. She watched above and over her shoulder for prying and condemning eyes. She knew that if word got back to Grand Ma Maw, her freedom would evaporate along with what remained of the family's good name.

Blossom often called Monique by her "old" name, Lai. Now, however, Lai plied her trade in a world of silk stockings and fancy lingerie as Monique LaFontaine, and she peppered her rendezvous conversations with "oui" more often than not, since "yes" was the answer to most requests from patrons.

Blossom remembered when Lai's parents died. The girls were both fourteen and Lai had no other family members who were able or willing to take her in. She confessed to Blossom that she saw no other choice but to strike out on her own. In a city teeming with men in need, Lai quickly became Monique. Before the rough-and-tumble streets of San Francisco could suck out her joy of life, or her *joie de vivre* as she would learn to say, Monique was taken under the wing of Madam Claudine Bijou, who taught her the ways of the world at far too early an age. Adding French to her repertoire was her mentor's idea and was accomplished under her tutelage. It paid off handsomely over time at the bordello just on the fringe of Chinatown.

Monique always came to see Blossom, so that she'd never have to set foot in a brothel or be seen doing so. This morning, Blossom faced the door and was about to take a reputation-battering step. She bit her lip, noticed how dry her mouth was and felt queasy. She entered Madam Bijou's parlor unannounced, though a small chime hanging above the door signaled her arrival.

Blossom whispered as she took in the visual assault. "Whoa! So this is her world!" The parlor was unlike any room she'd been in before. With nothing that looked like Chinatown, the French-influenced, gold-colored wood furniture had floral silk cushions, and the large mirrors reflected images and light in all directions. The air was filled with a stew of stale cigar smoke and sweet perfume. The room felt dreamy and unreal to Blossom.

Madam Bijou sashayed into the room with a series of tiny but quick steps. She was surprised to find Blossom standing next to one of the painted urns that held arrangements of long ostrich feathers.

"*Bonjour. Enchanté.* Welcome, my dear, to Maison Bijou. I was a bit shocked when I heard the chime. We don't usually receive many guests in the morning, especially on Sunday. I was just getting ready for a superb luncheon of haute cuisine at the Poodle Dog. Have you dined there?"

"No ma'am, I haven't had the pleasure," replied Blossom as she gazed up at a massive chandelier with crystal necklaces draped over it.

"What a shame. Perhaps someday you will dine there too. Are you looking for someone in particular? Or perhaps you are looking for employment at our Parisian paradise?" she asked as she outstretched her arm gracefully to direct Blossom's attention to a wall of portraits. In the center was an oil painting of Madam Bijou—in her younger days—in a grand gold frame, flanked by framed photographs of coyly posed women dressed in décolletage for the evening, their low-cut gowns showing more shoulder, chest and bosom than Blossom was accustomed to seeing.

"I do hope you're looking for work. Please don't be offended. A half-caste girl with your lavender eyes, skin tone and hair will suit you well in the business of entertaining gentleman callers," Madam Bijou said as she reviewed Blossom's attributes.

"Oh, oh no, ma'am," Blossom choked out as she cleared her throat. She turned and ran her fingers through the feathers as she thought, *How dare she call me a half-caste! I may look different, but 'haft-caste'?* Then she focused herself back on responding to the woman.

"I'm here to see Monique...ah...Monique LaFontaine. We're old friends, and I need her advice...yes, um, her advice on an urgent matter."

"*Quel dommage.* What a pity," said Madam Bijou as she shook her head in disappointment.

"Ah, yes, Monique is a special girl. I'm sure whatever advice she gives you will be wise and kept *entre vous*...between you two. Discretion is an essential part of our business, you see?"

"Yes, ma'am," replied Blossom.

Madam Bijou ascended the stairs to tell Monique that she had a visitor. A girl was leaning against the wall on the staircase landing.

"Madam Claudine," said the girl with a distinctly boozy drawl. She was looking at Blossom with a furrowed brow. "This girl's got bigger teats than me and she's a Chinese chickadee. That ain't right. Chink sluts are usually flat as washboards."

Oh, I feel naked. Monique, where are you?

The girl twirled the white-feather boa that hung from her neck as she began to blurt out more observations. "What's wrong with you anyway?

Your parts don't all add up. I bet your folks both ain't Chinese, right?"

Blossom's eyes opened wide like a goldfish's.

"Hold on there, you fat cow. Chantilly or Filet Mignon—or whatever the hell you're calling yourself these days—get your nose out of my business and drag your lopsided ass and mismatched *teats* back upstairs," announced Monique as she descended the stairs.

In contrast to what was spewing out of her mouth, Monique delicately tied a bow in the wide rose-colored ribbon that secured her peignoir above the waist, which made her appear taller than she was.

"Don't mind her. She's more than a little rough around the edges for this place, but she's a wildcat in the sack and she brings in more than her share of men."

"Shoo!" screeched Monique as she goosed the girl on the bottom as she went back upstairs.

Monique walked over to the front door, opened it and looked out in both directions.

"It's not out there."

"What isn't?" Blossom looked at Monique with a cocked eyebrow.

"Your mind. Have you lost it? What were you thinking? You, here in broad daylight! Has someone died? That's about the only thing that would bring someone like you to Maison Bijou!" Monique walked toward Blossom and adjusted her ebony hair rolled at the nape of the neck in its chignon. She caught Blossom staring at the wall of portraits.

"Honey, if this was a restaurant, that would be our menu. Only the best girls get their portraits taken and hung on the wall. Look there," said Monique as she pointed to her photograph at the top of the arrangement. "I'm up here for all to see…and order!"

She continued, "Did you know that *bijou* means 'jewels' in French? Madam Bijou says we're like the jewels of a *priceless* necklace that surrounds her on the wall there. But we all have a price, don't we?"

Monique shook her head. "So why are you here?"

"I'm so sorry that we weren't able to stop and talk last night, Lai…I mean Monique. We were in such a hurry and—"

"Don't worry about it. What were you in such a hurry to do with Anna Mae?"

Blossom looked beyond Monique to avoid making eye contact. Her fingers from both hands were woven together and nervously wiggling.

"Come on, let me have it," prompted Monique. "Do I have to coax the words out of you like I do some of my shy gentleman callers?"

Blossom was relieved that Monique had provided the smoothest of transitions to move their conversation along.

"How oddly coincidental that you should mention gentlemen. I followed through on our dare and now I'm getting into unfamiliar territory with a man. As far as I can figure, you're an expert on the topic," Blossom blurted out in a way that only friends can.

Monique smiled. She'd become an expert in the types and ways of men. She had to if she was going to survive in her occupation.

"So is he an upstanding Chinese man? Did your father pick him out for you?"

Blossom began to squirm. *Clearly this isn't going to be an easy conversation.*

"*Au contraire.* See I can speak French too!" She dropped her eyes modestly and confessed, "He's white, lives on Nob Hill and is engaged to be married. Could I have made it any more difficult?"

"Yes, he could already be married or have some nasty disease!"

"You're not making what I have to say any easier. We met in our bakery. He's the one I flirted with because of the dare. Something sparked. I would have flirted with him anyway, whether or not we'd made that pinky swear. So then we met again in our restaurant. Last night, when you saw Anna Mae and me running down the street, it was to spy on him and his brother. And I told him I'd meet him today at noon."

Monique nodded. "I'm not sure you really want to know what I've learned about men, but if it'll help, I'm happy to talk. Besides, it'll give me a break. Business has been good, but I'm exhausted, and the morning is usually the only time to relax! Let's go up to my room. We'll have more PRIVACY there," she raised her voice as she spoke the word privacy, suspecting that someone might be listening to their conversation.

When they got to the final landing, Blossom said "Eight!" They'd climbed eight short sets of stairs that brought them to the fourth floor.

"I know, I know, it's the fourth floor. Most people around here are afraid of the number four. But for me it's the penthouse and most of my clientele is not Chinese. So, I'm choosing to believe that four is not bad luck in this case, even if it sounds like the word for death in Cantonese. But just to be on the safe side, don't say that word out loud."

She opened the door and they were greeted by high-pitched barking. Monique revealed not only her stunning golden-colored room, but her miniature poodle. She greeted the toy-like dog with sweet baby talk.

"I just got her. She's an apricot poodle. See her coloring? I just love my little Peaches to pieces," said Monique as she picked up the obviously pampered dog.

"Pull up a cushion and sit by us, *mon cheri*," instructed Monique from the luxurious settee she now rested upon.

Blossom patted Peaches on the soft tuft of fur on her head.

"Before I start, you have to understand that a bordello is a woman's world. Most people think it's a man's world, but they're wrong. The men come and go, but we hold the power."

She stopped, thought for a moment and dramatically added, "You might think what we do is wicked and depraved. But this is where young men discover the deliciousness of women and where old men relive past conquests. That makes it sound magical, and I suppose it is for the men." She stopped again to adjust the pillow that was behind her lower back.

"Kind of like a good shot of whiskey in a barroom, we girls are horizontal refreshment in a bedroom!" She laughed at the humor she thought she'd created. Blossom didn't laugh.

"Anyway, my time with men is all about fantasy. It's not real. There's nothing emotional about what I do, and I'm not entirely proud of some of the things I've done. It's usually kind of mechanical, you know, like an instruction manual—put Tab A into Slot B. Then there's the role playing."

"Role playing?"

"Sometimes I'm a saloon girl or a dairy maid from the French countryside or a princess in distress. I could be a pretty good actress when I think about the roles I've played. But I have a line that I don't cross."

"Really?"

"Yes ma'am. Like most women in my line of work, I don't kiss. It's too personal."

Blossom looked at her with pinched lips and a wrinkled forehead. *She doesn't kiss?*

"But I've learned a thing or two about men along the way. They're easily blinded by lust. Money doesn't buy class. Some of the classiest men I've been with had very little money. The bottom line is this: Men are pretty simple creatures, and they're predictable," she reflected.

"I'm known as a soiled dove. I'm a treat, a tart, and hopefully if I'm doing it right, a thrilling encounter. They come in all sizes, and I'm not just talking about their height and weight. Their manhoods range in size from firecracker to fire hydrant. The fire hydrants are rare, but when you're with one, brace yourself!"

Blossom looked at Monique with widened eyes. *A fire hydrant?*

"But, there are two things they all have in common: They want you to listen when they talk because they think they're always right, and they need to be told they are incredible lovers. Believe me, it's not hard to make them believe both of those things, even if it's not remotely true. If more wives and single women figured that out, I'd be out of work."

She continued, "Someday, though, I hope to find a real man and kiss him…and kiss him…and kiss him. I've got to escape this trap before my charms and body give out. Actually, I'm more afraid of the younger girls who're always trying to stake their claims on my clientele. I was one of those younger girls once, so I know their game. It's one that I can't win with some men. *C'est la vie*."

She looked at Blossom. "Is this what you want to hear?"

"Yes, please go on."

"This is not a business built on happiness. It's all about pleasure…for men, that is. There's nothing happy for me in this other than the money. Lovemaking without love is actually pretty sad when you think about it. To be with so many men and wake up alone, that's sad."

Monique paused. "This man that you're talking about, I hope he's worth it for your sake. You're putting a lot at risk to have a relationship with him. I don't want you to be disowned by your family and find you working here! I know what it's like to go out on your own, and I don't need any more competition. The way you look could set you apart and above me and most of the other girls here, especially those lavender eyes of yours. They're one of a kind, well, two of a kind. You have two eyes that match, right?"

The blood in Blossom's cheeks fired up. *It's always the eyes!*

Monique settled back in her settee and stroked the tiny dog resting on her lap. Her eyes gazed up to the ceiling as if she were going to pull her words out of the air. "You can tell a good man by his eyes. I know that because I don't see it often."

"Oh, my Mr. St. Clair's eyes are deep," said Blossom. "Even if I didn't want to look, they're like magnets that draw me in with a force so—"

"Did you say Mr. St. Clair?" interrupted Monique. "Not that shit

Austin? Damn him! He walked right past me twice last night and didn't even wink at me. Hey, you and Anna Mae were with him, weren't you? And after everything I've—"

Blossom took a turn to interrupt by asking, "You know Austin? That's Brock's brother."

"I guess I'm, shall we say, well-acquainted with only one of the Mr. St. Clairs!" exclaimed Monique. "I don't believe I've ever met Austin's brother."

"And let's just keep it that way."

"So, let's get back to our little talk about the men. Most of my gentlemen callers don't talk much or offer their real names. Usually, they look like men and smell like men. They definitely sweat like men. But they screw like selfish, impatient boys. Austin, now he's different. I'm mighty glad to see him visit. He's a true *bon vivant*. He enjoys the good life. I do like a man who knows how to live!"

Blossom quickly added, "Face it, you like a man—period!"

"I guess there's some truth to that, but Austin's a man who knows his way around a woman's body. Plus, he's a big tipper. When you have a legion of men climbing on your body and having their way with you night after night, a guy like Austin stands out."

She began to laugh. "He calls it his dragon, and sometimes the Eiffel Tower. But it's really more like the Leaning Tower of Pisa. It's slightly crooked I mean."

"Monique, that's not very kind."

"It's true though. And if his brother knows how to use what he's got, you're in for a treat! Every time, *la petite morte*…an orgasm…the little death."

"Monique, stop. *Tout suite!* See, I've done it again. I've learned a few words in French from you over the years. Remember, it's me, innocent little Blossom. You're embarrassing me, sort of!"

"*Excusez-moi!* You aren't so innocent! You just walked in the front door of one of the city's finest bordellos in plain daylight! You brazen hussy." The two laughed loudly at the situation they were in.

"I really don't know what I'm doing. This is so risky," said Blossom. "All I do know is that I couldn't stop looking at him and I can't wait to see him again."

Monique clasped her hands together in her lap. "Well, you could do much worse than spending some time with a St. Clair man. It's no secret that Butch comes to your restaurant every night in hopes of marrying you. He's the first-born son in his family, and that means he's used to having first choice and getting his way. He tells plenty of people that you're the one for him and he's going to make it happen. Not that he's got the guts to speak up and tell *you*. Has he? Or has he resorted to paying a matchmaker to work out the details for him?"

"He's not a talker, that's for sure," Blossom said.

"He may be part of the strongest of Chinatown's tongs and his family watches his back, but he's not much of a gang member. It's like he doesn't belong or want to fit in. And then there are his hands. He's missing a few fingertips. I guess that's what you get—or lose—when you're a butcher." Monique held up her hands with several fingertips bent back to appear as if they'd been amputated.

"You can ask any of the girls along the alley and they'll tell you there's nothing much below his belt. When he's not around, they all laugh and call him Mr. Chopstick Dick. He's not for you, my dear Blossom," said Monique as she waved her flattened hand back and forth as if shooing away a pesky gnat.

"You might as well know more about my line of work. That will help you understand what they like and how they go about getting it."

Monique explained that prostitutes generally land in one of three types of establishments: parlor houses, dance halls or cribs. There was also a fourth type, which was undoubtedly the worst form of prostitution: streetwalking. Though Chinatown's brothels featured mostly Chinese girls, there were also white, Latino, Filipino and black prostitutes. Being different or exotic could work to a girl's advantage. Many girls started at age seventeen and were either washed up or dead by twenty-three.

At the high end of the spectrum, gentlemen frequented multi-story parlor houses that once had been private homes. This was Monique's place in the hierarchy.

"We may be shady ladies who live on the Boulevard of Broken Dreams, but we're classy!" Monique stated with pride. "You won't find any tattoos here."

She was among the femme fatales at the top of their profession, charging ten dollars or more for an encounter, especially because she was a girl with a convincing French accent. At those prices, even the bed sheets were changed after each visit—a nicety not even considered in the city's other brothels.

"Unlike the girls who work in the dance halls or cribs, we put on rice powder and lip rouge sparingly and tastefully," said Monique as she pretended to apply cosmetics.

One rung down on the ladder of whoring, dance halls offered entertainment while featuring dancers and waitresses who discreetly and not-so-discreetly offered sexual services on the side. "You've heard of 'hurdy-gurdy houses,' right?"

Blossom's head bobbed as she said, "Sure have."

Monique described how they spend time with men listening to tunes churned out by a hurdy-gurdy music machine, the full-size and much more complicated version of Ting Ting's hand-held hurdy-gurdy.

"Now let's talk about the girls who are getting close to hitting rock bottom. It's more of an endurance test than a job. Most girls endure an awful lot. And the lot they get is really awful in the cribs," said Monique in an exhausted tone.

"A girl named Suzette worked here when I started. She really must have been something when she was younger. You could see it behind her aging face and the way she carried herself. She got sick. I heard she ended

up in the cribs and became known as Chop Suzie until she died not too
long ago."

"Want me to keep going?" Monique questioned.

"Absolutely," Blossom replied as she scooted closer on the settee, like
it was story time in some sort of sex kindergarten. *Seems like she's telling me
more about prostitution than men, but I'm learning.*

The most unsavory kind of prostitution was available in Chinatown's
darker corners. Known as "cribs," rows of stalls held little more than small
cots that were divided by haphazardly built partitions. A crib was often no
bigger than an outhouse. A group of cribs gathered under one roof was
called a cow yard.

"Those girls have faces like ghost towns. What's for sale there is time
with a woman's body, not with a woman. It's not for romance. The men are
looking for a convenient wet hole. That's it."

Blossom looked directly at her friend. "Monique, you speak dirty"

"Yes, I'm fluent!" Monique laughed at her own comment.
"Streetwalkers have it even worse. All they do is throw down a rug or an
animal hide on the ground outside and they're in business. I'll have to
find a new career before I ever come close to becoming a crib girl and
definitely before I hit streetwalker status," said Monique. "Either you have
it or you've had it! And I *have* it, for now anyway. Say, when I'm ready, will
your grandmother need another girl for the bakery or restaurant?"

"Well, there's hardly any money in it. By the time you think your back
is breaking from sitting on a stool in the bakery all day, it's time to work in
the evening until your feet are killing you. Does that sound good to you?"

Monique smiled and in her best French said, "*Oui, avec plaisir!* That
means 'yes, with pleasure.'" They laughed, but Blossom stopped abruptly
when the mantle clock announced that it was 11:30. "Honey, did you say
you were meeting your man at noon?"

Blossom sprang out of her chair. "I'll never get home in time to make
up another excuse—at least a convincing one—and meet Brock!"

"Relax. Living in a world of lies and deceptions has helped me perfect my skills of getting out of compromising situations and helping others do it too," said Monique.

She paused and pondered a moment. "I know, I'll loan you one of my white-girl dresses. There's no silk and no high necklines like your outfits. Don't fret. We'll get you to wherever you said you'd meet. I'll come up with something to tell your father."

"But I already told him I was visiting Anna Mae this morning."

Monique plotted. "I'll go to Anna Mae's and tell her what happened. Then I'll have her telephone your father and say that you're staying for lunch and then to help in her family's store. Will he believe that?"

Blossom responded, "I don't know, but I don't want to miss meeting Brock—and I don't want him going to the bakery looking for me either."

Monique transformed Blossom's entire appearance in less than ten minutes, but not without one misfire. The first dress was a tad too tight. Following the worried look that Blossom gave Monique, more dresses were pulled out of the small closet in the corner of the room. "Sweetie, we just can't squeeze ten pounds of sugar into a five-pound bag. Tightening your corset will help, but let's just try on another dress," Monique said cautiously, not wanting Blossom to think she was insinuating that Blossom was overweight. The second outfit was perfect.

"Are you sure Brock is going to like this?" Blossom asked as she looked at herself in the floor-length mirror.

"Is he a man? Of course he'll like it, even if you can't breathe, speak or move very well," replied Monique.

"This dress is so tight too, but the pale pink color is awfully nice. The heels on these buttoned-up white boots feel odd. I'll trip or tip over for sure! And look at my hair. I've never swirled it up like this, especially with a hat on top!"

Blossom reached up to adjust the petite pale-pink hat with a single pink ostrich plume. Monique playfully swatted Blossom's rising hand.

"Leave it alone. You look irresistible. Trust me. Besides, there's no time to undo what I've done, so you'll just have to make do."

Blossom kept looking in the mirror. *It's just like Yeh-Shen. I'm a Chinese Cinderella.*

"One more thing, you need a little white-girl frosting." Monique turned to her vanity and grabbed a small ceramic jar.

"When I'm working, bright colors do the trick. But other times, I use cosmetics to subtly enhance my beauty without overpowering it!"

"Monique, that sounds so calculating."

"It is. Now watch and learn." Monique dipped her index finger in the pink rouge and defined Blossom's check bones with a line of it. "This will give you a feverish, flush look on the apples of your cheeks." She dabbed it with blotting paper to soften its appearance.

"Now, to make your eyes look like a white girl's eyes, I'm putting a dab of pink on the outer corners of each eye. I'm dragging it under your eyes."

"Do I want white-girl's eyes?"

"You practically do already. I guess I never really studied their shape until now. And, yes, you need white-girl's eyes…today anyway!"

"I trust you."

"Here's the real corker…it's actually a cork!" Monique picked up a wine-bottle cork that had been whittled down to have a have a thin edge at one end. She lit a match and burned the edge of the cork. "Ready?"

"For what?

"Some black magic, of course." Monique carefully applied the charcoal dust created by burning the cork around Blossom's eye. She blurred the pink coloring and the burnt cork with her pinky finger.

"*Viola.* You're ready. Now I'm sending this pot of pink color and the burnt cork with you. Keep it in your handbag to touch up my fine work. And here's a compact mirror too…for your date with destiny!"

Monique opened her bedroom door and gently nudged Blossom out into the hallway. They carefully descended the eight flights of stairs. The girls were met at the bottom by Madam Bijou.

"*Coup de foudre!* I didn't see this coming so quickly, but, my child, how you have changed this morning. Are you sure that you wouldn't like to stay here and become another one of my protégés? Such beguiling beauty should not be wasted on just one man!"

Blossom responded half-jokingly as the pair scooted out the front door. "If I don't get to the cable car stop in front of the Tie Yick General Store by noon, we may need to have that discussion!"

Madam Bijou smiled, winked and waved from her front door saying, "*Au revoir*…until we meet again!" She added quickly, "I'll be waiting for you."

Chapter 11
The View From Twin Peaks

Sunday, April 15, 1906, 11:57 a.m.
Three days before the earthquake and firestorm

Out of breath but on time, Blossom nervously swayed back and forth in front of the Tie Yick General Store. She felt awkward and confined in Monique's clothes and yet somehow liberated. She caught a glimpse of her reflection in the storefront window. *I don't feel like me and, oh my gosh, I don't look like me*, she thought.

She watched how her body's movement gently billowed the pale-pink plume in her borrowed hat. *So this is what Yen-Shen must have felt like when she saw herself in her green gown and golden slippers before she went to the festival!*

Then the rush of the moment hit her. *I'm waiting for a man I hardly know to take me someplace where I've probably never been. How could I even think this might be a good idea? He probably won't even show up. And, if he does, he won't even recognize me.*

Her rapid-fire thoughts were interrupted by a deep voice. "Blossom? Is that you?"

Her breath was stolen from her. She looked to her right and saw Brock's reflection in the windowpane. He stepped down out of his carriage and removed his hat. The "ah-ooo-gah" sounds of the blaring horn of a new-fangled automobile luckily didn't unsettle the two black horses standing ready to pull the carriage.

"Hello," she said softly, letting the word barely escape her lips.

"Don't talk," Brock ordered gently. "Just stand there."

He looked into her eyes and then slowly gazed down to the ground and closed his eyes. There was a long, awkward pause.

"I've got it. I captured the vision," he said. As slowly as he'd closed his eyes, he opened them and grinned widely.

"Don't take this wrong, but for a moment I didn't think it was you. My God, you look incredible!"

"Do you really think so?"

"Yes, I mean…I couldn't keep my eyes off of you yesterday, but today you're…"

Blossom didn't know how to react. Having always been looked at as being odd and different in Chinatown, she was ill-equipped to respond. Her mind raced.

What a day this has been, and it's only noon. I've been to a bordello where I was asked if I wanted to become a prostitute. Someone hollered about how my breasts are too large. And now, Brock thinks I'm—

"Blossom, what are you thinking about?"

Snapped back to reality, Blossom looked around. While facing Brock's carriage, she asked, "We're not taking the cable car? I just assumed we were meeting at a cable car stop so that we could take one. Oh, I'm babbling, aren't I?"

"No, not at all. I brought a carriage for us this afternoon. Do you know how to ride a horse?"

"You mean I don't get to ride in the carriage with you?"

They broke into laughter at the same time.

At that moment, the strains of *Entrance of the Gladiators* being played on a hurdy-gurdy danced on the breeze. Blossom froze. She saw Ting Ting and Little Sunflower skipping down the sidewalk toward her. Without distracting Brock, she held up her palm to signal them to stop. They did, dead in their tracks.

Ting Ting smiled widely and cocked her head to the left with what Blossom thought was a sense of curiosity. She waved back to Blossom in a knowing sort of way and then turned to skip away, cranking her music maker. Little Sunflower waved, but didn't move. She stared at Blossom. Ting Ting grabbed her by the elbow and pulled her away. Blossom watched as Little Sunflower followed like an unwilling prisoner.

Brock walked Blossom over to the carriage step and helped her in.

"Did you hear that?"

"Hear what?" asked Blossom.

"Someone called my name. At least that's what I thought I heard," he said as he looked across the street.

Blossom scanned their surroundings to see if she could spot anyone who would have called out Brock's name. In the process, she discovered that her encounter with Brock was already a cat let out of its bag. From his street-side shop—comprised of a wooden chair and an upended crate— Sang Yuen, the local fortuneteller, was busy writing down a message from a client, but looked up to notice her. He often served as a letter writer for residents who wanted to send mail back to China.

Ruby the flower seller, though making a sale, also witnessed Blossom in Brock's carriage. Blossom realized how quickly the fabric of her somewhat sheltered life could be easily pulled apart thread by thread if those who were seeing what they were seeing today wanted to do her harm. *Certainly my secret is safe with Sang, Ruby, Ting Ting and Little Sunflower*, thought Blossom. *Any other witnesses?*

She looked around the area again quickly, stalling momentarily to focus on the storefronts just down from the general store. She didn't notice any other familiar faces on the street at that moment, though two unwashed men came up from the unusually steep stairs below a nearby building. They looked at her with inquisitive eyes. She returned a curious glance and then realized that she didn't look like her normal self. The men shielded their eyes as the sunlight was too much to bear all at once. They were among the many illegal immigrants who lived underground in tunnels beneath Chinatown.

Returning to Brock's earlier question, she answered, "No, I didn't hear a thing. I was too focused on stepping into your carriage without tripping on the hem of this blasted skirt." Blossom then peered in the direction that Brock had looked in. She caught a glimpse of a stunningly elegant white woman in a brilliant-green outfit wearing an extravagant hat adorned with cream and emerald plumes. *Boy is she and her hat out of place in this part of town!*

Faye Huntington was standing on the corner across the street in her signature color: green. She was on a fortune cookie-finding expedition. After making the friendly gesture of calling Brock's name moments ago, she thought twice about making her presence known and slipped behind an aromatic rack of dried fish in front of a store. There, veiled in a shadow, she watched what was playing out in front of her.

Who's that girl? She's no one I've ever seen before, thought Faye. Love the dress, hate the color. And why is Brock meeting her in this cesspool? She must be one of those bordello girls! Faye unavoidably noted how the air was heavy with a combination of stale cooking grease, fish and spices.

She observed how Brock looked into the girl's eyes. Faye saw how he paid more attention to his companion than on getting his rig moving. That was true until the horses bolted forward, slamming the couple against the back of the black leather bench seat.

As Brock's carriage drove out of sight, Faye continued her hunt for fortune cookies. Though uncomfortable with the idea that a dessert could predict her future, she was going learning more about fortune cookies.

As fate would have it, she'd just learned a lot more about the futures of some other people in her life without the aid of a cookie.

She grinned with great satisfaction at the possibility of being the bearer of news about Brock's whereabouts this afternoon, wondering what story he may have already fed Clarissa. Not being the type of person who needed all the facts before she made up her mind or opened her mouth, Faye knew that what she witnessed—or thought she witnessed—was sure to be some powerful grist for the rumor mill if she timed it right.

Blossom felt her stomach flatten against her spine as the carriage moved out into the street, giving her a fluttering sensation, as if butterflies were taking flight.

"I just saw a woman with the most incredible hat on. Someday, I'm going to have a hat like hers, with a whole flock of feathers that dance in the breeze." Blossom raised her fluttering hands along the sides and back of her head. She then realized the frivolity of what she'd just shared.

"I'm sorry. I bet the last thing you'd like to talk about is feathers and bonnets."

"If that's what you want to talk about and if a hat like that would make you happy, then it makes me happy too," said Brock. "I'll ask again. Can you ride a horse?"

"Of course I can. I may be a city girl, but I've ridden horses since I was a child," responded Blossom, stretching the truth to her advantage.

"Great! We're heading to my dairy farm and stables up near Twin Peaks. I've brought us a picnic lunch. We can go for a ride on the trails along the hilltops."

Blossom instantly regretted her fib about horseback riding, but realized that she had the perfect excuse: She was wearing Monique's pale-pink dress.

"I love surprises, but had I known you wanted to ride today I would have dressed for it."

"You're right. Well, we're on our way, so let's make the most of our time together. Does your family know you're with me?"

"Does your fiancée know you're with me?"

"Ouch!" replied Brock.

They stopped talking and both looked forward.

The journey to Twin Peaks was slow as they moved along the rutted dirt pathway. The pair reignited their conversation after a few minutes. The erratic rhythm of the horses' hooves hitting the uneven ground sounded like a bad heart in a stethoscope.

They talked about family and friends, Nob Hill and Chinatown, discovering that the many things that made them different in society's eyes were, in fact, fairly similar in reality.

Whether they had money or not, whether their families were large or small, whether their house was on a hill or above a restaurant, Brock and Blossom became more comfortable with each other. By the time they reached the stable, they'd learned more about each other than most people learn after several encounters.

Below the stable on the hillside was a broad patch of green grass and a stand of sycamore trees, with wide canopies that created areas of shade.

"Let's go over by the trees. It's my favorite spot." Brock reached out his hand to help her out of the carriage. She looked down and hesitated for a moment. Brock sensed it. She said something so softly that he couldn't hear clearly, except for the last word.

"Leap?" asked Brock. "You don't have to jump. I'll help you down."

"Oh don't mind me," she said as she put her hand into his.

Look before you leap, thought Blossom. *Look…before…you…leap.*

And what a sight she took in before she leaped into her unexpected future. The vista was spectacular.

As they walked, Brock admitted, "I come here to be alone and think. It's hard to find places to be alone, to just think, isn't it?"

"I can't remember when I was ever truly alone. There's always someone—whether you know them or not—near you in Chinatown."

They stopped walking and Brock spread out a blanket near several huge boulders at the base of the massive sycamore trees. Blossom set down the wicker hamper, not knowing if she should open it and remove its contents. She mindlessly hummed the tune that her father often hummed in the bakery.

"What's that song called?" asked Brock.

"I don't know, but my father sings and hums it all the time. Usually, he looks at me and throws in the words 'Iris eyes a-smiling.' Don't even ask me why he's so stuck on it and why he says 'Iris" instead of what I'm guessing should be Irish!"

"Hungry?" asked Brock.

"Actually, I'm very hungry. It's been quite a morning and I guess I've worked up an appetite."

When Brock didn't make the first move to open the hamper, Blossom took that as a signal for her to do so.

As she released the latch, Blossom asked, "Did you pack the lunch?"

"No, our cook, Clementine, put it together."

Fried chicken, biscuits and jam, a block of cheese, apples and red velvet cake were carefully wrapped inside. Blossom removed each item.

"All of my favorites. How about you?"

Blossom looked down. "To be honest, fried chicken and biscuits are not usually on our dinner table, but I do like them. And I guess I should tell you that in Chinatown we don't eat much cheese."

Blossom had told her second lie. She couldn't recall ever having fried chicken and biscuits before, but she wasn't about to admit to it now. "But

I have to say, I've never had a velvet cake before…red or any color." *But I sure saw a lot of red velvet at Madam Bijou's today,* she gleefully thought.

"Oh, it's Clementine's specialty. She says it pleasures her to see how much I like her red velvet cake. Those are the words she uses, *pleasures her.* Clementine has cooked for my family for as long as I can remember. She's from Dixie, as she calls it. Actually, she worked as a cook for a well-to-do Atlanta family. Because she could make both Southern and French meals, Clementine was hired by my mother to be our cook. There aren't many cooks who look or sound like her on Nob Hill!"

He went on with a twinkle in his blue eyes and more energy in his voice. "She's always baked a red velvet cake for me—and iced it with light-as-a-cloud cream-cheese frosting and sprinkled red cake crumbs over it—whenever I was celebrating something or needed to be cheered up. I guess it's always there when I needed it." He paused. "And here it is."

"So did she think you were celebrating and needing to be cheered up today?"

"Good question. I really don't know. But, depending on how our picnic goes, we'll know."

"So what's it like to have servants?"

"What do you mean?"

"You talk about Clementine like she's part of your family, not your cook. What's it like to have people all around you who do whatever you tell them to do?"

"They're my mother's employees…her helpers. Clementine is special though. She practically raised me. She knows more about me than just about anyone."

Blossom noticed how Brock softened as he continued to speak about Clementine. "She's always been there for me. And I don't mean her red velvet cake. Why do you ask about our servants, Blossom?"

"I guess you could say that we're our own servants. It would be nice to have helpers as you call them, at least on days when I'm just not running at full steam."

Blossom stared out over the hillside and closed her eyes. She inhaled deeply and noticed how the air was laced with the sweet smell of new grass, quite unlike the damp city air below.

"This may sound odd, but the air smells good up here."

"You like the barn smells and manure?" asked Brock.

"No, of course not, but the hillside smells so fresh, especially as the ocean air pushes the scent uphill toward us. Thank goodness the barn is behind us!"

The water in the bay glistened in the afternoon sunlight. Blossom let herself think that all was right with the world as the hours leisurely passed. *This...is...heaven.*

"It's wonderful up here," said Blossom with an audible exhale. "There's nothing but air, plants and animals...that is until the city folks spread out some more and move up here!"

She went on, "But what a spectacular place to build a new house and live. In Chinatown, we're so cooped up."

Brock smiled a crooked smile, with lifted eyebrows, and looked out over the bay.

The conversation shifted to families.

Brock learned that Blossom's mother died shortly after giving birth.

"I'm sorry for your loss. She must have been a beautiful woman. Not that your father isn't handsome, I guess, but your beauty had to come from somewhere."

"Yes, everyone says my mother was an exceptional beauty. There aren't any photographs of her since my Grand Ma Maw and parents were stirrin' up grub, as they call it, for the miners. They say that people didn't have much of anything except their mining tools, gold dust and a sack full of dreams. By the time I came along, most of the gold was long gone and so were the miners.

"My mother came from a different part of China and that's why I look the way I do, not like everyone else. All of my life I looked around and saw people who were just like me—and yet nothing like me."

She paused.

"I *really* don't look like anyone else. Whether it's good or bad, it's who and what I am. But I have to say, it's not easy being different," she said and looked away awkwardly, as if there was shame in not fitting in.

Brock added, "I know what you mean, sort of. I've never fit in either. People see me as an odd mix of rich guy and cowboy, with one foot in the parlor and the other in a barnyard. Huh, I guess I've never really talked about it before."

"Whenever I say something about my different looks, Grand Ma Maw says, 'China big place. Everyone not look same. Why you think you must look like everyone else?'" Blossom smiled at her mocking impersonation of her grandmother's words.

"After my mother died, Grand Ma Maw decided that the three of us should move to the Tangrenbu district, I mean Chinatown, and open a business using the money that they'd earned. Actually, it was gold dust. She felt I'd have a better life here and that I could go to school and learn to speak English well. She also thought that working in San Francisco would keep my father busy from sunup to sundown while his broken heart mended. I'm sorry if that sounded tragic the way I just said it."

"But look how fine you turned out, Blossom!" Brock looked as if he was about to say something more and then stopped. Blossom noticed.

"What were you going to say?"

"Actually, I have a question, but I'm not sure if it will offend you."

"What is it?"

"It's about the way your father and grandmother speak. I wouldn't expect them to speak perfect English. No one actually does. But, if it was so important to your grandmother to have you speak English well, then how is it that she speaks it with words missing and the order sort of backwards?"

Blossom gathered her thoughts before responding. "Think of it this way. I was taught to speak English since I was a child, along with Cantonese. My father and grandmother learned Cantonese first. Most people speak Cantonese in Chinatown because they came from Guangdong in southern China. Other people speak Mandarin, but not many."

Brock nodded.

"So, even though they're fairly fluent in English, they speak it from the perspective of someone who speaks Cantonese. Instead of saying 'This is my daughter,' my father says, 'This my daughter' because there really isn't a to-be verb...or *is* in the way they speak. Sounds academic, I know, but that's just the way it is."

To Blossom, it looked like Brock was following her train of thought. "Or my grandmother might ask, 'Fortune cookie good, no?' We would ask, 'Isn't this fortune cookie good?' My poor friend Monique learned English and Cantonese as a child. Then she learned French when she was fourteen, after her parents died. She told me there are sounds that you have to make when you speak French that our mouths and throats just aren't trained to do, at least not very well for most people. She calls the English that the elders speak Chinglish. I'm not so sure, but—"

Brock jumped in, "Please don't think I was being critical. I'm just trying to get to know you and your family better."

"No, that's fine, really," said Blossom. "The best thing to remember about speaking Cantonese—or understanding it—is tones. How you say something, the pitch you use, can completely change the meaning of what you might have *wanted* to say. Then there's writing!"

Blossom explained that it was no easy task to learn to write in Cantonese, which has about 40,000 symbols, each standing for a word or word fragment. But only about 5,000 are needed to communicate well.

"*Shay shay*," replied Brock. "Did I say it correctly?"

"You're close. How do you think it's spelled?"

"Is that a trick question? I couldn't even guess."

"It's spelled *xie xie*. That's how you say and spell the word thanks. And if you want to reply, you use the words *bu ke qi*. That's how you say that you're welcome…it sounds like *book itchy*."

There was a natural break in the conversation as Brock processed what he just heard.

"So, you're an artist. Your grandmother told me about it last night. I've seen a lot of artwork, but yours is…is…special and unique," said Brock, searching for words that didn't appear to come easily.

"Thank you. I've sketched and painted for as long as I can remember. It's just part of me."

As they continued to talk, Blossom learned that Brock's mother was from a fine, upstanding Bostonian family and that his father had whisked her away to the wilds of the western frontier, much to her family's dismay.

Brock patted one of the boulders to his right. "I've done a lot of thinking with these rocks!"

Blossom smiled.

"What are you thinking about…right now?" asked Brock.

"Grand Ma Maw used to tell me a story about how the leaders in China—long, long ago—treasured large rocks so much that they would send hundreds of men on expeditions for months and years, just to bring back one boulder of a particular shape. One boulder!"

"For what?"

"For their palace gardens!"

He replied, "Then aren't we lucky to have these rocks right here to enjoy, exactly where they've always been."

Blossom reached out and ran her hand along the smooth, weathered surface of a boulder.

"Lucky, yes, we're lucky alright."

Their conversation comfortably traveled among topics of significant and minor importance as the shadow of the sycamore tree shifted, exposing Brock to the full brilliance of the sun.

"Is it getting warmer, or is it just me?"

Blossom replied, "It's just you. You're in the sun now. What time is it?"

Brock looked at his pocket watch and announced that it was 3:37. He paused for a moment and held the gold watch in his hand.

"That's a beautiful watch."

"Thanks. It was a gift from Clarissa. It's attached to my vest with a fob made out of Clarissa's hair."

"Oh, that's her hair?"

"She braided it. I guess it's like a piece—actually, lots of pieces—of Clarissa are with me all the time."

Blossom's heart sank. *I'm sorry I asked.*

"Do you have to be home at a certain time?"

Blossom considered how to answer the question. *Depending on what I say, will I appear to be too eager: too eager to stay, too eager to leave, or just too eager?*

"We should probably get going. I still need to check in with Anna Mae to make sure we keep our story straight."

"Your story for who?" he asked.

"My father and Grand Ma Maw, of course. Like you didn't know! I don't want to spoil this afternoon, but do you understand the risk I'm taking by being here with you?"

As the words came out of her mouth, Blossom immediately wished she could take them back. She continued though, "Please don't misunderstand me. I'm here with you because I want to be, even need to be. I haven't known you long, but just the same, I feel closer to you than—"

Blossom lost her words.

Brock caressed her hand. Then, with one flowing movement of his right arm, his fingers and palm brushed Blossom's cheek and slid down far enough to cradle her chin.

Blossom cast her eyes down and raised them slowly to match Brock's in an innocent move that was not meant to be coy or flirtatious. He tilted his head to the left and leaned forward to kiss her.

I don't know if I've longed for this moment or dreaded it…or both. Do I dare kiss him? Dare! What if he finds out this is all because of a dare? What if—

Blossom's thoughts were instantly hijacked when Brock's lips touched hers. Their first kiss was warm, tender and feather light. Blossom's eyes were closed, but she saw it all in her mind, as if she was both a participant and an observer. *Can this really be happening? Can anything feel better than this?*

As she inhaled deeply, she realized it could feel better, especially without her dress's cinched-in waist and such pressure on her rib cage.

As they kissed a second time, a sturdy breeze released some of Blossom's hair. It taunted and teased their faces. She reached up to tuck it behind her ear but instead used the situation to explore Brock's face. She'd studied it with her eyes plenty today. Now, her hands examined this new terrain.

First she felt the strength of his brow. It was softer than she expected, but definitely not soft. Then her fingers traveled down his cheeks with their tiny golden freckles. His jaw was clearly defined and sunken in just enough to create highs and lows in his face. Her fingers swam through the waves of his thick hair, which ended at the nape of his neck. Blossom's hand landed on his shoulder as they continued to kiss, then it traveled down his arm.

Brock cautiously pulled away. He stood up and leaned against a nearby tree.

"Brock, are you okay? I can hardly breathe. I'll admit that I'm inexperienced, but that kiss was…um…well, it wasn't like any other kiss I've ever been part of!" Blossom rose to her feet and stood close to Brock.

"That's good to know. And it's a relief." he replied.

She initiated a third kiss, one with more confidence and passion, that sent a flash of heat down and back up her tingling body. Though she was out of breath, she couldn't help but noticed how firm, yet yielding, his lips were. Blossom sensed how the intensity of their kiss changed and was now more like two angry thunder clouds crashing together. As they kissed, his tongue tenderly followed…circled…the edges of her lips. She followed his lead and did the same in return.

Time held its breath.

As their hands began to move along each other's bodies, the ground jolted. Blossom pulled away.

The horses in the barn whinnied, and the pigeons foraging for seeds among the hay took to the air in a furious flurry, which further upset the horses. The cows made a collective clamor in the field and in the corral.

"Well, honestly, I've heard about men making the ground move under a girl in a moment like this, but I never believed it. I do now. The earth actually moved for me!"

"You're right about the earth moving," agreed Brock. "I felt it too. It wasn't because of our kisses, though I'd like to take the credit. I think the ground actually moved. We just had an earthquake, or something like an earthquake."

"Well, either way, I'll never forget that kiss, ever."

"Neither will I. Every time I see you now, I'll think about kissing you…every…time."

Blossom raised her right hand to cover her feverish cheeks.

He removed his pocketknife and started carving an X on the trunk of the nearest sycamore tree.

"What are you doing?" asked Blossom.

"Marking the spot—like on a pirate map—with an X."

"The spot?"

Brock answered, "The spot of our first kiss, our first *earthmoving* kiss! Now we'll always know where it happened."

Blossom smiled as she ran her fingertips over the freshly carved X. She looked into Brock's eyes and whispered, "Always."

Chapter 12

*E*ast Wind Blows At The Mahjong Table

Sunday, April 15, 1906, 3:40 p.m.
Three days before the earthquake and firestorm

Taking time for herself was not something Grand Ma Maw was very good at. She put others first, herself last. She didn't begrudge anyone for it or complain about it. While many elderly women resigned themselves to being the honored one at the dinner table or having others seek their advice on matters ranging from tea service to burial traditions, Grand Ma Maw was as active and as vibrant a woman as her worn-out body permitted.

Her one indulgence was the game mahjong. When she, Chang and infant Blossom arrived in Chinatown, she befriended several other women who were looking for a social outlet and a trusted pipeline of information to share about their tight-knit community.

For a time, they played pai gow. Then they experimented with fan-tan. But it was mahjong that stuck with the women, and the women stuck together with it.

There was no set day or specific time each week to play. They liked it that way. Games were quickly initiated with a brisk phone call. The games were played based on the acquisition of some red-hot gossip or an actual event in Chinatown.

The agreed-to rule was that no rumors about any of the four women or their families would be discussed at the table. That was forbidden territory not to be entered. And up to this point, the agreement had not yet been broken.

In a city in which everyone talked and was talked about, Chinatown still had its secrets, despite the most vigilant eyes and ears.

Grand Ma Maw's group included Grand Auntie Lim Kee, Berty Chin and Dulcie Chow.

Today, Dulcie arranged the game to share news about a new girl at a bordello on Duncombe Alley and what she purchased at her husband's medicine store.

The other three players soon arrived at Dulcie's home, which was spacious and well appointed due to her husband's retail success.

The women took their usual places at the square table. Proving that people come in all shapes and sizes, the table of four was a mixed bag. Grand Ma Maw was small and delicate. Her hearty appetite, firm views and loud pronouncements made her seem bigger than she was.

Grand Ma Maw looked to her right and made a quick study of Grand Auntie Lim Kee. She was taller and thinner than the others. She was also the oldest, and it showed. She was married to a short, petite merchant. They made such an odd-looking couple. In her youth, Grand Auntie Lim Kee had been "as enchanting as cherry blossoms in a spring breeze, but she was as barren as the Gobi Desert in August." That's how Grand Ma Maw described her to Blossom as soon as she was old enough to understand the word barren. *All beauty, but no babies*, Grand Ma Maw thought. She was given the courtesy title of Grand Auntie by Blossom and many other children in Chinatown.

Across the table, Grand Ma Maw noted how Berty Chin was getting balder by the day, her thinning hair a sign of the worrying and stress that consumed her life. After decades in a marriage that was a rickety bridge, her husband died twelve years ago. Since then, she took in boarders for income.

"How are the many, many men in your life, Berty?" asked Grand Ma Maw.

"They just bed renters. Nothing more. Nothing less. They either at work, eating in restaurant, or doing nasty things I not wish to discuss." Berty slowly turned her head side to side. "But money good. So many shifts and jobs they work, my beds rarely cool off. Someone always sleeping in them, always."

To Grand Ma Maw's left sat Dulcie Chow. *She getting rounder and rounder.* Her love of food and her disdain for physical activity of any sort resulted in her body looking to Grand Ma Maw like overgrown melons that were stacked on one another with the largest in the middle. Her husband owned three stores—a meat market, a vegetable stand and a Chinese medicine shop. He adored her and provided her with a life of comfort and inactivity, much to the envy of Grand Ma Maw.

Their game always began the same way, with the selection of the dealer. Grand Ma Maw looked down at the tiles' colorful images that included combinations of circles, bamboo, and Chinese characters and numbers, along with the four winds and eight flowers. She and her three lady friends referred to the flower tiles as "blossoms" in honor of Blossom.

Dulcie poured the tea. Much to Grand Ma Maw's delight, she won the dice competition and was the first dealer. The game progressed in her favor. She was feeling lucky as tiles and turns moved around the table. She was in possession of three of the flower tiles that represented the seasons. She was missing the winter tile. She had the spring flower tile in her hand when a wave of dizziness swirled in her head. She noticed that they all were looking at each other with scrunched up faces.

"You feel that?" asked Dulcie uneasily.

"Yes, you too?" replied Grand Ma Maw.

The three-story building gently swayed as the women looked around the room. There was a sudden bump against the building that Berty said felt a lot like when one of her "fat-as-an-oxen" renters has been pushed out of bed and onto the floor so that the next renter could rest.

Grand Ma Maw noticed the ripples of motion in her tea cup. "Earth moves. Earth Dragon upset," she said matter-of-factly.

She accidently dropped her spring-flower tile onto the table.

"Bad sign you drop your blossom," announced Dulcie.

"No sign at all. My Blossom fine!" Grand Ma Maw replied with an uncharacteristic edge that did not escape the ears of her friends.

Dulcie pointed her index finger at the tile on the table while saying, "That blossom. Not *your* Blossom."

The heads of the women bobbed up and down. Grand Ma Maw quickly realized that her comment and reaction had sent a signal, a loud and clear signal that the three women would be following up with their gossip sources around town. Her stomach ached as she realized that the seeds of suspicion were planted in fertile soil, and she planted them.

Blossom, you on watch now! Grand Ma Maw knew that any misstep by her granddaughter could trigger a wildfire. *Whatever you doing Blossom— and whoever you doing it with—please be good girl.*

Chapter 13

$\mathscr{S}$ ixpence For Good Luck

Sunday, April 15, 1906, 3:48 p.m.
Three days before the earthquake and firestorm

"Thank you so much for having me for tea today, Mrs. St. Clair," said Clarissa as she was greeted by Brock's mother in the parlor. Clarissa rose from one of the many chairs in the room.

The overabundance of chairs was as an ostentatious show of wealth. It was a sign of good fortune and a display of good manners. Since it was considered rude for a man to offer his seat to a woman because the cushion might still be warm, having the extra chairs resulted in there always being a fresh seat available when ladies entered the room.

A few minutes earlier, a maid greeted Clarissa at the door since it was the butler's day off. She escorted Clarissa to the parlor, a formality that was no longer necessary for someone who was about to join the family. To pass the time, Clarissa scanned the names on the calling cards that had gathered on an ornate silver tray on a nearby table. One of them, from Mrs. Phillip Stanton, was edged in black, signifying that she was in mourning. She picked it up just before Mrs. St. Clair entered the room.

"Goodness, you should not have been made to wait here. I'll speak to the staff about how you're to be received in the future." She noticed the sad look on Clarissa's face. "Oh, yes, you knew that Gladys Stanton lost her son to the fevers, didn't you? The poor dear—" She looked down to the floor and collected herself. "Come, let's go into the conservatory. The flowers open in the afternoon sun. That will cheer us up," said Mrs. St. Clair as she led Clarissa to the glass-enclosed garden room.

Clarissa noticed how her soon-to-be mother-in-law's dress made a scratching sound with each step. Clarissa thought the cream-colored lace overlay made the stiff taupe-silk dress look elegant. *Faye would probably think it looked like an oversized doily*, she thought. Clarissa quickly cleared Faye from her mind.

"I was born in the fog of Boston, and I'll die in the fog of San Francisco. Let's enjoy the sun while we have it, shall we?" asked Mrs. St. Clair in a genuinely welcoming way.

As the two settled into their chairs, Minnie, one of the household's maids, entered the room. "Ready now, ma'am?" she inquired.

"Yes, you may begin, Minnie."

"As you wish," she said gently and disappeared.

Clarissa knew that a late-afternoon tea service was an ideal setting for an intimate conversation. However, it could be a complex ritual depending on the household or hostess. The hazards were numerous. *A slippery tea cup on a slippery saucer, boiling-hot water, one lump or two, gloves on or off, China or India tea, milk first.* The thoughts swirled in her head. However, successfully navigating this mine field gave all the participants a secure feeling that they belonged to their class.

In no time at all, Minnie rolled in a tea cart with a three-tier service piece graced with delicate triangular sandwiches and petit fours.

"How lovely," remarked Clarissa at the sight of the pastel-colored treats.

"I don't know about you, but I actually like crust on my sandwiches! I know it's not proper, especially at tea time, but I learned to like crusts when Mr. St. Clair and I were young and making our way in the world." With that, Mrs. St. Clair sighed and dismissed Minnie to return to the kitchen. Minnie backed out of the room and quietly said, "Very well, ma'am."

"Funny, isn't it?" asked Clarissa.

"What's that?"

"It's funny that people call us the 'upper crust' and yet your lovely kitchen staff cuts your crust off even though you prefer it!"

"Yes, it is ironic, I suppose." Brock's mother looked down at her well-trimmed sandwich and then up directly at Clarissa.

"How are you and Brock getting along? Any wedding jitters?"

"Everything's on schedule. But I have to say that Brock doesn't always seem very interested in what I'm saying or what we're doing lately. Is that just how men are about these things?"

"Men do see the world differently than we women see it. And Brock, he's always been more comfortable around a barnyard than a boardroom or a ballroom. But he's a real jewel, though I must admit I'm a bit partial!" exclaimed Mrs. St. Clair. "He's a good man who's driven to make his own way in life. And he's chosen you to be at his side while he's doing it."

She cleared her throat politely. "Now on to the real reason why I asked you here. I wanted to spend some time with you before the wedding."

Clarissa responded quickly, "And I couldn't be happier to be here with you…or to marry your son."

"Before you receive yet another gift of a crystal bowl for fruit or an epergne to arrange flowers in, I have something for you," Mrs. St. Clair said as she revealed an odd-looking coin.

"It's for your shoe." She carefully placed it on Clarissa's open palm.

"My shoe?"

"Why yes, your shoe. My mother gave it to me just before my wedding. Since my two girls didn't live long enough to see their wedding days, or even their first birthdays, I'm giving it to you, my new daughter."

Clarissa knew that Mrs. St. Clair was very guarded about speaking of the deaths of her two infant girls. She wasn't sure how to respond about the coin or the girls. This was growing increasingly uncomfortable for her and it showed on her face.

"It has to do with the English rhyme: Something old, something new. Something borrowed, something blue. And sixpence for her left shoe." She placed her hand on Clarissa's when she said "her left shoe."

Clarissa was familiar with the saying, but now it all made sense in this situation.

"Of course, and how thoughtful of you to share it with me."

"Have your mother and bridesmaids already given you the other items?"

"No ma'am, not all of them yet," Clarissa responded. "But, I'm sure everything will be in place by Saturday."

"Now if I could just get Austin to find the right girl and settle down. Perhaps one of your friends would be a suitable match?"

"I'll give it some serious thought, ma'am."

Mrs. St. Clair poured the tea. Even though she knew Clarissa liked two lumps of sugar, she asked anyway. "Two lumps, please," was the response. Clarissa unfolded and laid a lace-trimmed, crisply pressed white napkin across her vibrant turquoise-skirted lap. Above it was an eggplant-purple blouse with turquoise accents and trim. It was tight at the neck, waist and wrists, and puffy everywhere else.

"Your colors today are so exotic, like a peacock feather. I would not have thought to put them together. You've done it so beautifully."

Clarissa replied, "Oh, thank you. It's a tad loud I suppose, but the combination is arresting, like your son's eyes. I just melt away every time he looks into my eyes."

"He has his father's eyes. I know that feeling well, though it's been some time since I've looked into Mr. St. Clair's eyes, bless his soul."

"I am truly sorry that our conversation keeps turning to your losses," said Clarissa, resting her cup and saucer down on the white napkin covering her lap.

"Now, now. We must not focus on what we've lost. We have so much to look forward to, together. My mother taught me a saying that comes in handy more often than I'd like: Just because a cloud blocks the sun, it doesn't mean the sun is gone. You keep that in mind!"

Clarissa smiled weakly at first and then widely as she thought of her wedding day. "Thank you. I will. Now I have to share something with you. I'm afraid Brock is going to reduce me to a pool of tears when we're saying our vows," confessed Clarissa. "I know brides are supposed to blush, but I don't want to be a blubbering bride."

"Tears show everyone how happy we are or how unhappy we are. I'm certain that your tears of happiness will sparkle like the diamonds in your wedding tiara. I helped Brock pick them out, but your tears—and your love—are worth far more than diamonds."

"I hope so, Mrs. St. Clair."

"It's high time that you call me something other than Mrs. St. Clair. What do you think?"

"How about Mother? That's the way I feel about you."

"Don't you think your mother will mind?"

"Not at all. She's gaining a son and I'm getting a second mother."

Clarissa reached over and selected a pink petit four with a sunny yellow flower bud made of icing on it.

"Our life together is going to be as sweet as this piece of cake."

Mrs. St. Clair added, "Yes, my dear, your marriage is going to be an absolute dream."

Chapter 14

*S*omething Borrowed

Sunday, April 15, 1906, 4:04 p.m.
Three days before the earthquake and firestorm

"Blast! This dress is not only uncomfortable, it's downright dangerous!" Blossom tugged at the skirt to loosen the bunching at the hemline.

"Then why are you wearing it?" asked Brock.

"It's not even mine. I borrowed it from a friend who thought it would help you see me as something more than a bakery girl from Chinatown."

"It worked. But you didn't need a dress to do that. From the minute I first saw you, I knew there was something special about you. And it didn't have anything to do with what you were wearing."

"Well, that's good, because you'll never see me in this dress again!"

They smiled at each other. Brock took her left hand in his right and they walked over to the barn. She tripped on the hem of her skirt and her body jerked.

"Agreed," he said with conviction. "From this point on, we'll just be ourselves."

She looked at him with a puzzled expression. "Were you pretending to be something or someone today?"

"No. I've always been a what-you-see-is-what-you-get kind of person.

I may have had the benefits of wealth, but I'm making my own way in life with this dairy farm. So, for better or worse, I'm not at all complicated and I'm definitely not a game player."

A vision of Faye flashed through Brock's mind. "I know someone who fits that description well."

"Do you like that person?"

"Not particularly, but she is my fiancée's best friend."

The word "fiancée" halted the conversation.

Blossom realized they were no longer holding hands. Painful silence took over. She faked a smile so he wouldn't see how the awkwardness of the moment affected her. Blossom mustered her strength and asked, "Your fiancée, what's she like?"

"Do you really want to know?"

Blossom looked off toward the bay. "Yes, I do. If she means so much to you that you want to marry her, then yes. I want to know what makes her so special to you. I bet she has everything I have to do without."

Brock licked his upper lip.

"Clarissa, that's her name, lives on Nob Hill and comes from a good family. She's everything—"

Blossom interrupted, "No, what is it about her that you love?"

"Everything, I guess…not just one or two things in particular." *What is it that I love about Clarissa? I've never thought about it that way,* he thought. "We're comfortable together, like a hand and glove."

"Has the earth shaken when you've kissed her? Oh, I've gone too far with that question, haven't I?"

"I can honestly say that's something that's only happened with you, and you haven't gone too far with your question." Brock began to clearly see that he and Clarissa were like perfect strangers who knew quite a lot about each other and wondered if that was enough to result in a lasting marriage. He knew it was on Nob Hill.

Brock took Blossom's hand again and they walked together.

"What are the girls like, I mean women, on Nob Hill?" asked Blossom.

"Usually, their lives are planned out for them. They're raised by nannies and maids. They're schooled in all the right subjects. Their social calendars are carefully tended to. They learn how to direct the household staff. The goal, I guess, is to put the best package together that leads to a marriage that's mutually beneficial to both families." Brock stopped talking and digested what he'd just said. *Sounds more like merging two businesses than a marriage between two people.*

"I think not having to work would be great! I work so hard. But everyone works hard in Chinatown, so it's not something to complain about, I guess. In Chinatown, you're never alone and yet you can be so lonesome. Or you just keep yourself too busy with work to get lonesome."

"Actually, work is good," said Brock. "Ladies obsess about the pattern on their dishes, the color of the table linens and the placement of silverware. Don't get me wrong. I like to eat, but all the rules and the fussing make me crazy. It's just dinner after all!"

They stopped walking. Blossom looked at Brock. "But maybe you're wrong. To your mother, it's much more than dinner. Besides, your life—as a man—seems so much more direct and to the point. You work. You eat. You sleep."

"You make us sound so boring."

They started walking again. "Oh, I didn't mean to. I guess I was thinking about how living in Chinatown is more complicated. It's not all about work and food and sleep. It's that there's no privacy. Everyone knows everyone else's business."

"Blossom, it's the same way on Nob Hill. Everyone knows about everyone else. Maybe it's because so many people have so much more time to sit around and talk about each other."

He turned to face her and held both of her hands. His heart skipped a beat and began to race. "I've never met anyone quite like you, Blossom, and I've never been so comfortable and open before."

"I feel the same way. What makes it confusing is that I've never really had the chance to get to know someone who wasn't part of Chinatown," admitted Blossom. "There might as well be walls around that place with one gate in and out. Not that I'm complaining. It's all that I know. But there's so much more of the world that I want to be part of."

"So what's holding you back?"

"I'm not sure that it's a case of being held back. My father and Grand Ma Maw and our business keep me busy. I just don't think there's been a reason to push out beyond Chinatown...until now."

They stopped walking again.

"Brock, why are you here with me and not Clarissa?"

He pulled her close into an almost stifling embrace.

"You're not at all like Clarissa. You're not what I thought I wanted in life."

"Oh."

"Wait, that didn't come out right. You're different. It's the way we talk and laugh. It's your eyes, your smile, your touch. I can't seem to get enough of you. You've made me see that I may not feel—or ever feel—that way about the woman I'm about to marry. I'm not sure if I should thank you or despise you for it."

"Oh."

"I'm not clear about why, but it's you that I want to be with right now, not Clarissa."

"Oh. Oh no!" She brought her palms up to her mouth. A thunderous belch escaped. Blossom looked at Brock, her eyes unusually open.

"I suppose I could blame my corset or say that the fried chicken is talking back to me, or *clucking* back at me—" She started to laugh and couldn't complete her sentence. He joined her in diffusing the breach in good manners.

"You're just full of surprises, aren't you? I don't think I've ever heard a woman burp before, other than Clementine. She burps like a sailor who's swallowed too much beer too fast. She curses like a sailor too, when she thinks nobody is around."

"Please excuse me," said Blossom.

"Any other surprises for me?"

"I'm sure to surprise you again if you stick around long enough!"

"I think I'll do just that."

Chapter 15
An Experienced Single Woman

Sunday, April 15, 1906, 4:47 p.m.
Three days before the earthquake and firestorm

"Hello, Mrs. Donohue. Is Clarissa at home?" asked Faye as she was greeted in the parlor of the Donohue estate.

"Why yes she is, honey. She just got back from Brock's house. I'll send someone up to get her from her room."

"Oh, that won't be necessary. I'll just scoot right up there myself."

"As you wish, honey," said Clarissa's mother.

Zelda observed Faye's arrival and went about her daily chores. She left the kitchen and headed down the hallway. "Jesus, Mary and Joseph, I swear this house actually grows dust," she muttered to herself. She randomly swished her feather duster—which felt to her like an ever-ready extension of her hand.

As she passed by, she smiled sweetly at Faye and as soon as she was beyond Faye's line of sight, she stuck out her tongue and crossed her eyes. The passive-aggressive act did not escape the sharp eyes of Mrs. Donohue, though she shot a smile and a nod in Zelda's direction in a subtle display of approval. Faye quickly turned, only to find Zelda's back moving down the hallway toward the kitchen.

Zelda plopped herself down next to Katie Malloy at the servants' table. The staff was taking a quick break as the dinner hour quickly approached.

"Why Mrs. Donohue tolerates that snake in the grass, I'll never know!" announced Zelda.

"These rich folks stick together," said Katie. "And I mean stick, like pine sap on the bottom of your shoe. They tolerate each other's shenanigans more than they ought to so as not to upset anyone or cause folks to talk behind their backs about them. They're more concerned about what other people think about them than we are of putting food on the table or having a bed to rest on at night."

Zelda jumped into the flow of what Katie was sharing. "That's because they don't have to! They have everything. The only thing they could lose at this point is their precious reputations. Makes me sick in the stomach," she said dramatically, putting the back of one hand against her forehead and the other on her stomach.

The two laughed. Katie looked at the wall clock and jumped to her feet.

"Enough of that. Some of us have real work to do, and not fill up our days with dress fittings and tea sipping!"

Up the stairs and down the hall to the second door on the right, Faye stood outside Clarissa's bedroom door listening with great interest to assess what was going on behind the closed door.

The sounds of a woman sitting at her vanity could be heard…a hairbrush being set down on the counter, dainty cabinet drawers opening and sliding shut, the sound of a perfume atomizer being sprayed liberally blending with the sweet melody of a hummed tune.

There's nothing going on in there that's worth standing out here in the hallway for, thought Faye.

Faye rammed her words through the keyhole. "Clarissa, are you in there?"

"Yes, come on in. You know that you don't have to knock or call out before coming in. This room is practically as much yours as it is mine. Now when Brock and I share a bedroom, then you'll need to knock!" Clarissa giggled like a young schoolgirl who'd seen a painting of some naked Romans for the first time in a fine-art book.

Faye noticed how the room smelled of rose essence and lilacs. "Couldn't decide which perfume to put on, could you?"

"I sprayed both."

"Yes, I can tell," replied Faye as she entered the room. *And so can my stinging eyes and burning throat,* she added in her head.

"So what have you been doing today, Faye?"

Weighing her options and determining if the time was right to drop her Brock-and-the-other-woman-in-Chinatown cannon ball, Faye said, "Oh, nothing much. I went into the city to do a little shopping. How about you? Where's Brock?"

"I'm having a quiet day at home. Brock is probably still playing gentleman farmer up on Twin Peaks. He told me they're breaking in a new filly."

You can bet your Aunt Bertha's bloomers that he's breaking in a new filly— only she's wearing a pink dress and he's not in a saddle, thought Faye.

Clarissa continued softly, "I'll never understand the pleasure he gets from those smelly cows and horses, and that fly-infested barnyard out in the middle of nowhere. But there are worse things a man can do with his time. Horses are fine by me…just so I don't have to spend any time with them or Brock up there."

"Are you two planning to have dinner tonight?"

"Yes, after he cleans up, he's coming here for his favorite meal: corned beef and cabbage. I detest it, but he'll never know because I devour it as if it's my favorite too!"

"My, my, my…how devious and deceptive of you. This whole marriage thing is changing you into a person I don't think I know anymore."

"I hope I'm not being devious—well at least not much. I'm sure that our mothers did the same thing as newlyweds. Like twirling around a dance floor, it's best to follow the man's lead. There will be plenty of time to guide things later," said Clarissa in a crafty sort of way.

"I'm sure you're right. You usually are. I'm going to miss spending so much time with you. I'll just have to rush off and get married myself so that we can experience wedded bliss together."

"Is Burt Lovell still interested in you? Or should I rephrase that question and ask if you're at all interested in Burt?"

"Burt's nice enough, I guess. But there's just no spark between us—not like the one you and Brock must share. Burt needs a woman to teach him how to kiss, and I'm not that woman. That's not to say that I haven't done my share of teaching boys about girls, but Burt just isn't worth the effort."

Clarissa was well aware of Faye's encounters with men, since she'd always told Clarissa about each one in great detail, whether she wanted to know or not. Much to Faye's frustration, Clarissa was particularly guarded about the romantic aspects of her relationship with Brock.

"I wouldn't know much about other men, since I've only dated Brock," confided Clarissa in a slightly self-righteous way. "He's such a polite and sensitive man, not at all pushy or demanding like the men you've told me about, Faye."

"Heavens, you're practically married! You mean to tell me that he hasn't forced himself on you yet? Not even the slightest bit?"

"No, absolutely not. Should I be worried?"

"You bet your garters you should be worried, especially if you plan on keeping him your husband or having a passel of babies!"

"Faye, you are too, too bad!"

"Oh, it's good to be bad! But honestly, I'm not bad. I'm just an experienced single woman." *Brock's way too polite. I'm going to do my damndest to make her suspicious, especially after what I saw in Chinatown.*

Chapter 16
Not A Good Idea

Sunday, April 15, 1906, 4:58 p.m.
Three days before the earthquake and firestorm

"Clip-clop. Clip-clop. Clip-clop." Brock's carriage slowly pulled up to the front of Chinatown's Tie Yick General Store. Blossom took a quick inventory of her surroundings. *Whew! Ruby must have sold all of her flowers and gone home. No familiar faces in sight this time*, she thought with relief.

The pair of black steeds heeded Brock's firm tug on the reins. Blossom watched his hands. *Too bad I can't pull the reins on time itself and make this afternoon last longer.*

"I'm not sure what to say...how to end this—"

Blossom interrupted, "Then don't."

"When can I see you again? I don't dare come into the bakery or restaurant, do I?"

"No, that's definitely not a good idea. It's the exact opposite of a good idea." *He said "dare" again. Should I tell him about the dare I took—*

"How about we meet at Anna Mae's?"

"No."

"Can we meet here, right here?"

"No," Blossom replied again.

"Can you say anything other than 'no' right now? If you want today to be the beginning of something, then you'll have to say 'yes' at some point. If you don't and you keep trying to push things off to tomorrow, you'll just end up with a heap of hollow yesterdays. I sound like some poetic old man, don't I? Sorry."

"It's fine, really."

"Can we meet somewhere outside of Chinatown? Let's go back to the stables."

"I'll meet you right here tomorrow at three o'clock. Now I'm off to Monique's to return this dress. Take one last look at it and me. The next time you see me I'll look like the bakery girl you first met."

Brock scanned her body from toe to top and leaned in for a quick kiss. As their lips met, the horses lurched forward and yanked the carriage.

"What is it with you? The ground keeps moving underneath me every time we kiss," said Blossom.

Brock got out of the rig and came around to Blossom's side to help her down. She sighed with relief that she'd made it to the sidewalk without tripping.

"Would you rather have me drop you off at your friend's house, the one you borrowed the dress from? Monique, wasn't it?"

"No, this is good. I'll tell you about Monique another time. It's probably best that you don't visit her house today, especially in the daylight!"

Brock looked at her curiously as she grinned.

"See you soon."

"Not soon enough."

Several doors down, Butch was speaking to a man outside his butcher shop. The girl in pink caught his eye. She stood there as the impressive carriage pulled away. He squinted to clearly see the girl's face before she turned and began to walk away in a hurry.

She was hardly recognizable, but he knew it was Blossom. He'd know her anywhere, anytime. He felt the cold stab of jealousy and through tight lips he forced out the word—and only one word—"Mine!"

The man Butch was talking with looked confused and turned to see in the direction Butch was staring.

"Mine!" Butch said it again and then once more, "MINE!"

Chapter 17
$\mathcal{S}$omething Blue

Sunday, April 15, 1906, 5:39 p.m.
Three days before the earthquake and firestorm

Stepping out of the hot bathtub in a steamed-up bathroom, Brock reached for the pale blue towel that was mysteriously no longer on the counter where he thought he'd left it.

"Looking for this?" taunted Austin, as he wildly waved the towel in the air from his hiding place just outside the doorway leading to the connected bedroom.

"Does big brother need a towel?"

"Austin, give it to me now!"

In a girlish falsetto, Austin replied, "Oh, Brock, you big hunk of a man. If you want it, then you'll have to sashay over here and get it yourself."

It was no secret that Austin rejoiced in teasing and taunting his older brother. It was a well-perfected game they'd played for years in about every situation imaginable. Austin did all he could to upset the golden apple cart.

"Just a few more days and this will be over. You're such a child. What are you, twelve or twenty-two? Honestly, give me the towel or—"

"Or what? You'll walk down the hall buck-naked to the linen room wagging your dragon around, or should I say your newt? You can't call

Wanda—or whatever the new maid's name is—to bring you a towel? Come on, face it. You're at my mercy."

With that, Brock opened the hallway door and immodestly strutted down to the second-floor linen room. Luckily, no one else was around or there would have been hell to pay, and Austin would have been the one to pay the bill. But in the early evening, the entire staff was likely enjoying their dinner in the kitchen. Brock was betting on it.

The satisfaction of forcing his brother to walk the main hall of their house naked should have been enough, but not for Austin. He walked passed Brock and lunged forward in a feeble attempt to pull off the towel and run. But Brock was wise to his brother's antics and kept a firm grasp on the towel.

"You better get moving, Austin, before I kick your ass so hard you'll be wearing it like a hat!"

"Dinner in Chinatown again tonight, Brock?" Austin yelled at the top of his lungs so that he could be heard throughout the house. Towel or no towel, Austin always exhausted every possible opportunity to embarrass his brother.

Brock didn't respond to Austin's outburst with words. Rather, he made eye contact. He made a hand motion around his neck and pulled an imaginary rope up like a hangman's noose. Austin got the message.

"Brock," called his mother from the base of the staircase. "Did I hear Austin correctly? I thought you were having dinner with Clarissa?"

He walked over to the top of the house's formal staircase in nothing more than a towel around his waist.

"My stars! What are you doing parading around like a toddler escaping his bath? Oh, I should have known better. It was Austin up to his tricks again, right?"

"Right," replied Brock with indignation. Clementine emerged from the kitchen to see what the commotion was about. She stood next to Mrs. St. Clair with a dish towel in her hands.

"I have to say, this place won't be the same without you two boys and your constant bickerin' and fightin'." Clementine nodded and smiled up at Brock.

"Right now, I can't say that I'll miss it, but someday I might!" Brock grinned at his mother and Clementine.

Mrs. St. Clair turned to Clementine. "Pretty soon I won't have to ask you to keep an eye on Austin and whatever mischief he's up to."

"Yes ma'am. I'll be able to do better. I'll keep *two* eyes on him!"

The women smiled at each other and Mrs. St. Clair tenderly put her hand on Clementine's wrist.

"Brock, if you are going to Clarissa's, why did Austin mention Chinatown?"

"Mother, Austin must be talking about that wild-goose chase Clarissa sent me on to get a special dessert for the dinner with her bridesmaids."

"Fine." She added in a hushed voice, "While I'm comfortable with our Chinese servants, I've never been very comfortable even passing by Chinatown. It's just so unsavory down there."

"You say *down there* as if Chinatown is in a sewer. I think it's a pretty fascinating place. In fact, it's a *particularly* fascinating place if you ask me."

Brock was thinking of Blossom and their afternoon conversations. *How am I not going to think about this afternoon during dinner with Clarissa?*

"Well, I'm glad that you're braver than I am at trying new things."

Oh, if she only knew just how brave I'm becoming at trying new things.

Chapter 18

Broomstick And Black Cat

Sunday, April 15, 1906, 6:18 p.m.
Three days before the earthquake and firestorm

"Sweetheart, how was your afternoon at your precious barnyard?"

Oh fine, the first full sentence out of her mouth tonight immediately plants Blossom's face in my mind, thought Brock.

He walked into the foyer of the Donohue mansion and kissed Clarissa on the right cheek.

"Lots of flies and manure. You should spend more time with me up there. Let me rephrase that, you should spend some…a little…time up there with me."

"That's your special place and I have no intention of interfering with it," said Clarissa.

"I can't say I'm surprised by that," Brock admitted. "But I did have a surprise today. Did you have one too? Did you feel the earthquake?"

"No. And you'd think I would have since I was alone in my room most of the day, except for when Faye stopped by."

This evening was looking dicier by the minute.

"Did she bring her broomstick and black cat with her?"

"Be kind. You're clearly spending too much time with your crass little brother. We'll soon fix that, now won't we?"

Brock nodded.

Following their meal of corned beef and cabbage, during which Brock had three heaping helpings and Clarissa—with a smile—managed to swallow one serving, the pair retired to the parlor.

Mrs. Donohue walked by the half-opened pocket door and greeted Brock just as he raised his hand to cover his mouth. He sneezed violently. "Good thing you covered your mouth. That should keep your soul from escaping," said Mrs. Donohue.

"Oh, Mother, you can be so superstitious," Clarissa playfully whined.

"While I may not totally subscribe to the superstitious beliefs of others, I'm not going to tempt the Fates. You can pooh-pooh it all, but I'm still going to get out of bed and step on my right foot first to make sure I have good luck each day. As for people who cut their fingernails or change their bed sheets for fear of having bad dreams on a Friday, that does seem a bit extreme," said Mrs. Donohue, shaking her head dismissively.

Clarissa added, "Faye's mother told me she believes that the tip of a peacock's feather has an evil eye, but she has a whole bunch of them in a vase in her parlor. What do you think about when someone dies and the body is in the house, and the family stops every clock in that room at the time of death or they think they'll have bad luck?"

"Well, I don't know. But I suspect you womenfolk are doing some things with our wedding that might be questionable in the minds of some respectable people."

"As for weddings, Mother, I'm sure you'll agree that some superstitions are part of our plans. I remember learning in Miss Merriwether's etiquette class that there supposedly are lucky and unlucky days and months. Sayings like 'Monday for health, Tuesday for wealth' and so on certainly dictate wedding dates for some."

Mrs. Donohue added, "Also, warnings like 'Marry in May and rue the day' and 'Marry in Lent, you'll live to repent' are definitely heeded by brides and mothers everywhere, I suspect."

"Hmmm." Brock rested his chin between his thumb and index finger in a mocking sort of way. It didn't stop Clarissa from going on. He picked up what looked like a magazine that was on the settee. It was, in fact, a catalogue from Cawston Ostrich Farm. Brock flipped through the pages that featured beautiful women wearing magnificent plumes on their hats, fans and parasols.

"I've heard that brides must never try on their entire wedding outfits before their wedding days. Oh, here's one that I just learned. The final stitch in a bride's gown is not to be completed until just before she leaves for the church."

Brock's attention was completely stolen when he came across a photo in the catalogue of a man feeding oranges to ostriches. There were several oranges stacked up and bulging in the ostrich's throat.

"Where did this come from?" he asked.

"That's the ostrich farm that Faye and I went to last summer when we visited her relatives down in Pasadena. They send catalogues from time to time," said Clarissa.

"Let's focus on something real. The corned beef was outstanding, as always. My compliments to the cook!" said Brock with satisfaction.

"I'll be sure to pass along your compliment, honey," said Mrs. Donohue as she continued down the entry hallway toward the kitchen. She turned around and poked her head in the doorway.

"Can Zelda get you two lovebirds some coffee or sweets? Perhaps some brandy or a cigar for you, Brock?"

As Mrs. Donohue said "lovebirds," Clarissa's pair of caged birds in the conservatory began to chirp.

"Romeo and Juliet, please be quiet," Clarissa reprimanded the pair of winged pets. They disobeyed by chattering a bit more and then settling down.

"No Mother, we're fine. But thank you for the offer," said Clarissa loudly, adding softly, "and the interruption."

"I heard that. I haven't lost my hearing yet!"

Clarissa grinned at Brock as he noticed over her shoulder that two Scandinavian-looking servants walked by. Brock noticed how their skin looked as white as lace and their hair was the color of the dried grass in the late-summer sunshine up on Twin Peaks.

"Are all of your servants white?" asked Brock.

"Absolutely, that's the way my mother wants it. She distrusts people if they aren't white," replied Clarissa matter-of-factly.

"Truly," was Brock's initial response. "My parents, especially my father, hired people who weren't white—on purpose—when he ran the mining business. He said his Chinese employees worked harder than two white men put together. That's why he paid them more and it caused a big fight with other mine owners whose Chinese workers left to work for Dad."

Clarissa looked at Brock with mild disinterest. Talk of work did not usually hold her attention, but especially leading up to the couple's wedding and all of its taxing details.

"That's nice, Sweetheart."

"It was Dad who found Clementine working in a restaurant and hired her to be our cook. He made sure that my mother hired Lily to be one of our maids. She's the wife of a miner who lost a leg while working for Dad at the mine. I've grown up with a Southern Black cook and a Chinese maid, just to name two, and never thought it was different from other households, like yours. Our other servants are—"

Brock noticed that Clarissa's mind was wandering. She covered her inattention with, "I didn't know that."

"Anyway, how are the wedding plans coming along? Has your checklist gotten shorter?"

Clarissa beamed. "I think we're set, thank goodness."

She paused.

"I guess that little paper in the cookie I opened last night was right."

She reached for her heart-shaped locket, opened the hinged section and handed it to Brock.

He unfolded the tiny strip of white paper that read, "Confucius say, 'Wherever you go, go with all of your heart.' What happened today that made you think this message held some truth for you?"

So, two cookies can have the same fortune. What are the odds of that happening? Blossom would know.

"I just feel like we're so close now, that our hearts beat as one. I know that sounds nonsensical, but it's how I feel."

With that, Brock rediscovered something he admired about Clarissa. It was her clarity and confidence in things like love and relationships.

At that same moment, he confirmed to himself how unclear and unconfident he now was in his ideas and feelings about love and relationships.

"You're the only one for me," said Clarissa.

Brock held her close, but didn't utter a word.

"I could use some fresh air. How about you," Brock asked as he began to stand up.

"Yes, if that's what you want."

As he walked away, Clarissa admired his six-foot frame, which was built like an upside-down triangle—broad at the shoulders and narrowing all the way down. Appropriately inexperienced, but knowledgeable about the male body from studying sculptures in art galleries, she felt naughty as she imagined Brock's heavy brown suit being peeled away to reveal the muscular body that would be hers after they took their vows.

Having felt the brush of her glance, Brock turned back. *What's that strange look on her face?* "What are you thinking?"

"Oh, nothing you need to know just yet."

Mrs. Donohue passed by a nearby doorway, made eye contact with Clarissa and nodded. "Everything fine with the upcoming nuptials? Brock, no second thoughts or cold feet?"

Clarissa's body stiffened at the candidness of the questions. Brock took the lead and responded, "Yes and no."

"Good, very good," said Mrs. Donohue.

"You know Brock, with you I have simply *everything* life has to offer," Clarissa said as she walked toward him.

Brock reached out his hand and escorted her to the garden.

Yeah, and with Blossom I found something I didn't know I was missing.

Chapter 19

Deception

Sunday, April 15, 1906, 6:21 p.m.
Three days before the earthquake and firestorm

"Oh, there you are, my child. Seeing you always bring me great joy. But, odd thing happen today," said Grand Ma Maw as Blossom closed the door behind her and the street noise was quickly muffled.

"Anna Mae's father come to see if his treasured daughter still here with you. I not show my surprise to him. Did you not say this very morning you go spend time with Anna Mae's family? Why then her father come here in search of you two?" probed Grand Ma Maw, certain that Blossom was cornered like a mouse in the pantry with a broom aimed at it.

"And at my mahjong game this afternoon, ladies interested in you more than usual," she added.

"You caught me. What can I say?"

Grand Ma Maw was shocked for the second time today as Blossom actually admitted to what might be a transgression.

"Our work was done around lunchtime, and Anna Mae and I went to visit Monique at Maison Bijou."

"Yes, everyone know of your Monique. She make quite a show of herself," said Grand Ma Maw with a growing anger that could erupt at any moment. Grand Ma Maw recalled in her head how Monique's internal compass seemed to always point her in the wrong direction, even as a child.

"Why in name of our ancestors would you go there? Have you no common sense? Anyone see you go in or out? Your good name—and our family's reputation—already a mess," said Grand Ma Maw authoritatively. "Monique, that whore who sells and sells and sells herself. She just empty oyster now. No pearl to give her husband. No man want new wife with no pearl. I know she your friend, but she worse than a used handkerchief."

She looked at Blossom with intent eyes. "And what you do to your hair? It looks like a pile on your head, like mountain. And make-up on face. Only people on stage and good-time girl on street wear make-up!"

"We were trying out some new looks for me at Monique's."

"Just stop right there. Tell me no more," interrupted the old woman with her palm raised and facing Blossom.

"Oh, Grand Ma Maw, Monique's home is beautiful. I wish you could see it. I'll ask Monique if we can stop by sometime soon. You've never seen such fancy furniture and wallpaper. It's like walking through photographs of a mansion in Paris. There are mirrors everywhere, even on the ceiling!"

"Heavens, child, you promise me now you never go there again!"

"Oh, but I didn't tell you the best part! There are golden statues of naked women holding up candelabras that drip with sparkling crystals! Then, in Monique's bedroom I saw—"

"Stop…right…now," commanded Grand Ma Maw. "I not wish to hear any more, and I not want you to bring visions of that horrible place into your mind or mine! I ask again, did anyone see you?"

"I suppose I did say 'hello' to a few shopkeepers along the way. I wouldn't want to be unfriendly in our own neighborhood."

"No way to fix now," said Grand Ma Maw. "Hurry up and dress. We need your help in dining room. It may be Sunday evening and people have eaten big lunch, but that never stop them from coming out for nice dinner. Best of all, Ming Yang waits for you. He ask for you earlier. You ever going to show him some attention? He not wait forever!"

"Grand Ma Maw, I'll bring out his meal and I'll take away his dirty dishes every day of my life if I have to. But it will be in this restaurant only, and it won't be as his wife. I just wish…oh, what's the point?" With that, Blossom turned and headed up the back stairs to her room to put on a proper outfit for serving in The Golden Palace's dining room.

Grand Ma Maw shook her head, confounded by Blossom's apparent lack of good judgment and planning for the future.

"What I do to deserve such a girl?" she said aloud to herself. Then she reconsidered her question. *Could Blossom end up like me here in 50 years, still running the restaurant…doing same thing…day after day? This good living, but very hard life…little room for wishing or making wishes come true. I must find way to help bring her happiness.*

Chapter 20
$\mathcal{L}$isten With Your Heart

Sunday, April 15, 1906, 7:23 p.m.
Three days before the earthquake and firestorm

Hand in hand, Clarissa and Brock strolled on the gravel pathway in the rose garden. The glow of the light inside the house appeared golden and warm from the outside looking in.

"Brock, the roses remind me of something I read today." Clarissa pulled from her waistband a small piece of paper that was neatly folded and tucked in. "I wrote it down to share with you tonight."

She unfolded the paper. "It's about love, the gentle and romantic kind of love that poor President Garfield had with his wife, Lucretia. It was before he was assassinated, of course. Apparently, she wrote him these words as they were separated on New Year's evening in 1856. I know. I know. Just get to the point, right?"

"Nonsense. Go on," urged Brock.

"Thank you. She wrote—"

Clarissa looked down. "I'll read each word to get it just right. 'Wherever you may be I know you are with me in spirit, and upon my lips I almost feel the fond kiss your ardent love places there.'"

She stopped. Brock rubbed the back of his neck and sighed loudly.

"Doesn't that just melt your heart? It gets better, though. He wrote back, saying, 'Your dear little message of love passed over the wide wintery waste that lies between us, to reach me…your letters are like dear little drops of yourself, sweet roses from the full garden of your heart.'"

He cleared his throat and put his hands behind his back.

"Say, tell me about the progress on our new house. Is your father still driving the construction crew crazy?" asked Brock, referring to the mansion Clarissa's parents were building for them just down the street within the Nob Hill district.

"He's one to pay attention to the details, isn't he?" Clarissa asked rhetorically, knowing that his success in business could be attributed to his precision and persistence.

"It should be ready for us to move into after our honeymoon this summer. I visited it on Thursday, and the men were installing the tile counters in the bathroom and the sinks were about to be dropped into place. I do wish you spent more time there to be sure the work is to your satisfaction, not just Daddy's."

"If I've learned anything from your father, it's to know when to get out of the way and when to stay out of it."

"But this is our house, our home. I want it to be perfect."

"Nothing is perfect in life," Brock reflected. "I'm not sure that striving for perfection is something we should ever do."

Clarissa stopped walking. The garden pathway's gravel no longer made the familiar grinding noise beneath their feet. She turned to face him and with her right hand lifted his lowered chin to look him straight in the eyes.

"Talk to me. What's going on behind that handsome face of yours? I've never heard you sound so doubtful and unsure. Is it the wedding?"

Brock remained silent, staring directly into Clarissa's eyes.

"Honey, talk to me," urged Clarissa.

"I don't know exactly what it is, so I can't talk about it. Maybe I should leave."

"No, don't go. We can talk about whatever it is tomorrow or the next day. I want to be with you. I get so little time alone with you as it is."

He took Clarissa's hand in his and began to stroll again.

"It's so clear tonight. The moon is huge. Look at it rising over Oakland across the bay. You can always count on the sun and the moon, can't you?" asked Clarissa.

"Yes," said Brock. "You can always count on them."

"Before you leave, I have a surprise for you inside," said Clarissa excitedly. She led him into the music room, where her harp stood proudly as the center of attention, with ornate chairs scattered around the room. Hand-painted murals of violins and harps adorned the walls. Mrs. Donohue encouraged her daughter to add playing an instrument to Clarissa's list of accomplishments. Mrs. Donohue made it known she would have preferred the selection of the piano, because Clarissa's choice of playing the harp produced calluses on her fingers, which were never desirable for a true lady.

"Sit down next to me," she urged as she pulled a gold-painted chair next to the harp's red-velvet-covered stool. With a hand on his shoulder, she pushed him down into the chair. Then, she situated herself at the harp.

"Close your eyes and listen with your heart. I wrote this for you and I only used the best notes! It's your song."

Clarissa played her original composition with passion. There was more to this tune than the mere plucking of strings. It was stirring, soaring and even subtle at times.

Her eyes closed as she played. It was as if Clarissa could hear a full orchestra behind her as the music swelled and subsided. It was intoxicating to her.

As she plucked a single string to make the last note, she sighed with relief. She awaited his reaction.

"I'm not sure what to say. No one has ever written a song for me... much less played it on a golden harp," admitted Brock. "However, I don't believe the harps of angels could sound any sweeter. That was something I'll never forget, Sweetheart, never."

Clarissa beamed. "Whenever you want to hear your song, for the rest of our lives, all you'll need to do is ask."

"Does it have a name?" he asked.

"Yes. Well, it didn't until the other day when we were at the Cliff House and I read the Land's End sign. That's when your song got its name: Land's End. On Saturday, we'll leave behind our past lives and start a new one together. It will be like soaring off the cliffs and out over the ocean. Just you—" she paused and gently placed her left index finger on his heart. "And me," she said as she placed her right index finger on her heart.

Then, she whipped her fingers in swirling circles over the harp's strings and laughed loudly.

"But let's not be so serious," she said. "I'm glad you like it."

He looked into her eyes and said, "I do."

Chapter 21
The Time Had Come

Sunday, April 15, 1906, 7:58 p.m.
Three days before the earthquake and firestorm

The Golden Palace crowd was thinning. Blossom traveled through the dining room, checking on her remaining patrons to ensure unwanted plates were cleared and tea pots were hot and full. Her body was going through the same routine motions, displaying poise and confidence.

A nagging piece of hair broke free from Blossom's bun and needed to be tucked again. With her left hand, she captured it and slid it behind her ear. Then she touched her upper lip with her index finger, holding it there. She stopped walking and stood there.

"You ill, Blossom?" asked Grand Ma Maw.

"I'm fine."

The old woman looked at Blossom with curious and probing eyes. They were the eyes of a suspicious and protective caregiver who was seeing what she had dreaded for years: the awakening of the woman who was no longer the little girl and constant companion in this Chinatown bakery and restaurant. The time had come. Grand Ma Maw was sure of it.

Chapter 22
The Rice Bowl That Never Empties

Monday, April 16, 1906, 2:42 p.m.
Two days before the earthquake and firestorm

Under the veiled guise of visiting Anna Mae before the dinner rush, Blossom left the bakery with Grand Ma Maw waving goodbye, then shaking her head as she often did.

"I do not believe Anna Mae getting a special visitor today. But I do believe Blossom visiting *someone* special," she said aloud, but softly.

"You talking to me?" asked Blossom's father.

"No, my son, I talk to hole in wall."

"Now that we talking to each other, you notice how much time Blossom say she spending with Anna Mae's family lately? We do something to drive her away?"

"I not believe we drive her. I believe she drawn to something," said the old woman as she watched Blossom blend in with the traffic and disappear down the street.

Grand Ma Maw stepped back in the doorway and closed the door behind her. The bells mounted to the top of the door rang out.

Grand Ma Maw had always welcomed the ringing of the bells on the door. That meant a customer had entered and business was going to be transacted. For the first time, she heard the bells in a different way. At this moment, they meant someone had left and the door closed behind them. She didn't like this new feeling, not at all. She looked pained.

"What you looking at? Have you no work to do? Chang, dinner rush here soon enough, and we not be ready."

Chang turned away and entered the kitchen.

The door's bells rang out loud and clear again. It was Ting Ting and Little Sunflower.

"How are you two this fine afternoon?" asked Grand Ma Maw.

"I'm great," Ting Ting replied as she reopened the door to release the hanging crimson-fabric banner that was deliberately placed too close to the door opening. It was Grand Ma Maw's plan for it to get stuck in the door regularly, as it drew more attention to the message on it as people opened the door to set it free.

The banner's vertically arranged characters made the following wish to everyone in luminous golden threadwork, "May good fortune follow you on your path through life." While the message escaped Ting Ting's notice, the banner did not.

Little Sunflower made herself quietly comfortable on a chair in the corner of the restaurant entrance. "I'm great too."

"How's the rice bowl today?" Ting Ting eagerly asked. She had an unusual fascination with the bowl on the shelf. The cobalt-blue dragon painted on its sides intrigued most children. But for Ting Ting, it was the rice inside the bowl that commanded her attention. Grand Ma Maw knew that Ting Ting loved the idea that the rice bowl would never be empty. Being a girl of substantial appetite, endless food was a dream come true for her.

"You like to put new rice in bowl?" asked Grand Ma Maw as she lowered it down from the shelf. Ting Ting nodded eagerly. "You handle bowl with great care."

Ting Ting did as she was instructed. Grand Ma Maw recalled a young

Blossom as Ting Ting scampered away.

When Ting Ting came back, Grand Ma Maw returned the rice bowl to its place and thanked her with a softly spoken *shay shay*.

"Ting Ting, our great ancestors in Mt. Penglai—land of the Eight Immortals—thank you too," she added. "Rice bring us together in Chinatown. It bind us, like sticky rice in mortar that hold Great Wall of China together, century after century."

Ting Ting hugged the old woman around the waist and looked up at her with a beaming smile. Little Sunflower smiled from her seat in the corner.

"I read this question in a storybook today: Has a moment ever hugged you, hugged you like this," the little girl asked as she embraced the old woman more tightly, "and never let you go?"

"A moment? Hugged?" asked Grand Ma Maw. She thought about what the girl had really asked with her choice of words.

"Yes. Yes, just now. Your hug never let me go, right?"

"Right," replied Ting Ting with a sweet giggle.

Grand Ma Maw's lip quivered. She looked at the door that led out of The Golden Palace.

"Yes, my Ting Ting, I not let this moment go…ever."

Chapter 23
The Unforeseen And The Seen

Monday, April 16, 1906, 3:06 p.m.
Two days before the earthquake and firestorm

To Blossom, it felt good to be back in Brock's carriage, beside the man she couldn't stop thinking about. They'd been traveling for a while when she caught him staring at the brown-paper-wrapped package that she held on her lap. He didn't ask about it, but he was staring just the same.

"I want to show you something, Blossom. Chinatown isn't what I expected it to be, or at least it didn't live up to its reputation."

Blossom jumped into the conversation, "You clearly haven't seen the darker parts of town."

"Anyway," said Brock, "it's different from other parts of the city, but not necessarily in a bad way. You can find kindness and cruelty in any neighborhood. That's what I want to show you."

"You want to show me some kindness and cruelty?"

"Yes, and here it is."

The carriage stopped in front of a home of palatial proportions.

"A museum?"

"No, that's my family's house. This is Nob Hill."

Blossom quickly estimated that fifty Chinese families could live in that one building alone.

"I want you to see—"

"Brock, giddy-up those horses and get us out of here! Someone's sure to see us!" said Blossom as she quickly rummaged through her handbag and produced a fan. She unfolded it in an attempt to mask her face.

"I don't care."

"Well you ought to. The windows in Chinatown have eyes, and I believe the same is true here," said Blossom as she studied her surroundings from over the black fan with cherry blossoms painted on it. She'd had the fan since childhood. It was a gift from Grand Ma Maw and it had her name spelled out in white Chinese characters. While she knew it was unnecessarily risky to be here, it was unavoidable not to gawk at this place.

"How many people in your family live here?"

"Um, the three of us and the help."

"You have half a city block for just three people? It's hard to believe!"

"Believe it. It's all I've ever known, and I wanted you to see it so that you have a clear picture of who I am and where I come from."

The playing field was leveled now. Each had been exposed to the other's world, only separated by a handful of street names on a city map.

"Do you know how lucky you are?" asked Blossom.

"Yes, I met you on Saturday and today you're in my carriage. How could I be any luckier?"

"That's not what I mean and you know it."

"Yes, I know that I've lived what most people consider a charmed life. Now let me charm you!"

He signaled to the horses to get moving. They were off at a full gallop in no time, with the carriage surging back and forth randomly until its movement synchronized with the horses.

Blossom held onto Brock's arm tightly. *This is nice*, she thought. She took in the sights as each mansion appeared grander than the next. He pointed out the homes of the Crockers, the Stanfords and the Huntingtons.

"If you think these houses are amazing, you should see the one that's being built for Clarissa and me. And it's just for two people! It's complete insanity. I'm beginning to think that I'd rather live up at my ranch," said Brock. He looked forward at nothing in particular. "But that's never going to happen."

Before long, the houses grew smaller and then nonexistent as they left the city. Blossom firmly held the package on her lap. As she looked down at it repeatedly, Brock had to ask, "So what's in there?"

"I suspect you haven't had to want or wait for much in your lifetime. Where I come from, it's not only good to want and wait, it's unavoidable. It makes you appreciate what you get when you get it. Oh, that sounded high and mighty of me, didn't it? That's not what I meant to say. Well, it is what I meant to say, but not the way I meant to say it." She paused. "I'm babbling. My father would have shushed me long ago."

"I'm not your father, and I want to hear everything that you want to say to me," Brock said as he focused on the curving, winding rutted road that led to his dairy and stables. He made a clicking sound with his mouth and the horses knew to pull harder and move faster.

"Well, here's something you may or may not want to hear me say," Blossom announced, intriguing Brock with such a set up.

"All of my life I've been taught what to think and believe about being Chinese, being respectful and being obedient. I've been fine with most of it, but being obedient…I've never been too good at that. You know what I mean?"

"Yes."

Blossom went on, "One…single…solitary…day in the bakery can stretch on for what seems like a month. Don't misunderstand me. I love my family and our business. But time practically stands still there. And I don't sit or stand still for long. It's not in me."

She stopped and realized that she was speaking much too openly and freely.

"Now that was babbling. Why didn't you stop me?"

Brock looked at Blossom the way he did the first time they met, intimately and deeply. "You're so different."

"Different from the girls on Nob Hill?"

"Different from anyone I've met. I mean that in a good way, in a *very* good way."

It was getting breezier as they reached the stable on the hill. A gust of wind pushed and pulled the carriage canopy. They both felt it and braced themselves.

Brock handed the reins to a grizzly looking old man named Gubbs, a hired hand who came with the ranch and stable when Brock's father bought the place for his son. Trying to study him without getting caught, Blossom noted that Gubbs had a face that was marinated by life.

"It's time for your surprise," said Blossom as she lifted the package and the carriage was parked near the tree they'd kissed under yesterday. In a flash, Blossom replayed that moment in her mind and smiled.

"I'm glad that you're happy to be here," said Brock as he helped her out of the carriage.

"What makes you think I'm happy?"

"The smile on your face was my biggest clue."

Blossom looked down at the ground.

"Yes," she recovered, saying, "I could get used to the animal smells at some point, but the view—and you—make me happy right now. Thank you for bringing me here again. I can see why you want to live here. Is it safe that your stable man knows we're here?"

"Oh, sure, Gubbs talks to the animals more than to people, I think," said Brock reassuringly. "The other men who work here don't really notice when I'm here or not, or who my guests are."

She handed him the package.

"This is for you. I hope that you like it."

He knelt down, setting it on the ground. Blossom studied how Brock's hair was streaked with sunlight as he gently unwrapped the package. A ball of string rolled out in one direction as the wind picked up and stole the rest of the package's contents.

"Quick, a thief has stolen my gift!" announced Brock with a playful sense of urgency.

"That's a good thing. We need the wind to take this gift. It's a dragon kite. I'll put it together."

Blossom unfolded a sheet of paper that had a diagram of how to assemble the kite. She organized the rows of circular hoops wrapped with bright tissue paper stretched across, arranged like a centipede with an outrageous dragon face on the front disc. Soon she was ready to help Brock launch it into the blue sky.

"Here, you hold the string and run when I tell you to. I'll be over here holding the kite."

"Blossom, I was a boy once. I know how to fly a kite."

"Not one like this!" replied Blossom. "But first, I have to take my shoes off."

"Your shoes off?" asked Brock.

"You might as well know now. I like to be barefooted or in socks. Shoes are too restrictive," she said. "Take yours off too and see for yourself."

Blossom looked at him in a playful way.

He hesitated. As he began to remove his boots and socks, Blossom watched. When he was finally finished, she found that she had to hold back her first reaction.

"How did that happen?" she asked, pointing to his feet and putting her hand softly on Brock's arm.

"It was years ago, when Austin and I were little boys. We were playing cowboys and Indians in the cellar under our house. I was the cowboy and I let him tie me up to a wooden support beam. We were going to pretend that he was going to burn me at the stake. What I didn't know is that someone had taught him to tie really good knots and how to set a fire. And he did both!"

"He set you on fire?" she asked sounding outraged.

"We were playing. He put newspaper and pieces of wood around my feet and lit it. Once it started, he ran away thinking he'd be in trouble and—"

"He ran away?"

"Yes, but luckily Clementine was in the kitchen and smelled the smoke. She came running down and saved me, but not before the skin on my ankles and calves was burned. I had to be in bed for weeks. She said she hadn't seen flames like that since she was a little girl…when she watched the Yankees burn down Atlanta near the end of the war. Ever since then, I've done my best to stay away from fire."

He stopped talking.

"Brock, we all have scars," assured Blossom. "Yours show."

"Thanks." He stopped talking again. His eyes opened abruptly.

"But Clementine made me fried chicken and biscuits…and red velvet cake…every night for my dinner for a long, long time!"

Blossom smiled back at Brock. "That's why you liked our picnic lunch so much."

"No, I liked it so much because I was sharing it with you."

Brock's comment embarrassed Blossom, but pleased her too.

"So let's get this dragon into the air!" she announced as she ran a good distance away, holding the kite.

She instantly let go and laughed loudly as Brock wrangled and wrestled with the unleashed dragon. It was a racing blur of crimson and gold with black eyes. It felt alive in Brock's hands, fighting, swirling, pulling and yanking wildly.

"You're right. I've never flown a kite quite like this one. You can stop laughing now and help me get a grip on it," said Brock.

Blossom moved close behind Brock, in the way someone lovingly teaches an inexperienced person how to swing a golf club or tennis racket.

But this closeness served another purpose as well.

Her hand guided his to calm the unruly dragon.

"Thank you. I haven't done this in years."

"You are most welcome." *I'll never forget this moment, no matter what happens next*, she thought.

They stood united on the crest of Twin Peaks, the wind tugging at their clothes and swirling their hair. The sky was unusually clear. The sun warmed them as they looked beyond the kite over the sparkling bay and the endless blue sky.

Blossom knew that he now also had a tight grip on her heart, and she didn't want him to let go.

He turned to look at her. A gust completely took hold of her hair, making it fly in all directions. Brock studied her and then stared deeply into her eyes. Just as he'd done in front of the Tie Yick General Store, Brock asked Blossom to stand silently. He slowly looked to the ground and closed his eyes. After a long pause, he announced, "Okay, I've got it!" to let her know that he'd captured the vision of her. He slowly opened his eyes.

"Brock, look up...not at me!"

"No, I'd rather let go of this kite—of everything—and just be with you." He held up the ball of string and deliberately dropped it. The dragon took off. Neither immediately reached to grasp the escaping string.

Blossom, however, knowing how hard she'd worked for the money that bought the kite and ball of string, broke away to run and firmly plant her foot on the string. He followed.

They embraced as if nature's forces pulled them together. Brock's lips forcefully parted Blossom's. He nibbled softly on her upper lip. Blossom inhaled irregularly and then calmed down. She slowly slid her hand down Brock's back, over his hips, and she crouched down in a slow swooping motion that surprised and intrigued Brock. She burst out in laughter as her hand scooped up the ball of string.

"Let's fly this kite right."

"I'd rather continue what we've started," said Brock.

"So would I, and that's why we need to fly this kite."

Chapter 24
$\mathcal{I}$rreplaceable

Monday, April 16, 1906, 4:58 p.m.
Two days before the earthquake and firestorm

"Where Blossom?" asked Grand Ma Maw. The urgency was apparent in her tone. "It one thing to storm out of here. It entirely another to not help in restaurant tonight."

"Yes, my honored mother, she know her obligations. I believe she return soon. Can I help?" asked Chang.

Grand Ma Maw grunted in frustration. "Unless you can wear women's clothes, carry heavy trays and smile entire time to dining room packed with hungry people, you cannot replace your daughter."

The reflective blue mood Grand Ma Maw was in a few hours ago passed. She was clearly back to her feisty ways again.

"People waiting to be seated. At least do your job before asking if there anything else you can do! Now go tend to them while I see if I can get someone to fill in for Blossom tonight."

Grand Ma Maw reached for the telephone receiver, but looked at the door. *No one ever replace my Blossom.*

Chapter 25

The Last Place On Earth

Monday, April 16, 1906, 5:02 p.m.
Two days before the earthquake and firestorm

"Brock, can we go any faster? The dinner rush already started without me."

"I'll see what I can do," replied Brock as he snapped the reins, giving a hurry-up signal to the horses.

"Aren't these the houses we saw going up to Twin Peaks?" Blossom put her hand on Brock's thigh. "Do we even dare use this street twice in one day, with me in plain view?"

"Sure."

Blossom continued, "Speaking of dares, I need to tell you something... to confess something. I—"

The horses suddenly got spooked and Brock's full attention diverted to them and away from Blossom. "Whoa. Whoa," he said.

Brock turned the carriage to the right. "We'll take a different way."

"See that yellow one on the left with the scaffolding in the front? It's the new house I told you about, the one that's being built for Clarissa and me."

"It looks very nice," said Blossom, immediately feeling left out of Brock's future life. "So getting back to what I want to tell you, Brock, I...

uh, who's coming out of the front door?"

The wheel of fortune suddenly stopped spinning in Brock's favor. Clarissa and Faye stepped out from under the scaffolding.

"Isn't that Brock's carriage coming this way? I thought you said he didn't take much interest in the new house," said Faye to Clarissa.

"Why, who is that Chinese-looking girl with him? Oh, just one of his family's maids, I guess. Such generosity and attention his family gives their servants, sightseeing trips around Nob Hill no less," Faye chattered on. She delighted in the clandestine moment that fate laid comfortably in her lap. *Now things are really going to get interesting*, thought Faye.

"Brock, honey, is that you?" asked Clarissa with a tentative wave of her hand.

Blossom quickly reached into her handbag to retrieve the fan from Grand Ma Maw. She opened it and shielded her face.

"Sweetheart," he said as he turned his head. "And Faye, how wonderful to find you here too."

Faye wasted no time. "Are you going to introduce us to your passenger?"

"Yes, of course. This is Blossom," he said. There was a long break before he continued. "Her brother works at the stables and I offered to take her home to Chinatown so he could finish his work and she could start hers ... yes, um, waiting tables in a restaurant."

"Your stable boy's sister, you say?" asked Faye, hoping for another verbal stumble. With the assistance of Faye's almost photographic memory, she knew this was the same girl she'd seen Brock with in Chinatown. *Now this girl has a name: Blossom.*

"That's right," he responded and refocused his attention on Clarissa. "How's the progress on the house?"

Blossom kept her head in a demure and downward position. She fanned herself briskly to cool the heat that was stinging and staining her cheeks.

Brock made small talk with Clarissa about the work crew's progress. Faye nodded from time to time to appear engaged in the conversation, but she never took her eyes off of Blossom. Faye's action bordered on rudeness for someone who should know better.

"Can we offer you ladies a ride home?"

"Are you kidding me?" Faye fired back. Her eyes shifted squarely on Brock, which was a relief for Blossom. "I won't be caught dead behind horses these days! I only ride in automobiles now. They smell too, but not of manure."

"Thank you, but we have a driver coming to fetch us any minute now," Clarissa responded.

Faye scrunched-up her face and wrinkled her nose. "Besides, we wouldn't want to delay Blossom from getting to her job waiting on tables, now would we? Just think of all the hungry Chinese men down in that part of the city. They must be waiting, simply desperate for the kind of service she provides!"

While I've been told that I can be a one-note shrill of criticism, Mr. Brock St. Clair, I also can be a dreadful symphony of sarcasm, anger and jealousy. This just gets better and better. And I don't even need to lift a finger!

"That's very considerate of you, Faye," replied Brock.

"By the way, I hope that the bachelor party Austin is hosting for you is something you'll *always* remember. Where is it being held? I thought I heard it's going to be at Prickly Pete's," announced Faye in a more-than-sufficiently loud voice considering the decorum of the neighborhood.

"Yes, Prickly Pete's it is." Brock flicked the reins. "Ladies," he announced with a nod of his head and a tip of his hat, "have a safe journey home in your automobile, even if it's just around the corner."

"I am so sorry," said Brock in a hushed voice. "I didn't know what to say or do. Understand?"

"Understand?" she replied as she folded her fan and returned it to her handbag. "How could anyone have been prepared for that? I was so mortified that I couldn't even speak. It was like my head emptied. They probably think I'm deaf and dumb!"

"Yes, I noticed that you didn't talk."

"Well, even if I could, what would I say? 'Hello. I'm the girl whose heart races for your fiancé!'"

"It does?"

"Yes, silly, it does," said Blossom, shaking her head much like Grand Ma Maw did a thousand times a day.

Blossom started to laugh, slowly at first. Then it was a belly-shaking kind of laugh. "What are you so amused by?" asked Brock. Blossom regained her breath. "It's like when I was a kid, when I'd spin in circles and get so dizzy I couldn't stop laughing." She laughed more, and he joined in.

As they began to settle down, Blossom observed, "This was the last place on earth that I expected to meet her. Oh, that's not right. It's your new home. That should be the first place on earth to meet Clarissa." She paused and began again with, "Clarissa seems nice. Though I can't put my finger on it, there's something evil about the other one."

"Yes, Faye is special that way. How perceptive of you to see that in her. Is it that obvious to someone who's just meeting her? I've known her for so long that I guess I'm dull to her sharp edges. But she's always been like a shot of strong whiskey in a porcelain tea cup."

Blossom admitted, "For the first time, I felt wrong and sort of dirty, as if she suspected or knew about us. Do you think she does?"

"Faye is suspicious any time of the day or night, and I think she enjoys looking for people's flaws and unsettling them in the process. She's not someone to ignore or underestimate. But I also wouldn't live my life based on what Faye thinks, gossips about or imagines in her own twisted way," said Brock.

"Do you really think you can live in that house...be happy there? I've seen the house you live in now. I've seen the one that you'll live in soon. And I've seen the ranch, twice. Well, to me it just doesn't look like a good fit."

Brock did not acknowledge her remarks.

"So, what do we do next?" Blossom fanned her face.

Brock pulled the reins, slowed the horses and stopped the carriage. He turned, leaned toward her and pulled her close across the smooth leather seat.

"Not here, Brock. We've been far too unlucky today already. Neither of us—"

Her words were cut short as their lips merged. A passionate kiss consumed the air from her lungs. Despite being parked along a curb in the Nob Hill neighborhood, they were in a world of their own for a few brief moments as they focused completely on each other.

The subtle, yet screechy squeak of the Flood mansion's front gate spooked the horses and they sprang into action. Brock looked up and forward to get his bearings and then to the side from which the squeaking originated. There stood Mrs. James Flood, who unquestionably held one of the highest slots on the list of Nob Hill's elite. Brock and his family, along with most of their neighbors knew that Mary Leary Flood was an Irish immigrant who had tended bar with her husband in a saloon before they amassed a great silver-mining fortune. She had an affinity for diamonds, the larger the better. Mary was none too bashful about wearing her jewels anytime of the day. She was especially known to shimmer on nights at the theater.

"Mr. St. Clair, your public display of affection truly warms my heart," she said with an exaggerated wink at Brock. "However, your lack of discretion may ultimately break yours."

She adjusted a stunning diamond bracelet on her right forearm and turned, saying nothing more. She glanced at them to be sure they noticed her jewelry and then walked toward the attendant who was holding her motor car's passenger door open.

"She sparkles." That was the only thing Blossom could summon to say.

"Yes, but her words sting."

Chapter 26
A Time To Celebrate

Monday, April 16, 1906, 8:23 p.m.
Two days before the earthquake and firestorm

"Boys, raise your glasses!" bellowed Austin to the barroom full of revelers at Prickly Pete's establishment in the notorious Barbary Coast district. It was a breathtaking kind of place, literally. However, Austin paid no mind to the unrelenting and pungent mixture in the air of unwashed men, writhing snakes of cigar smoke, and musty floorboards that hadn't been touched by a broom, mop or soap in far too long.

For years, the number of bars, saloons, gambling houses, dance halls and brothels grew to meet the demands of sailors, laborers, criminals and brave-hearted tourists. The practice of Shanghaiing unsuspecting sailors was legendary, with victims being shipped out to sea before the booze or opium wore off.

But Austin and his guests were here for one reason: to celebrate in a larger-than-life and obnoxiously boisterous way.

"Like real men say, 'It's time for booze and teats at Prickly Pete's!'" The crowd roared in agreement, including Pete, who was behind the bar. He lived up to his prickly name in both looks—a wild unruly red beard and shock of hair—and behavior. Austin reveled at how Pete could string together the crudest words and bark them out in such a way to shock even the grisliest sailors who regularly bellied up to his bar.

"Let's toast the best things in life...women, and more women! You'll be giving them all up but one, Brock. But we're sure that you'll be getting much more in return. When you find out exactly what that is, be sure to let us all know!"

Spitting arcs of chewing-tobacco juice glistened in the air as the room broke out in a roar of laugher. All eyes turned from Austin to Brock, who was never comfortable being the center of attention. That was painfully evident right now. *I only have to do this once, right?* he thought.

As the general sobriety of the partygoers diminished, Brock's less-than-festive mood was not very apparent among the back-slapping, "hey-hey-hey" howling and beer spilling. Not unfamiliar with stag parties, the barmaids were good humored about their treatment by these fine men of society, and they were plenty experienced at holding their ground if need be.

Brock became intrigued by the unfamiliar music the piano player was banging out from the other side of the room. He made his way over to ask about it.

"Hello there. I'm Brock," he yelled to the musician.

"I gather that you're in the spotlight tonight. But if you don't mind me saying, you don't look much like someone who's celebrating. I'm Max... Max Morath. Pleasure to meet you."

Not acknowledging Max's observations, Brock asked, "What kind of music are you playing?"

"Ragtime, man. Ragtime! It's the *Maple Leaf Rag*. A clever Texan named Scott Joplin wrote it." The seated performer with a worn and craggy face—and a sly smile—energetically went on. "Watch how ragtime combines two enemies: discipline and chaos. My left hand pounds out a steady beat, kind of like a march. But my right hand's gone wild and syncopated. Looks like it's lost its mind, doesn't it?"

"Yes it does."

As Max talked and pounded his fingers on the ivories, Brock considered the metaphor of ragtime in his life. He'd always been disciplined, doing what was expected of him…adhering to society's playbook. But now a wild and chaotic world was coexisting in his life, creating a ragtime of his own design.

"How did you find ragtime?"

"Ragtime found me and I can't shake it loose," Max said with contagious delight. "Rag's rhythm can seduce you if you're not careful, like some of the ladies around here."

"It was good talking with you, Max," said Brock as he began to move back toward his table.

Despite the clanking of glasses and the testosterone overload created by too many drunken men in too small a space, Brock's behavior remained subdued.

Rather than bragging about female conquests or predicting his between-the-sheets performance on his wedding night, Brock was contemplative. His mind escaped the confining saloon and traveled back to his kite-flying afternoon with Blossom. Lately he was finding it harder and harder to clear his mind to focus on anyone other than Blossom.

Memories of Mrs. Flood barged in. He could hear her parting words to him: "Mr. St. Clair, your public display of affection truly warms my heart, but your lack of discretion may ultimately break yours."

Brock knew that he was no longer playing with fire. He was dancing in an inferno that was sure to burn a lot of people before it subsided. The thing that surprised Brock at the moment was that he really didn't care. Not that he wanted to hurt anyone, but he was focusing on making himself and Blossom happy.

He was jarred back to the realities of the party with a bear hug and a manly slap on the back. "I hear that your personal stud service is booked for Saturday night, buddy. For a city boy who spends as much time as you do in the country with those animals of yours, I bet Clarissa is in for the ride of her life!" loudly announced an inebriated and foul-mouthed partygoer. "She's a real lady, so you better break her in easy, if you know what I mean!" Drunken, sloppy laughter and elbowing with winking eyes took over the room.

Brock summoned a smile to appear to be playing along with these boys. This bachelor party could not end soon enough to suit him, and yet it had only begun. He hadn't even finished that thought when the girls who Austin hired for the night poured into the room like beer out of a keg. Not one, not two, but five shimmering, sparkling beauties surrounded Brock on cue. Their hands rubbed all over his body. He was uncomfortable before. Now he was being made the center of a sexual spectacle.

A Chinese girl with smoky almond-shaped eyes and a suggestively sassy grin appeared in charge. She signaled to Max to crank up the volume of his music. Brock took a deep breath and grinned with everything he could muster in his body.

"Hey all you stags, it's time to add some va-va-voom to this party. I'd like to introduce you to a very good friend of mine and some very good friends of hers. Yep, these are some friendly ladies from around the globe led by none other than Mademoiselle Monique LaFontaine. Here they are: Monique's Mistresses of Pleasure. The only rule tonight is: there are no rules!!!" yelled Austin with all the pride and bravado of a circus barker.

"I don't know about you, but I'm tired of it always being 'this or that.' I say that's horse shit! My bosom buddies, now it's a time for 'and.' You don't have to pick either one or the other tonight. I'm the host, and this is an 'and' place where you can have it all. So, have some fun. Hell, have anything you want!"

Monique secured some of the most noteworthy—or perhaps notorious—prostitutes in the region, each of a different flavor: Mexican, Creole, French and good-old American. It was a female buffet, an international rainbow of carnal delights. The men in the room responded enthusiastically with catcall cheers and the tongue-wagging exuberance of backwoods miners striking the Mother Lode. And it was just that, striking the whoring equivalent of the gold miners' Mother Lode.

As several of the girls ran their fingers through Brock's hair, they flaunted their heaving bosoms and their round, full bottoms in every possible direction around Brock.

"Damn, your dumplings are boiling out of their pots," Austin exclaimed. He quickly followed that remark by slapping the girl's backside while saying, "Your bottoms are tops!" The crowded room filled with cheers of delight.

Austin looked to Brock for his reaction and approval. He knew this entire evening was going to be profoundly painful and awkward, considering Brock's inexperience with women and the darker side of being a wealthy man in a boomtown where hearing "no" was not an option in just about any situation.

"Brock, my brother," said Austin as he put his right arm around Brock's shoulder and forcibly pulled him over to Monique. "I'd like you to meet my lightning in a bottle!"

In his intoxicated state, Austin then pulled Monique in close with a single grab and jerk. Monique did not appear to be offended by the roughness.

"Monique," Austin said. Then he robustly released a loud, foul-smelling belch and an equally explosive laugh. "Oh, pardon me, Monique. I'd like you to meet the guest of honor, my brother, Brock."

Monique responded, "You rascal! You didn't tell me the party was for your brother." Austin rolled his eyes down as a signal to Brock to emphasize that they were in the company of women who sported an excess of bosom covered by an insufficiency of fabric.

"Nice to meet you," Brock said in a loud voice to compensate for the noise level in the room. He tried not to focus on her nearly exposed breasts, but it was impossible.

"Pleasure's all mine," responded Monique as she sized up Brock, scanning his body from top to bottom. "It's like I already know you somehow," she said with an arched eyebrow.

Austin belched again and interrupted with, "I don't see how that could be possible since Brock doesn't whore around like he should, and you don't spend much time in a horse barn or on Nob Hill with the Stanfords, Huntingtons or St. Clairs."

"Just the same," said Monique, "I have this feeling."

"Well, feel *this*, Baby," Austin said as he grabbed Monique's hand and placed it on his crotch.

"You've always had a handful. You'll always *be* a handful. So get over yourself already, my devilishly handsome Big Boy. There's nothing down there that we haven't explored together, now is there?"

Austin proudly smiled, made clear eye contact with Monique's breasts and generated a growling tiger sound. "I just love those melons of hers. Want to feel them?" he directed to Brock.

"And to think, even after that, I'm not immune to your charms! Now simmer down, Austin. This night is about your brother and his wedding this weekend. I'm sure you'll make your fiancée's dreams come true," said Monique as she ran her right index finger across Brock's chest and tapped on his heart.

"She must be a mighty fine catch to tie down a big hunk of man like you."

Brock smiled politely.

"She's not one of those high-and-mighty rich bitches is she? Oh, that came out a little harsher than it should have," Monique apologized, recoiling a bit, since she was well aware of his dalliances with Blossom while he was preparing to marry a high-bred show pony of a woman. In Monique's world, situations can get dicey fast, but she had to admit to herself that tonight took the prize for awkwardness and clandestine meetings.

"Better watch yourself around Monique. You may have a girl named Clarissa in your life to arrange flowers for you. But, if you're lucky, Monique will—in a heartbeat—rearrange your *bouquet*, if you know what I mean," blurted out Austin as he swiftly reached down to grab the front of his brother's pants. Brock's quick reflexes enabled him to intercept Austin's reach. He grasped Austin's wrist and twisted it firmly until it was behind his back.

Monique snickered.

"Come on and laugh a little. What happened to you?" Austin asked with a tinge of pain in his voice.

Brock replied, "I grew up!"

"Well then, grow back down, would ya!"

Brock released his grip on his brother.

Austin scanned the room to see that his guests were having a good time. Brock was sure that he was witnessing his evening curdle into a toxic mess.

"I'll leave you two to get to know each other better while I get to know some of Monique's exotic companions," said Austin as he turned and stumbled across the room to approach a statuesque black beauty from the South.

A brisk pull on his elbow forced Austin to swing around to face a new partygoer: Faye Huntington. She'd come to a party that she was neither invited to nor welcome at.

"Well don't you put the *hell* in hello!" she said too loudly for their proximity.

Equally loud, he added, "Well, don't you put the *good* in goodbye!" He tried to back away. "Now get your damned claws off me," he said in response to being woman-handled and at having the bride's best friend at a bachelor party. "Get yourself out of here, now! Shoo! Scat!"

Austin stared into Faye's eyes. "There's something about you that always pisses me off whenever you're around me. You're like an un-locatable itch that makes my skin crawl!"

"Oh no, my pet. This may not be the most respectable thing I've ever done, but that's never stopped me in the past, now has it?" Faye offered a paper cut of a smile. "I have every right to enjoy some refreshment at this *dump* if I wish to. In fact, I just knocked back—as you boys would say—a shot of Devil's Spit and it burned like hell fire all the way down."

She cleared her throat and went on, "I'm just keeping an eye on your dear brother so I can report anything unseemly to Clarissa who, by the way, doesn't know that I'm here. My driver is right outside waiting to whisk me away to Clarissa whenever I wish."

"You sure know how to spoil a party, don't you?"

"Austin, my alley cat, you have *no* idea!" said Faye, almost purring.

She added, as if stating a fact, "You and I are alike, you know."

"I have to disagree with that pile of horse shit you just shoveled at me. But, if I was a conniving, manipulative, frigid shell of a woman, then I'd agree," retorted Austin with a sense of pride in his word choices given his inebriated state.

Faye seethed. She pulled him in close and replied, "Nicely played. On second thought, we're not that much alike at all." A verbal swordfight had begun. "If I was a puny, lost boy who lived with both hands in his mother's wallet, then we'd be alike. So, you're correct."

She paused. "I have a feeling—a strong feeling—that I'll be battling with you until hell freezes over. And then I'll fight you on the ice," predicted Faye. She turned with a flourish and headed for the saloon's front door, displaying her finest high-and-mighty strut.

Austin grabbed her by the elbow and swung her around. "I'm going to try something." He planted a boozy kiss on her lips and forced his tongue into Faye's mouth so that it could dance with Faye's. He abruptly stopped and she slapped him across the face with every ounce of strength she possessed.

"Hey, hold on there, young lady! They say opposites attract. But I just proved they're wrong. No attraction. Just opposites. What a relief!"

Austin went on and announced loudly to Prickly Pete at the bar, "Pour me something stronger than that red head who's about to exit your fine establishment!"

At the same time, Monique took Brock by the hand and led him to a table and chairs where they could talk without needing to yell. As they crossed the room, they parted the thick, smoky air and made it swirl like heavy cream stirred in a cup of coffee.

"Discretion is absolute in my profession," said Monique. "But what I'm about to say has nothing to do with my profession and everything to do with friendship."

Chapter 27
Tonight Is The Night

Monday, April 16, 1906, 8:49 p.m.
Two days before the earthquake and firestorm

The Golden Palace was empty except for one uneasy customer: Butch. Blossom studied him, though she didn't want anyone to notice. He was alone at his usual table, which had been cleared long ago. He fumbled with his napkin. He looked uncomfortable, like he had a stomachache or was surrounded by a bad smell.

For someone whose family did much to feed Chinatown's bad reputation for dives and dance halls, opium dens and hideouts, Butch didn't fit the profile of a tong member. Blossom and her friends called the gangs that controlled well-defined sections of Chinatown the "Six Companies." They regularly and publicly fought to gain ground from a neighboring gang. Butch displayed none of the usual bravado and posturing of his family members. His attention was on his butcher shop and marrying Blossom. Butch's business was successful. His love life was not.

Chang stood in the doorway. Grand Ma Maw observed from her stool as Blossom tidied up the tables so they'd be ready for tomorrow's business. Butch fixated on Blossom. She didn't fixate on Butch.

"Ming Yang!" Grand Ma Maw said loudly, with an edge sharp enough to chop through the raw carrots in her kitchen. "You sit there like a too-old head of cabbage." She came closer. "Your name means wind! Push some wind through those lungs of yours and say something! Have you something to ask? You need something more this fine evening?"

Blossom thought that he looked even more uncomfortable now.

"Yes, Grand Ma Maw. I mean, no, Grand Ma Maw," Butch muttered.

"Honestly, I believe you have more—"

"Tonight's the night then," answered Butch as he turned to Chang. "Yes, tonight. With utmost respect, I ask for your daughter's hand in marriage. Do I need to hire a matchmaker to make this match?"

Before Chang could answer, Blossom abruptly joined the conversation.

"Pardon me, but I'm right here in this room! Would someone like to ask *me* what I think or what I'd like?"

Blossom knew it was proper for Butch to ask her father, though Butch might have chosen a time to ask his question when Blossom wasn't present. *It sounded so formal, so rehearsed*, Blossom thought.

The telephone in the reception area rang. Again. Again. No one moved to answer it.

"At long last, my friend, you speak up. However, you not only man in town to admire my Blossom. Her beauty and grace, they prized possessions. Much time pass and I begin to believe our only relationship destined to be between restaurant owner and young butcher who bring meat for our meals," said Chang. "My answer: yes, yes, yes. No need for matchmaker." *It's just like him to say "yes" three times, as if a single "yes" wasn't intolerable enough.*

Butch briskly rose from his chair, shook Chang's hand and nodded his head. As he dashed toward the door he added, "I'll be back with a gift to honor you and your decision."

The crimson banner got stuck in the door as he left. Grand Ma Maw walked over to release it and read its message aloud with a few changes to mark the occasion. While looking through the door's window to watch

Butch hurry away, she said, "May good fortune follow you *and Blossom* on your path through life—*together.*"

She turned and added, "And so it begins." With her arms folded in front of her, Grand Ma Maw had a visible sense of satisfaction.

"The beginning. The *beginning?* The BEGINNING!" said Blossom in three distinctly different ways. "He practically ran out the door. That looked more like an ending than a beginning to me!"

"My child, you wrong," replied Grand Ma Maw with a knowing look. Blossom read the signals loud and clear. Blossom's throat got tight. Since she was a little girl, Blossom was taught to respect and honor her elders and their thoughts while silencing her own. Other children could swallow it back, but Blossom usually surrendered to the overwhelming urges to speak her mind. This discussion was one of those boiling-over times. She knew it was a time to disagree and offer another point of view. However, she chose to bring the boiling down to a simmer. She restrained herself from commenting further, knowing that her words could trap her.

"We shall see what begins now," said Chang without his triple-repeat pattern. Blossom didn't know if that too was a signal.

Chapter 28
*I*n Over Her Head

Monday, April 16, 1906, 8:57 p.m.
Two days before the earthquake and firestorm

Monique leaned in toward Brock, closing the gap between them and reducing the chance of someone overhearing what she was about to say. Loud enough to be heard over the gyrating group of revelers around them, yet soft enough to be discreet, Monique started.

"I'm a let's-get-to-the-point kind of girl. Are you fine with that?"

"Sure," Brock replied with a slight turn of his head.

"Blossom's completely in love with you. It's her first time, and you'll destroy everything that's good in her if you get married on Saturday."

Brock was stunned into silence. That was definitely "to-the-point," as she had warned, but it was not what he expected to hear at his bachelor party from a woman of Monique's profession and talents.

"Yes, I know all about you and Blossom. She's one of my best friends. Despite, shall we say, our occupational interests and differences, we've been good friends since we were schoolgirls. As you heard, I didn't know this party was for you when Austin asked me to supply the entertainment. But now that I'm here—"

"Blossom told you about us?"

"She sure did. I guess she thought our paths would never cross. Boy, was she wrong!"

Brock slipped into deep thought—not panic, just deep thought. Monique gave him a few moments to consider his next move.

"Austin has kept me a busy girl at the Maison Bijou for some time now. I don't think he's ever talked about you. When we're together, it's all about him."

"Now that doesn't surprise me one bit. That's my *little* brother."

Monique leaned in closer. "Blossom came to me with a lot of questions about men. She figured I was an expert. Well, I don't claim to be an expert, but I have picked up a thing or two about what motivates and satisfies a man. I admitted to her that what I've learned is not about love, though, just lust and laughs." She looked around the room.

"Blossom is special. She's special in a lot of ways. And you're the first guy that's captured her attention, and clearly something more than that," she said as she pointed at her heart.

"Honestly, we shouldn't have dared her. She's in way over her head. When news about you two gets out—and it will in a small place like Chinatown—it will destroy her reputation. What's so amazing is that she knows it, and she doesn't seem to care. You mean that much to her."

"What do you mean *dared?* Is this some kind of game?" Brock was growing visibly uncomfortable.

"Hold your horses, cowboy. It was all innocent girl games. It may have started as a dare to flirt with a customer, but it's gone far beyond that for Blossom. And, to top it off, you're getting married in a few days and it's not to Blossom!"

Brock took in what Monique shared and was no longer on edge. "Thank you for caring so much about Blossom that you talked to me tonight. You could have sat back, kept this to yourself and then reported what happened to her. With Austin in charge, I knew this party was going to be awkward, but this, well, this is—"

"I don't expect you to open up and share your plans with me. But what the hell are you going to do? Say, you're not one of *those* guys who, after they get what they want, they don't want it anymore, are you?"

"No, I'm not one of *those* guys. I honestly don't know what I'm going to do. Is it possible to be in love with two women at the same time?"

"Hey, wait a second, did I hear you right? Like I told Blossom, I live and work in a world of fantasy, pleasure and a wagonload of lies, not *love*. You'll need to talk to an old happily married couple to learn about love. Say, I'm pretty sure that I heard you just say you *love* Blossom."

"Yes, that's what I said and how I feel. I do love her. She's so different from my fiancée."

"Are you going to flip a coin?"

"What?" asked Brock.

"You have to pick one. Saturday is going to be either the happiest or the saddest day in Blossom's life. It's your call."

"So, do you have a coin?" Brock asked in a somewhat defeated way.

"In this outfit? Are you joking? There isn't even room for me in here! I couldn't fit a butterfly's wing inside this corset. There's barely enough give to it for me to breathe!"

"I get it."

Monique looked directly into Brock's eyes. "Without thinking too much, can you answer a question?"

"Of course I can."

"Does Blossom make you happy?"

"Yes, but—"

"Could she make you happy for the rest of your life?"

"Yes, but—"

"Then Blossom's your girl. You just said it in very few words," concluded Monique.

Austin broke into the conversation by painfully wedging himself between Brock and Monique. Brock took a deep breath. *God, he can be like a wood sliver under my fingernail!*

"If I didn't know any better, I'd be worried about you horning in on my action, big brother. But, in all honesty, as inexperienced as you are, Monique would be way too much woman for you to take on."

Brock blushed, and Monique playfully slapped Austin on the cheek.

Brock noticed how Monique looked at Austin…not as hired help, but as someone who has feelings for Austin. *Or, she's a good actress.*

"So who's going to lead whom on your wedding night, Brock? You two will be fumbling around like two virgins playing the I'll-show-you-mine-if-you-show-me-yours game." He amused himself to the point of having to hold his stomach as he guffawed.

"Maybe Uncle Alec needs to take you back to The Kensington Club for a few more lessons, if you know what I mean!" teased Austin.

Monique turned her head slightly and looked knowingly at Brock as she was all too aware of the exclusive clientele that The Kensington Club's prostitutes entertained.

"That was really classy of you to say, Austin. I should threaten to reveal something embarrassing about you to Monique, but I'm sure you've already done plenty to embarrass yourself and her in the past 24 hours!"

"Oh, you have no idea!" Austin responded.

"He's right. You have *no* idea," added Monique.

Sadly, thought Brock, Austin was right about what was really a triangle of inexperience with Clarissa and Blossom. But he knew somehow that anyone's questionable lack of expertise would not be an obstacle on his wedding night.

The real obstacle: choosing which girl to be the bride.

Chapter 29
*I*nto The Fire

Monday, April 16, 1906, 9:16 p.m.
Two days before the earthquake and firestorm

In the St. Clair family, it was a rite of passage that when a boy turned fourteen, an elder male family member took him to a bordello to introduce him to the pleasures of women.

Austin's earlier remark about Uncle Alec brought back a mixed bag of memories for Brock. Once Monique moved on to other bachelor-party guests, Brock's thoughts traveled back to the night of his fourteenth birthday, and to what he did and didn't learn.

While visiting a bordello for the first time was a family tradition, it wasn't something that was celebrated openly or discussed in mixed company.

For weeks leading up to Brock's birthday, his mind was filled with wild and racing thoughts of what his first encounter with a woman would be like. Adding to Brock's expectations and uneasiness, an eleven-year-old Austin immaturely and inappropriately brought up the subject at the dinner table. Brock found that he was unable to look his mother in the face when the topic was raised. Austin couldn't wait for his turn and was none too shy to say so to the men of the St. Clair family.

The morning of his fourteenth birthday, Brock was confronted by his mother, who would only acknowledge what was going to happen that night with one remark and without eye contact: "Brock, what a man and a woman share in love is *not* what will be shared with you tonight." That was it.

While he was too young to fully grasp the wisdom of what she said, he was old enough to appreciate the courage it took for her to say it. It would be a number of years before he'd experience what she described: true love rather than consuming lust.

But lust was what that night was designed to be all about. For Brock, the lessons in navigating the landscape of a woman's body would be taught by Chloe at The Kensington Club, one of San Francisco's finest bordellos. Brock had been told time and again that no heir of a Nob Hill millionaire was going to lose his virginity at "a two-bit flophouse." There would be time for that later in life, as was discussed by the family's men when they were among themselves. But the first encounter was to be special. For Brock, in many ways it was.

Brock was handed off like a father hands off a bride at a wedding altar. He looked back at Uncle Alec—fondly referred to as Uncle Smart Aleck—to see the pride in his face. He did his best to block thoughts of what Uncle Alec's fourteenth birthday night must have been like. After all, this was the man who taught Brock and Austin at much-too-early ages how to play poker, smoke cigars and drink a shot of whiskey like a real man, slamming the empty glass down on the counter. The crusty brother of their deceased father, Uncle Alec—even with only a horseshoe of hair left—could have easily been mistaken as Austin's imaginary father with his wise-cracking wit, girl-chasing escapades and self-centered approach to life.

Living up to his "Smart Aleck" nickname, Uncle Alec not-so-gently stuffed a roll of paper money into the bodice of Chloe's black-lace outfit with an all-knowing wink. Her corset was so tightly cinched that her body took an unnaturally curvaceous hour-glass shape. Then, for all to hear as Brock was being escorted away to lose his virginity, Uncle Alec yelled, "Bring him back to me as a man with one of those lacy garters for a souvenir. And he better be exhausted and spent."

For the love of God, could he please be quiet, thought young Brock.

Chloe replied, "He'll be well spent, just like the money you just gave me. It's my pleasure to be of service." She nodded and, in an exaggerated gesture, swiped back her wavy cascade of blonde hair as if to indicate she meant business.

To make matters even worse, as Chloe led Brock out of the bordello's parlor he noticed a hand-embroidered sign above the hallway opening that read, "Into the fire." *Oh fine,* thought Brock. *Fire is the last thing I need to think about now.* It almost made the burn scars on his ankles heat up just to think about fire.

"You're in good hands. I'm going to teach you wrong from right."

"You mean right from wrong?" Brock hesitantly asked.

"No, there's nothing right about what we're going to do. So, relax," purred Chloe as they entered a door with the number six on it. Brock noticed that the room was filled with peacock feathers in bouquets in vases, on fans…even laid loosely on the counter of her vanity. He scanned the walls that were draped with swags of purple, green and turquoise cloth. The space glowed softly with flickering candlelight emanating from scattered candles that were short and tall, thick and thin.

She struck a match and lit five candles that stood erect in an ornate silver candelabra. There was a red candle in the center and four white ones, each poised atop one for the arms that extended from the base, which was a sculpted naked woman.

"This one's for you," she said as she removed the red candle. His mind raced with possibilities, some not entirely erotic. She placed the candelabra on the nightstand.

"It's my experience that men make love with their eyes, or at least that's what stokes the flames inside them," said Chloe knowingly.

Questions flew through Brock's mind. *All this talk about flames and fire? A room full of flickering candles? And I'm going to make love with my eyes?*

She continued, "I'm going to teach you that it's more about the touch than the look."

Brock peered at her curiously and with obvious apprehension.

"Now, you take your shirt off and lay back on my soft bed. Or would you like me to help you with that?" she asked as she approached him with the burning and now dripping red candle in her hand.

"No, I can do it," Brock quickly replied as he shed his shirt to avoid the need for her to get any closer with the flame.

"Close...those...dazzling...blue...eyes," she directed. Her every syllable flirted. He did as he was told. She soothingly ran her fingertips from his forehead, over his eyes and down his cheeks.

"That's right. Now take a deep breath and release it slowly." As he did, he felt a sharp pain in the center of his hairless chest, which startled him. He began to sit up and open his eyes.

"Shhhh. Close your eyes and lay back down, lover boy." Again, he did as he was told.

Within a few seconds he felt a concentrated hot spot, just above his navel.

"Feel the sting and then the warmth that follows," she said with restrained excitement.

Brock did his best to block out the vision of the flame that he had in his mind. In no time, he sensed a thrill each time a drop of liquefied candle wax stung and then caressed his skin. The frequency of the sensations slowed until they stopped. Brock kept his eyes closed and couldn't imagine what might come next.

Then his boots slid off of his feet and Chloe firmly tugged at his trousers.

"Take a deep breath because I'm going to take you places you've never dreamed of," she said as she continued to do what she did best.

Brock never told anyone about what he experienced that night, even when pressed as more fourteen-year-old boys in the St. Clair family were poised to unlock the mysteries of women.

He would forever remember his adventure "into the fire," as the embroidered sign at The Kensington Club foretold and, indeed, delivered. And he would never look at a candle in quite the same way again.

Chapter 30

Stirring The Pot

Monday, April 16, 1906, 9:32 p.m.
Two days before the earthquake and firestorm

"Are you ever going to have your bedroom redecorated? It looks like an eight-year-old lives here!" exclaimed Faye.

"With the wedding coming up, I just don't see the point. Brock and I will be in *our* new home before we know it," replied Clarissa dismissively.

Clarissa scanned her room. She looked at how the hooded chimney piece was flanked by quaint little galleries and shelves of treasures and ever-changing transient objects. Bows and sashes adorned just about anything that could accommodate them. Plumes, pictures, dried flowers and countless little mementoes spoke loudly about Clarissa's life and choices.

"Why don't you just stay the night?"

"Clarissa, my dear, I think I'll do just that. Even though I just got here a little while ago, it seems like we've chatted the evening away while your fiancé has been tomcatting around as part of the bachelor party his darling brother put together."

Faye looked directly at Clarissa and reached out to hold her hand. "The least I can do is stay and distract you from fretting about the depraved things he's doing at this very moment and might try out on you Saturday night."

Faye turned and faced the vanity. She grasped a pair of Clarissa's long evening gloves. "Oh, it just makes my head spin to think about the riff-raff and debauchery he'll be subjected to tonight. Skimpily clad trollops traipsing *to and fro*." To emphasize to and fro, Faye added a flip-flap of the pair of gloves in her hand.

"By the way, how many pairs of gloves do you have?" she asked as she noted the numerous colorful glove boxes lined up on several of Clarissa's shelves.

"You are so easily distracted tonight!" replied Clarissa. "I don't know how many I have…a dozen or two. How many do you have? There are short gloves for the daytime, long gloves for the evening and heavier gloves for the country—not that I ever go there. So, we must have quite a supply, right?"

"Back to what I was saying about bachelor parties—"

"Your imagination is running wild," interrupted Clarissa. "What could you possibly know about bachelor parties?"

"My brother has gone to plenty. From what he was willing to share with me and what I forced out of him, an innocent girl like you best not know too much before your time. Trust me."

"Well, men should have their private time, just as we women should. Whatever wild oats Brock is sowing tonight, well…I just hope he gets them all out of his system. Starting Saturday, the rules change, right?"

"Usually," agreed Faye, "but not always. Do you think that all of the skirt chasing that goes on in San Francisco is being done only by our city's strapping young *single* men?"

Clarissa looked unsure about how to answer. She wasn't so naïve as to think that all married men were monogamous, but she didn't want to give Faye too much pleasure in one-upping her in a I'm-more-worldly-than-you contest.

"Oh, pish-posh! I can't speak for other girls' men, but my Brock is a one-woman man. I'm not the slightest bit concerned that he could be unfaithful. It's not in his nature."

"Nature?" asked Faye. "That's the whole point. Don't have the audacity to disagree that men are by nature always on a hunt to woo and possess women. Yes, Brock is truly a gentleman, but even gentlemen stumble and fall sometimes."

Faye consciously prepared herself to speak in a coy voice to ask, "Clarissa, what did Brock tell you about going to Chinatown? Did he discover anything exotic there?"

Clarissa rolled her eyes up to the ceiling as if to pull down Brock's remarks from inside her brain. "Ummmm, he said it smelled different." *You can say that again dearie*, thought Faye.

"He said the people were friendly and showed him to a bakery to get the cookies for my party. He told me the difference between moon cakes and fortune cookies, and something about the yolks of duck eggs. Why do you want to know?"

"Has he gone back there?" she managed to squeeze out of her unnaturally smiling mouth. Faye ran her fingers delicately along the beaded fringe of a nearby lamp shade. *This is going to be good.*

"If he did, he hasn't told me. If he hasn't, I wouldn't know that either. I'm going to ask you again, why do you want to know about Brock and Chinatown?"

"Oh nothing, just making conversation," said Faye. *I've stepped into something here and it's not a bed of roses! Clarissa may learn from me to never trust a pretty girl with an ugly secret.*

Clarissa signaled that she'd had enough of this inquisition by not-so-gently removing a fresh nightgown from her chest of drawers and presenting it to Faye.

"Pink! Oh, you know how I adore pink," said Faye upon seeing the pale-pink cotton sleeping gown. "But do you have anything in green?"

"Yes," replied Clarissa, who had already pulled out a lime-green gown, knowing full well that Faye only wore green.

"I thought you'd lost your mind there for a moment. I had to be as polite as possible when you began to hand me that ghastly pink nightgown," admitted Faye.

"Mother was telling me today about how New York's high-society women are wearing a lot of pink these days."

"Well, the Astors and Vanderbilts can have all the pink they want. They can have all of New York City, along with the entire East Coast for all I care!" exclaimed Faye, demonstrating her haughty Huntington West Coast attitude of affluence and arrogance.

"Just put this on," Clarissa remarked as she turned and left the room to allow Faye some privacy to undress.

"Heavens, we're closer than most sisters. You don't need to leave the room. I don't believe God equipped me with anything he didn't give you."

Clarissa turned as she walked through the doorway. "That may be true, but just the same, I'll check on Mother and be back with some warm milk for us in a few minutes."

"Milk! Are we drooling babies or grown women?"

Clarissa just kept walking down the hallway shaking her head, softly mumbling an answer: "Both."

Chapter 31
$\mathscr{A}$ Veiled Discussion

Monday, April 16, 1906, 9:54 p.m.
Two days before the earthquake and firestorm

Clarissa re-entered her bedroom with two glasses of warmed milk on a tray, along with half a lemon and a saucer. She nearly dropped the tray at the sight of Faye twirling around in front of the vanity mirror wearing Clarissa's bridal tiara and veil.

"Pardon me!" Clarissa announced with great force as she entered the room.

"Don't get all superstitious about this," replied Faye as she sat down in the fancifully frilly chair that matched the vanity. In a move to avoid eye contact with Clarissa, Faye picked up an ornate silver jewelry casket from the vanity's surface and began to fidget with it.

"You had no right to open that box, much less put my tiara on!" Clarissa snapped back as she set down the tray.

"I know, but it just called out to me and pleaded, 'Put me on...put me on...and pretend for a moment that *your* wedding day is coming.' But, you're right," admitted Faye.

"It's against tradition! It's against the rules," pointed out Clarissa.

Red-handed, caught red-handed! An awkward pause of silence provided

Faye with the opportunity to plot her next checker-board move.

"As you well know, as a rule I avoid rules! Anyway, I had no business dreaming for even a moment that I'd have this diamond-encrusted, silver tiara given to me by a man as wonderful as Brock." Faye stopped there and made a pouty face at Clarissa in hopes of worming her way out of an awkward position. She removed the tiara and veil.

Doesn't she know that there's only one person who matters in this world, and that's me, thought Faye. It's always been about me, and it will always be about me, except Clarissa's wedding, I guess.

"With this tiara, he'll make you his princess and you'll never have another thing to worry about. Your dreams will have all come true," said Faye in a syrupy sing-song way.

"Well, I hope I have a few dreams after we're married."

"I wouldn't. Marriage is going to solve all of my problems. I won't be a second-rate Huntington anymore. I'll leap to the top of the heap. Status, obscene luxury...everything will be mine and I will be ecstatically happy and content."

"You? Content?" asked Clarissa.

"I don't want to *ever* lift a finger."

"But you don't now!"

"Precisely, and I'm going to make sure that I never have to. The right man will take care of all that. There may not be a white horse or shining armor. He may not be a real prince. But there will be legions of servants and massive houses and anything and everything I could ever want."

"Fine. Just give it here," said Clarissa with an unmistakable sense of urgency as she eyed the tiara.

"Afraid I might muss the lace, are you?"

"No. I want to put it on you correctly and take a good look at how you'll appear to your husband-to-be when you walk down the aisle someday soon."

They smiled at each other. *She's so sweet she makes my teeth hurt.*

"After the wedding, these two stones will become tear-drop earrings. The rest will be used for a brooch and necklace, all using the silver from the tiara," explained Clarissa.

"You're going to have it melted down? I understand putting this bundle of diamonds to good use, but not destroying the tiara."

"With all of the silver I'm marrying into, the little clump this melted-down tiara is going to become won't make any difference at all," replied Clarissa with a shrug of her shoulders. "Besides, changing things is good."

"That's all fine and well, just so you don't think you're going to change Brock," Faye said. "It's the greatest fantasy for women, you know!"

"Know what?"

"Clarissa, since the beginning of time, women have thought they could change the men in their lives. It doesn't work and it won't work. What you marry is what you get. So you better get used to that ranch of Brock's. I think he was born with dirt and hay in his veins! Keeping him on Nob Hill, well, it's just not going to happen."

Clarissa gazed off in the distance.

Faye added, "Face it. You're Nob Hill. You're lace. He's leather. You're slender tapered candles. He's a scrap-wood campfire. Something's going to have to give. And someone's going to have to give in. Are you ready for that?"

"Sure," said Clarissa with a slow nod.

"It could very well be you who ends up giving in. How are you at milking a cow?

Clarissa patted Faye's back. "Don't worry. I'm sure the milk in my kitchen on Nob Hill will be delivered to my back door and received by my cook…with no hide nor hair of a cow in sight."

Clarissa adjusted the veil after she placed it on Faye's red hair. "Take a look. You're going to make a stunning bride."

Faye did her best to beam with excitement for Clarissa's sake. "Let's toast to our future happiness."

"With milk?" asked Clarissa.

"Yes, milk."

Their glasses clinked.

"Now on to the lemon. I've been applying it to my face as a tonic for weeks to have the smoothest, whitest skin on all of Nob Hill for my wedding day."

"Yes, none of that tanned working-class skin for the future Mrs. St. Clair!" added Faye.

"Before we know it, I'll be a married woman. That tiara will be at the jeweler's shop while Brock and I tour Europe on our honeymoon. My dream is coming true."

You better hope Brock doesn't have the jeweler melt down your heart too, along with that precious dream of yours.

Chapter 32
*R*evelations

Monday, April 16, 1906, 10:17 p.m.
Two days before the earthquake and firestorm

Blossom peered out her bedroom window into the alley with worried eyes. She hugged her knees while sitting on a wood crate draped with a golden silk cloth. Everything was dampened by the wet evening air. Despite her increasingly frail body, Grand Ma Maw insisted that she and Blossom still share the third-floor bedroom. She told everyone it was to breathe the fresh air that travelled above the streets of Chinatown. But most people knew it was a prime position for observing activity in the alley…activity that could be discussed in great detail in the market, over the sale of a smelly fish or gnarled root, or across the mahjong table.

Grand Ma Maw was breathing loudly. It was only a matter of minutes before the snoring began. Every night it was the same routine.

Blossom's thoughts were interrupted as she looked down on the people passing in the alley below, some strolling hand in hand, others scurrying as if they were late for an important appointment. She zeroed in on a young couple, looking more at each other than where they were walking. The girl tripped over a block of wood that had been left in the main pathway. She teetered, but the man supported her arm and kept her from falling. *That's just how Brock caught me*, she recalled. *Brock, where are you and what are you doing…right now?*

Her face felt flushed, so she reached for her collapsible handheld fan. She quietly opened it up. Blossom gazed at the black fabric with the simply painted cherry blossoms on it. She looked back out the window and rhythmically fanned her face.

"You more restless than usual. You not think I notice these things?" asked Grand Ma Maw from her bed.

Blossom continued to look out the window and fan herself as she replied. "I know there isn't a *thing* that you miss here or anywhere in Chinatown."

Grand Ma Maw inhaled deeply. "Blossom, I notice you change…like little girl in you now gone away."

"I believe she has. She may be gone, but I'm right here. But I'm changing…and I can't help it," responded Blossom as she cast her eyes down and rested the fan on one of her knees. "But that's not necessarily bad."

"You meeting that rich white man, yes? I find pot of make-up in your handbag when looking for your comb. You wear make-up for him, yes?"

"Yes, just once."

Though shocked by the directness of the elder woman's words, Blossom was almost relieved to be confronted by her grandmother.

"You think you love him, yes?"

"I *didn't* know, but I do now. Yes, I love him. And he has a name: Brock."

The room went silent.

"But you engaged to Ming Yang."

"You and Ba Ba engaged me to Butch. I had nothing to do with that." Blossom's restrained energy was released like someone had just broken the seal on a jar of jam and the pent-up pressure escaped. *I said it out loud. I love him.*

"Then now is time to say things that remained unsaid for far too many years." Grand Ma Maw spoke in a gentle but concerned voice as she sat up in her bed. "You now going where I and your father been before."

Blossom looked puzzled.

"Our time here, it like a flickering candle with a short life to live. You, my granddaughter, must make most of what in front of you. What behind you, in past, you must now learn. These things you deserve to know before you give your love to this Brock man. Come, sit with me."

The old woman went on to tell her love story and about how marriages in China were almost always prearranged by families, though romantic love was encouraged and allowed. She recalled how a band of musicians banging gongs and blowing flutes accompanied the bride's procession to the groom's house.

"You look at me and see old woman. My body get tired, but young girl inside just like you. Many seasons ago, I young inside *and* outside on my on my wedding day. I make a big racket even then! And I not even have to say a word!" said Grand Ma Maw with a large grin. Blossom grinned back, but wondered why she was telling this story that she'd heard many times before.

Grand Ma Maw continued the familiar story that included a tea ceremony served by the younger family members and gifts brought by older couples as tokens of their best wishes.

"I not Grand Ma Maw then. My parents name me Lei after cherry blossom buds. I meet your Grand Ba Ba only four times before we marry," she said holding up four fingers. "I scared. But love bloom for us."

Her words stopped flowing.

Blossom nestled beside her just as she had when she was a child. The old woman reached out her weathered, withered hands to cup Blossom's chin.

"I know you always felt different. That because you different. You special. A treasure—"

She stopped again for a moment.

"Your mother not one of our people. Iris Lancaster, that her name. Cameo Rose, that her working name."

Blossom broke in. "Are you telling me that my mother is not Chinese and that she's alive? You decided that *this* is the right time to tell me?"

Blossom quickly considered what she'd been told and then asked, "She has a working name? What does she do for work? Does she need a stage name because she's a beer hall singer?"

Grand Ma Maw slid her hand across Blossom's lips.

"Perhaps it best to be silent, my child. Let me tell you our story... your story."

Blossom slowly nodded in agreement.

"Love be wonderful. Love be messy. Love even be wonderfully messy. You the result of wonderfully messy love," observed the old woman.

"Your Grand Ba Ba and I raise your father the very best we could. You know all about how we come here to *Gum Saan*, the gold mountain. We make food to feed prospectors. Miners just put things over fire and take what happens. My cooking, they like! We wash dirty clothes of other people for extra money. That where your father met your mother. I always call her by her real name, Iris, because her eyes not like any eyes I ever seen...until I see your lavender eyes. Men along river nickname her Cameo Rose because she always wore cameo brooch." She paused. "Go to my dresser."

Blossom obeyed her grandmother.

"Open top drawer."

Blossom did.

"Now, pull it out of dresser. Take light and shine it inside."

She did.

There, resting against the back wall of the dresser was a worn cameo brooch.

"It yours now. She give it to me to give to you when I think it right time. Now is time."

Blossom sat down next to Grand Ma Maw. She studied the oval-shaped brooch, with its white and caramel-brown carved set of three blooming roses. It was a "three stages of love" brooch with a bud, a half-open bud and a fully blooming rose. It was surrounded by a beaded edge of silver. A single pearl dangled freely from the center of the broach's bottom edge. She ran her fingers over it again and again as if it would conjure up an image of her mother.

"It not a crystal ball," Grand Ma Maw whispered.

"You said the men along the river called her Cameo Rose. I get the cameo part and the rose part, but not the working-along-the-river part. Was she a prospector?"

Grand Ma Maw inhaled deeply again. "No, she not. She was artist. Make beautiful drawings and paintings. That one she paint," said Grand Ma Maw as she pointed to the life-like portrait of Chang that hung on the wall near Grand Ma Maw's bed.

"Look at the love in his eyes. She see it. She paint it. Perhaps that where you get your talent with pencil and paint brush. Her sketchbook was your sketchbook all along. First pictures in book from her eyes and hands."

Blossom smiled slightly. In the past, she'd wondered who had been the previous owner of the book. But years ago, she stopped thinking or asking about it.

"But you also must know this. Iris was like your friend Monique."

"A prostitute? You're telling me that my mother was a prostitute?" a now pop-eyed Blossom replied.

"Yes."

"Did she work in a parlor house, a dance hall or a...what was it that Monique called it? Oh yes, a crib. She wasn't a streetwalker was she?"

"I not know what you mean. But most people call her good-time girl," Grand Ma Maw replied and added, "But your father, he love her with all his heart. And she love your father. She involved with young man from family of bakers who made special bread. It tasted sour. It sturdy and last a long time. We ate a lot of it. Anyway, she became pregnant. No one know your father and her was lovers. That would have ruined her life among the white men."

Blossom was doing her best to listen and not ask questions. But it was impossible to remain silent.

"If she was a prostitute, how did anyone know who the father—*my* father was? It could have been anyone along the river, right?"

Grand Ma Maw looked out the open window. "Think of it, my child. Iris had pale white skin with eyes the color of lavender iris. She white and laid down only with white men—until she met my Chang. They fell in love, despite my many warnings. I try to keep them apart. But their love pull them together. It meant to be. You meant to be. Iris stop working soon after."

Blossom listened, waiting for more.

"We all knew that a couple—Chinese man and lily-white woman— never be accepted anywhere. It against law. Then add baby. Their love must be hidden. So, she give you to me to raise, along with cameo. She left and it destroy her…and your father too. Not like heart ache. Not even like heart break. This worse. Like glass that fall and shatter into too many bitty pieces to put back together." Grand Ma Maw made a sweeping motion with both hands toward the floor as if the glass shards were scattered in all directions.

"You too young to understand, but there come time when you notice how life stop giving you things and how life start taking them away. For your father, this time came too early. But, what we do was right thing to do. My mother told me young ones always stand on shoulders of generations that come before them. She said her mother told her same thing. Older lift up younger for better life."

Grand Ma Maw stopped before continuing her story.

"I can't believe that I caused their sadness and separation. It was my fault, wasn't it? What am I thinking, of course it was my fault," Blossom acknowledged painfully.

"No. This not your fault. We move here to Chinatown and start new, like springtime. Start our business. No laundry this time. I hate washing other people's clothes. We told everyone your mother die in childbirth. And, until now, story worked."

Grand Ma Maw noticed the hurt feelings that were not the least bit masked on Blossom's face.

"She send me some letters and some money, from time to time. She never give return address, so I cannot tell you where she is. She visit once. But it not go well. You very small. What left of your father's heart shatter all over again. She never come back. "

Blossom was stunned as the pieces of her past came together.

"But what about the photo of my mother on Ba Ba's nightstand?"

"She one of our relatives who we knew would never come here," explained Grand Ma Maw.

"Do you have a photo of my real mother?"

"Yes. You find Iris in frame behind your cousin's photo."

Blossom got up to retrieve it, but Grand Ma Maw's hand tugged her back.

"You sure you want to see her now? You been through too much already?"

"Yes, I want to know and see it all now. I'm feeling like my life is a series of questions that I didn't know I had to ask!"

"Alright, but do not disturb your father. Let him sleep one more night not knowing that you know truth about him and your mother. Tomorrow come fast enough, I believe, and he tell you more. He hold this in so long that he be happy to tell you, even if it mean reliving it and it breaking heart all over again."

"Relive it? Don't you think he does that already?" asked Blossom. "If they loved each other the way you described, how could he have held the truth in so long and not relived it in his mind every day?"

Grand Ma Maw listened but did not respond.

"What I think I've learned about love with Brock makes this whole thing seem unbearable. I couldn't do it. I *won't* do it if Brock loves me the way I believe he does and says he does."

"Blossom, learn from those of us who walk path before you. Maybe we make wrong decision, maybe right decision. This—" Grand Ma Maw stopped to collect her thoughts. "This your time for choices and decisions. Choose your path wisely and have no regrets. These words come from a woman at end of her life. You have much to look forward to."

"But I don't feel like I have any choices to make, Grand Ma Maw."

"Oh, my treasured one, you always have choices. Don't ever forget that. If you remember anything—anything—that I say to you in your lifetime, know that you always have a choice even if you do not see it. Your courage and ability to make choices separate you from other peoples. Do not ever, ever lose that."

"I hear the words you are saying, Grand Ma Maw, and I know you are speaking with wisdom in your heart. But it's hard to see too far into the future, considering that the man I love with all of *my* heart is getting married on Saturday…and not to me."

Chapter 33

The Morning After

Tuesday, April 17, 1906, 9:03 a.m.
One day before the earthquake and firestorm

"Rise and shine, my pet," announced Austin sweetly. He held his head in a wince-inducing attempt to soothe the throbbing brought on by too much liquor and fun the night before. "Sonofabitch" he yelled, all the words smashed together into one angry word outburst.

"Oh, well, that was useless, now wasn't it?" he continued, discovering that Brock was not in the room and his bed was made.

"What fresh hell is this? I can't remember how the night ended, but I'm here and he's not. I wonder which of us had the better time?"

He looked into the hallway mirror. A purple lump on his forehead was clearly visible. He pulled his hair forward to cover the mysterious addition to his face.

"I guess that's why they call them bangs after all!" Austin rubbed his unshaved chin and headed down to the kitchen for some much-needed coffee.

Upon entering the room, he placed his order. "Coffee, black. Toast, dry. Shot of whiskey, straight up. Ice, wrapped in a towel." He plopped himself at the servants' table and placed his forehead on the cool marble tabletop with an audible thump.

"Ugh, another bad move on my part!"

"Mr. Austin, do you want it brown or burnt today?" asked Clementine in a response that had become a routine between them.

"You pick. My head might explode if I think too hard."

Clementine replied, "Yes, sir."

Austin summoned the energy and fortitude to softly sing some lyrics in a slurry and somewhat unclear way.

"In a cavern, in a canyon,
Excavating for a mine,
Dwelt a miner forty niner,
And his daughter, Clementine.

Oh my darling, oh my darling,
Oh my darling Clementine,
Thou art lost and gone forever,
Dreadful sorry, Clementine.

How I missed her! How I missed her!
How I missed my Clementine,
Till I kissed her little sister,
And forgot my Clementine."

Clementine shook her head. Austin had been singing that song in her presence since he was a boy. Even then, he would scramble the lyrics to make it his own song.

"Did my precious brother come and go already? Off to see his blessed cows and horses, I'd guess."

"Yes, sir, indeed he did," said the woman with a slow Southern accent, drawing out her words as if they were stuck in melted caramel.

"Did he have a hangover?"

"No, sir. How was the party?"

"It was wicked, like it should have been," he replied and raised his eyebrows several times in a synchronized pattern.

"And between us girls, would you believe that snotty Faye Huntington showed up…at Prickly Pete's! There's something about her that makes me crazy!"

"Your parents and her parents were mighty close…until you kids came along. Usually that brings folks together," said Clementine as she poured Austin's coffee. "Not your folks." She placed his two drinks down in front of him.

"Here's your coffee and whiskey. Toast will be ready soon."

The South was known for strong coffee, and Clementine made it that way. "My Pa, may he rest in peace, used to say that coffee should be black as night, strong as love and hot as hell!"

"He was right!" Austin sipped slowly from his cup until he thought about Brock again.

"Cows and horses. Horses and cows. He's stuck in the past. It's like he can't see the future…the future that's right here on our streets."

Clementine listened as she fussed with some just-washed kitchen utensils.

"I'm going to get me one of those automobiles. That'll show him. They're all over the city now and I'm not going to be left behind, even if they do have trouble with the city's hills."

He went on, "I'm leaving the horses—and the never-ending trail of horse shit—behind with Brock. I'll have a shiny new automobile. He can keep his hay-burning *oatsmobiles!*"

A searing bolt of pain drilled into Austin's forehead. In a half-hearted attempt to distract himself, he took a long drag on the cup's edge as if he was inhaling the heavy smoke of a cigar.

With great satisfaction, he sighed. The distraction appeared to work.

"Burns my britches, yes, it burns my britches. I live for nights that I can't remember while he's off playing farmer and marrying a beautiful woman. On top of that, he's the apple of Mother's eye. Could anyone's life get better?"

The cook slid a plate of bone-dry burnt toast in front of Austin. "I couldn't rightly say, sir, but this toast might help you see the world differently. There's nothing like black coffee, golden whiskey and burnt toast to set you straight. That was my Pa's remedy too."

"It may set me straight, but straight toward what?"

"You'll find your way, Mr. Austin. With your brother married and out of the house soon, you'll have your mother's undivided attention for the first time in your life. Maybe she'll help you in ways that she hasn't been able to in the past."

She put her hand on his shoulder and patted him.

"Yeah, that's exactly what I need, my mother's undivided attention. That ought to do me as much good as a brand-new Bible in a brothel."

"Let's face it, I've always been like leftovers around here. I got what was left from my parents after Brock got the attention and praise."

Austin moved the chair next to him out and away from the table. He motioned Clementine to sit down.

"You know I can't sit with you, even here in my kitchen. If your mother saw that, well, it just wouldn't be good." She didn't sit down, but she did lean against the counter's edge.

"Ya know, all I am is…what I'm *not*. I'm not like Father. Not like Brock. Not like Mother. I'm just me and that doesn't seem to add up to much. But, and this is a big but, I might have hit on something the other day, Clementine. It fascinated me, and the men who were doing it fascinated me too."

Clementine looked intrigued. "And just what was *that*, if I might ask?"

"I was on Market Street and it was the usual chaos. Motorcars, streetcars, carriages, wagons, pedestrians and newspaper boys were all hurrying in every direction, with no one in control of the whole mess. It was kind of like when you kick an ant hill."

Clementine nodded.

"I walked in front of a stopped cable car and noticed everyone was waving at it. I got on the cable car and on the front end of it were two men and a hand-crank camera. The cable car was facing the bay and the Ferry Building at the end of the line."

Austin stopped to sip his coffee and have a bite of toast.

"So what happened next?" asked Clementine, her interest piqued.

"The cable car started moving and the two men started taking turns wildly cranking the camera. When I asked them about what they were doing, they said they were making a travelogue that would be shown in cinemas all over the country."

"Tell me more."

"They cranked like mad men. They sang *Daisy Bell* over and over again. It helped them keep the rhythm of the cranking the same. You know…'Daisy, Daisy, Give me your answer, do; I'm half crazy; All for the love of you.'"

Austin stopped and rubbed his forehead. "It was nuts I tell you, just nuts. If I heard them get to the point of 'a bicycle built for two' one more time I thought I'd jump right off the cable car and head to a saloon. But I couldn't. I had to see what happened next."

Clementine blinked in an exaggerated way.

"I looked ahead and to the sides to see what the camera was recording. I saw the biggest dray being pulled by teamsters with a line-up of horses hauling the delivery. It was like a barge moving through town! Anyway, they cranked all the way from 8th Street until we got to the Ferry Building and turned around on the turntable. I offered to help crank, but they said 'no.' I got their card. It's in my wallet upstairs. I think their last name was Miles, and they were brothers."

"Sounds fascinating."

"You should have seen how people stopped and stared, but most waved and smiled and acted a little crazy. Even a flock of nuns with wings on their hats waved—modestly, of course. No one stood still, like you have to when a photograph is taken. These pictures were being taken in motion and, believe me, everyone was in motion!"

He took another sip of coffee and nibbled on the dry toast.

"I haven't seen you this excited about anything in years," said Clementine.

"There's something there. I'm not sure what it is yet, but I've got to learn more about taking pictures in motion."

Clementine nodded and patted Austin on the shoulder again.

"There's an old saying where I come from," she said with a glistening eye. "It says, 'Pray, then move your feet!' You can't just wish and dream all day or your life will pass you by. Look at what your father earned in his life, and he earned it with hard work."

Austin nodded in return, though he was never too keen on the idea of work, much less hard work.

"You might be onto something. People like to watch people, now don't they?" she asked. "Just look at all the benches in the parks…so folks can watch the parade go by even when there isn't a circus in town."

He rested his chin on the palm of his hand. His elbow was firmly on the tabletop.

"Yes, yes they do."

"Then, before too many other people get the same notion as you, you best get on that idea of yours quicker than a grease fire in a grimy kitchen!"

Austin smiled at Clementine and asked, "What would I do without you?"

Chapter 34
*I*t Must Be Love

Tuesday, April 17, 1906, 9:43 a.m.
One day before the earthquake and firestorm

"May I work with you again?" asked Ting Ting. Little Sunflower was in tow, silent as usual. "There's no school today, and I'm going to need to be able to help your father and Grand Ma Maw after you marry your Mr. St. Clair!" She smiled impishly, waiting for a response from Blossom.

"What did you just say?"

"You heard me, and you know it's true," said Ting Ting with a snicker. She began to crank her ever-present music box as a distraction.

Blossom realized how obvious her feelings must be if a child could sense them.

"Why do you think I'm going to marry him?" she asked in a hushed tone to keep their conversation as private as possible.

"You're different now. You're sparkly most of the time. But now, you seem kind of sad. That must be love, right?"

If only Ting Ting knew everything that I'm feeling with Brock and the mother I just found out about and the lie I've been living with Ba Ba and Grand Ma Maw, thought Blossom.

"Hey, are you going to help me learn to make fortune cookies or not?"

asked the little girl, bringing Blossom back to the reality of the bakery.

"Yes, my little one, I will teach you—both of you—more about cookie making. How many lessons have you already had?"

Ting Ting interrupted, "Can you teach us about Mr. St. Clair too?"

They all grinned. Blossom hugged Ting Ting, ruffled Little Sunflower's hair and pulled two extra stools next to her work station.

"First things first. Slip off your shoes, but be tricky about it. Grand Ma Maw will bang her walking stick on the floor really hard if she sees that your shoes are off."

To make the dough, Blossom beat egg whites, oil and vanilla extract. "Our family secret is to add almond extract too for taste and a sweeter smell. You must never give our secret away," cautioned Blossom. Ting Ting replied with a crisp, "Never!" Little Sunflower turned her head to the right and left and pursed her lips.

Blossom instructed the girls to mix flour, sugar and salt in another bowl. The contents of the two bowls were mixed and enough water was added to create a runny batter.

A spoonful of batter was placed in the hot iron's circular indentation. "Watch it now. When the edges turn brown, it's done. If we wait too long, the cookie gets too hard."

Blossom selected a slip of paper. "This is when we get to become fortunetellers, picking out the future for whoever opens the cookie," she said dramatically as she put the paper in. "If the paper goes in too soon, it will sink into the dough that hasn't cooled enough."

She folded the circle of dough in half and quickly pulled the two ends of the straight edge to create the unique crescent shape.

"Now we put each one of them into its own little cradle to rest and cool off," instructed Blossom as she placed the newly formed cookie into one compartment of what looked like a massive muffin tin. "We must not disturb them while they nap!"

Ting Ting giggled. "It's like they're little babies in a nursery."

"Yes, I guess so!"

Before long, the topic of discussion shifted in a not-so-masked way from cookies to men. Blossom answered Ting Ting's questions much like Monique answered hers.

"Why him? He's not like you."

Blossom cleared her throat. "That's a big question for a little girl. But I'll do my best to answer it."

Blossom made sure that her voice was hushed. "I like Brock *because* he's different. He's not like the men here in Chinatown. And I've always thought that I'm not really like the women in Chinatown."

In fact, I now know that I'm not like the Chinese women in more ways than I could have imagined.

"When I see him, I feel alive. I feel different, in a wonderful way. When we're together, we can't stop talking about anything and everything. I don't think those feelings will ever change."

Ting Ting winced as she burned her finger on the cookie iron.

"Oh, please pay attention to what you're doing."

"But he's a rich white man. You're Chinese."

Blossom replied, "Yes, we're not alike when you see us with your eyes. But inside, in our hearts, we're the same."

Ting Ting cocked her head to the side while maintaining eye contact, not quite understanding what Blossom just said.

"So is he your prince, the man of your dreams?" Ting Ting sweetly asked with the innocence and hopefulness of a child. Little Sunflower looked at Blossom and grinned.

"Prince?"

"Yes, is Mr. St. Clair going to take you away from all of this and make your dreams come true?"

"Like Yeh-Shen?" Little Sunflower broke her silence.

"Yes, like Yeh-Shen. I was reading it to her the other day. I really think she likes the pictures more than the words! I told her that learned in school that there are Cinderella stories all over the world, like in France, Germany and Russia."

"Can you tell me the story Blossom, please?" asked Little Sunflower.

"Only a short version, though, we have work to do!"

Blossom went on to tell the tale of Yeh-Shen, whose father had two wives. "The father died. And so did one wife, the one who was Yeh-Shen's mother. Her stepmother raised her, but favored her own selfish and lazy daughter. Even though she had to do the worst chores, Yeh-Shen remained kind and gentle. And she was pretty. She only had one friend. It was a fish with golden scales and big…golden…eyes!" Blossom put her open palms next to her ears and waved them like gills.

"Yeh-Shen got very little food. She was always so, so hungry. However, she loved her fishy friend and shared what little food she got each day with him."

"I don't like this next part," Little Sunflower whispered to Ting Ting.

"One day, the stepmother followed Yeh-Shen to the water's edge and watched. Later, the stepmother captured the fish and cooked him for dinner."

Little Sunflower frowned. "I've never liked eating fish."

"Me either," added Blossom. "Well, Yeh-Shen cried and cried and cried because she felt so bad about her friend. But out of nowhere, an old man appeared and told her to save the fish's bones. He told her to speak to the bones and ask them for help if she was ever in trouble."

"I get in so much trouble that I would be talking to those fish bones every day!" Ting Ting laughed and held her belly.

"It was time for a festival that only happened once a year, where young women dressed in their finest clothes to meet young men who might become future husbands. Oh, and how Yeh-Shen wanted to go. And do you know what happened?"

Little Sunflower perked up. "Her stepmother wouldn't let her go, right?"

"That's correct. She didn't want Yeh-Shen, even in her dirty clothes, to spoil her own daughter's chances of making a good match. So, Yeh-Shen spoke to the fish's bones and pleaded for new clothes to wear to the festival. Before she could end her pleas, she was wearing a gown of sea-green silk, a cloak of kingfisher feathers and the most, most, most beautiful golden slippers."

Ting Ting looked down at her stocking feet and wiggled her toes.

"The fish's bones made Yeh-Shen promise not to lose the slippers. Against her stepmother's wishes, Yeh-Shen walked to the festival. Along the way, people stare at her because she looks like royalty. She has a wonderful time until she sees her stepmother and stepsister. She thinks they recognized her. Yeh-Shen runs away so fast that she steps right out of one of her golden slippers."

Little Sunflower raises her stocking feet and joins in the toe wiggling.

"Yeh-Shen is devastated. She knew that she was not to lose her slippers, even one of them. She speaks to the fish's bones, but they remain silent. Then a man finds the shoe and gives it to the king. The king is mesmerized by the small slipper. He figures that such a beautiful shoe must belong to a beautiful woman, and he must find her. The king announces that he'll marry the girl whose small feet fit the shoe. He has a pavilion put up along the roadside to display the slipper and so that all the women who pass may try it on. The line is long outside the pavilion, but every woman's foot was much too big to fit into the dainty slipper. Yeh-Shen hears about the slipper in the pavilion, but not the marry-the-king-part of the story. So, when all of her chores are done, she sneaks out of the house to go get her other slipper."

"Now it gets good!" chimed in Ting Ting.

"The king's men capture Yeh-Shen, thinking she's a thief, and they take her to the king. He's very angry that a peasant girl would have the nerve to steal the precious golden slipper. She tells the king about how she lost her mother, her father, her fishy friend and now her slipper. As she tells her story, he notices how small and dainty her feet are. And he notices how kind and gentle she is. The king and Yeh-Shen go to her house to get the other slipper. She puts them both on—"

Little Sunflower couldn't contain herself. She added, "Then her gown appears and the king falls in love with her. And he wants to marry her! She marries him and brings the fish's bones with her to the palace, leaving behind her stepmother and stepsister who die when the sky rains down fiery stones on them."

"Oh, let's not end the story like that. Let's make it happier. Let's finish with, she marries the king and becomes a loving and generous queen!"

Ting Ting added, "And all her dreams came true. That's my wish. That's what I want to have happen."

"If I've learned anything lately it's that you have to make your own dreams come true, and it takes more than wishes. As someone wise told me, it takes 'pluck and luck.' A prince would be nice, though, I have to admit. For now, I'll let you dream of your prince coming to save you from Chinatown. Or maybe you and your prince will live right here in Chinatown. Now let's focus on our work."

"Okay," said Ting Ting. "At least with fortune-cookie making, we might help someone discover a dream with just a few words on a little piece of paper."

"Yes, there's some magic in what we do," replied Blossom, "even if it involves spoons and bowls and not golden slippers!"

"We gotta go now," Ting Ting said as she pushed her stool away from the work table and grabbed Little Sunflower's hand.

Chang entered the room, looking over his shoulder to see if the coast was clear. Grand Ma Maw was not in plain sight. He handed each girl a piece of hard candy. "A sweet for my sweets," he said softly.

Looking at Blossom, he added, "Don't tell Grand Ma Maw what I did."

"Yes, Ba Ba," replied Blossom. She—and it was likely that Grand Ma

Maw—was fully aware of this candy-dispensing habit.

"Ting Ting, you no tell either," said Chang as he left the room. "That go for you too, Little Sunflower."

Ting Ting smiled and groaned a sound that resembled an "uh-ha" from her full mouth.

Blossom thought, *that's the only secret he and I shared. But, after last night and what Grand Ma Maw revealed, he and I are going to be sharing a whole lot more secrets.* She refocused her attention on the girls.

"Come by later and I'll draw pictures of you in my book. If you have any more questions about you know who, you'll come to me, right?"

"Right."

Blossom added, "This must remain our secret."

"Just you, Little Sunflower, me…and *Mr. St. Clair,*" said Ting Ting. She pronounced Brock's last name in a silly school-girlish way.

Just then Chang re-entered the room to survey what was going on.

"We were just leaving," said Ting Ting as the girls scampered away.

Chang turned and left the room as well.

Blossom was alone with her thoughts, a handful of cookie dough and a pile of paper prophecies.

She picked one up and read it aloud. "Sometime fortune smile. Sometime frown. Today fortune do both."

She put the slip of paper down and whispered, "So which one is going to come first?"

Chapter 35

$\mathscr{B}$eing Held With Hungry Arms

Tuesday, April 17, 1906, 10:02 a.m.
One day before the earthquake and firestorm

Blossom perfected the art of making fortune cookies with machine-like precision years ago. She mindlessly deployed that precision as her thoughts painted elaborate scenes of her mother coming back and apologizing for abandoning her.

Her father returned to the workroom. Blossom noticed how he hovered more than usual. He kept staring at the brooch she was wearing. Blossom broke her rhythm and put her hands on her lap. "Will you stop staring and start talking? Please."

Chang pulled up a stool next to Blossom, sat down and started to talk. "I know Grand Ma Maw told you about your mother last night. I so…so very sorry I not tell you before. Last time I see that brooch was last time I see your mother. She was the most, most, MOST beautiful woman I ever met, until I see you and your iris eyes a-smiling."

Blossom interrupted, "Before we go any further, we have to talk about that song. I cannot believe that every time I heard you sing that awful song and I corrected you about it being 'Irish' not 'iris,' you were singing about my mother. You were actually saying her name, leaving me in the dark the *entire* time!"

"I not sing it to be cruel. It comfort me to talk your mother's name around you. Seeing your lavender eyes help me feel your mother not far away."

He handed Blossom a photo of her mother that she assumed was the one Grand Ma Maw described as being in the picture frame on Chang's dresser.

"See, she beautiful like you, yes?" he said with wounded pride.

"Yes, she's beautiful," replied Blossom as she gazed at the face of the woman who brought her into this world and then abandoned her.

"This for you. You keep now," commanded Chang. Blossom tucked the photo in her pocket. "It not one from the picture frame. This I keep somewheres special for you."

"Thank you," said Blossom quietly.

"You look like your mother. I miss her, but she always with us…in sketchbook…in your face. She here in bits and pieces, around you your entire life. You just not aware," admitted Chang. "We try hard not to have love for each other. But not try hard enough. Our love like swirlpool in river. It powerful and take control."

Blossom fought the urge to correct her father's use of the made-up word.

"I wish that I could say that I miss her too, but I've never met…" Chang's raised fingers touched Blossom's lips and cut off the stream of words.

"I know. I sorry. Now you learn truth. Perhaps she here for you in brooch," said Chang as his fingers lowered to touch the brooch as Blossom lifted her hand to touch it. Their fingers tips collided and they smiled, each pulling their hands away and then looking downward to the floor.

Blossom couldn't help herself from looking up and asking, "Grand Ma Maw said my mother visited once. What happened?"

"Another time I tell you. Hurt too much. For now, know she held you with very hungry arms. She love you," said Chang tenderly.

"Did she still love you?"

"I believe so. I know so. But she leave to give you best chance at happiness."

"But it cost you your happiness."

Chang nodded slowly and lifted his shoulders as if to signal that there was no other good choice to make.

"How could you go on day after day, year after year, living such an enormous lie? Didn't you think I'd eventually find out?"

Chang put his hand on Blossom's. "Once I tell lie, it easier to tell again and again. Soon, I almost believe it. Can you forgive me?"

"Honestly, I'm not sure I can, at least not right now. But there may come a time when I need to ask for your forgiveness, and I hope you'll be able to find it in your heart to forgive me."

Chapter 36
Meant For Each Other

Tuesday, April 17, 1906, 10:07 a.m.
One day before the earthquake and firestorm

Clarissa's daily routine was in full swing, but her mind was not engaged with the tasks at hand. She rested on the edge of the master suite's bed and closely watched her mother pick and poke at the tightly woven swirl of hair that Zelda just created. Zelda had many duties, and she was skilled at hair dressing. Clarissa noticed that some hair rebelliously escaped the elegant coiffure.

"No matter how well she styles my hair, it always requires a few more touches. I should just do it myself from start to finish. But your father won't hear of it. He doesn't want me to lift a finger these days." She cleared her throat and began speaking mockingly in a deep manly voice. "Mother, you've worked hard enough in your life. By the sweat of our brows and the grace of God Almighty, we've hit *our* Mother Lode and you should live like royalty now and forever!"

She broke her act and began to laugh as she saw in her vanity's mirror how Clarissa was moving around the room with an all-too-familiar swagger while she peered in the mirror too. *Between the voice and the walk, it was almost like having him in the room*, Clarissa thought.

Zelda knocked at the door she'd closed behind her moments ago. "Anything else I can help with, ma'am?"

"No, that will be all for now. Thank you."

Zelda stood outside the door and continued to listen as discreetly as possible, her morning duties nearly complete.

"When did you know you loved Daddy?" Clarissa sat back down on the edge of the bed.

"Well, where did that question come from?" She looked closely at her daughter. "I don't know that it was like I didn't love him one minute and then loved him the next. It was gradual. But when I knew it, I knew it."

She gazed at the vanity's mirror again. Clarissa thought it looked as if her mother was almost looking through it like a window to her past. She waited for what seemed like an eternity. "So, when was it? How did it feel?"

Mrs. Donohue began slowly, but soon the words came easy and swift.

"You've known since you were a child how your father and I met, so this isn't going to sound like a fairy-tale romance, because it wasn't. Really, it wasn't! As a young married couple, we were out among the prospectors, as dirty and covered with God's good earth as you please. Back then, we weren't quite as tidy as we are today. I tended a vegetable garden and washed clothes to earn extra money. We were happy enough, or at least we thought we were. Our whole future was out in front of us."

Clarissa asked, "Had he just hit it big? Is that when you knew you loved him?"

"No, it was quite the opposite. He was about to give up and never prospect again. I knew it was his dream, maybe even his destiny, to be successful in a big way at something. It might as well have been mining silver. I looked at him, and at that moment, when he needed me the most to encourage him to keep on trying, I wiped off my hands and pulled his face close to mine…one hand on each cheek. I told him I wasn't about to stay married to a quitter. I knew that would get his attention. And it did," she said and winked.

"A few days later, he hit the silver deposit that paid for the house we're sitting in right now. He needed me. I needed him. It's as simple as that. That's when I really knew we were meant for each other. We've been together ever since."

Clarissa looked at her mother, admiring her in a way that she hadn't before. She also realized she didn't have a story she could someday tell her daughter before her wedding day about the moment she knew she loved Brock. She looked at the wall and then out the window. These actions did not escape her mother's knowing eyes.

"Brock is a good man and he loves you. I can see it. You know it in your heart. So why the long face and distant look in your eyes?"

"I know brides and grooms usually have doubts before their weddings. I don't, at least I don't think I do. But, I also don't have a story to tell about the moment when we shared the spark or whatever it is. To be truly honest, our love is comfortable, even reassuring most of the time. We didn't have to face the challenges you and Daddy faced. Do you think our kind of love will stand up over time too?"

"That's up to you two. Our love was literally forged out in the wilderness. Our gift to you was a better life, the niceties in life. Love doesn't have to come from adversity."

"But what if it's been too easy for us?"

Zelda, who had been leaning on the door to hear more clearly, made the door creak loudly. For a moment, Clarissa and her mother looked at the door. Zelda scurried down the hallway as quietly as she possibly could.

Figuring it was nothing, Mrs. Donohue responded to Clarissa's question. "Listen to your heart and follow what it tells you. Don't think about it so much. Besides, the ladies are coming to lunch today to celebrate with you, and we can't have you looking unsure or uneasy, now can we?"

Clarissa sat up straight. "No, we mustn't!" She rose to her feet and left the room with her mother's hopes trailing behind her like a loose thread from the hem of her skirt.

Chapter 37
Trouble In Paradise

Tuesday, April 17, 1906, 10:27 a.m.
One day before the earthquake and firestorm

"You'll never believe what I just heard!" Zelda exclaimed as she entered the kitchen. She gasped to catch her breath.

"Don't you mean *overheard?*" fired back Katie. "Have you been eavesdropping again? What did you hear this time? Ain't, I mean isn't this place gossipy enough without you adding more carrots to the stew?"

"Stew! Schmoo! Here's the tasty morsel. Mrs. Donohue told Miss Clarissa about being surrounded by prospectors and how she fell in love. And, she talked about being covered with God's good earth. I know what she's talking about—"

Katie broke in, "This is not about you and your time in the mining camps. What did you learn about the Donohues?"

Zelda got herself back on track. "I have to admit I've been too hard on them. It sounds like they've had their share of rough times. But, here's where it gets even better. The princess sounds like she's having doubts about her prince."

Katie added, "So there's trouble in paradise, eh? What did Mrs. Donohue say to encourage the bride-to-be?"

Zelda looked out the kitchen window. "Um, I didn't quite hear that part."

"Why in heavens not?"

"I leaned on the door to hear better and it creaked. I ran down here as quietly as I could before their talk was over."

Katie put her hands on her hips.

"I know. I know. I'll do better next time," said Zelda reassuringly. "But whether or not Mrs. Donohue turned Clarissa's frown upside down, like you said, there's trouble in paradise."

Chapter 38
Making A Whopper Of A Decision Lickety-Split

Tuesday, April 17, 1906, 10:32 a.m.
One day before the earthquake and firestorm

The smell of hay was particularly strong in the damp morning air at Twin Peaks. But Brock didn't notice.

"What's bother'n yuh, Pork Chop?" asked Gubbs without his usual ornery seediness. "Yuh been as quiet as a hangin' tree on Sunday."

Brock turned toward the plain-spoken cuss with leathery skin who was inside the horse barn. "I guess I have…been quiet, that is. I've been thinking a lot."

"Where's yuh're gumption? A man who's gettin' hitched in a few days outta be thinkin' a lot…thinkin' and not regrettin'—"

"Yeah, you're right," replied the younger man in a slow and drawn-out way, on the heels of a sigh. For as long as Brock could remember, Gubbs had called him Pork Chop. It was an odd term of endearment, but Brock never considered it disrespectful or inappropriately playful.

"Does tha 'a lot' yuh been thinkin' about include that purty gurl China doll yuh been sneakin' up here? Didn't think I'd missed that, did yuh, Pork Chop?"

Brock wasn't surprised. He assumed Gubbs observed the couple's visits to Twin Peaks.

"She's not a China doll. Her name's Blossom. She works in her family's bakery making cookies during the day and in their restaurant at dinnertime. And, yes, I've been thinking about her. What do you think?"

"About what?"

"Blossom and me."

"Tain't what I think that counts much right about now."

Brock sat on a bale of hay and rubbed his palm across the back of his neck. "You know me in a way that most other people don't. I'm at my best when I'm here. What keeps you here, Gubbs? You never talk about your family or a wife."

"Tain't much to tell."

"Tell me anyway."

"If yuh're askin' if I been in love before—like yuh're with that Blossom of yers, not with some dame who's no smarter than a box of rocks—then tha answer is yes. But it didn't work out fer me. Actually, I didn't do what it takes to make it work out. That's somethin' I reckon I'll regret until I drag in my last breath. At my age, I ain't sure there's a whole lotta regrettin' left to do. These days, I'm just a rusty chunk of barbed wire. Prickly and long past my prime."

"I had no idea," said Brock.

"I ain't so much of an open book as I could be. So what are yuh fixin' to do? Yuh can't be marryin' two women, at least not here in California."

"What do you mean, Gubbs?"

"Lemme point something out fer yuh. Blossom comes here. Miss Clarissa don't. Are yuh lovin' the one yuh can't have?"

Brock stopped to consider that while Gubbs didn't usually talk much, he excelled at dispensing white-haired nuggets of wisdom.

Gubbs quickly added, "I hope I ain't overstepped myself, but if yuh're asking me—and I think yuh are—who likes tha things that make yuh

happier, I think yuh already know, Pork Chop. It's long past time to make
a choice. Seein's that yuh haven't, yuh hafta make one whopper of a choice
lickety-split. What I'm seein' now is what I walked away from years ago.
This oughta be clear and not hit yuh like a sack of hammers. Yuh could do
some learnin' from my mistake or yuh gonna end up smack-dab where I
am today."

"Why did you walk away?"

"Myrtle Elaina Stae, that's *her* name, was perfect in my eyes. First off,
she would have none of me! But, over time, she saw things in me that I
didn't see. She was from Norway and was still learnin' to speak English.
Tha way she spoke in her old-country ways was like music to my ears. I can
still hear how she'd say my name. She didn't call me Gubbs. No siree! She
called me my God-given name, Gilbert."

He paused.

"My family, my pa and ma in particular, didn't take a shine to her.
When tha day came fer me to tell 'em about my feelings fer Myrtle, I'm
pretty damned sure that Pa's ass clenched up tight enough to snap tha
handle off a shovel!" Grubbs smiled, but the lightness faded quickly from
his face.

"Over time, they planted doubt in my mind, and I guess yuh could
say I listened to my head and not my heart. Looks and sounds kinda
familiar, eh?"

Brock neither agreed nor disagreed.

"Son, I didn't have yer choice between two women, but I walked away
from tha one I could've had," he said as he rubbed his grizzled beard and
then scratched his scalp.

Brock rubbed his rough hands together and looked carefully at Gubbs,
whose face now looked like a skull shethed in callus.

He broke his own heart and chose not to put it back together again, thought
Brock. Listen to me...God...I sound like a love-sick girl...broken hearts...
back together...I have got to sort this out!

"Yuh know, that's more than I've told anyone about that part of my life. But yuh need to hear it and think on it. Like my Myrtle told me once, 'If yuh want tha fruit in life, yuh have to go out on a limb sometimes.' Got it?" He made a giddy-up sound with his mouth.

Gubbs turned to walk away. Brock called out, and Gubbs swung back around. "Got it, and thanks," said Brock with the awkwardness appropriate for two men talking about things more personal than men typically talk about.

Gubbs smiled. Brock returned the smile, even though he felt more like frowning in frustration.

Chapter 39
$\mathcal{W}$indows Have Eyes

Tuesday, April 17, 1906, 10:46 a.m.
One day before the earthquake and firestorm

Dulcie Chow requested this morning's game of mahjong. She didn't know it at the time of the telephone-called invitation, but Grand Ma Maw would not like what she was about to hear. Nor would she like the game that was about to be played.

Berty and Grand Auntie Lim Kee arrived at Dulcie's apartment soon after Grand Ma Maw had begun to make herself comfortable. The mahjong table was set and a pot of boiling-hot tea was ready to be poured.

The women took their places, dispensed the tea and waited for Dulcie to unleash what was expected to be a prized jewel of gossip.

Berty turned to Dulcie and gently said, "*Shay shay*. I am grateful for your most generous hospitality. What news will you share today?"

Dulcie raised her hand to signal that Berty should end her questioning.

Grand Ma Maw didn't win the role of first dealer, and consequently she didn't have the honor of being the East Wind as the game began. That omen, and a quick glance at the tiles she had in front of her, told the old woman this was not going to go well.

"About Blossom," said Dulcie abruptly with a look of great concern.

"We must talk."

"Ah, you heard that Butch ask for her hand in marriage last night? Already such good news being talked about?" replied Grand Ma Maw.

"There is talk about the engagement of the butcher and Blossom. But also talk—troubling talk—about Blossom only," added Dulcie.

With a wispy wave of her hand, Grand Ma Maw tried to redirect the conversation. "Must we? Activities of other people far more interesting, I believe."

"I believe *not*," responded Dulcie with a subtle, yet upset smile.

Grand Ma Maw looked down at her tiles.

"Years ago, yes, years ago we agree never to speak of our families at this table," Grand Ma Maw reminded the other three players, even if it was unlikely that they might have forgotten this cardinal rule.

Despite the history lesson, Dulcie went on. "It pains me to say this. Yesterday afternoon, near my loving husband's very successful tea store, Blossom enter carriage of white man. Fancy carriage with big, very big black horses. She have package on lap," reported Dulcie.

Grand Ma Maw listened intently and watched the shopkeeper's wife for facial expressions of emphasis that might tell more than her words.

"Blossom return at end of day in carriage, says my dear husband. He see with his own eyes. No package on lap this time. What you say about this?" she asked.

All eyes were on Grand Ma Maw. Everyone looked uncomfortable and tense. Grand Ma Maw focused downward on her tiles again.

Dulcie observed aloud, "You *not* saying anything about as loudly as a person can."

"I look at my tiles. I must plan two or three moves ahead, not dwell on tiles already played," Grand Ma Maw replied. She said no more. Her tears fought for room in her eyes.

Despite many tales of tragedies and triumphs these four women had shared over the years, they had never seen Grand Ma Maw shed tears.

Now, she was.

Tears of pain. Tears of joy. Only in private. That my mother taught me. What she think of me, hot tears on my cheeks?

"My Blossom make choices we never had," Grand Ma Maw squeezed the words out of her tightened throat. "In future, I guide her best I can."

Dulcie put her hand on Grand Ma Maw's hand in a way that only a caring friend can. Grand Auntie Lim Kee, to Grand Ma Maw's right, put her hand on Grand Ma Maw's other hand. She patted it in a slow, soothing rhythm with a very strained smile of encouragement on her face.

As much as Grand Ma Maw knew she was among friends, Blossom's actions would soon—if not already—be the topic of gossip and innuendo in the alleys of Chinatown.

"Our buildings have eyes. Our buildings have mouths. How loud will they speak this time?" Grand Ma Maw asked the group. *What has begun cannot be undone.*

Chapter 40

onfusion

Tuesday, April 17, 1906, 11:47 a.m.
One day before the earthquake and firestorm

"Hello," announced Brock as he entered the front door with a bouquet of daisies. He firmly planted a lingering kiss on Clarissa's lips as he moved her to the point of being backed up against the foyer wall's flocked rose-patterned wallpaper. *Whoa, now that's a kiss. Where's he been hiding them?*

"Hello to you too," said Clarissa as he handed her the bouquet.

Brock didn't often visit Clarissa for lunch on weekdays, since he was usually out at Twin Peaks. So today's visit was especially important to her considering Brock's uneasiness during their recent times together. *Wedding jitters aside*, Clarissa thought, *he just hasn't been himself lately. But this…this I'm liking!*

Brock kissed her even more passionately again and then again. Clarissa felt her back against the wall more solidly with each kiss. She dropped the flowers on the floor with a rustling thud.

Clarissa's mother entered the foyer and silently stepped backward, retracing her footsteps, hoping not to be noticed or to interrupt what she hadn't seen between the couple before: unbridled passion.

The passion, however was only one-sided and it was bridled.

Moments earlier, Brock stood outside the Donohues' front door for about five minutes mustering up his courage. Compared to kissing Blossom recently, this encounter with Clarissa was nice, but not earth-moving.

"So, what's for lunch?" he asked matter-of-factly as he pulled away from her and looked at the sideboard in the dining room. Clarissa scooped up the daisies.

"Eureka! That's more like it! I saw the whole thing!" blurted out Faye from the staircase landing. "Bravo!" Unlike Clarissa's mother, Faye had no problem pushing herself into this private moment. "You're a real tiger! Grrrrrrr!"

Clarissa pulled herself together, took a cleansing breath and glared at Faye. She took Brock by the arm, walked him to the kitchen and pointed out the wicker hamper.

"Surprise! We're going on a picnic. Well, not exactly a picnic. We're going to have our first meal together at our new house. I already checked with my mother about any superstitions that might apply, and I think we're fine. It's not like seeing me in my wedding gown before the ceremony or anything like that."

"That's a surprise, a wonderful surprise."

Knowing his favorites, Clarissa made sure the hamper included fried chicken and biscuits.

He stopped and objectively asked himself, *How could I not love her? She's kind, thoughtful and now even spontaneous. I do love her. Or do I like her a lot? And, if I do, is that enough?* He decided it was too much to think about right now.

As if hollering from the staircase wasn't rude enough, Faye barged into the kitchen just as the couple was about to leave.

"Oh, you two lovebirds make my heart sing! Just a few more days and you'll be eternally united."

The two shook their heads, gathered up the hamper and the blanket that was set out, and headed for the front door.

Brock stopped at the entryway to the dining room. "Sure we shouldn't just eat here? Faye could join us then."

Clarissa took Brock firmly by the arm and proceeded to the front door as Faye followed in quick pursuit. She waved goodbye to them from the stoop as if she was a resident of the Donohue home.

She walked back into the house to the dining room archway and passed under it. On the sideboard she saw the fortune cookie that she had refused to open during Clarissa's bridal dinner on Saturday night. She picked it up, looked it over carefully and set it back down precisely where she found it, as if disturbing it might disturb something else.

She was nearly startled out of her high-heeled shoes when Mrs. Donohue asked from behind, "Faye, honey, what are your plans for this afternoon?"

"Oh, this and that. I'll just get my little handbag and be on my way."

"Alright then, I'm sure we'll see you soon."

"Tootle-loo!" said Faye energetically as she collected her belongs and headed out the front door.

"There's a world of opportunities out there," she said softly to herself. "Opportunities for me to catch people behaving badly. Let the search begin!"

Chapter 41
A Taste Of Their Future

Tuesday, April 17, 1906, 12:17 p.m.
One day before the earthquake and firestorm

With a little imagination and a set of blueprints that were tacked to the wall, anyone could sense the opulence of the newlyweds' new home. It was like a dressmaker's mannequin, ready to be draped in the day's latest fashions.

Clarissa had been working feverishly in recent weeks with a decorator to perfectly appoint each room. Along with the parlor, the dining room would be a showplace to entertain and impress their guests. The combination of emerald green, ivory and gold leaf would add life to what now were simply four wood-stud walls in the shape of a rectangle. By the bay-window frame, a swatch of the green velvet that was to be used for the draperies hung limply.

"Did Faye put you up to this?" asked Brock as the velvet swatch slid through his fingers.

"Having lunch here today? No, this was completely my idea."

"I meant the green in this room. Faye only wears green, right?"

"Yes, she does."

"Every time I see these drapes, I'm going to think of her, and I'm not sure I want to do that," admitted Brock.

"They're just drapes and it's just the color green. But if you want, I'll speak to Jean-Pierre and change it. What color would you like?"

"How about some of that red-and-white checkerboard cloth, like the curtains in the cabin at Twin Peaks?" Brock cocked his head and grinned.

"Let me think about it and I'll get back to you," replied Clarissa. "Ummm, no."

"What if we just leave this all behind and live up at the ranch? It would be so much easier."

Clarissa's eyes opened wide. "No. Absolutely not."

"Is it the cabin? If it is, we could build another one of these houses up on Twin Peaks. We've got the blueprints."

"As I said, absolutely not. Our place is here on Nob Hill. End...of... discussion."

"Then how about blue velvet drapes?" Brock sighed and began to walk away.

"I'll check with Jean-Pierre, but I think blue will be fine. What do you think about putting the birdcage in this corner, near the window? Romeo and Juliet can live happily ever after right here."

She caught up to him and they wandered through the quiet construction site. Before she'd arrived, Clarissa had instructed the foreman to release the crew for the day.

The couple did their best to envision what it would look like when it was finished.

When they arrived at the master-bedroom suite upstairs, Clarissa felt a surge of courage. She slammed Brock's back against the bedroom wall and kissed him just as passionately as he had kissed her earlier.

Her left hand slid behind the nape of Brock's neck, and she drew him in closer to her, taking control of the situation. Brock didn't resist.

Clarissa's kisses grew more intense and immediate, her lips pressing against and gliding across Brock's. Her hands raced urgently around the curves of his shoulders and over his upper chest. He inhaled deeply.

"Are you alright?" asked Clarissa breathlessly. Before he could answer, she started kissing him again. He emitted a long, low groan to acknowledge her question as his back slid down the wall until they were both on the unfinished floor.

Now I have his undivided attention, thought Clarissa, whose face was now flush with heat. In fact, her whole body seemed to be on fire from within. Her senses were heightened, smell and touch especially.

She had never been so aggressively affectionate. Whether she was politely waiting for the signal she got from him earlier today or was simply releasing her bottled-up passion, Brock didn't seem to care.

Her warm, delicate hand slipped inside the front of his shirt, which she mysteriously had been unbuttoned. Her wandering fingers moved slowly down the center of his chest. *I can't believe I'm doing this*, she shouted in her head.

For the first time, she felt the firmness of his pectoral muscles, skin to skin. She slid her index finger from side to side, following the defined, curved contour under each of his breasts. With her thumb, she playfully rolled over his hardened right nipple. He twitched and then groaned again.

"Can you feel my heart pounding?" he asked as if he was racing to catch his breath. Clarissa opened her right hand and gently placed it over Brock's heart. It was pounding, no doubt about it, but not as fast as hers.

Clarissa withdrew her hand as he ran his right hand down the back of her dress, feeling her corset. He pulled her in close with a firm hand at the small of her back. She moaned. *So this is what the poems and songs are all about*, Clarissa thought as her feelings shifted from aggression to submission. She sensed everything within her going soft and limp. But, within seconds, she was back in her aggressive mode and seeking out new pleasures.

Clarissa was becoming intoxicated with the heated sensations. She was sharing a building firestorm.

They separated abruptly when they heard something horrible downstairs that could have included a hammer, a pane of glass and a metal bucket of nails.

With that, it was over. Clarissa froze in the moment.

They started to button what needed buttoning and fasten what needed to be refastened. She began to giggle uncontrollably, but covered her mouth with her hand. The noise they generated prompted a person below to ask, "Luke, is that you upstairs? I've got the nails we needed, but I need to pick up the mess I just made. You heard that, I'm guessing."

Clarissa replied, "Luke isn't here. It's Miss Donohue. Weren't you given the afternoon off?"

"No, ma'am, at least I don't recollect so."

Brock looked at Clarissa and shrugged his shoulders, not having played a part in making or messing up her plans for today.

"I'm here with…ah, with Jean-Pierre." Brock silently mouthed the name Jean-Pierre and gave Clarissa a questioning look, along with a mocking smile.

"We're um, getting a better feel for this, ah, room." Brock laughed without making any detectable sounds. "Go ahead and clean up. Then you may leave for the day."

"Thank you, ma'am. I'll do just that. I'm sorry if I disturbed you and Jean-Pierre up there. My mother always said I was as clumsy as an ox and—" His voice trailed off as Brock walked toward the bay window and gazed down the street. Clarissa snuggled closely behind him and rested her cheek on the side of his left shoulder. They looked in the same direction, a view she'd dreamed for some time now that they'd share each morning as they began their day together looking at the sunrise.

"This is going to be our special place. Every morning, I want you to kiss me right here in this alcove. Brock, I want to feel the warm morning sun and your touch before I do anything else."

Church bells tolled the half hour. They looked at each other. "Church bells will be ringing for us soon," said Clarissa. "Won't they?"

Brock reached around his side to hold Clarissa's left hand. He felt the engagement ring he'd given her, and its existence jarred him back to reality.

"I can hear them now!" he replied.

He was about to marry this woman, live in this house and look out this window for the rest of his life. Day after day, night after night, they'd form a routine, a comfortable routine like every other married couple on Nob Hill. At this moment, that sounded pretty good. Considering how Clarissa revealed her desires moments ago, Brock might have everything a man could want, except a girl named Blossom.

Chapter 42

Rendezvous With The Girls

Tuesday, April 17, 1906, 12:31 p.m.
One day before the earthquake and firestorm

Blossom was standing in front of the bench in the alley with her lunch in her hands as her friends approached. Monique usually stopped by the China 5 Operator office to pick up Anna Mae.

"Why so glum, Sugarplum? I know that we're later than usual. And why are you standing there?" asked Monique tenderly as the pair came closer.

"We have to eat somewhere else today, someplace private," replied Blossom.

"Oh, this is going to be good," added Anna Mae with obvious interest.

"I'm not sure if it's good or bad, but I can't tell you here." Blossom began to walk away.

Monique and Anna Mae raised their shoulders in unison, looked at each other in a confused way and followed.

"Let's go down by the cribs," suggested Monique. "Nobody talks or listens down there. There's just a lot of grunting. Men in and men out, the girls barely come up for air. We can talk safely there," she added, directing them toward the row of prostitutes' shelters a few blocks away.

They found a bench in the area and sat down. Instinctively, none of them opened their lunches, knowing that this was not a time to eat.

Blossom cleared her throat. "You know how I've never felt like I fit in here."

"Who does?" asked Monique as she looked all around herself.

"If this is about your lavender eyes, we've always thought they made you exotic, not different," reassured Anna Mae.

Their conversation was interrupted by two men who were looking for a good time during their lunch hour. Monique sent them away with a few choice words and redirected their attention to several crib girls who were standing outside their doorways, advertising their wares.

"So get on with it. Tell us more," urged Anna Mae.

"But what about my hair color and my skin color? What about my mother?" Blossom asked.

"Your mother? She gave you all of that," said Monique. "You can tell because your father doesn't look exactly like you."

Blossom spoke again. "It's about my mother. She's alive."

"She's what?" the two said at nearly the same time.

"Grand Ma Maw told me last night that my mother didn't die when I was a baby. Her name is Cameo Rose. Actually, her name is Iris Lancaster. She's white and a prostitute. Or maybe she was a prostitute then and isn't now. I really don't know."

Monique and Anna Mae did not make a single noise or gesture.

"She left me to be raised as a Chinese baby by my father and Grand Ma Maw. She left me this brooch."

The girls each reached out and touched it, tipping it in several ways to take in the beauty of its three blooming white roses against the caramel-brown background.

Blossom continued to speak to her silent lunch mates. "She writes letters and sends some money every now and then, with no return address. So we don't know where she is, but she's out there."

Blossom reached into her pocket and pulled out the photograph of her mother.

Still silent, the girls took turns looking at the photo. With unusually wide-open eyes, they took in everything they were hearing and seeing.

"My life has been one…big…fat…lie. I thought I knew who I was and now I'm somebody else. The woman who brought me into this world has not left the planet, she's out there somewhere." Blossom took a deep breath.

"She's kept her distance. How does a mother do that? Was she just being selfish and moving on with *her* life? Or did she love me so much that she had to leave me behind…for my own good?"

Blossom looked at her friends. "What's the matter with you two? I just told you all of that and you don't make so much as a peep! You've never been this quiet before."

"Are you done?" asked Anna Mae.

"Because we have lots of questions. At least I do," added Monique.

"Yes, I'm done."

"First of all, have you told Brock?" asked Monique.

"No. I just found out last night and it's only lunch time," Blossom replied. "When would I have seen him? When I do see him again, I doubt that I'll start the conversation with this news. But it does explain a lot. I've only known him for—" Blossom looked up and counted in her head. "It's hardly been four days. I guess he might as well know all there is to know about me, even as I'm finding it out too."

"You…are…so…in…love," cooed Anna Mae.

"Hey," added Monique, "I'm in love too. I'm in a serious relationship with prime rib and baked potatoes!" Her humorous comment broke the conversation's intensity.

The pair went on to ask their questions.

Blossom felt relieved after confiding in her closest friends, but then tensed up. "You have to swear to tell *no one* about this."

The pair acknowledged the secret nature of what they'd been entrusted with just as a drunk dock worker approached.

"How much for all three of you—together—at one time?" he slurred.

"Mister," replied Monique, "first of all, what you said is completely redundant." The man looked confused. "And second, while your offer is almost irresistible, we can resist. So move on. There are plenty of good times for you to have in any of the stalls down the alley."

"Are you sure about that?" he asked as he farted and scratched his crotch.

"If we weren't before, we're completely sure now!" replied Anna Mae with a giggle.

"Let's get out of here," said Blossom as she rose to her feet. "I don't want anyone to see us down here. I have enough secrets to keep…and now you two do too!"

Chapter 43
$\mathcal{N}$ot A Misfit After All

Tuesday, April 17, 1906, 3:11 p.m.
One day before the earthquake and firestorm

Every time the bakery's front doorbell jingled, Blossom's heart skipped a beat. One time, Blossom thought, *Brock will come through that doorway again.* She knew it. Until then, she had to settle for her memories of last Saturday afternoon.

"Work, work, work, my precious daughter," said Chang, bringing Blossom back to the task at hand. "Grand Ma Maw see you daydreaming again, you in big, big, big troubles."

"Yes, Ba Ba. Yes, Ba Ba. Yes, Ba Ba," Blossom replied, mocking his triple-repeat speech pattern.

"But first, I need some fresh air. I'm going for a little walk."

"Where you go, my child?"

"Oh, here and there. I need to get the flower for tonight's arrangement. Perhaps it will be a scarlet carnation or a yellow mum. You never know what Ruby's going to have in her flower basket. I'll be back in 10 minutes. You can time me if you wish."

"Yes, I wish," said Chang as he caught his last glimpse of Blossom as she headed out the back door into the alley.

With the ringing of bells, Grand Ma Maw entered the front door. The look on her face got Chang's immediate attention.

"Where Blossom?" demanded the old woman.

"She just leave out back door," Chang responded matter-of-factly.

"When she return, we must talk…we three."

Blossom walked slowly and found herself at the Tie Yick General Store. She peered into the window pane that she'd been gazing into before Brock took her to Twin Peaks. Blossom noticed her pulse speed up and her face warm. She pulled at the stiff mandarin collar of her scarlet blouse, which showcased her mother's brooch. Then she brushed away the flour and any other evidence of her life at the bakery.

I wonder if Brock would think I look incredible now.

Just a few steps away, Blossom found the flower seller at her usual spot.

"Hi Ruby, what's in your basket today? I know I'm later than usual, so my choices will be limited."

"My Blossom, I set aside something very special for you on this fine day," said Ruby as she reached behind her chair to pull out a flaming-red tulip, with a canary yellow center.

"Oh, it's spectacular. Thank you so much for saving it for me. The colors will certainly grab our customers' attention tonight!"

As Blossom passed a few coins to the old woman, Ruby replied, "You bring sunshine to me when you visit. I not speak of this before, but I see you bring your sunshine to someone else on Sunday. You wearing someone else's clothes. Your hair up. Your smile wider than I ever see it before. He special to you, yes?"

"Yes, he's special to me."

Sang Yuen, the street-side fortuneteller, was close enough to hear Blossom's admission.

"Then my heart soar for you, but my mind…it worry for you. Be wise. Be wiser than your age," warned Ruby. "You must know that your secret is my secret, but others may not be so protective of you."

"I too look forward to your visits," said the fortuneteller. "Each day I say 'good fortune is yours today.' But now—" He stopped speaking to study her more than usual. "Come close. Give me your hand."

Blossom held out her right hand. Her left one held the red tulip. The fortuneteller placed one of his hands above and below her hand, closed his eyes, inhaled deeply and then opened his eyes widely to connect with hers.

"Something different today. Something different in your *future*. A matter of the heart I think. This man you talking about with Ruby, he change your heart. He change it for good. Chinatown is not—"

Blossom pulled her hand back. "Oh, that reminds me. I'm already late getting back home. I must go. Thank you, thank you both."

As she turned to head back to The Golden Palace, a white family—a father, a mother, two daughters and a chubby son—walked by, commenting about the sights and sounds of Chinatown. Blossom noticed how they, especially the mother, walked with their noses so high they could drown in a sudden April shower.

She politely watched them pass by as the mother said loudly, "Children, don't touch that ching chong. You never know when the plague might come back to this part of town, and you might catch it on *these* streets and from *these* people." The woman turned to her husband and added, "Why did you bring us to this *filthy* chink-filled place?"

The boy pulled his pumpkin-shaped face with his hands to make his eyes slanty. He stuck his tongue out of his tightened lips.

"Do you see any cats?" she asked.

"Cats?" replied the father.

"Yes, Mrs. Ford told me that when you look for a Chinese restaurant to eat at—not that we *ever* would—you should look for cats."

"I repeat, cats?"

"Yes, if there are cats out and about, then that restaurant isn't cooking with them."

Blossom thought that this woman must have been raised with better manners, and how the woman incorrectly assumed that she, Ruby and Sang didn't speak English.

"Such blindness they have," said Ruby.

Blossom fought the urge to set the record straight about the plague in Chinatown and how it had been eradicated. As she thought it over once more and gazed into the window pane, the reflection of what looked like three ostriches passed by. She looked a second time. If anyone only looked at them from the shoulders up, the three women who had just strolled by with elaborate ostrich-plumed hats could have been mistaken for birds. Blossom was mesmerized by the way the air made the feathers flow as the women walked.

Someday I'll have a hat like that, piled high to the sky with feathers and ribbons. Brock's fiancée probably wears hats like that and she shops with girlfriends like those women and...

The ringing of a nearby church bell announced that it was 2:30. Blossom brought herself back to reality. *There's no way not to be late now.* She looked down at the flower petals that rested at Ruby's feet.

"You know what? For the longest time I thought your job was called a 'flower petaler,'" she said as she brushed the ground and captured a few wayward petals with her hand. "Even though I know that you're a flower peddler, I still think of you as a petaler. I just thought you should know that!" said Blossom as she tossed the petals to the passing breeze and waved goodbye to Ruby. Blossom made her way back to the bakery with the red tulip.

"Ten minutes, you say," Chang reminded Blossom of her earlier commitment as she entered the door.

"I know, but I got distracted." She twirled the tulip gently between her fingers and looked her father straight in the eyes. "It's not like this was the first time it's happened, but why do white people look at us as if we're part of some exhibit in a museum? Is it ever going to end? A woman said that we serve cat meat in our food, and she called me a *chink* and a *ching chong* in one breath. I'm embarrassed to admit it, but now that I know that I'm partly white, it makes me even madder that they look at me as if I just arrived from Shanghai and can't speak a word of English."

"What inside matter most. Not outside. Not clothes. Not shape of eye. Not skin. Not language." He continued and pointed to his eyes with both index fingers, "My eyes see your beauty. Their eyes, they see something exotic and mysterious. Or, we look *evil* and mysterious. Not much in between."

"That's it. I'm in between. I don't belong with them and I don't exactly belong here either. I'm in between, a misfit."

Grand Ma Maw came up from behind Blossom and wrapped her arms around her. "You are no misfit. You fit perfectly right here in my arms. You always have. You always will."

"Thank you, Grand Ma Maw," Blossom whispered as she clung closely to the old woman, knowing that Grand Ma Maw would not always be there to help pick up the pieces when her life fell apart.

Blossom noticed how Grand Ma Maw's hug stiffened and then she dropped her arms.

"It pains me, but I must tell you both something." She turned Blossom around and looked at her, then at Chang.

"For first time, Blossom, you topic of ladies' discussion today at mahjong table. And it not good discussion. Humiliated. Embarrassed. Those my feelings."

Blossom gave a sideways look toward her father.

"Oh, the China 4 must have really been bored if they had to resort to talking about me. Did someone see me going to visit Monique at the Maison Bijou?" asked Blossom as she tried to finagle her way out of this situation. She quickly sensed that it wasn't working.

"As you been told many time before, we not China 4," clarified Grand Ma Maw. "You seen with white man in carriage. Not once, but twice," she said holding up one finger and then a second.

"Your Mr. St. Clair, yes?" Grand Ma Maw asked.

Blossom knew this was serious and decided that a straightforward response would be best.

"Yes, I was with Brock."

"You bring shame upon yourself, also upon our family. This must stop," commanded the old woman.

"Yes, must stop," seconded Chang.

Blossom was silent for a moment. Then, fully knowing the disrespect she'd be showing, she fired back a crisp and defiant, "No."

Grand Ma Maw banged her walking stick onto the floorboards and instructed, "Speak no more, unless you can improve the silence."

The old woman walked away.

To Blossom, the silence was painful.

Chapter 44
An Inconveniently Placed Piece Of Paper

Tuesday, April 17, 1906, 4:20 p.m.
One day before the earthquake and firestorm

"You're home!" announced Mrs. Donohue as Clarissa and Brock came through the front door. "Eleven more gift packages were delivered today!"

"More pickle castors and cruet sets I expect," replied Clarissa, waving her right arm with a flourish toward a special table set up near the dining room to display their wedding gifts.

"Honestly, I don't care if you get 100 pickle castors, and I don't care if you ever serve your guests pickles from them. You'll receive them graciously and enthusiastically, even if no one else is around," Mrs. Donohue reprimanded.

"What about the broken pickle castor and the shattered glass wedding basket? Should I graciously receive trash?" asked Clarissa.

Zelda's snickers from down the hallway were not muffled enough. They didn't go unnoticed.

"I wonder if someone *might be dropping my packages* after she receives them from the delivery boys. I wonder who that might be?"

Brock, Mrs. Donohue and Clarissa all turned in the direction of the hallway, but could hear or see nothing.

Mrs. Donohue changed the topic quickly with, "Say, how was that picnic of yours?"

Brock unlatched the hamper so she could see its emptiness.

"That's just as it should be at the end of the afternoon," she said.

"But I'm still hungry," Brock admitted as he looked into the dining room and spied the fortune cookie on the buffet.

As swiftly as he could said, "Oh look, an extra dessert," Brock cracked open the cookie.

"I know Faye didn't want to open it," said Clarissa in a cautionary way, "but I don't know if she wanted anyone else to open it either."

"It was Faye's? Well, too late now. Want to hear her fortune?" Brock responded playfully. He read it to himself, mouthing each word. Then he read it aloud.

"Tomorrow will bring you problems that you do not have today."

Clarissa looked at Brock and didn't say a thing.

"Now I can see why she didn't want to open it," said Brock. "I wonder if the fortune is now mine, since I opened it? Or is it still Faye's because it was hers to begin with?"

Clarissa looked at him with a puzzled expression. "I don't know, and considering the prophecy, I don't even want to think about it."

Mrs. Donohue chimed in. "I've always felt the future is what you make it. A prophecy wrapped in a sweet cookie is just an inconveniently placed piece of paper if you ask me."

Clarissa theatrically swirled her hands in the air and announced, "I'm surrounded by pearls of wisdom from cookies, from mothers and from my fiancé. How lucky can a girl get?"

Chapter 45

*L*iving Dangerously

Tuesday, April 17, 1906, 5:30 p.m.
One day before the earthquake and firestorm

Blossom looked twice, not believing what she saw through the restaurant's front window. It was Brock, no doubt about it. He was doing his best to catch her attention. She smiled at him, but quickly turned to see if her father or Grand Ma Maw had observed the exchange. Luckily, both were uncharacteristically unaware. However, Butch was aware. Brock made some hand signals that Blossom deciphered as "I'll meet you out back." She nodded and made her way to the kitchen.

Butch looked around, left his dinner on the table and stomped out the front door.

"Are you trying your best to make a mess of everything?" Blossom asked as she hurried out into the alley and into Brock's arms. She looked all around and up to the open windows as well.

"Ah, to hell with it!" she said and smiled for a brief moment before Brock's lips made it impossible to speak.

They blocked out the world and kept kissing, swaying side to side. They moved in a circular motion as if they were slow dancing to a song no one else could hear.

"Do you feel like someone's watching us? I do," said Brock.

"Even when there isn't anyone watching, it always feels like someone is. Brock, get used to it. I have!"

If the brazen, public kiss wasn't risky enough, Blossom was about to say something that would definitely get attention.

"If my heart was a balloon, it would have burst by now," whispered Blossom. "I am so filled with love for you. I can't understand how that's possible in four days, but it is. I'm sure of it."

Brock didn't know how to react to Blossom's use of the word "love" and the admission of her deep feelings, so he kissed her again.

"What's this?" asked Brock as he gently ran his finger over the cream and caramel-colored cameo brooch on Blossom's collar.

In a serious tone she answered, "I have something to tell—"

"Is it about the dare?" Brock interrupted. "Monique already told me that—"

"Have you no sense? Have you two lost your minds!" Anna Mae announced in a false voice that sounded like Grand Ma Maw.

"Shoo-shoo," she added, as if she'd come across two stray dogs coupling in the alley.

Anna Mae burst into outrageous laughter and hugged them.

"You really know how to live dangerously," she added in her own voice this time. "If Butch saw you…well, there's no telling what he might think or do!"

Blossom responded, "Don't you have someplace to be, like…um… let's say…not here?"

"No, my break just got started, so I have a full fifteen minutes. Wouldn't you know it, though, that gossip Kitty and I are on the same shift tonight. Every time I want to bust out of there to be with you, she's watching me and the clock. Blossom, hopefully we can talk a minute or two, if you can pull your *lips* away from his. I ran over here to catch up on your romance, but I've seen it now for myself since you're so public about it. I'll just be on my way and leave you two to carry on and let all of Chinatown know your private business."

Anna Mae turned in a mockingly dramatic way and started to walk away.

"Hold on there, little missy."

Anna Mae pivoted around to make eye contact with Blossom.

As the girls conversed in Chinese, Brock began to question his intentions with Clarissa and Blossom. *Am I being totally selfish? How's this going to end?*

The two friends chattered away as Brock was thinking and looking distant and removed. He spied Ting Ting taking in the sights and sounds from a window above the alley. He didn't let her know he'd seen her.

Brock heard the snapping of fingers. "Hey, farmer boy, where are you?" asked Anna Mae. "We're here in this alley. Are you with us still?"

"Yes, of course."

When I'm with Blossom, she's the one I want. When I'm with Clarissa, I'm pretty sure she's the one I want. I can't believe I'm playing—

"Honestly, Brock, would you rather be somewhere else?" asked Anna Mae.

"I have to get back in the restaurant. I'm surprised they haven't sent out a pack of search dogs to find me," said Blossom as she turned toward the door to open it.

"Bark! Bark! Bark!" announced the old woman in the doorway. "This dog found you. What your next move, my dears?"

Blossom turned and kissed Brock on the cheek and scampered back to her customers. Grand Ma Maw looked up and into Brock's eyes.

"Her heart is full of you now. That no secret to anyone. What you do next, that your choice. She carry that choice in her heart forever." She stared at him for what seemed like a painful amount of time to Brock.

What is she saying? Does she actually want me to choose Blossom? Is she telling me to leave and never come back even if it breaks Blossom's heart?

Brock stood there, immobilized. Grand Ma Maw walked slowly back into the building.

"Well, she told you!" said Anna Mae.

"Yes, she sure did!" added Ting Ting from above. She waved to Brock.

"Don't you need to get back to work?" Brock asked Anna Mae. "And don't you have something better to do, Ting Ting?"

"You sure know how to make a girl feel welcome. Yes, my time here is over. I'm on my way, see?" Anna Mae started to walk away. "But you, Brock, are still standing there."

He was. He stood there motionless as she rounded the corner and disappeared. Brock felt lightheaded and loosened his collar.

Now what?

Chapter 46

Totally Happy And Totally Miserable

Tuesday, April 17, 1906, 6:17 p.m.
One day before the earthquake and firestorm

After wandering around the streets of Chinatown unsuccessfully attempting to collect his thoughts, Brock ended up at the front window of The Golden Palace yet again. He looked in and watched Blossom control the attention of the men in the restaurant. She glided around the room with grace and elegance in an atmosphere that was neither graceful nor elegant. Comfortable? Yes. Graceful and elegant. No.

It was inevitable that she'd look up and catch his image in the window. She smiled at him warmly, lowering her shoulders and cocking her head slightly to the side as if to ask, "What am I going to do with you?"

He made the same hand gesture as before and mouthed the words, "I'll be back at ten o'clock." Then he began to head for the alley, but stopped.

Blossom looked to the restaurant's entry to see if Chang was there. He wasn't. She pointed to the door in a gesture Brock couldn't miss.

They met in the building's front entry.

"We have to talk this through," Brock blurted out with a sense of urgency and impatience.

Blossom responded, "What's *this?* What do you need to talk through exactly?"

"You…and me. We…or I…have to sort this out. I know it's up to me, and I feel totally happy and totally miserable at the same time. I can't take it."

She jumped in, "You can't take it! What about me? And what do you mean, it's up to you?"

"You're right. We can't take it, and it's up to us," acknowledged Brock.

But, at that moment, Brock didn't realize that he should be including Clarissa in that reference to "us."

"I'll be in the alley at ten o'clock to meet you, and we'll go somewhere to talk. Will your grandmother still be awake? Or, should I come later?"

"Ten is fine."

He took a risk and quickly kissed her, and gently pushed her back into the restaurant.

"Bye for now."

"You can bet your—" said Blossom. She looked up and down Brock for a visual cue to complete her statement. She continued, "You can bet your boots it's only bye for now!"

Chapter 47

*C*andles And Cologne

Tuesday, April 17, 1906, 8:10 p.m.
One day before the earthquake and firestorm

Austin's outrageously loud belch at the base of the staircase reverberated throughout the St. Clair house. It should have come as no surprise to anyone who knew him, since he always could be counted on for inappropriateness.

"Honestly, are you *ever* going to act like a gentleman?" asked Mrs. St. Clair in an exasperated way. "This is not a barroom or a barnyard."

"Speaking of barnyards," spoke up Austin, "where's your fair-haired son, the one with the polished manners and the manure on his boots?"

"Austin, I don't keep tabs on Brock's every move. He's got a business to run and a fiancée to attend to. I sometimes wonder if he even lives here anymore with his comings and goings. Though, I have to admit, he's been more preoccupied and distracted than usual when he's here," reflected Brock's mother.

"Oh, if you only knew. He seems so *smitten* these days. Have you noticed?" asked Austin in a probing way.

She looked at him quizzically, but wasn't willing to take the bait.

"In no time at all, Brock and Clarissa will be guests in this house, and you'll finally get all the attention this household can shower on you. Won't that be dandy?"

"Dandy," said Austin as he wrinkled his nose. He turned to walk away. "Yeah, more attention, that's just what I've been looking for all of my life." He then thought, *I know where I can go to get some real attention.*

Austin left and headed straight to the Maison Bijou in Chinatown. An evening with Monique would set the world right.

The bordello's foyer was unattended when he arrived. So, Austin raced up the stairs as quietly as he could.

Without as much as a knock on the door, he entered Monique's fourth-floor suite. This was an impolite practice he'd started some time ago. If the door was locked, she was entertaining a client. If it was unlocked, the rush of his entry was delightfully met with a squeal of naughtiness, as if he'd just seized his own personal heaven on earth.

He scanned the room, only to find Monique missing. Her poodle, Peaches, whined with excitement at the possibility of being released from her confining, even if plush, kennel in the corner of the room. Austin noted how the shiny gold duvet was neatly covering the bed. Though the room was bathed in the glow of moonlight, there were no burning candles to shimmer in the many mirrors scattered around the room.

He thought about how much less interesting and intriguing the room was without her there. He took Peaches out of her cage, petted her head, gently pulled her cotton-ball-like tail and put her back in her kennel.

Austin wandered down several flights of stairs. On the first floor, he headed toward the reception area to ask Madam Bijou about Monique, trying hard not to hear what was unavoidable in the hallway of a whorehouse. The audible expressions of passion and pleasure only heightened his need to find Monique.

With a kiss on an outstretched and welcoming right hand, Austin asked, "Madam, where might I find Monique on this very fine evening?"

"*Mon cheri*, she is out running an errand, as her engagement had a change of heart at the last moment. *C'est la vie!*

"Well, that poor sap's 'change of heart' will be my good fortune, when Monique returns, that is."

He eyed Madam Bijou from head-to-toe and then toe-to-head. *She must have been quite the complete package in her day*, he mused.

"Is there something I can do for you?" she asked, giving him a head-to-toe and toe-to-head glance in return. The motion of her eyes stopped on the way back up on a bulge in the front of his pants, but off to the side in an unusual position. Austin followed her stare. To solve the mystery, he reached in and pulled out the wad of money he always carried.

"People tell me that I carry too much cash. But I like it, and it's impressive. Don't you agree?"

"Oh, yes," she said and smiled. "Very impressive!"

Austin returned the smile, winked and went back to Monique's room to wait for her to return. Once there, he lit a few candles and sprayed cologne from the gold-toned glass atomizer on her vanity. The room glowed in a golden way and smelled of vanilla and essence of rose.

It wasn't long before Monique returned with several wrapped boxes. Slightly out of breath from climbing the numerous flights of stairs to get to the top floor of the building, she paused at the door and then entered.

"Well, hello," announced Austin. "I thought something bad might have happened."

"Don't worry," replied Monique. "With you around, it will!"

"Let me help you with those."

"What a nice surprise to see you. Do you have any other surprises for me tonight?"

He put the packages down on the table and pulled her close with an abrupt sense of urgency. "I don't know. But I bet if we put our heads together, we can come up with a surprise or two. You know me!"

"Yes, I do know you and somehow I still like you! In fact, I like you quite a lot." She pulled away and took a few steps. "Stop toying with me."

"But I'm a child and I like toys. I especially like *your* toys," added Austin.

"So, how long are you planning to be here?" she asked.

"I'm all yours...for the whole night."

"Isn't that something I should say to you?"

"Either way, I don't want to be home. I'd rather be here with you."

Monique nodded. "I guess that's good enough for this girl. My night is your night. Say, did you feel the earthquake? Everyone around town is talking about the Earth Dragon moving."

"I don't know about any Earth Dragon moving, but do you want to see my dragon move? Wait. Don't answer that question. I know you do!"

He stood there and stripped away his clothes like unpeeling a banana. Liberated shirt buttons flew in all directions. Monique watched his magician-like performance until he was completely naked and a pool of clothes swirled around his feet. She took measured steps toward him to slow down his pace.

"Whoa, we have all night!" Her comment was pointless. He was ready to go. The warm, flickering candlelight revealed his "dragon" twitching and dancing erratically. For added effect, he raised his arms and made his biceps flex to an unheard drum beat. For his average size, he was more muscular than many man—especially businessmen and the city's non-laboring elite.

"Well, I can see there's no stopping you now!"

"No. But I'm not one to rush, am I?"

Before Monique could respond, Austin pulled her close. He cupped the back of her head and swung her down as if they'd just finished dancing the tango.

He kissed her right cheek. He caressed and kissed her left check.

Austin brushed the runaway hair from her forehead and kissed there too.

He's good. Maybe he's the one for me. A kiss on the lips, someday, a kiss... *on...the...lips.* Her thoughts became fractured as he kissed her neck and expertly removed each piece of her clothing and pooled them with his nearby.

Monique glanced in one of her room's mirrors. *Now that's a beautiful sight,* she thought referring to the firm slope of his derriere. She watched how the candlelight illuminated and shaded the hallowed, smooth indentations on each side of his buttocks.

He continued to kiss her neck while he turned her around, kissing each bit of flesh on her neck as she rotated. She knew he craved her. And she craved him. Her need was overpowering like a vampire needs blood.

He kept guiding her to spin slowly. Again she peered into one of the looking glasses and witnessed Austin caressing her breasts. *One...blessed...* *nipple...at...a...time.* He rubbed and nudged their firmness. His soft fingertips traveled down to her waist as she continued to turn. His fingertip circled her navel and wandered slowly downward. His fingers swirled in curves and circles. It was as if he was elaborately frosting a cake. *And how I do love icing on my cake!*

Monique sensed that Austin could contain himself no more. He guided her back to the gold duvet that covered the bed. Though she was moving backward, Monique knew that their lovemaking was only going forward at this point. Most times, Austin used his body to worship her like a goddess. *A goddess, yes, worship me like goddess!*

However, like a starving man entering a banquet hall, Austin soon engorged himself until he was satisfied...and, as fate would have it, so was she.

Her contentment was clear by the tension escaping her naked body and the slowing pace of her racing heart. Austin sprawled on his back next to her. She could hear his breathing calming down.

"We'll live happily ever after, you and me," said Austin contently. He wiped the sweaty sheen from his forehead.

"Austin, people like us don't get happily ever afters. We're lucky to get an 'ever after.'"

"I'm fine with that. So long as we're together."

Hmmmm, I like the way "together" sounds. I could get used that!

Chapter 48
$\mathcal{S}$tardust

Tuesday, April 17, 1906, 10:06 p.m.
One day before the earthquake and firestorm

At last, some cool air and a chance to sit down, thought Blossom. She'd worked extra hard to close and clean up the restaurant in order to get her father and Grand Ma Maw off to bed. She was not about to miss the first possible chance to slip away to talk "things" over with Brock. She sat in the alley with her tattered sketchbook, drawing the flower pots on the shadowy window sill across the way. She often drew to calm herself and pass the time when time needed to pass quickly, even if the light was as low as it was in the alley.

The sound of heavy feet and the silhouette of an approaching man distracted her. As the figure entered a more well-lit section of the alley, Blossom saw Butch's face. *That's all I need right now!*

Down the alley in the other direction, Brock arrived in his carriage. "Blossom, I'm over here," Brock announced discretely to get Blossom's attention.

She realized that Butch was getting too close to ignore or pretend not to notice. "Butch, I hope you're having a good evening. Bye now."

She took off toward the carriage before Butch could get close to her.

She thought she heard the word "mine" and she turned around to check. But Butch was standing there, silent as always. "Mine, *gwai lo*, she's mine," Blossom thought she heard, but did not turn back this time. *Gwai lo? A white person? A 'ghost person'...is that what he said?*

Brock began to properly greet her and help her into the carriage, but she helped herself and climbed into the rig in one swift move. She put her sketchbook on her lap and her purse on the seat. "At least I don't have Monique's blasted skirt to trip over this time! Let's go."

She looked down at her silky pale blue jacket and billowy pants, and her flat black shoes.

"I like what you're wearing. Do you?"

"I suppose. But Brock, all of my clothes look like this, and I guess they always will."

"Well that suits me!"

Blossom swiveled on the seat and stared straight into Brock's eyes. "Wait. Before we go, are you saying goodbye? Tell me. I can take it. But I won't be able to bear it if you drag it out. Just say it now if you're going to. Go ahead."

The horses lurched forward as Butch came in their direction.

"No, not to you," Brock said to the horses with a tug of the reins.

They smiled at each other as Brock leaned forward to kiss her, but she didn't respond. Instead, she looked in Butch's direction and said, "Let's go, really...let's go."

Brock gave the horses the signal to go, and they did. The conversation, however, did not move forward. Silence prevailed as Blossom considered what to say next and how to say it.

Once they got to the outskirts of Chinatown, Blossom broke her silence. "Why do I have the feeling that I'm going to remember this night for the rest of my life? Will it be a good memory or a bad one? Come on, tell me."

Brock stopped the horses by a glowing street lamp. He reached into the back of the carriage and pulled forward a large, white hatbox tied shut with an immense pink bow.

"Whether it's good or bad, that's up to you, Blossom."

"Fair enough."

"This is for you. It's my turn to give you a gift," said Brock with an ever-widening smile. "I hope you like it. I remembered something you told me, and I wanted to make that wish come true."

He didn't say goodbye. That's a start. Blossom felt more at ease. In fact, she was stunned and at ease at the same time. She'd never received such a lavish package, especially with that kind of thoughtful sentiment.

"May I open it now?"

"If you want to."

Want to? Of course I want to. But, it's so beautiful. Maybe I should wait. No. She placed her sketch book on the carriage's seat next to her handbag. Gingerly, she coaxed the ribbon's knot free, which released a single long-stemmed red rose. Setting the rose to her side, she lifted the lid and pulled back the white and pink polka-dotted tissue paper that protected and concealed the box's contents.

"Oh!" Blossom forced from her tightened throat. "It's the most amazing thing I've ever seen!"

She lifted out a cream-colored hat embellished with an array of beads, pearls, lace, ribbons and elegant ostrich feathers. Also in the box was a hat pin in the shape of a pine cone that was encrusted with faceted black stones and clear crystals. Even in the nighttime light it shimmered. The hat's wide brim sloped down in the front, which would naturally draw everyone's attention right to her eyes.

"Brock, it's breathtaking, it's truly breathtaking. I don't think I can breathe!"

"I remembered what you said the other day when you described the woman you'd seen wearing a hat with feathers on it. But what I really remembered was *how* you described it. I could tell you wanted one badly."

"Thank you. I love it! Brock, you can't possibly know how much I love it." She smiled with every part of her face.

"I think I can *see* how much," he replied as he signaled to the horses to move. "The rose is for your next flower arrangement, but you better not tell Grand Ma Maw where you got it or who you got it from."

Blossom beamed.

They sat close: shoulder to shoulder, arm to arm, leg to leg. It was a seamless matching that was reinforced as she gracefully laid her left hand on his right thigh. It helped to steady her as the carriage jostled the pair on the way up to the stables. That was one benefit of their contact. The other benefit was simple: it felt good, even reassuring to Blossom. With both of Brock's hands on the reins, she couldn't hold them during the ride.

"Can we just vanish? I never knew I could feel like this. I don't know if I can go on *not* feeling like this."

"I'm guessing you want to start our conversation before we even reach Twin Peaks?" Brock responded.

"You guessed correctly," said Blossom as she patted his right thigh.

"Where do we start?" he asked as he checked the road ahead and then her face.

"Where do we end?" she added.

The last question killed the conversation. Brock ultimately got his way, and the pair rode in silence the rest of the way to Twin Peaks.

After the carriage stopped on the hilltop, Brock helped Blossom down onto the hard-packed dirt near the horse barn. He lit one of the hand-held kerosene lamps and grabbed a large folded blanket.

Gubbs peered around the corner to make sure all was well, this being his place of work as well as his residence. Seeing a familiar face, he motioned to Brock to come over to him. He took Brock around the building's corner, leaving Blossom standing alone for the moment.

"I got one last piece of advice fer yuh. Then I'll be as quiet as tha prairie just before a tornado. Pork Chop, yuh can't ride two horses with only one ass. Yuh need to make yer choice and be done with it."

His crass assessment of Brock's situation was all too true. The time had come.

"You're right. Tonight's the night. That's why we're here." Brock thought, *I just wish I knew exactly how this is going to turn out!*

"Well, right now there's a woman standin' around the corner who I 'spect won't be makin' cookies in Chinatown no more." With a wink of his eye and a pat on Brock's back, Gubbs disappeared into the dark stable.

Brock returned to Blossom. "Let's go down on the hillside." He took her to the same spot where they'd spent time together before. It felt entirely different at night for Blossom. The hazy, fog-veiled view of the city lights and the moon on the bay were magical, even with the awkward situation. It was difficult to see where the earth ended and the heavens began. But as Blossom's gaze went upward, above the haze she discovered a glistening tapestry of stars. *Heaven on earth, that's what this is*, she thought.

Brock spread out the blanket, smoothing one crumpled corner. He placed the lantern at the back edge of the blanket closest to the tree. As the couple sat down, the light flooded behind them, creating a flickering amber glow on everything close to the blanket.

Blossom put her hand on Brock's hand, her fingers intertwined with his.

"You're trembling," she said with a note of concern.

"I'll be alright." He exhaled and deeply inhaled, then leaned toward her. He began to form a word with his lips, but closed his mouth in what appeared to Blossom as frustration. His lips parted again and his words flowed. "Blossom, it seems like my life began the day we met. I have feelings when I'm with you that I've never had before. You make everything seem brighter and more interesting. You don't take anything for granted. That's how I want to be. And, when I'm with you, I am."

Whoa, did I just hear that right?

He went on. "I know what's expected of me on Nob Hill. That was all fine until I met you. Now, everything's changed."

Brock stopped and then swallowed purposefully as if to set the stage for what he was about to say.

"I love you, Blossom. There, I've said it. Now you know."

Blossom looked into his eyes. "I know. I already knew. My heart beats for you…it's beating very fast right now!"

Oh my ancestors, help me…help me to say this without it coming out a babbling mess!

She continued, "What we do with our love is up to us now. Grand Ma Maw says there's always enough love to go around. Do you love me enough to share your life with me?"

"Yes," he said and kissed her on the lips. "Yes," and he kissed her more firmly. "Yes," and he kissed her a third time.

Blossom's heart beat even faster. It didn't go unnoticed that he said "yes" once, twice and then three times. *Surely that was a sign of good fortune.*

"From now on, any step I take away from you will be a step in the wrong direction. I'll end it with Clarissa tomorrow morning. I'm not sure how, but I will. I'm going to break a heart to follow mine…to you." Brock paused and sighed. "Nothing will come between you and me again."

He chose me! He...chose...me!

"What are you thinking about?"

"That you made your choice, and it was me."

Brock replied, "Loving you is not a choice."

She looked up at him, slowly this time. She gazed at an ecstasy that had been out of reach, until now.

"Don't talk," she said, turning the tables on Brock. "Just sit there." She slowly looked down to the ground and closed her eyes. "Okay, I've got it!" she said to indicate that she'd captured the vision of him. She opened her eyes slowly and grinned somewhat timidly.

She moved closer to Brock and rested her head on his chest. His heart was beating so strongly that she could feel each beat. Blossom noticed everything. Every sound. Every smell. Her senses were alive. Her mind raced through the last few days. About how he listened to her. About how he watched her. About eating fried chicken and flying a dragon kite. About seeing his face through the window of The Golden Palace. She felt satisfied and completely comfortable.

Brock leaned back and rested on his elbows. He looked skyward. Blossom moved so that her head still rested on his heart and her body was close to his. Brock's left arm wrapped around her.

"I have another gift for you," said Blossom tenderly. "I'm giving you my 'forever.'"

"Your 'forever?'"

"Yes, you know, that 'forever and ever' people always talk about. I'm giving you my 'forever.'"

Everything feels right. I'm not going to say another word. This is perfect.

Before long, their reclined embrace and star-gazing lulled them into a quiet slumber.

Chapter 49

$\mathcal{T}$he Earth Dragon Stirs

Wednesday, April 18, 1906, 5:12 a.m.
The day of the earthquake and firestorm

With incomparable force and explosive energy, the earth shook beneath Brock and Blossom at 5:12 a.m. They woke up to an ungodly grinding in the ground and the startled cries of the livestock. Everything around them seemed to spring to life, surprised by the violent movement. The shaking went on for what seemed like an eternity as they held each other.

While according to Chinese tradition, this was a sign the Earth Dragon was moving, according to science, two of the world's greatest tectonic plates, the Pacific and the North American, were no longer able to bear the geologic tension. With the fury of two battling fire-breathing dragons, they lurched past each other.

"This is bad, really bad," said Blossom as she realized they were not only experiencing a major earthquake, but she wasn't going to be in her bed when Grand Ma Maw woke up. "When's it going to stop?"

The ground shouted and growled at them. Everything seemed to slam against the earth again, as if God was a blacksmith at his anvil and he'd just hammered the ground. "It's twisting now, and going up and down. Brock, when's it going to stop?"

She could hear Gubbs in the barn doing his best to quiet the horses, but they would have none of it. The earth was moving and the barn's weathered wood beams were creaking and cracking overhead. No amount of shushing could override what the horses were feeling. When the shed next to the barn collapsed, Gubbs' efforts were even more futile. The rooster and hens broke loose in a cloud of feathers and a deafening chorus of cackling.

He yelled for Brock and Blossom to help. The look on Gubbs face showed his relief that they were already on their way.

When the grinding finally stopped, they noticed something else started. The quake had knocked over a lit kerosene lamp in the horse barn, quickly igniting the straw that was strewn on the ground. It traveled to a pile of hay bales. By the time Gubbs could return with two pails of water, it was clear that it would not be enough to make a difference. It was spreading too fast.

"Gubbs, let's get the horses out…now!" Brock assessed the vulnerability of the barn and its contents. The hungry flames feasted on anything within reach. Blossom made sure the released horses ran away from the barn by swinging her arms and yelling. "Honey, Mother Nature already taught them to run away from fire."

"Then what can I do to help? I have to do something!"

Just as the cows appeared to be settling down in the yard, with their mad pushing, butting and shoving coming to an end, the earth exploded with more angry movement.

"Damn, we's in fer it again!" hollered Gubbs. With incomprehensible force, the ground rolled and snapped sharply, this time like a housewife shaking out a dusty rug.

The barn's windows revealed a glowing fire that was quickly consuming the fuel inside. Blossom watched the horses running freely on the hillside, whinnying and galloping randomly as the uneasy earth moved below their hooves.

Again, the shaking stopped.

"Gubbs, let's get the wagons out of the barn," yelled Brock. He stopped and contemplated the flames, flashing back to his childhood burning-at-the-stake experience. *Austin, I'll never forgive you for what you did that day.*

Blossom saw the look on his face, sprang to attention and embraced him. She knew she could help pull or push a wagon as good as anyone at a time like this, but also she could calm his nerves about entering a fiery building.

During the last quake, some cows broke through the split-rail fencing of their corral. Like logs breaking through the pinch-point of a logjam, they poured out to freedom. However, once free, they didn't know what to do with themselves other than to moo loudly.

"We're going to lose the horse barn," said Brock as the trio delivered a second wagon out of the barn with some saddles that they'd quickly thrown into the back.

"How can we keep it from spreading?" Brock urgently asked.

Blossom grabbed a rake that rested against the barn's outer wall. "I'll clear away the loose straw and dried weeds between the horse barn and the dairy barn. That should separate them, so long as the wind doesn't pick up much more."

"Good idea. Gubbs and I will tend to the cows." A couple of hired farm hands stumbled over from the faraway bunkhouse.

"What can we do?" one asked in a weak voice, clearly out of breath.

The noise of the animals, the fire and the increasing wind required everyone to yell.

"Where have you been? We're losing the horse barn!" hollered Brock over the horrific sounds emanating from the blaze. As the words streamed out of his mouth, Brock noticed the blood on the one man's forehead. The other couldn't lift one of his bloody arms that clearly was not only broken, but likely crushed.

"The bunkhouse fell down on us with the first quake, and while we tried to get out, the second one hit. We didn't hear any other men, so we made our way over here."

"God, I'm sorry. I didn't know. Are you two able to help?" asked Brock more sensitively now.

"We're beat up, but not washed out. We'll be fine," said one man.

"What would you like us to do first?" asked the other.

"Let's work together to get the cows back in the corral."

"Brock," screamed Blossom. "Look!" She pointed to the city. Fires were flickering all over San Francisco, resembling the stars they'd gazed at earlier that night. But this time the sight was horrifying.

"The city, it's on fire! I've got to go home and help Grand Ma Maw," she said, her voice spilling over with fear. "What about your family, Brock? What about Clarissa?"

"I'm not sure the streets will be passable," said Brock as he looked down at the glittering city with barely visible plumes of smoke rising in the early-morning light. "You said you could ride a horse, right?"

"Well, you're right. I said that. But I wasn't telling the truth. Actually, I haven't told you the truth about something else."

"That will have to wait. Now, I guess you're going to learn to ride a horse and learn fast. Gubbs, can you saddle two of the horses? Then finish up with this firebreak in the dirt."

"You got it, Pork Chop."

Gubbs winked reassuringly at Blossom.

"Yuh'll be fine, miss. Just be sure tha horse knows yuh're in charge," he yelled.

For the first time in her life, with all the chaos swirling around her, Blossom actually felt in charge.

Chapter 50
From The Roof's Edge

Wednesday, April 18, 1906, 5:17 a.m.
The day of the earthquake and firestorm

Clarissa's parents were moving around their house to ensure that everyone, including the staff, was safe. However, Zelda could not be found. Rudely awakened from her crystal and silk dream world, Clarissa nearly smothered herself as she buried her face in her mother's bosom, a frenzy of sobs and tears exploding from her. Seated on the main parlor's settee, Clarissa's mother stroked her distraught daughter's hair and did what she could to calm Clarissa down, as only a parent can do.

At first glance, it appeared that their opulent and ostentatious home stood strong and sturdy through the shaking, though many of their treasures were hurled to the floor from the walls and curio shelves. As a result of the first quake, Clarissa's harp had fallen over and was leaning against the wall. However, as the house settled the golden instrument slide down and hit the floor, creating a nightmarish noise that prompted everyone to turn and look. It sounded nothing like the rapturous and hypnotic melody Clarissa played for Brock just a few days earlier.

The earth began to move violently again.

"It feels like our house is out on the open sea," declared Clarissa's father as he visually took in the unnerving movement of things that don't normally move by themselves, including the entire structure of the house. "It's like we're getting the old heave-ho!"

Romeo and Juliet were flying freely around the house since their cage fell in the conservatory, its door now wide open.

"Too bad Brock's not here to see you flying free," Clarissa said in a sing-song way to the birds. Her mother looked at her queerly.

"You're fine. See, the shaking stopped. Your father and I are fine. Our house is fine, for the most part. We must pray that our friends and neighbors are as fortunate," said Mrs. Donohue, with what Clarissa sensed was an odd calmness.

"Mother, you didn't mention Brock. Do you think Brock is fine?" A rush of doubt and fear raced through Clarissa's body. She sat up straight with a noticeable look of someone who had just realized something she didn't want to realize.

Mrs. Donohue gently touched her daughter's chin and turned her head so she could make eye contact. "Brock is fine too. I'm sure of it."

Mr. Donohue said in a hushed tone meant only for his wife to hear, "Don't make promises you can't keep."

Mrs. Donohue turned back to Clarissa. "Honey, I couldn't bear to see you with a broken heart."

Clarissa coolly replied, "Well, you better look the other way, because I'm halfway there."

"Ma'am! Oh, Mrs. Donohue!" shrieked one of the maids. "It's Zelda. She's...she's...dead!"

"You must be mistaken," Clarissa's mother stated dismissively and calmly.

"No, ma'am. I just checked outside the servants' door." The maid stopped to catch her breath. She looked at Mrs. Donohue with a cocked head, as if she wasn't speaking to the gentle woman of the house she'd always known. She cleared her mind and went on, "Some of those huge, stone urns that are up on the roof's edge came down. One of them hit Zelda!" As the words came out of her mouth, a horrible picture was painted in everyone's mind.

Since gracefully taking charge was something she did best in this household, Mrs. Donohue consciously blinked, inhaled deeply and said, "Then we must go to her right away." She rose to her feet and began to walk. They all followed the matriarch in a formation that looked much like a funeral procession.

Chapter 51
*S*carlet With Blood

Wednesday, April 18, 1906, 5:20 a.m.
The day of the earthquake and firestorm

Austin survived in more than his share of barroom brawls and taken his hits. But being on the top floor of a four-story building that collapsed on itself like a squeezed accordion was a sensation unlike any he'd ever felt. Monique held onto him for dear life. Peaches barked and whined in her kennel.

When the movement stopped and the dust began to settle, Austin hollered, "Horse shit! Let's get out of here!"

Monique spoke up immediately. "I'll second that!"

"I used to think a good shake in California would not be half as bad as a twister or a hurricane somewhere else, but I'll take a tornado over what we just felt!" Austin said rapidly as he made his way out of the bed.

Monique looked at him and instructed, "Wait a minute there, cowboy. Let me see the side of your head."

He complied with her request. He put his hand up to his left temple and felt moisture. He looked at his hand and it was scarlet with blood. "I thought one of those pieces of wood landed close to my pillow."

Monique scanned the room for something to wrap his head with. The mirrors that once reflected light and lovemaking transformed into shiny slivers of bad luck all over the floor. She grabbed a long stocking from the end of the bed. "That'll do," she announced with pride. Peaches continued to bark sharply.

"Good thing we dropped our clothes right near the bed. Lust pays off in more ways than one, eh?"

"Austin, how can you say that at a time like this?"

"It's better than being serious at a time like this!"

The pair cleared the freshly fallen debris off of the bed so they could get out. Timbers from the ceiling's structure dangled in various lengths and angles. They got dressed and Monique rummaged through the drawer that had flown out of her dresser. She scooped up a handful of stockings. She balled them up and put the wad on Austin's temple. She used a loose one to wrap around his head as a bandage.

"Does it hurt?" she asked with an empathetic wince on her face.

"It didn't, but now it's throbbing like a sonofabitch," he replied with eye-squinting, breath-stealing pain.

They collected Peaches and made their way out the window that now functioned as a door. It was nearly at ground level as three stories of the building were flattened beneath them.

In the street, the air was thick with dust and smoke. Coming in and out of sight were prostitutes and their gentlemen callers running around fully or partially nude, hysterical and wholly indifferent to what they were—and were not—wearing.

"This is something I'm never going to forget!" announced Austin as he squinted and put his hand on the stocking wrapped around his head.

Monique fired back, "Come on. Put your eyes back in your head and let's get out of here."

Peaches barked in agreement.

"My big brother isn't going to like these fires."

"What do you mean? Won't he be like everyone else and be afraid of the earthquakes?"

"Nope. He's used to riding unbroken horses. So the earth moving wildly underneath him is nothing compared to an open flame."

"Really?"

"Really."

"Why's that?"

Austin said meekly, "Because of something I did to him when we were kids."

"Really, you were immature even when you were immature?"

"Yep. I tied him to a wood pole in our cellar, like the Indians do."

"You better tell me you didn't try to burn him at the stake?"

"Okay, I'll tell you I didn't try to burn him at the stake if that's what you want me to say, but I did it...well, sort of. But only his feet got burned. Clementine came to the rescue after I ran out through the servant's entrance."

Monique shook her head. "Even after that, you're still playing with fire—fire of all kinds."

She looked around. "Well, there's plenty of fire out here today. I just hope Brock can cope with it all."

"Don't worry about my big brother. He always has everything under control. I take it back. Maybe we should worry about him!"

Chapter 52

Taking In Sights That No One Should Have To Witness

Wednesday, April 18, 1906, 6:07 a.m.
The day of the earthquake and firestorm

Brock led the way atop a shiny black workhorse he called Ebony. He guided Blossom's horse by holding the reins.

"Brock, wouldn't it be easier for us both to ride on just one horse?"

"Yes, but I bet both horses will be needed in the city to help out."

"You're right. Always thinking of others, aren't you?"

"Not always."

As they entered the outskirts of town, Blossom repeated her earlier statement, only with tears this time. "This is bad, *really* bad."

It was like hell itself yawned before them.

Collapsed buildings. People wandering and weeping in the streets in their pajamas. The smell of smoke set against an eerie silence of the new morning. It was more than unsettling. Sunrises were supposed to be heartwarming, not heartbreaking.

Unfurled blankets of broken bricks and masonry from building fronts made streets difficult to navigate. Severed water mains gushed streams of water down roads that pooled in low spots. Pavement was shoved in all directions. And it was accented by cable-car tracks that had broken loose from the ground and reached upward to make themselves unwelcomed obstacles. It looked to Brock like the world was being ripped apart at the seams and the tearing was happening everywhere.

How could this get any worse? thought Brock. *It's on fire. That makes it worse!*

"Let's get you home first. We'll have a lot to talk about with your father and Grand Ma Maw." In his mind, he added, *if they're still alive.*

The destruction seemed to get worse the farther into the city they went. Perhaps it was the taller buildings. Perhaps it was the older, less-secure construction. Maybe it was fate or Mother Nature's cruel randomness. Whatever *it* was, Brock saw a decimated city before him.

They became unavoidably aware of fires that resulted from toppled chimneys and crumbled flues. More aggressive blue flames danced sharply from broken gas lines. Sparks spewed from the erratic, snake-like movements of downed electric power lines. There was an unmistakable randomness of debris in the streets that buildings had violently spit out. The ripping action created harsh barricades. In contrast, costly draperies, tangles of clothes and broken furniture littered the roadway as well. All of it was being drenched by geysers rising from broken water mains.

The unleashed and writhing electrical-power lines pushed the horse's limits. Ebony reared up and whinnied in a way that sounded more like a scream of fear, nearly bucking Brock to the ground. He held on to Ebony, but unintentionally released the reins of Blossom's horse. Not even an experienced horseman like Brock could summon the dominance needed to bring Ebony back under control. Overwhelmed and sensing more freedom to its movements, Ebony bolted down the street with Brock on his back at a speed that made the horse's mane fly.

As the two raced down the street, nearly avoiding the obstacle course of rubble, Brock realized they were about to pass the house Clarissa's family was building for them. It was in flames. The crackling was loud enough to be heard over the noise of Ebony's hooves on the street's bricks.

"Brock! Come back!" he heard Blossom scream in desperation. "Don't leave me! DON'T LEAVE ME!"

He turned to look back and as he did an ear-piercing explosion caused Ebony to rear again, neigh wildly and dash farther down the street and away from Blossom. They turned the corner and Blossom was out of sight.

For the first time, Blossom's mind focused on the wailing and cries for help coming from every direction. It was incomprehensible. "Help me!" she squeezed out of her throat as it sealed shut and her heart raced in scared-rabbit beats.

Nearby, a clean-cut man witnessed what happened and helped Blossom off of her horse.

"He'll be back for you," the stranger said.

"Thank you. I'm not very good with horses. I guess that's pretty obvious," replied Blossom, though not making much eye contact with the man as she scanned the area in all directions in hopes of spotting Brock.

"Look behind you, I think I see him coming for you," he said as Blossom heard her horse shuffle. Within a matter of seconds, the man climbed up on the horse and was on his way.

"That's my horse. Come back here. You can't take my horse. What's wrong with you?" she yelled pointlessly at the thief who was quickly traveling down the street.

"Thank you, ma'am. There's nothing wrong with me, *everything's* wrooooong," she heard him say as his silhouette faded, making him a hazy shadow man.

"Now what?" she asked herself out loud. Blossom stood there, horseless and with a growing sense of hopelessness. Burning-hot tears slid down her cheeks as smoky dry breezes swirled around her.

As she desperately looked around for Brock, she began to take in sights that no one should have to witness.

People were moving in all directions. Many had physical injuries, but more looked like they'd been emotionally damaged to Blossom, as if a trusted friend had suddenly and severely wronged them. The earth was not supposed to move under their feet. They were to move over it.

Somehow, though, Blossom had never felt so alone and isolated. A deafening explosion tore the air and a writhing fireball shot skyward like the dragons she'd long seen in Chinese picture books.

Blossom continued to assess her surroundings, but now in an almost detached way. Currents of breezes came and went. A rain of cinders began to cloak every tree, fence railing and cobblestone in a wispy garment of ash. It was as if she was observing it all but not part of it.

Everything was moving unnaturally slow before her eyes, and the clamor of noises was muffled. Her mouth opened as her jaw slackened involuntarily.

Another loud explosion pulled her back into the horrors of the moment.

She spied a young woman, fully dressed with her hat properly pinned in place. She was sitting on the street curb. Next to her was a carpet bag of rich velvet brocade in gold and wine tones. Her hand firmly grasped the leather and brass handle.

But instead of looking prepared for a cable car or a carriage coming to whisk her away to an appointment, she looked frozen. Her face was emotionless. Her body was motionless. Blossom studied her to see if her eyes were blinking. They were. However, that was the only sign of life in the young woman.

Blossom moved in her direction. "Miss, is there anything I can do for you?" There was no response. A riot of barking dogs passed by, adding to the chaos along the street.

A teenage boy carelessly ran into Blossom and dropped two of the overstuffed pillow cases he was carrying. In a racing thought, she hoped those were his belongings and not loot that belonged to someone else.

"Hello," Blossom tried again. "Is there anything I can do for you?"

Still, there was no response from the stranger on the curb. Blossom turned to move on.

"Wait," she heard the woman say. She coughed on a stream of smoke as it traveled by. "Wait. Is that you? Mother, is that you?"

Blossom stopped and turned around. The woman's blank stare had turned to a wild-eyed expression and she grinned like a lunatic. Blossom instinctively knew she needed to move on, so she did. She didn't look back.

"Mother? Mother, is that you?" now could be heard over and over again.

Within a few moments, Blossom's determination to get home overrode her feelings of fear and helplessness. Something inside her grew stronger. She needed to find her own way home.

With or without Brock, I'm going home.

Chapter 53

$\mathscr{S}$addled To A Tornado

Wednesday, April 18, 1906, 6:22 a.m.
The day of the earthquake and firestorm

Ebony was in full control. Brock never rode a trained horse that was behaving in such an unbroken way. He figured it was understandable since the streets were in complete disarray. As Brock processed the blurry and jerky glimpses he was taking in, he sensed the familiarity of the neighborhood.

He tried every trick in his book to regain control of Ebony. But Brock was riding a tornado. The horse's energy and force were not to be reckoned with, but respected.

However, in front of the Flood estate, Ebony decided to stop, rear up and then gallop in a tight circle. The street was nearly clear of debris.

"Finally! Now let's get you turned around so we can get back to Blossom," he said forcefully to Ebony.

"Mr. St. Clair," he heard called out in his direction. "MISTER St. Clair," he heard again, but with more emphasis and clarity this time.

"Is there not enough chaos in our fair city without your cowboy antics adding to it? Why just last night I was at the opera taking in the most uplifting performance by Enrico Caruso and mingling with the likes of that new actor John Barrymore. He paid me quite a compliment about my pearls. And now, here we are…you and me! Who could have imagined?"

Mrs. Flood was out in her generous yard, fully dressed, with her hair styled from the night before and her usual conspicuous amount of jewelry on display. The enormous pearls she'd just referred to were impossible for Brock to miss, even at a time like this.

"You seem to have a problem confusing my street with Lover's Lane and now a rodeo arena."

"Hello, Mrs. Flood. Pleasure to see you again," Brock replied as he held the reins tightly with both hands.

"By the way, how is that pretty young thing who I saw you kissing the other day…the girl who I believe was not Miss Donohue, your fiancée?" she asked as she shooed away flying embers as if they were pesky insects.

In the middle of this disaster, she's talking about the opera, actors, pearls and what she witnessed the other day with Blossom. God help me, thought Brock. *And, Blossom is all alone right now and I'm here!*

Ebony was finally beginning to settle down, allowing Brock to continue to speak with Mrs. Flood.

"How kind of you to remember our meeting the other day. I was up at my stable when the first quake hit and I'm doing my best to get back into town to help any way I can. Are you being well cared for?"

"Oh, yes, my staff sees to my needs whether the earth is moving or not. I expect no less and I pay for no less. But, I must say, I'm not entirely sure that I wish to live here in the future," she announced with an air of measured politeness and concern.

"Yes, I understand fully. Your home looks fine, but there are fires all around. I've seen row houses and estates that are total losses."

"Nothing in life is a total loss, Mr. St. Clair. My husband saw opportunity in everything, even in life's worst experiences. I trust you will learn to do the same."

"Yes, ma'am, I'll do my best to—" Brock's reply was violently interrupted by an immense explosion a street or two away that triggered Mrs. Flood to cover her ears with the palms of her bejeweled hands and for Ebony to instantly return to his erratic, energized bolt-of-lightening speed. Brock was unable to say a proper farewell to Mrs. Flood, as he focused his energy and attention on gaining control of Ebony once again.

Everything raced by like airborne leaves in a harsh wind: the spikes that topped wrought-iron fences, the swaying trees, the yet-to-be-used fire hydrants and the unlit street lamps. He and Ebony burst through foggy-thick bands of smoke that spanned the street, while the glow of raging fires added eeriness to the billowing smoke.

Air currents pushed the smoke, sparks and ashes in all directions. Just as the city's people were moving chaotically, it appeared to Brock that Mother Nature had lost control of her own destructive forces.

He hastily created a mental checklist. *Get back to Blossom. Get Blossom home. Check on Mother and Austin. Make sure Clarissa and the Donohues are alright. Get back to Twin Peaks.*

Ebony tired eventually and voluntarily stopped in his tracks, as if to mourn the lifeless team of horses alongside the street they were now on. Beautiful, productive work animals lay wasted in the rubble, observed Brock. There was no sign of the driver, and no one seemed to care enough to stop and offer assistance or clear the carnage out of the way.

People of all walks of life were out and about, moving with no clear direction or conviction. The screeching of casters on the legs of beds and settees being dragged and pushed over the broken streets was ear piercing. They were piled high with what refugees could salvage, using the wheeled pieces of furniture like lifeboats in an ocean of destruction and loss. Brock knew he would never forget this moment, though he knew he would do his best not to retrieve it from his memory in the future.

Brock considered dismounting and walking alongside Ebony, but he realized the horse's brute strength would easily separate the two when the next explosion or other terror triggered Ebony to bolt. He decided it was better to stay in the saddle and ride out the storm.

The earth suddenly lifted and dropped, like a possessed elevator car. Ebony bucked and was off and galloping again. For the first time that day, Brock noticed the sound of Ebony's horseshoes colliding with the street's surface. The usual rhythm did not exist, but a random and unsynchronized clamor rose from the horse's fast-moving hooves.

Brock could not believe his eyes as a ribbon of cobblestones ahead of him surged up like popcorn kernels in hot oil. The street literally separated, with stones violently jumping out of their previously cemented positions.

Ebony would have none of it and on his own decided a severe left turn at the next intersection was the best escape route. His choice was not a good one, as the side street was completely blocked by the remains of a building that had lurched off of its foundation. Its many pieces not only littered, but blocked Ebony's passage.

"Someone have mercy and help me."

Brock looked down and spotted a middle-aged man who looked fine from the waist up, but the lower half of his body was hidden by debris.

Brock calmed Ebony down enough to dismount, and tie a rope around the saddle's horn and a jagged piece of decorative rooftop cornice that was crushing the man.

"I'll do my best to get you out, sir," yelled Brock.

"Bless you. Hurry, I can't feel a thing down there," he responded in unmasked agony.

Brock pulled Ebony by the reins to drag away the large chunk of cornice that appeared to be the culprit. As he did, the man shrieked. The movement not only revealed his crushed legs, but it released the pressure on his severed arteries. Blood explosively sprayed in crimson geysers like an unimaginable scene from Yellowstone National Park.

"God, what have I done?" asked Brock as he tied Ebony to a nearby fire hydrant. A trickle of water escaped the base of the hydrant and meandered down along the street's edge. He hurried over to the fading man.

"Thank you," he whispered. "I can see there's no hope for me. You best move on and help someone else who's got a chance." Brock was splattered with an explosive stream of blood as the dying man began to cough uncontrollably as smoke engulfed the small street. It was clear to Brock that pain was coursing through the man's entire body. With each cough, a rush of blood was forced from his body. Brock watched the blood and water mixing and flowing as one down the street.

"Thank you…thank youuuuuu—"

Brock felt the man's neck for a pulse. There was none. Brock was ambushed by a rush of feelings and emotions that he did his best to keep in check. The world and everything on its surface seemed to be upended. He grabbed a nearby curtain that not long ago gracefully hung near one of the building's windows. He draped it over the man's face.

He wiped his bloody hands on his shirt, untied Ebony and headed back to where he had been separated from Blossom. For the time being, Ebony was complying with Brock's every command. Brock thought about what just happened and how the very same scene must be playing itself out all over the city: people helping people as best they could. At least, in his heart, he hoped that was happening.

Chapter 54
Church Bells Are Ringing

Wednesday, April 18, 1906, 6:47 a.m.
The day of the earthquake and firestorm

Ting Ting heard—with each thunderous movement of the earth—church bells across the city ringing like an unholy choir. They rang loudly and hauntingly long after the shaking stopped. The ruckus of dogs barking preceded and overlapped the clanging bells, making it impossible for Ting Ting to question whether or not the ground had moved again. There was unavoidable proof all around.

While some buildings looked unharmed to the young girl, others were destroyed in tragic chain reactions. Rows of toppled structures looked like knocked-over dominos after a child had his destructive fun. But the stores and apartments above them were not domino game pieces, and this was not fun. Ting Ting was having anything but fun.

She watched as orange, yellow and scarlet flames chewed on the bottom of vertical Chinese-language banners. In a flash, burning words took flight and escaped the confines of their paper prisons.

Ting Ting, Little Sunflower and their parents were able to get out of their building after the first quake. It was the subsequent ones that were doing the most damage. They clustered and commiserated with their

Chinatown neighbors. Rumors about people who lived, and those who did not, spread like the wildfires that were incinerating the city.

"Have you seen Blossom? How about you? Or you?" With Little Sunflower as a shadow, Ting Ting asked anyone who would listen to her if they'd encountered Blossom. She became more frantic as time went on and no one could account for Blossom, or Blossom's father and grandmother.

Ting Ting cranked her hurdy-gurdy music box so wildly that her father reached over to grab it from her, but he stopped himself. He looked at her with caring eyes. She looked down, clutching the one thing that brought her close to Blossom.

"Please Ba Ba. I beg you. Come with me," pleaded Ting Ting as she pulled her father by the hand toward the smashed building that had been The Golden Palace. "Blossom must be in there. She needs us!"

"No, no," yelled Little Sunflower. "We shouldn't go near there. Fire and smoke will—"

"Blossom! Blossom! Are you in there? Let us help you!" she desperately asked. Two of the unstable floors collapsed onto one another. "Ba Ba, you're hurting me," said Ting Ting as her father briskly pulled her away to a different section of the alley to join Little Sunflower and their mother.

"Our business is ruined. And fireworks will begin to explode soon. We must gather what we can and get out of Chinatown," said Ting Ting's father. "Now!"

They scooped up what valuables were in sight and started the process of saying their goodbyes to cherished neighbors with the hope they would meet once again.

"We'll head to the Ferry Building and the docks along the bay, secure passage and be with relatives in Oakland in no time at all," assured Ting Ting's father.

Her world was being destroyed before her eyes. Her dearest friend was missing. And above it all, Ting Ting dreaded the next time she might hear church bells ringing.

Chapter 55
The Most Precious Thing
This World Holds

Wednesday, April 18, 1906, 6:59 a.m.
The day of the earthquake and firestorm

The morning was unfolding like a fever dream, everyone not quite sure if what they were seeing was real.

"Blossom!" she thought she heard Brock yell.

"Blossom!" she heard his voice plead again. It came from behind her. She stopped running in the direction of Chinatown and turned around to see Ebony delivering Brock to her. He guided Ebony slowly and closely to Blossom. He dismounted and embraced her so tightly that all of the air escaped her lungs.

"I thought I'd lost you!" he said with relief.

She pushed him away in order to take a breath and then pulled him back in tightly.

"I thought I'd lost *you!*"

"I'll *always* find you, no matter what," he replied. "Always."

Then she quickly sensed something was wrong with Brock.

"You're covered in blood." She had only focused on his face up to that point. "We need to get you to a doctor."

"No, I'm fine. I was helping a man and…um…it didn't end well for him." Brock mounted Ebony. "I see there's only one horse and two of us now. Give me your hand. I'll pull you up."

"Yes, a man who I thought was being helpful…well, he just *helped* himself to my horse and bolted."

"Alright then, give me your hand," he instructed.

"I can't."

"What do you mean, you can't? Of course, you can. Give me your hand!" He didn't want her to emotionally unravel yet. *There will be plenty of opportunities for that later*, he thought.

She complied and Brock pulled her up behind him. She wrapped her arms around his waist and wove her fingers together. He put his hand over hers.

"Don't let me go!"

"Not a chance," replied Brock. Ebony walked with no speed and plenty of caution.

"Isn't that the street your new house is on?"

"Was on, not is on. It's destroyed. I got a glimpse of the broken pile while Ebony took me on a wild-ass tour of the neighborhood. Just when I thought I'd seen something bad, I'd see something worse. The new house is rubble."

"I'm sorry."

"I wasn't going to live there anyway, right?" he asked.

"I suppose. I mean, right."

They came close to a man and woman who were walking strangely with what appeared to be great effort. On closer inspection, Brock realized they had several layers of clothes on at the same time. The couple noticed Brock studying them, and the woman called out as they passed, "We figured it was easier than packing a trunk. We put on our best clothes first and layered outfits that would take the smoke and ash better. Clever, eh?"

"Yes, ma'am, very clever," Brock said.

The many distractions cleared from Brock's mind as he refocused on their mission to find Grand Ma Maw and Blossom's father.

"Let's go. Chinatown can't be too far away, can it?"

"No, it's just down the street, around the corner and down the hill. We should be there soon," Brock assured.

They entered the edge of Chinatown and saw billowing and boiling clouds of smoke nearing. Brock heard Blossom crying. He wondered how she'd held herself together this far. The street before them was rippled and sharply ripped open, creating a jagged trench to navigate around.

"Do you want to stop and rest?" asked Brock, trying to disguise his growing fear.

"No, I just need to get home." She reached up to hold her mother's cameo brooch, which still rested just below her neck.

Random piles of bricks clogged sections of the streets, unlike the collapsed brick walls that looked like spread-out blankets they'd seen earlier. Jagged, splintered timber was everywhere, as if wooden buildings had burst at the seams. Brock figured the wood must have flown through the air like renegade arrows. The rubble here was unlike other areas. Architectural wreckage was mixed with fresh produce and shop wares that spilled out into the streets. The carcasses of butchered animals and ruptured burlap sacks of rice added to the mess.

As the minutes passed, noticeably more smoke reached for the sky. The unmistakable crackling of fires could be heard in all directions.

When they arrived at The Golden Palace, they were stunned to find it missing. Or, more accurately, floors of the building were missing. It appeared to have pitched forward, collapsed and sandwiched on top of itself. All around, the earth's gluttonous appetite was visible. It had chewed up the city, swallowing some buildings entirely and leaving chunks of others behind like gnarled gristle.

Blossom looked at the wreckage with her mouth open, but she closed it without speaking.

It was like the restaurant, the bakery and her home had vanished. Instead of a swarm of firefighters and rescue workers on site, only a few neighbors were searching and calling out for survivors. With everyone tending to their own problems, there were few extra people to take the lead and address other matters at hand.

"Wait!" yelled Brock after Blossom jumped down off the horse and immediately started to climb into an open window on the building's new first floor.

"Let me tie up Ebony, and tie him up well. He doesn't take kindly to fire and commotion." *Not that I do either.* "I don't want to make it easy for someone to steal him. Let's go in together. I don't want to lose you again."

Blossom hesitated momentarily but waited for Brock.

"Grand Ma Maw! Ba Ba! Are you in here?" hollered Blossom with all the voice she could summon. "Please be alive. Please."

Brock took her by the hand and led her through the window's opening. While the outer wall was intact, its floor was not. Everything from the floors below heaved up and through the wood flooring. It was a dangerous maze of debris.

"Grand Ma Maw! Where are you?" Blossom's voice was clearer and stronger now. However, tears were streaming down her cheeks, and she trembled so much that climbing through the mess was becoming impossible.

Smoke was filling their space, and the crackling and popping of a wood fire grew closer.

"Grand Ma Maw! Ba Ba! Please! Father, are you here?" she screamed desperately.

"You stay here. I'll keep going," assured Brock.

"No, don't you leave me. Don't you leave me." Panic was rioting within her.

Brock held her hand more firmly and continued to lead them deeper into the ruins.

"Blossom...my Blossom," they heard a weakened Grand Ma Maw say. Her words were like a beacon. They made their way to the rear part of the building, only to find the roof had collapsed in that section as well. A fire was moving inward from the alley.

Blossom yelled as loudly as she could, "Grand Ma Maw, talk more so we can find you! There's a fire and we need to get you out of here."

"I know...about fire. I smell it," confirmed the entombed old woman, ending with a weak cough. "With fireworks next door, you go far from here. Now! It be the biggest New Year's celebration ever in a few minutes."

"What can we do?" Blossom asked Brock in a subdued tone.

"Try...try anything we can to get her before the—" Brock stopped himself before saying what they both knew but couldn't say. It wasn't necessary to say it.

The compressed chunks of the building below their feet, combined with the collapsed roof, made a nearly impenetrable wedge of debris. The elderly woman was somewhere below.

Blossom realized they hadn't heard her father's voice. "Grand Ma Maw, talk some more. Where's Ba Ba?"

"I do not know," she replied. With that response, they pinpointed her location. Rafter beams, shingles and a tangled web of interlocked pieces of building separated Blossom from her grandmother. The pair pulled away smaller pieces to try to uncover the woman before the flames could reach her.

"Can you move?"

"Have you no sense, girl? Of course I not move. I have building on top of me," she replied with her sharp-as-a-tack wit intact.

"Yes, I see that, but is there room to move your arms or legs?"

"Honey, I can move nothing."

Blossom looked deeply into Brock's eyes, transmitting the desperation she felt.

"In all my years on this earth, I never good at goodbyes—"

"Stop right there, Grand Ma Maw. You're not going to say it now either. Brock and I will get you out. We have to," interrupted Blossom as she clawed away at the building remnants under her feet, like an excited child digging in the sand at the beach.

"Your Mr. St. Clair with you, yes? That as it should be. You together. I go now and know you be fine." Her voice got weaker and she started coughing more heavily.

Blossom began to sob, recognizing the futility of their efforts to reach Grand Ma Maw.

"I love you, Grand Ma Maw. I always have and I always will."

The old woman weakly replied, "I love you too. And you must promise me…you must talk to your father…your mother left you that brooch, but she took something with her when she leave us…something else you must know about."

The woman's voice went silent.

"Grand Ma Maw?" asked Blossom desperately.

"I still here," she choked out. "You know you the most—" Her coughing was getting more strenuous. "You the most precious thing this world holds for me. Mr. St. Clair, you hear me?"

"Yes, yes I can hear you," he replied.

"*Shay shay*. Thank you. My Blossom…she your Blossom now."

As Brock took in those words, the debris pile groaned and the ground roared again. The ruined building shifted and dropped out from underneath them about two feet. They fell abruptly, adding their bodies to the debris pile. The force pushed flames, sparks and smoke in all directions.

They made their way back onto their feet, even though their footing was unsure. Brock had a look of panic on his face. He couldn't conceal it anymore from Blossom. Fire and smoke disarmed him like nothing else on earth.

Shaken, Blossom called out again and again. "Grand Ma Maw? Are you there?"

There was no response. As she was about to ask again, the question died in Blossom's throat.

Brock took Blossom in his arms. She knew what that shift in the debris meant.

"Grand Ma Maw!" Blossom screamed with everything she had left in her, as if the life was being drawn out of her body as well.

He held her tight, so their connection couldn't be broken. She couldn't have moved even if she wanted to.

"Not Grand Ma Maw too," said Anna Mae as she climbed through the wreckage to get to the pair, swishing away the sparks and smoke from her face.

"Oh, Blossom," she said as she hugged the couple. The flames were dancing across the timbers a few feet away, and the wind was picking up. Gusts scattered sparks in swirling circles and rolling waves. The sun was gone. The gyrating smoke had eaten it, just as the fires were feasting on the city.

"We have to get out of here. People are dying all over town. First your father. Then Grand Auntie Lim Kee. I saw her in her little husband's arms. He could hardly carry her body and walk at the same time."

Anna Mae told how every time he had to stop to rest, he caressed Grand Auntie Lim Kee's face and kissed her lifeless lips. "And now Grand Ma Maw! Blossom, who could be next?" asked Anna Mae in dismay.

"My father? You saw Ba Ba?"

"No, but I heard that he was helping next door when the brick building fell on top of the men. No one survived."

"I can't breathe, Brock. I can't breathe."

"Yes, yes you can, Blossom. Slow down. Think about each breath. In and out. In and out. I'm here. Anna Mae is here. Breathe in and out."

"We have to leave. Between the fires and the quakes, we have to get out of Chinatown," said Brock hoarsely.

"Fine. I have nothing to keep me here," she said in the most defeated voice imaginable.

Blossom covered her mouth as if to trap something that might escape. She turned and a wave of smoke swept across her loosened hair. As she reached up to pull the hair away from her eyes, some papers skipped across the debris. She took another step and heard glass crack. It was a picture frame. She reached down. She saw her mother's photo, the one that had been tucked behind another woman's photo in the frame from the dresser top. She picked it up and discarded her Chinese cousin's photo. *Now I have two photos of Cameo Rose...of Iris...or whatever she calls herself now.*

"She's out there somewhere," Blossom said repeatedly as they walked away from the blaze as it engulfed The Golden Palace.

"Who's out there?" asked Brock. "Who's the woman in the photo?"

"She's out there. She just has to be." She paused, and then added, "And she has whatever it is that Grand Ma Maw wanted me to ask my father about."

She grabbed his arm for support and didn't let go. He walked as carefully as he could, though a curled band of metal wrapped around his boot, making a bell ring. A long piece of crimson fabric was tangled in it. Blossom stopped moving.

"It's the doorbell," she said as she looked down at Brock's foot. "After we first met, my heart skipped every time that bell rang because I thought it might be you again."

"I'll keep it then," he said reassuringly.

"Thank you. I hoped you'd come back to me in the bakery. Now when I hear it ring, it'll remind me that you'll always come back to me."

"Then I better take it off of my boot or I'll be ringing like a peddler's junk wagon!"

Brock pulled off the red fabric and held it up. Golden Chinese characters were embroidered on it. "What's this?"

"It hung by the front door. Grand Ma Maw put it there so people would read it as they left."

"What does it say?"

Blossom looked at him. "Do we have to talk about this now? Look around us!"

Anna Mae reached out and unfurled the fabric. She could see Blossom was in no state to keep the conversation going, so she answered. "It says, 'May good fortune follow you on your path through life.'"

Brock gently took it from Anna Mae and wrapped it around the doorbell.

Blossom held Brock's arm even more tightly as they continued to walk. Fires were burning all around and out of control, and they were linking up like ladies at a family reunion.

They reached Ebony.

"Anna Mae, how is your family?

"Battered and beaten, but alive."

The chaos got even more intense and physical when a strong hand grasped Blossom's left shoulder and separated her from Brock.

"Come with me, now!" a deep voice commanded.

Blossom turned to look and break the grip on her shoulder. She turned, but the grip didn't break. She was confronted with Butch's angry face.

"You are mine. You *belong* to me. Your father said so," he yelled. She saw he had fire in his bulging eyes and a vein in his forehead looked like it was going to burst.

"I'm not yours," Blossom coughed the words out of her tightening throat. "You've got it all wrong. I don't belong to you. I belong *with* him."

Brock looked at Blossom and then at Butch and then back at Blossom. "Is there something I should know?"

Butch cold cocked Brock in the left temple. The flesh-on-flesh impact sounded like a melon hitting the pavement.

"Stop that! What are you...some kind of animal?" Blossom hollered at the butcher. Brock held his hand to the side of his head.

Brock swung his fist and made a direct hit on Butch's stomach, causing him to exhale the wind in his lungs. Butch crouched down to recover.

"Damn, that hurt," Brock announced as he rubbed his knuckles.

An opaque wall of smoke closed around them like a blindfold. The smoke burned their nostrils, throats and lungs as involuntary coughing robbed them of being in control of their own bodies.

"Blossom, give me your hand!" Brock reached out in the direction of her coughing. They connected and Brock pulled her toward him. Ebony whinnied, giving them an audio target to aim for. When they reached the horse, Brock lifted Blossom on its back.

"Anna Mae, come with us," begged Blossom.

"Yes, come with us. You two can ride. I'll walk," Brock said.

Blossom turned to see who was making the staggering, erratic sounds of footsteps behind them.

"No you don't," said a voice new to the conversation. It was Austin's. He was behind the butcher.

As the air cleared, Austin reached down and grabbed a timber from the rubble at his feet. He stood up and in one unbroken movement swung the timber and made full-force impact with Butch's head.

Butch screamed in agony and collapsed lifelessly.

Austin bent down and put his hand close to his victim's nose. "Yeah, he's still breathing. Let's get the hell out of here before he wakes up with a killer headache...or the headache of a killer!"

Austin stood up. "I thought I might find you here, big brother. Monique and I—and sweet little Peaches—are heading up to the house to check on Mom. Come with us," he said easily, as if the catastrophe around them was only a minor inconvenience and the catastrophe's twin sister—calamity—wasn't already present.

"Blossom, welcome to the family," Austin added.

"What do you mean?"

"Brock's here with you. I take that to mean you won. It's the way it should be. Clarissa just wanted to collect you, my brother...like miniature statues, hat pins and caged birds. Say, if you two had the wits of a snail, you'd hightail it out of here and start a new life together somewhere far away." He stopped for a moment and then continued. "No one will know, except us. You've just been handed the ultimate ticket to escape your lives here."

Brock looked at Austin and didn't know if he should pound the life out of him or hug him. Brock realized what Austin recklessly suggested could actually work. The disaster lent them a helping hand. Brock and Blossom could simply disappear.

He hugged Austin. "This could be the last time I ever see you."

"Geez, lay off, would ya!"

Brock pulled away. "Tell Mom and then Clarissa that you...uh...that you saw me get crushed by a collapsing building that was on fire. There was nothing you or anyone else could do to save me." Brock stopped and looked around at the chaos. His shoulders drooped as he looked at the ground. "No, I can't ask you to do that. This is all wrong...so wrong. God, it's wrong and I can't—"

Austin forced his words into Brock's, "No, *you're* wrong. This is right. It's what's meant to be. Now take Blossom's hand and go. Go now!"

Brock reached for Blossom's hand. "Let's go. We need to—"

The shriek of a little girl stopped the conversation.

"Blossom. Stop!" yelled Ting Ting from down the street.

Blossom turned to see two girls running toward her, dodging debris of all sorts along the way. Ting Ting stumbled as she neared Blossom, having kicked the white-and-blue porcelain rice bowl that Grand Ma Maw had regularly tended in the entrance of the restaurant. Brock thought that the rice bowl looked like it had been spit out of the collapsed building.

Ting Ting's family's shop was ablaze. The flames were only one wall away as The Golden Palace became fully engulfed in fire. Blossom watched how everyone was uneasily moving away from the wreckage. *A store full of fireworks and open flames don't make good roommates.*

"Your parents, Ting Ting…they're fine?" asked Blossom as she ran her fingers through Little Sunflower's hair.

"Our parents are fine. They want to leave Chinatown to be safe and go to Oakland to be with some cousins I've never even met. We were on our way there. I looked back and then I saw you! Oh, Blossom, I'm so glad to see you."

Blossom bent down to be at Ting Ting's height. She struggled to summon the strength she needed to say goodbye.

"I'm so glad to see you…both of you. But I'm leaving too and I need you to be strong for me. I'm not sure when I'll see you again."

Ting Ting began to cry loudly as if in physical pain. She kicked the damaged rice bowl again. Several chips of the bowl rested on the cobblestones nearby.

"So much for the Immortals keeping this rice bowl always full for Grand Ma Maw. Where is she?" asked the girl between sobs. Feeling an overwhelming sense of mortality, Blossom raised her eyes to the heavens. She could not bring herself to say that her grandmother was dead, her broken body resting in the burning pile of rubble. Blossom just shook her head.

"Can I have the bowl…to remember Grand Ma Maw by…even if it is broken?" asked the girl with the sincerity of someone much older.

"Of course you can," choked out Blossom. "We have to say goodbye now so you and your family can safely get to Oakland. But we'll see each other again. I know it in my heart. Ting Ting and Little Sunflower, you must not tell anyone that you saw me and Brock, no matter what."

Ting Ting sadly nodded. Little Sunflower nodded as well.

"No one?" asked Ting Ting.

"Yes, absolutely no one must know. Hug me as tightly as you can. It's going to have to last me a long time."

Ting Ting did as she was told. The embrace was as tight as a vise's grip. Little Sunflower hesitated. Blossom freed a hand and outstretched it to the little girl. Little Sunflower added her vice-like grip to the two who were already hugging.

"I promise we'll be together again. But you must run to your parents and get to safety. Goodbye." Blossom could hear a hissing, sizzling sound as the wind gusted strongly again.

Ting Ting showed Blossom the hurdy-gurdy music box that had been in her pocket for safekeeping, the one Blossom had given her. Sobbing, she scooped up the pieces of the bowl. The pair dashed away, looking back several times. Through the high tide of smoke that was again filling the street, they waved one last time to Blossom.

Blossom quickly turned to her other friends. "Anna Mae... Monique...I can't take losing anyone else today. I don't know where we'll end up, but I'll let you know when we get there. I'm going to miss you more than you'll know."

"Go on. Live your life. You got your man and his love. That's more than a lot of people can say today," replied Monique.

"Maybe you better not tell us where you are or we'll move there too!" added Anna Mae as she came up close to Blossom. "Are you sure?" she whispered in Blossom's ear. "Are you sure he's the one? He's leaving his fiancée for you. Who's to say he won't leave you for—"

"I'm sure!"

"Sure of what?" asked Brock.

Blossom's eyes blinked hard and her shoulders abruptly rose repeatedly as the first string of firecrackers ignited.

"There go a few more evil spirits," announced Austin. "Lighting firecrackers drives them away, right?"

Within a few seconds, a fireball pinwheeled aimlessly down the street. Other fireworks that were usually devoted to New Year's celebrations shot skyward, leaving a trail of stars behind. The falling embers joined the wild dance of swirling sparks.

"There go some more!" Austin added as he erratically pointed in several directions.

Peaches nearly escaped Monique's arms, the noise making an already high-strung dog even more anxious.

Brock pulled Blossom away from the girls with his arm around her waist. As they hurried to their now-agitated horse, she looked over her shoulder at her friends, Austin and at the blazing ruins that had been her home.

Just as they mounted Ebony, the fireworks from Ting Ting's family's shop exploded with greater regularity. Peaches began to bark with even more intensity than before. The crackling and booming spooked their horse, and together they bolted down the street that was strewn with what was left of Chinatown's buildings. Blossom didn't dare look back over her shoulder again for fear of falling off. She knew it was definitely a time to look forward, and the fireworks made sure of it.

Once they were a few blocks away, Ebony settled down and they made their way back to Twin Peaks.

"Who could have ever dreamed this nightmare?" she asked.

Brock turned and looked her in the eyes deeply as only he could. He lovingly responded, "And who could have dreamed this dream?"

Chapter 56
Broken Hearts

Wednesday, April 18, 1906, 7:49 a.m.
The day of the earthquake and firestorm

Faye called out to Clarissa, "For Pete's sake, is the world coming to an end or what?" Clarissa left the mansion's front door open behind her and, seizing the moment, Romeo and Juliet noisily darted out the opening and circled overhead before disappearing. Clarissa covered her mouth with her hand and caught her breath, helplessly witnessing the caged birds set free. She came down the house's front steps to the gate at the street's edge.

"I don't know if the world is ending, but I'm not leaving it without Brock. Now that you're here, I won't be leaving it without you either, Miss Huntington!"

Clarissa continued as they began to walk, "Come on, my parents are fine. As you just witnessed, Romeo and Juliet have flown the coop. Unfortunately, Zelda is dead in the garden."

Faye stopped walking in an exaggerated jerk and looked at her friend. "Do I know you?"

"What on earth do you mean?"

"As cool as a cucumber, you just said Zelda was dead in the backyard, didn't you? Are you in shock? Denial? What was she doing in the garden at a time like this?"

Clarissa wiped away a few loose strands of hair that tickled her forehead. "She was having her head smashed in with a stone urn as she cut fresh flowers for our breakfast table. That's what she was doing in the garden!"

"There's a body in your yard and you described the situation with all the emotion of announcing how a string on your harp needs tuning."

"I know, I know," admitted Clarissa. "I just can't think about it right now. I've got to go down to the St. Clairs' house to see if Brock and his family are alright. My parents didn't let me go until now. Are you coming with me?"

"You mean he hasn't been here yet to check on you?" Faye replied. "My stars, I could count on my nipples—and that would be two—how many minutes it would take for my fiancé to come check on me. That is, if I had a fiancé."

Clarissa paused to admit to herself that Faye was correct. *Why hasn't Brock come to my rescue yet?*

"I just hope he's safe. Now, stop talking and start walking." She grabbed Faye's hand. They headed down the street toward Brock's house.

The pair side-stepped debris on the sidewalk, finally deciding it was easier to walk in the middle of the road beyond the immediate dropping range of the house fronts. The two moved among people who were going in all directions, but without any real purpose. Clarissa sensed anxiety and despair floating in the air like the wind-blown smoke and ashes.

It was those who were dragging trunks who captured Clarissa's attention and wouldn't let go. She was certain she'd never forget the grinding sound of people who correctly sensed the gravity of the disaster and were dragging everything they had left in the world in steamer trunks. Some had children trailing behind them. Some were empty handed. Others carried prized possessions and cherished keepsakes. Still others, focused on their own needs, appeared to be heading out alone. In the distance, huge mushrooming clouds of smoke reached skyward. Closer to them, the smell of smoke grew heavy and pungent, adding to the disaster's feeling of urgency. A dangerous momentum of destruction was swelling with no end in sight.

"It must be chaos in other parts of town if people have already packed up their belongings and started to move on," observed Clarissa.

There was another tug at the earth's crust. Church bells erratically rang out a confirmation of the tremor. Everybody stopped to assess what was happening and to brace themselves. It was over nearly as soon as it started, but it didn't escape anyone's heightened senses.

"That was a real bell ringer," remarked Faye as she started walking again, only to be stopped abruptly as she tripped over a chunk of brick. She fell to the pavement. As Clarissa bent over to offer her friend a helping hand, the earth's pressure erupted yet again, forcing Clarissa to fall on top of Faye.

"Damn it," cursed Faye as she and Clarissa separated and got back on their feet. It was a swift aftershock. Houses creaked as beams split and more loosened bricks and mortar fell.

"Watch your language, please."

"Truly? Now is not the time for etiquette and manners, my dear one," said Faye as she wrinkled her nose and narrowed her eyes. "This whole city and everyone in it can go to hell!" She looked around. "Hmmmm, I see we're already there!" she said as she shrugged shoulders.

They began to walk again and passed—and tried not to look at—a dead horse in their path.

"Ugh! This is totally unacceptable."

Displaying her inner strength and some restraint, Clarissa simply fired back, "Oh, Faye, just shut up!"

"Fine."

"Fine," said Clarissa crossing her arms.

"FINE!" ricocheted Faye.

"FINE!" said Clarissa firmly to end that exchange.

Clarissa watched as smoke blew through in waves, like a typical evening fog from the bay but at a brisker pace. Inhaling it was unavoidable. The smoke didn't smell like a familiar wood or coal fire in a hearth. It was a foul mixture of scents, of things the women had never smelled burn before. They both instinctively raised their hands to cover their noses and mouths.

When they got closer to Brock's house, Clarissa's pace quickened along with her heart rate. However, her hope of finding her fiancé unharmed began to slide down a slippery slope as Silverado came into view, or what was left standing where the silver-encrusted mansion once stood proudly, even arrogantly.

The front was gone. It looked to Clarissa as if a giant had peeled it off so anyone could look into it, much like her childhood dollhouse. The rooms appeared as if the giant's little brother ran his fingers through that dollhouse and knocked over and upturned just about everything in sight. The glass-covered conservatory was no longer glass covered. It stood like a fleshless skeleton.

Brock's mother and her maid, Pearl, were standing in the side yard. "Oh, Clarissa," Mrs. St. Clair called out in a crazed way. "You're alive. Thank goodness. I was so worried."

"And you, you are—" Clarissa stopped speaking. The full sight of the rubble was too much to take in while speaking and thinking coherently. Clementine, the cook, was walking toward the front of the house from the side yard.

"Pearl and I were in the kitchen," Mrs. St. Clair recalled as the pair approached. "I woke up and couldn't get back to sleep, so I came downstairs to make some tea. Pearl heard me and came out of her bedroom to see who was in the kitchen." She stopped and swallowed.

"Then Clementine heard the two of us. As noisy as we are, we'd make terrible mice, wouldn't we? Anyway, all of a sudden…well, I have to say it felt like a miner set off some dynamite right under us. Everything was shaking and swaying and falling. The crystals on the dining room chandeliers were crashing against each other and making a horrible sound, almost like an alarm telling us to leave. We got outside as fast as our feet would carry us. The house was coming apart."

She put her hand to her chin and shook her head. "If Mr. St. Clair was alive to see this happen to his dream house, well, it *simply* would have killed him!"

Clarissa looked at Faye and whispered, "She's losing her mind, or maybe she's already lost it."

"Sweet child, I know what you're going to ask, and I don't have an answer," the woman said plainly, as she sobered and stopped her ranting. "Brock and Austin, I don't know if they're here…in there, I mean." She couldn't speak anymore.

"Brock!" Clarissa screamed at the tangled ruins of the mansion that was Silverado.

"Austin! Bang on something. Yell at me!" Faye shouted with a strained voice and then coughed. "You may never get that offer again. Come on!" The smoke from the burning city continued to make its way across Nob Hill. Heavier than before, the smoke made it harder to see. A breeze parted the murky cloud to reveal that a mansion down the street was ablaze and no one was tending to it.

"I never thought I'd see this again in my lifetime," muttered Clementine loudly enough for others to hear her. "It's like how I remember Atlanta at the end of the war, the flames, the chaos, the tears. God Almighty, it brought out the best and the worst in folks. Indeed it did!"

The ground jolted sharply under their feet, and all eyes went to the house as the creaking and crashing turned much louder as ceilings fell in. The chandeliers were sounding their alarm again. Great puffs of dust were exhaled out of the structure's many new openings.

Mrs. St. Clair looked on. "I'm already a widow…and I could be childless now and not even know it." She asked herself softly, "What have

I done to deserve this?"

"Mother! Mother!"

Mrs. St. Clair turned to Clarissa and Faye. "You didn't hear that did you? Must be ghosts. I better get used to having ghosts around."

Faye looked down the street as far as she could. While the smoke made it difficult to see and all of the noises made it hard to hear, she heard, "Mother! Mother!"

Mrs. St. Clair turned in the direction of the voice.

"We're coming for you!" It was Austin, with Monique and Peaches in tow.

"You're safe—" was all he could get out before his words dried up and disappeared. He gasped at what appeared before him.

"I can see we don't need to ask where *you've* been," said Faye as she eyed Monique. "Why do you have your lover's lingerie wrapped around your head? Oh, don't answer that. I'm not sure I want to hear your answer." *Oh, but I do…I really do!*

"Have you seen Brock?" asked Clarissa in a guarded way that revealed how she almost didn't want to hear Austin's response.

Austin started to cry. His lips quivered. His chin quivered as well, with a patch of dimples forming on it. Austin reached out for his mother. Her arms hung limply by her sides in a gesture of disengagement. From her body language, it was clear to everyone she didn't need Austin to speak anymore. He'd already delivered the news without having to utter a single syllable.

Faye braced Clarissa around the shoulder with her right arm. Clarissa bit her lip as tears streamed down her cheeks.

"He's gone…he's gone," squeezed out Austin, raising his hand to his wounded temple. Monique stood by comforting the poodle she was clutching, not having an obvious role to play in the conversation.

He continued after clearing his throat. "We were on our way here when we saw him. I called out and he turned to look, just as we had another shaker. He was helping an old man who was sprawled out in the street, bloody and broken, in front of a building not far from here. It was completely on fire."

Austin stopped speaking. All eyes were on him, waiting for him to finish the story. Heavy smoke swirled around them, helping him choke up for real, not pretend. He winced and slightly adjusted the stocking around his head.

Faye watched Austin and Monique as if she was studying a pair of insects in a glass jar, with a mixture of close-up scrutiny and repulsion.

"The entire building fell forward out into the street, like someone had pushed it from behind. Down it came. He didn't have a chance to get out of the way. The last I saw, Brock was crouched down and over the old man, as if he could protect him from the burning building. And then—"

He said no more.

Faye gave Austin a glance as he delivered the final punishing words…a glance Austin knew all too well himself. He'd given it before, many times. It was a look that replaced all spoken words.

He's up to something, that lying shit heel. I don't know what, but he's lying like a corpse in a cheap casket. Faye held her tongue and avoided yet another barb-for-barb verbal assault on Austin. She knew there was plenty of time for that in the future.

"And then," Monique added, "everything seemed to explode in flames. Bricks were falling. Horses were running wild in the streets. Even cattle were loose. Poor little Peaches hasn't been able to settle down since then." She looked down and then got back on track by saying, "There was nothing for us to do, except save ourselves before we were crushed too."

The word "crushed" brought an impossible-to-miss wince of pain to

Mrs. St. Clair.

The wind started to blow fiercely in not one or two directions, but in every direction. Smoke, ash and sparks were everywhere.

Clarissa stared off to the distance, hearing what was being said by those around her and being mesmerized by an undulating cyclone of smoke that was spinning so powerfully that it was picking up pieces of lumber and roofing materials along with flames larger than she could have ever imagined in her worst nightmare. The whirling, burning funnel was carrying away life as San Franciscans had known it.

"I am so sorry, Mrs. St. Clair," said Monique tenderly. "Clarissa, I can't imagine what you must be thinking or feeling."

Monique turned away slightly and whispered to Austin, "That's the nastiest lie you've ever told...but now your brother is truly free to go."

Faye no longer could support the weight of her friend with one arm. Clarissa dropped to the ground in one limp movement, like when the air is let out of a balloon. What once filled it up and made it buoyant abruptly escaped.

Mrs. St. Clair hugged Austin, patted his wound and bent over to comfort Clarissa, who was now crying uncontrollably. One crazed woman feebly attempting to help another crazed woman—a woman who would have been her first daughter-in-law in just a few days.

"I did everything I was told. I did everything I was expected to do," mumbled Clarissa as she got back on her feet and paced among the group. Then she raised her voice. "I can set a blessed dining-room table to *perfection* for a man who doesn't exist in a new house that probably doesn't exist either!" She stopped pacing. "What am I going to do? What are *we* going to do without Brock?"

She walked toward the ruins of the house.

"Honey, stay away from there. You could get hurt too," pleaded Mrs. St. Clair.

"I don't care. Let it hurt me. Let it hurt me *more*."

Mrs. St. Clair's face went blank, as if a curtain was drawn. It appeared she could take no more of it either.

"Snap out of it," Faye urged Clarissa.

"Snap out of what? When I went to bed last night, I had everything to look forward to. Today, I'm a widow before I was even a bride! Look at me. Really look at me. I'm a…I'm a boarded up house on a dead-end street." She held the heart-shaped locket on the necklace that Brock gave her. "One minute everything is golden—and silver—and then it's ashes the next. Brock's taken my life with him."

Austin held his mother, but gazed at Monique. There was nothing more to be said. His work was complete.

Chapter 57
$\mathscr{S}$aying Goodbye Is Only The Beginning

Wednesday, April 18, 1906, 10:36 a.m.
The day of the earthquake and firestorm

"It's hell on earth down there!" Brock said to Gubbs. "And it's going to get worse before it gets better. There are broken buildings, broken people and fires burning *everywhere*. We're going to leave...leave it all behind."

They looked at the inferno, with the sky full of ashes and memories.

Gubbs cleared the rustiness from his throat. "Pork Chop, yer gonna do what?"

Brock gazed at Blossom. "Her family is dead. From this point on, we're dead too."

"Yer dead, are yuh?"

"Yes. Austin is going to say he saw me get crushed under a burning building that collapsed, which is entirely possible. My mother and Clarissa will believe him and get on with their lives. We will too, but we'll do it somewhere else. It's almost as if this disaster was meant to be."

"Meant to be, yuh say?" Gubbs repeated. "I don't reckon what yer doin' is right. But I don't reckon it's wrong. It's probably somewheres in between. If yer askin' me to be part of it, I will. If someone comes askin',

I don't know anythin' and I won't say anythin'." He took a labored breath.
"What ken I do to help?"

"The sooner we get out of here, the better. Hitch up a wagon and fresh
team. Blossom and I will get the supplies we need."

"Where yuh headin'?"

"South. I think we can get a clean start there."

"Then let's git yuh on yer way," said Gubbs as he turned to get a wagon.

Blossom stood at the top of the hillside and took one last look. Intense
red hotspots dotted the city like periods at the end of some horribly written
sentences. She cupped her hands and covered her eyes to block it out. She
had to.

Brock came over and embraced her gently from behind. He turned
her away from the horrific sights, breaking her momentary paralysis. It was
like being in the last row of seats at a chaotic circus of the damned.

When the wagon was full of provisions, Brock shook Gubbs' hand.
But that didn't seem nearly enough considering how their friendship
deepened in the past few days.

"I'm going to miss you, Gubbs," said Brock as he pulled the crusty old
man in for a hug. Gubbs patted Brock on the back and then pulled away.
This was more affection than Gubbs had experienced in some time.

Blossom stepped forward to face Gubbs. "Thank you," she said and
looked down at the ground.

"I'm truly sorry about yer family, Miss. Brock here will take good care
of yuh."

"I know," she replied as she looked up and placed a soft kiss on his
cheek.

"Oh, there's a few more things yuh need to take with yuh," Gubbs
said while gesturing for them to wait. He came back with the large white
hatbox, Blossom's sketch book and the handbag she'd left behind earlier.

"I don't have no use for nothin' like this," he said with a slight smile
while handing over the hatbox. "That picture book, now that's down-right

precious to yuh, eh?"

"Thank you, Gubbs. You're too sweet," replied Blossom. She looked at Brock and then down at the box that contained her first feathered bonnet.

"Is this all possible?" asked Blossom.

Gubbs quickly replied before Brock could. "Anythin' is possible. You taught Brock to fly a kite, didn't yuh?"

The earth lashed out once again, spooking the animals and the humans as well.

"Either we're getting used to the earth moving, or these quakes aren't as strong now," Blossom said.

"It's probably both, but I'm all for getting out of here and not finding out what happens next," added Brock as he reached into his rear pants pocket to get his wallet. He removed some paper money and reached out to hand it to Gubbs.

"Much obliged, but no," refused the old man. "You'll be needin' that more than me."

"Gubbs, you're a cowpoke whose beaten death before by lassoing it and dragging it out of town like a despicable outlaw."

Gubbs grinned.

"And I have no doubt that you'll beat whatever's ahead of you."

As Brock quickly stuffed the money back into his wallet, the small slip of white paper from the fortune cookie was jarred loose and made itself known. Brock slid it completely out and read its message to himself.

He smiled at Blossom and read it aloud, "Confucius say, 'Wherever you go, go with all of your heart.'"

Brock helped Blossom climb up into the wagon.

Once he was in too, Brock directed a firm "Giddy-up" at the two-horse team, with a third tied to the back of the wagon.

"Three horses?"

"Yes, a pair and a spare!" Brock replied.

Blossom did her best to muster a smile, though she felt like she had a rock in her stomach.

They waved to Gubbs and turned to face forward. To Gubbs, it looked more like 1846 than 1906 as this young couple struck out like pioneers facing the wilderness and their uncertain future. Nothing was ahead of them, and yet everything was ahead of them.

"They's stuck on each other like sap to a tree trunk," Gubbs said to a horse standing at the nearby fence railing. "They'll find their place in this here cockeyed world. Yep, they've got gumption and they're gonna be just fine."

Blossom put her hand on Brock's shoulder to steady herself as she began to turn around.

"Don't look back," Brock urged. "We have a blank slate now."

"When we meet people and when we get to wherever we're going… we'll have to rewrite our story, won't we?"

"Blossom, we're going to be *writing* our story…a very long story."

The End?

Author's note: As Lao Tzu, the philosopher and poet of ancient China, is reported to have said, "New beginnings are often disguised as painful endings." To discover how Blossom and Brock reinvent themselves and make their way to a new future, be sure to read an excerpt of *Blaze*, the second installment of the Blossom Trilogy, which appears on the next page.

Excerpt From *Blaze*, Book Two In The Blossom Trilogy

"I've heard people complain about how sore they got from sitting in a saddle too long. But who knew a wagon's bench could do the same?" asked Blossom as she adjusted her weight from one side to the other. "Don't misunderstand. I love sitting side-by-side with you on this seat hour... after...hour. Just the same, I'll be glad when this trip is over."

Brock grinned. "You need to spend more time in the saddle. Then you'll appreciate this bench."

"I'll have to think about it. Until then, here's something I have been thinking about. What are we going to do for work when we get to wherever it is we're going?" By saying it the way she did, the future seemed all the more uncertain to Blossom.

"Where are we going? I don't mean exactly where, but where?"

Brock turned to look at her. "You know, for the first time in my life I honestly don't know."

"It's kind of fun not knowing where we'll end up," admitted Blossom. "It's like the frog at the bottom of the well."

"It is?"

"You know...the frog thinks the universe is the well, because that's all it can see. But if the frog climbs out, it discovers the well is part of a much bigger world. So, I'm like a frog. You're like a frog too. We can see all kinds of possibilities now that we couldn't see a few days ago."

Brock's head bounced up and down.

"Are you nodding because you agree or because the ground is so bumpy?

"Yes and yes."

Brock cleared his throat. "Back to the topic of work, from what I've heard, there are plenty of farms, orchards and ranches around Los Angeles. There's even an ostrich ranch—"

Blossom broke in, "An ostrich ranch? That's something I'd like to see."

"Good," replied Brock. "Then it's all decided."

Blossom squinted her eyes as she turned her head to face Brock. "What is 'it' and what's been decided about it?"

"The 'it' is the Cawston Ostrich Farm near Pasadena. I've seen photos and read about it. I've even thought about breeding them at Twin Peaks. Their feathers are like gold, especially for ladies' hats, as you well know!"

Blossom recalled seeing San Francisco's finest women parading through Chinatown with undulating clouds of feathers on their heads. She remembered how she longed to have a hat like that someday, and then she got one from Brock. *There could be a whole lot of feathers in our future,* thought Blossom.

"You want to work there?" she asked.

"I can't be Brock St. Clair from Nob Hill anymore. But I do have skills that can earn us a living."

"Yes you do. And you've got the tanned skin and leathery hands to go with the skills," Blossom said as she slid her left hand under Brock's right upper arm. She leaned over and put her head on his shoulder.

"Ostriches? They're so ugly. And I bet they're mean," she said. "Are you going to be safe?"

"Let's not get ahead of ourselves. We haven't even been there, and I don't have a job, at least not yet. They're ugly though. I saw a photograph of a man feeding whole oranges to an ostrich. It already had three in its throat you could see bulging out of its neck! I'll never forget it!"

Blossom added, "Sounds awful! But those feathers...oh, those feathers. Every lady on Nob Hill must have an entire ostrich worth of feathers in her dressing room!"

Brock quickly became quiet and kept looking forward over the horses.

After a time, Blossom broke the silence. "It's your mother, isn't it? You're thinking about her."

"As far as she knows, I'm dead. I can only imagine how my *dear little brother* Austin told her. Do you think her mother's intuition is telling her something different?"

"I don't know much about a mother's intuition. But I'm learning more and more about hearts. If her heart is full of love for you, she's thinking of you and doing it with a broken heart." As the words "broken heart" passed her lips, Blossom wished she could take them back. *You idiot! Now why would you say that?*

"Brock, are we doing the right thing? I didn't leave much. You left everything."

He passed the reins to his left hand and put his right arm around Blossom. "Yes, there's nothing more 'right' than what we're doing."

"But what about Clarissa and your business up on Twin Peaks? And what about Austin? Can we trust him to keep our secret?"

"Clarissa and the business will be fine. I'm sure of it. I'm not so sure about Austin. He doesn't have the best track record."

Blossom reached around to the back of the wagon to find her sketch book and a pencil. She'd planned ahead by placing the items just under the backside of the wagon's seat. She swiveled to the side so she could look at Brock and began to sketch. This was the first time she'd drawn him, and it allowed her the uninterrupted opportunity to truly study his face, his hands, his hair and how he attentively led the team of horses. He turned to look at her briefly.

"Face forward, please," she said sternly, as if in control of the situation.

"Yes, ma'am," he barked as he smiled widely and gazed out beyond the horses' heads.

Blossom slipped off her shoes, pulled up her legs and folded them like a pretzel. In her own special way, she studied his features to identify the two or three most powerful lines to follow that would capture his essence. She got lost in her work as he did his work at the reins.

However, with each bump in the road, a bell rang a bit louder. It was the doorbell they salvaged from Blossom's family's bakery and restaurant just before the fire destroyed everything. It must have wiggled itself loose from its place in the wagon. Blossom reached back to find it, though it wasn't hard to miss. A crimson banner was still wrapped around it.

"What was it that Grand Ma Maw's banner said?" asked Brock.

Blossom unfurled it and ran her fingers down the golden Chinese characters that were embroidered on it. "The banner reminded everyone to be hopeful. It says, 'May good fortune follow you on your path through life.'"

They hit a deep rut in the road and the bell rang loudly. Blossom smiled at Brock. Just days earlier, the sound of that bell ringing was a signal that a customer had entered the building. Once she'd met Brock, every time the bell rang she wished it signaled his return. Now, the bell was a reminder of the life she'd never lead again, and she didn't need to listen for a bell to know that Brock was coming back to her. He was hers. She was his. They were sharing a common path through life, as the banner prophesied.

Blossom started to sketch, but stopped and looked away from Brock.

"I've been waiting for the right moment. This is it."

She laced her fingers.

"Brock, I have something to confess."

This is an excerpt from the forthcoming book Blaze *by Christopher Lentz. It has been set for this edition of* Blossom *only and may not reflect the final content of the forthcoming edition.*

Epilogue: From The Ashes

In April 1906, souls were lost, hearts were broken, and dreams were shattered. While *Blossom* explores this time period, it does so with fictional characters and creative license. For the men, women and children who experienced and survived the quake, aftershocks and fires in real life, it likely stayed in their memory banks throughout their lifetimes. One survivor likened the quake to a bulldog, with the city "a rat, shaken in the grinding teeth."

In looking at the facts, here are a few things to keep in mind about this disaster that included a destructive blaze that surpassed even the Chicago fire of 1871:

- Lasting less than one minute, the main quake—with an equivalent to 8.3 on the Richter scale (though some have revised it downward to 7.8)—struck at 5:12 a.m. on Wednesday, April 18, 1906, along the San Andres Fault, which runs the length of California. The Pacific and North American tectonic plates lurched past each other by as much as 21 feet in some places.

- Beyond the major quake and the additional 26 aftershocks, uncontrollable fires destroyed much of the city during the next three days. Ruptured gas mains, fallen lanterns, crossed electric wires, dynamiting and lighting fire breaks contributed to the blaze, while broken water mains crippled efforts to extinguish the inferno. Some of the fires were estimated to be as hot as 2,700 degrees, making the firestorm more catastrophic than the earthquake itself. An estimated 28,000 buildings were destroyed by fire.

- It's reported that someone cooking breakfast on a stove whose chimney was damaged during the quake started the 24-hour-long

"Ham and Eggs Fire" that was responsible for the destruction of a
30-block area, including parts of City Hall and Market Street.

- The death toll resulting from the disaster is estimated above 3,000,
though hundreds of casualties in Chinatown went ignored and
unrecorded.

- As much as 80 percent of San Francisco was estimated to be
destroyed by the quake and fire.

- Around 300,000 people were left homeless, which was about 75
percent of the area's population. Refugee camps along the coast
were still in operation two years after the quake. Two refugee
cottages still exist in the Presidio.

- The cost of the damage from the disaster was estimated at the time
to be around $400 million, which is more than $9 billion in today's
money.

- Even with an official order to shoot and kill looters, as many as 100
people died in looting situations. Significant looting by civilians
and military personnel was reported in Chinatown.

- To obtain its valuable real estate, there was an unsuccessful attempt
by San Francisco leaders to permanently relocate Chinatown.

- While San Francisco takes top billing when the 1906 quake is
discussed, significant damage also was done to Alameda, Berkeley,
San Jose and Santa Rosa. People in locations as far away as Southern
California, Nevada and Oregon reported feeling the earth tremble.

- In a move to protect the region's economy, local papers downplayed
the devastation and warned people not to send souvenir photos to
out-of-towners. There were claims by the Southern Pacific Railroad
that newspapers around the country exaggerated the devastation.

- The quake is considered the first major natural disaster to have its
effects widely recorded by photography.

- While thousands of before-and-after photographs exist, little film
footage survived that captured life in motion before the quake. To

get a real sense of the energy and atmosphere of the city just days before the disaster, take a few minutes to watch the film at http://www.cbsnews/video/watch/?id=6964752n.html. It's moving and fascinating when you consider how everyone who's captured in their daily lives is about to be forever changed by Mother Nature's fury. In *Blossom*, when Austin describes the filmmakers on the cable car, he's describing the real Miles brothers who recorded a ride that was the length of Market Street. Within a few minutes of silent observation, you'll visit the heart of San Francisco in 1906 and get a glimpse of a joyous city on the brink of disaster.

- In 2011, history buffs could view the devastation of the 1906 San Francisco earthquake in living color photographs taken by photography pioneering Frederick Ives in October 1906. Six months after the disaster, the devastation that left a majority of the city's population homeless is still clearly evident. The Smithsonian Institution uncovered a set of six photos taken after the quake that appear to be not only the first color photos of the ruins, but the first color photographs ever taken of San Francisco. Unlike colorless photos that have been "colorized" at the time, these are in fact color photos. Color photography was invented in 1861 by Thomas Sutton, so it was actually old technology by 1906.

- Will Irwin wrote a eulogy for San Francisco in the New York *Sun* called "The City That Was." It began, "The old San Francisco is dead. The gayest, lightest hearted, most pleasure-loving city of this continent, and in many ways the most interesting and romantic, is a horde of huddled refugees living among ruins."

- But even as the ashes smoldered, the city's boldest and brightest people were hatching plans for the city's future. They—along with their city—had beaten disasters before, and they'll likely have to do it again. One of the major milestones in the city's recovery occurred less than a decade later. San Francisco hosted an "open house" in

1915 known as the Panama-Pacific International Exposition. With a bejeweled tower and Beaux Arts palaces and monuments, it was opulent, artistic and impressive. It accomplished the goal of proving to the world that San Francisco had bounced back with brilliance and self-confidence. You can visit the picturesque Palace of Fine Arts that stands proudly today as a reminder of one of San Francisco's finest hours.

- As for Nob Hill, the New York-style brownstone Flood mansion was one of the only grand houses that survived the disaster. Once the home of James C. Flood, a house-proud hill-dweller who made a fortune in mining, it's the Pacific-Union Club today, an exclusive men's club that dates back to 1852.

- A rebuilt Chinatown is as colorful and bustling as ever. If you ask the right person, you can visit the backroom of a bakery and meet women who make fortune cookies, one at a time. Like Blossom, it's within their power to grant wishes and offer warnings with small slips of paper tucked just so in the warm dough of the cookies. However, it's up to you to select the cookie…and your fortune!

$\mathcal{R}$eading Group Questions

Questions and topics for discussion

Here are some questions for your reading group to reflect on and react to

The suggested questions are offered to help you and your reading-group members discuss *Blossom*. Though the story takes place more than 100 years ago, there's much to relate and react to today.

1. Whose life was more restricted and controlled: Clarissa's or Blossom's? Why do you believe that to be true?

2. Did men hold all of the cards when big decisions needed to be made in 1906?

3. Who blossomed the most in the book?

4. Who fits in and who's a misfit in the story?

5. Is there such a thing as love at first sight? Or, is it more accurately described as *infatuation* at first sight?

6. As a reader, you know that the earthquake and fires are coming while no one in the book does. Do you like knowing the future? Would you tell other people if you knew what was in their futures?

7. When Blossom learns about her family's past, is her reaction appropriate? If you were Blossom, how would you react to the information about your mother?

8. Think about the parent/child relationships of Chang and Blossom, Mrs. St. Clair and Brock, and Mrs. Donohue and Clarissa. How do their bonds differ? How are they the same?

9. Considering how the buildings "had eyes" in Chinatown and no secrets were kept for long, how do the social media tools of today create the same challenges for young couples? Do they bring those challenges onto themselves by sharing too much information in public spaces?

10. Is it possible to be in love with the idea of love and not the actual person in a relationship?

11. Clarissa arranges roses by the dozen. Each day, Blossom makes an arrangement with just one flower. What does that tell you about these two women? Is there beauty in bounty and scarcity?

12. Is Faye Huntington evil or just misunderstood?

13. Is Austin St. Clair a self-centered man-child or has he just not found his path in life yet?

14. How different or the same are Grand Ma Maw's mahjong club members and Blossom and her best friends who have quick lunches on a bench in the alley?

15. How do you think young Ting Ting and Little Sunflower will turn out as teenagers and adults?

16. What role does Clementine play in Brock's life? How about Austin's life? Has anyone played similar roles in your life?

17. Do disasters bring out the best in people or the worst?

18. Do disasters bring more people together or separate them?

Author's Note

The earthquake was real. The firestorm was real. Chinatown was real. Nob Hill was real. Here are a few more real things you might want to know:

- Musician Max Morath is real.
- The Palace Hotel is real.
- The Flood mansion is real too.

Just Google search them to learn more and see current photos. You can even hear Max's ragtime recordings.

Now let's move on to things that aren't so real.

I'll be the first to admit that I willingly got lost many times in whirlpools of research. And despite this need for accuracy and attention to detail, I took some liberties and sacrificed historical accuracy in the name of creativity and storytelling.

There's quite a controversy about the origin of fortune cookies. Some believe they were introduced at the California Midwinter International Exposition of 1894, in the Japanese Tea Garden that's now part of San Francisco's Golden Gate Park. Others believe the cookies have a Chinese heritage. I chose to reference the dispute in Blossom, but allowed Chang to insist that the Chinese should get credit for the fortunetelling delights.

Yes, for you music buffs, the song "When Irish Eyes Are Smiling" wasn't published until 1912, well after the San Francisco earthquake. For the sake of full disclosure, the lyrics were written by Chauncy Olcott and George Graff Jr., and the music was by Ernest Ball.

For you bakers out there, red velvet cake has long been considered a Southern specialty though its origins are not well documented. A very similar cake's recipe—Devil's Food Cake—made its publishing debut in 1902. Plus, there's an urban legend that it was introduced at New York

City's Waldorf Astoria Hotel in the 1920s. The one thing I know is that I like red velvet cake, and I wanted Clementine to make it as a comfort food for Brock. And that's that.

I hope these minor timeline-bending choices, and any others you discover, don't distract you from enjoying *Blossom*.

$\mathscr{A}$ Conversation With Christopher Lentz

Why set Blossom's story in San Francisco during the 1906 earthquake and firestorm?

Disasters bring out the best and the worst in people. Having lived in Southern California since the 1970s (I'm a teenage transplant from Detroit), earthquakes have fascinated me. The Midwest gets tornados and blizzards with some amount of advanced warning. With earthquakes, it's a random trick of Mother Nature. She literally pulls the rug out from under us when we least expect it. That's the price for living in paradise!

One of the triggers for writing the Blossom Trilogy came after watching the film Titanic for the umpteenth time. I read a quote from director James Cameron in which he talked about telling the epic disaster story though the eyes of engaging characters. And, he pointed out how everyone knows how the disaster ends, but they don't know what happens to his characters—who lives, who dies.

So, I looked in my own backyard, so to speak, to find a disaster to set a love story against. And that was the 1906 catastrophe in the Bay Area.

How did you learn about Chinatown and the Chinese culture?

I worked in downtown Los Angeles right out of college. I was part of a great team (Peggy, Karin and Amy, that's you) with a wonderful manager named Julie Edwards. We'd celebrate life's milestones by exploring the city on extended lunch hours on "creative field trips." More than one trip included LA's Chinatown. I'm not exactly sure why, but Chinatown always intrigued me—the food, the architecture, the color, the souvenir shopping.

After I was well into the first draft of *Blossom*, my family spent a few days in San Francisco, and we made a point to wander the streets and alleys of that city's Chinatown. We literally walked in my characters' footsteps.

Once *Blossom*'s story was fairly well set, my wife booked a once-in-a-lifetime trip to China. We were immersed in the Chinese culture, and we did every possible touristy thing we could cram into ten days.

Is everything historically accurate in your book?

Being a storyteller is a lot like being a travel agent, or perhaps it's more like being an airline pilot. It's my pleasure—truly, it's my pleasure—to help readers escape whatever is going on in their worlds and live vicariously with my characters.

For the most part, the details are accurate and precise, though some have been manipulated like sticky candy on a salt-water taffy machine to help enrich the story and the characters who inhabit it.

Is Blossom *a Cinderella story?*

Though *Blossom* was not written with Cinderella in mind, there are a number of Cinderella-like elements in it. Consider the following:

Blossom Sun is a generous, hard-working, thoughtful girl in a lower-economic situation who longs for something more in life

Brock St. Clair is living a charmed life above Chinatown on Nob Hill in what many would have considered a castle of a house

Monique LaFontaine is a prostitute with a heart of gold who helps Blossom transform herself

Sounds a lot like Cinderella, Prince Charming and the Fairy Godmother, doesn't it? Whether it does or not, Cinderella makes an appearance in *Blossom*—the Chinese version of Cinderella, that is. Her name is Yen-Shen.

As for the iconic ballroom scene, you'll have to wait until *Blaze*, the second book in the Blossom Trilogy, to experience Blossom's romantic waltz.

How would you describe your writing style?

I write so that readers can have an active and sensory experience. I'm inspired by the pace and brief-chapter construction of Dan Brown's novels. I do my best to always have my characters in touch with their feelings, thoughts and surroundings so readers can see, hear, smell and even taste the story. Most of all, I like to read books that feel more like watching a film. That's what I strive for when I write.

Why a trilogy?

Blossom started out as a self-contained book. Once I had a diverse group of beta readers provide feedback, I kept getting asked, "But what happens next?" People wanted to know more about the main characters after the disaster. So, I outlined the second and third books and then went back to plant the seeds for those stories back into the first book. You won't believe what's in store for them!

Who's your favorite character and why?

That's an unfair question. It's like asking a parent to pick a favorite child. I love all of my characters equally. But if I have to make some sort of choice, I would select the one who intrigues me the most: Austin St. Clair. He's a bad boy man-child. He's a conniver and a survivor. He's frustrated and frustrating.

Do you believe in the predictive power of fortune cookies?

I'm not so certain that a strip of paper that's packaged in a delicious cookie can tell my future. But I got one several years ago that I framed and keep on my desk. It says, "You have a charming way with words and should write a book." I'll leave the truth of that sentiment up to my readers!

What's next?

I'm currently working on the second and third books in the Blossom Trilogy: *Blaze* and *Bliss*. I'm also plotting several Christmas romances and an American version of *Downton Abbey*. And for Marilyn Monroe fans, I've got a whopper of a Cinderella-type romance that will knock your socks off.

Acknowledgements

Much of writing a novel is a lonely process, unless you think of the voices in your head as colleagues. But I could not have made it this far without the help of many loving and lovely people.

Thanks go to my wife, Cheryl, for being my one and only. Thanks go to my daughters Allison, Sarah and Miranda for their unwavering support and beta-reading skills.

Thanks go to my parents, in-laws, brother and sisters for showing me how love endures and that translated into the strength of the characters in *Blossom*.

And thanks go to my writing-warrior friends at Romance Writers of America for continuing to open my eyes and heart to the possibilities of telling stories in better ways. Anne Cleeland, Shannon Donnelly, Laura Drake, Melissa Crimson, Debra Holland, Tara Lain, Susan Squires and so many more authors who continue to graciously give me a hand up so my dreams can come true.

*A*bout Christopher Lentz

A man who writes romances, a self-starter who self-publishes and a dreamer who thinks growing old should take longer

Christopher Lentz writes stories about how love changes everything.

He loves living on the edge—of a continent that is. Having enjoyed far too much of Southern California's endless-summer sun and survived the onslaught of office life, he decided it was time for an extreme career makeover at age 50. He'd made his mark as a corporate marketing executive before he began writing novels. He burst onto the historical-romance scene in 2015 with his debut love story, *Blossom*.

He didn't always love words (in fact, he still has scars from those stand-up-in-front-of-class spelling bees that he was an epic failure at), but did learn to master words out of necessity. He was convinced there was a novel hiding somewhere inside him. With the help of some imaginary friends, he found it. Now his work is touted as Dan Brown meets *Downton Abbey* after surviving *Titanic*.

His first literary crush was Scarlett O'Hara. Then came Dorothy Gale, Jo March, Lizzie Bennet and Blanche DuBois. And truth be told, an infatuation with Mary Poppins transpired. Yes, Mary Poppins.

He loves—and devours—anything related to Disney like a ravenous kid inhales a bowl of Cap'n Crunch. It was a dream come true when he spent his college years immersed in Disneyland's turn-of-the-century Main Street USA selling everything from sticky lollipops to iconic Mickey Mouse ear hats. That experience resulted in a fascination with all things Victorian/Edwardian, not to mention a hoarder-status collection of antiques.

A teenage transplant from Detroit, he married his high-school sweetheart and raised three remarkable daughters and two adorable Yorkshire terriers.

As an active member of Romance Writers of America, this late bloomer looks forward to writing a bookshelf full of novels about misfits who find ways to fit in. He's currently working on his latest book, swimming for his life in research whirlpools and listening intently to the voices in his head.

He's convinced love changes everything. Always has. Always will.

To learn more, please visit www.christopherlentz.org or www.blossomtrilogy.com.